# A
# DARKER
# SEA

A

# DARKER
# SEA

A NOVEL

Master Commandant Putnam

AND THE

*War of 1812*

# JAMES L. HALEY

G. P. PUTNAM'S SONS
NEW YORK

G. P. Putnam's Sons
*Publishers Since 1838*
An imprint of Penguin Random House LLC
375 Hudson Street
New York, New York 10014

Library of Congress Cataloging-in-Publication Data
Names: Haley, James L., author.
Title: A darker sea : Master Commandant Putnam and the War of 1812 /
James L. Haley.
Description: New York : G. P. Putnam's Sons, 2017. | Series: Lieutenant
Putnam and the Barbary Pirates ; 2 | Includes bibliographical references.
Identifiers: LCCN 2017028230 | ISBN 9780399171116 (hardcover) |
ISBN 9780698164079 (ebook)
Subjects: LCSH: United States—History, Naval—19th century—Fiction. |
United States—History—War of 1812—Fiction. | United States.
Navy—Officers—Fiction. | GSAFD: Adventure fiction. | Historical fiction. |
War stories. | Sea stories.
Classification: LCC PS3608.A54638 D37 2017 | DDC 813/.6—dc23
LC record available at https://lccn.loc.gov/2017028230
p.        cm.

Printed in the United States of America
1   3   5   7   9   10   8   6   4   2

BOOK DESIGN BY LUCIA BERNARD
*Map © 2017 by David Cain*

*To the Millers,*

*Mike and Corina, and Becky and Kat,*

*with love*

To have shrunk, under such circumstances, from manly resistance, would have been a degradation blasting our best and proudest hopes; it would have struck us from the high ranks where the virtuous struggles of our fathers had placed us, and have betrayed the magnificent legacy which we hold in trust for future generations.

—JAMES MADISON,
PRESIDENT OF THE UNITED STATES

RUPERT'S
LAND

LOWER
CANADA

UPPER
CANADA

St. Lawrence River

Quebec

Montreal

Boston

New York
Philadelphia

UNITED

STATES

OF

AMERICA

Baltimore

Annapolis

Washington, D.C.

Pursuit and Escape
of the *Constitution*,
July 17-19, 1812

Chesapeake
Bay

CAPE
HATTERAS

N

0
Miles

Charleston

Sargasso
Sea

BERMUL

Map by David Cai

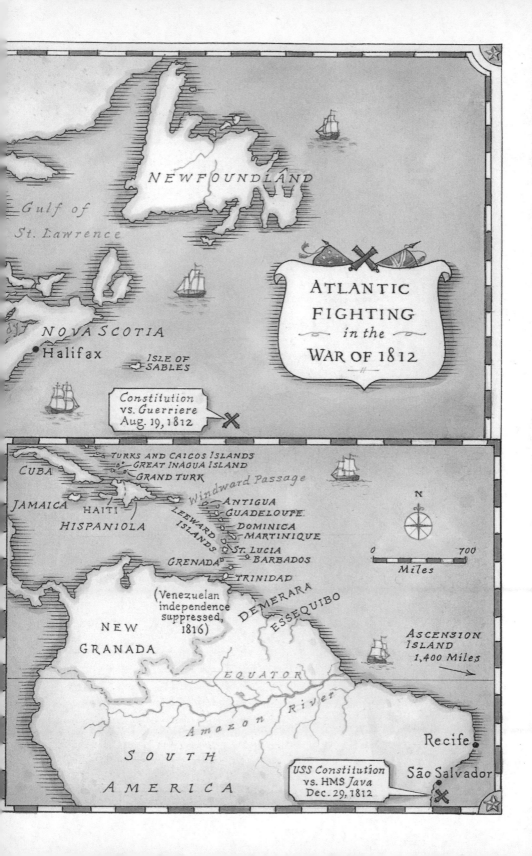

ATLANTIC FIGHTING in the WAR OF 1812

Gulf of St. Lawrence

NEWFOUNDLAND

NOVA SCOTIA
Halifax
ISLE OF SABLES

Constitution vs. Guerriere Aug. 19, 1812

CUBA
JAMAICA
HAITI
HISPANIOLA

TURKS AND CAICOS ISLANDS
GREAT INAGUA ISLAND
GRAND TURK

Windward Passage

LEEWARD ISLANDS

ANTIGUA
GUADELOUPE
DOMINICA
MARTINIQUE
ST. LUCIA
GRENADA
BARBADOS
TRINIDAD

N

0        700
Miles

(Venezuelan independence suppressed, 1816)

NEW GRANADA

DEMERARA
ESSEQUIBO

EQUATOR

ASCENSION ISLAND
1,400 Miles

Amazon River

SOUTH

AMERICA

Recife

São Salvador

USS Constitution vs. HMS Java Dec. 29, 1812

# CONTENTS

———⫫———

# A
# DARKER
# SEA

# PROLOGUE

## *The Hound in Blue*

In his cabin at the stern of the brig *Althea*, Sam Bandy dressed as he sipped the morning's first cup of coffee, rich and full-bodied, from Martinique. Sped into Charleston on a fast French ship with a dry hold, it tasted of neither mold nor bilge water. He was lucky to have gotten it in, avoiding the picket of British cruisers who, in the never-ending mayhem of the Napoleonic wars, sought to sweep all French trade from the seas. It might well have ended in the private larder of an English frigate captain. Now he had brought a quarter-ton of it to Boston, tucked into his hold along with the cotton and rice that one expected to be exported from South Carolina.

Yes, the life of a merchant mariner suited him, and it endlessly amused him. If one wanted a bottle of rum in Charleston, the cane was grown in the West Indies, where it was rendered into sugar and its essential byproduct, molasses. Thence they were taken by ship and, passing almost within sight of Charleston, delivered all the way to Boston, or Newport. There the scores of Yankee distilleries manufactured the rum, which then had to be loaded and taken back south to Charleston, which was halfway back to the Caribbean. And money was made at each exchange.

Sam ascended the ladder topside, coffee in hand, snugging his hat upon his head—a blue felt Bremen flat cap that a German sailor had offered him in trade for his American Navy bicorne. Sam had surprised the German with how readily he accepted the exchange, for in truth he felt no sentimental attachment to it at all. There were several considerations that impelled him to separate from the Navy. The death of his father during the Barbary War and the disinterest of his brothers placed the responsibility for their Abbeville plantation on his shoulders. And the Navy's penchant for furloughing junior officers for months at a time, and then recalling them without regard for the seasonal imperatives of planting or harvesting, he could not accommodate. Most important, on his voyage home from the Mediterranean on the *Wasp*, he had brought the daughter of the American former consul to Naples, and she had become his wife. Naturally he wished to provide her and their growing family the gracious life he had known, and shipping provided them a measure of comfort even beyond that of their neighbors.

And this would be a profitable trip. Their South Carolina cotton for the Yankee mills had brought him eighteen cents per pound and paid for the trip, leaving the rice, some indigo, and the Martinique coffee as pure profit. Topside, he observed his first officer, Simon Simpson, directing stevedores down into his hold. Simpson was astonishingly tall and brawny, dishfaced, with wild black hair; he knew his trade but was not overly bright, but then, apart from captains, what men who became merchant sailors were?

Their lack of schedule suited Sam; they had tied up halfway out the Long Wharf, selling until his hold was empty, and his taking on new cargo could not have passed more conveniently. As he reflected, Boston's famous Paul Revere was in his mid-seventies, but still innovating, still trying his hand at new business. His late venture into foundry was a rousing success, and Simpson lined the bottom of *Althea*'s hold with cast-iron window weights, fireplace accoutrements—andirons, pokers—and stove backs. Nothing could have provided better ballast, and atop these he loaded barrels of salt fish, all securely tied down. This left room for fine desks and bookcases from the celebrated Mr. Gould. Upon Sam's own speculation, apart from that of his co-owners of the ship, he visited Mr. Fisk's shop and bought a quantity of his delicate fancy card tables and side chairs, for which he expected the ladies of Charleston to profit him most handsome. Fisk's lyre-backed chairs were in the style of Hepplewhite of London, and when Sam visited Fisk and Son to make the purchase, it caught his ear that more than one patron expressed his pleasure that Fisk's fine workmanship had soured the market for Hepplewhite itself, so disgruntled had people become with the British interference with their trade.

The Long Wharf, with its glimpse of Faneuil Hall at its head, the taverns he had frequented in their nights here, the dockside commotion, the frequent squeals of seagulls, the salt air beyond his West Indies coffee, all left him deeply happy, but he was ready to go home. "Mr. Simpson!" he called out.

Simpson left his station at the hatch and joined him by the wheel. "Good morning, Captain."

"Good morning, Mr. Simpson. The tide begins to run in three hours. Can we be ready by then?"

"No question of it, we are almost finished."

"Excellent. Now, if you please, divert two of those Fisk chairs to my cabin. There you will find on my desk a package, addressed to the Putnam family in Litchfield, Connecticut. Take it to the post office and dispatch it. The Port Authority is right close by there. Arrange a pilot for us, come back, check the stores, and prepare to get under way."

Ah, the Putnams. Sam did not miss the Navy, but he missed Bliven Putnam. Their midshipman's schooling together on the *Enterprise*, their learning the handling of sabres together, their fighting Barbary corsairs together, even their fumbling attempts to bridge the cultural gap between Connecticut and South Carolina, and their punishment together at the masthead of the *President* mandated by Commodore James Barron for their having fought each other, all had bonded them in a way that would have been imperishable even had Barron not compelled them to swear their friendship to each other. Sam could not absent himself from the ship for a week, which would gain him only a day's visit to Litchfield, but he could send Bliven a sack of this rich coffee.

By ten Simpson had returned, and Sam hoisted the flags, signaling his imminent departure. With crew counted and hatch secured, Sam cast off, moving ever so slowly under a single jib and topsail into the harbor. The wind was from the northwest, which could not have served them better.

At the end of the wharf the pilot boat appeared, a small, sleek, low-waisted schooner, which hoisted *Althea's* name in signal flags. Sam answered and fell in behind her gratefully. In Boston's shallow bay the tides ran swiftly; once, he visited the other side of the city when the tide fell just to see the sight of Back Bay emptying out as fast as a man could walk; such flats were no place to get trapped. But this pilot very clearly knew what he was doing; the schooner was under a full set, and Sam had to loose his courses to keep up. They passed through the channel between Long and Deer Islands, and could see Lovell Island off their starboard bow. At this point the pilot came about, wishing *Althea* fair sailing; Sam signaled his thanks and steered east-southeast for the northern curl of Cape Cod. If the wind held, they should round the cape and be halfway down that seemingly interminable spit of sand when dark fell. He would be safe on a southerly course and well clear of Nantucket by morning, when he could set a new course, if the wind permitted, west-southwest for Long Island.

If it were not for the knowledge of going home, Sam would not relish the southward voyage. South by west was the most direct course to Cape Hatteras, but that would place him in the very teeth of the irresistible, opposing push of the Gulf Current. More distant in miles but infinitely faster it was to steer closer inshore along the mid-Atlantic and follow the eddying cold-water currents that would aid him.

Their seventh day out, Sam awoke to the accustomed clatter of the cook setting the tray of his breakfast on his desk. He did not mind, for every morning it reminded him of the glorious luxury of not being in the Navy, that every morning there were eggs and bacon and toasted bread for breakfast. On this voyage he did rather feel obligated to share his Martinique coffee with the crew, but it was a small cost to see the men feeling favored, and thus working with a more congenial will.

He dressed and glanced at a chart on the table, estimating in rough how far they must have come during the night. Topside at the wheel he saw his tall, wire-haired first mate, keeping a firm grip on the wheel in a stout wind from their starboard quarter. "Good morning, Mr. Simpson."

"Good morning, Captain."

Sam regarded the wind and the set of sails. "Steer east-sou'east until noon, then make due south."

"Very good, sir, east-sou'east she comes." Simple Simpson eased the helm a few points to port.

There was no need to explain why. Their southerly course had brought them almost to the outer banks of North Carolina. Now it was necessary to stand out far enough to avoid those coastal shoals whose locations changed with every storm, shallows that had brought numberless crews to grief, yet not stand so far out as to meet the strongest opposition of the Gulf Current, which here compressed as it rounded the Hatteras Cape and was here at its swiftest. If they made that mistake they could labor all day with their sails bellied full out and end the day not five miles farther on than when they started. It was a delicate calculation, but they would know if they went too far, for old sailors had many times told Sam, and he had himself once discovered the truth of it, that the inner edge of the warm Gulf Current was so sharp and sudden that in crossing it, water brought up from the bow and the stern might be twenty degrees different in temperature.

———#———

At the same moment in the sea cabin of His Majesty's sloop-of-war *Hound*, twenty-two guns, Captain Lord Arthur Kington in his dressing gown poured himself a glass of Madeira. Two weeks out of Halifax, bound for Bermuda, but empty-handed. They had not raised a single French sail to engage, nor even an American merchant to board and harvest some pressed men. For days now they had been plowing through the drifting mess of the Sargasso Sea, no doubt snagging strands of the olive-brown weeds that would hang on their barnacles and slow them down.

How in bloody hell could he have fallen from command of a seventy-four- to a twenty-two-gun sloop? For six years he had sailed in purgatory like the *Flying Dutchman*, each morning asking and answering the same question of himself, unable to break the cycle of it. It was difficult to comprehend how that incident in Naples had precipitated such a consequence. In attempting the apprehension of a deserter from a dockside tavern he and everyone else knew he was carrying out Crown policy. His fault, apparently, lay in attending a diplomatic reception while his press gang was assaulted and bested by a clot of drunken American sailors. No captain of a seventy-four would be seen in the company of his press gang; the notion was absurd, and he the son of a duke. What did they expect of him? Apparently, that his press gang prey only upon victims foreign or domestic, beyond the protective circle of their shipmates. It was his lieutenant on the *Hector* who had acted imprudently, but in the long-established calculus of the Royal Navy, he as captain should have foreseen such a circumstance and ordered his lieutenant to greater caution. That junior officer had not suffered for the act, he had later been raised from the *Hector*'s third officer to second, but it was Kington himself who, in response to the diplomatic stink that the Americans had fomented, had to be punished. And yet he wondered if there were not more to it, whether some key bureaucrat in the Admiralty had simply conceived a dislike for him.

At least the Admiralty had broken him in command only and not in rank, an admission that they needed his service as one who would willingly overhaul vessels on the high seas and take off what men were needed to crew His Majesty's ships. The need was bottomless, for desertions were constant, and Napoleon simply would not be crushed. Kington's conclusion was that his value to the Navy lay in impressing men in ways that could not be readily discovered, and in six years at this he had come to excel. The Navy needed him but would not acknowledge him; it was a circumstance that left him feeling ill used. Yet, if he did but do his duty, without complaint, and without overmuch using family influence on the Admiralty, he would work his way back up to his former station. This was certain, for even now a new frigate was waiting for him in Bermuda to take command once he brought in the *Hound* with a merchant prize or two, and some well-broken American sailors.

Thus he served, secure in the knowledge that the Royal Navy

needed pressed men more than ever—and more particularly they needed him, for after that affair with the American frigate *Chesapeake*, their need for impressment was forced into still greater subterfuge. Infinitely more so than Naples, the *Leopard–Chesapeake* encounter had altered the dynamics of impressment. Doubtless, it had been less than prudent, or at least less than sporting, for Post Captain Humphreys of H.M.S. *Leopard* to pour broadsides into the unprepared American frigate in peacetime, but it was open and obvious that the Americans had been enlisting British deserters into their crews. The American captain, some fellow named Barron, had been court-martialed and suspended for not fighting his ship to the last, irrespective of the hopelessness of the contest.

Kington screwed up his mouth into a smile. That said much for the American frame of mind, but not their practicality. Barron had had no chance. His guns were unloaded, rolled in, their tompions in place. His decks were piled with stores in preparation for a long cruise; when approached by the *Leopard*, Barron, knowing they were not at war with Britain, had not beat to quarters. Had he resisted, his crew would have been slaughtered as they limbered up the guns. As it was, the American was lucky to lose only four killed and eighteen, including Barron himself, wounded. Humphreys had seized four men from the *Chesapeake*, and then, the worst insult of all, refused Barron's surrender—they were not at war, after all— and left him there on his floating wreck. God help them if they ever encountered Barron again; he would sell his life very dearly indeed.

Of the four men Humphreys had seized, one was a Canadian,

whom he hanged. They did have some color of justification for taking Canadians, to whom the Americans presumed to grant naturalized citizenship. How dare they? His Majesty's government of course refused to recognize American naturalization. They were naval pretenders even as they were still pretenders as a nation, and no great attention need be paid them except for taking likely-looking seamen.

Now Kington knew that his exile was at an end; a new command awaited him in Bermuda, but he had concluded that he could not enter empty-handed, and he had turned to the northwest, crossing and riding the Gulf Current into the waters of the American coastal trade. Even as he was thinking they must sight a vessel on this day, he cocked his head at the faint cry above the deck overhead, of "Deck sail ho!" He straightened his dressing gown and seated himself at his desk, waiting for the rap at his door, which came only a moment later. "Enter," he said quietly.

"Beg pardon, m'lord." A lieutenant stood at attention and made his respects. "The lookout has sighted a ship bearing to the southwest."

Kington affected not to look up from the papers on his desk. "What do you make of her?"

"An American merchantman, m'lord, a large brig, low in the water, heading south."

"Very well. Make all sail to overtake her. I will come up."

"Very good, m'lord." The lieutenant made his respects again and departed.

Kington pulled a pair of brilliant white silk stockings up his calves, and then donned equally white knee breeches, which he fastened at the waist and knees. The talk was that the Royal Navy was going to change at any time to trousers for officers, as well as the enlisted men, who already wore them. He hated the notion. Trousers—inelegant, egalitarian, shapeless—suitable for the common sailors but certainly not for officers. After regarding his shiny white calves in the mirror, he buckled his sword about his waist and selected a coat from his wardrobe, the blue frock, undress but bearing the dual epaulettes that signified a captain of more than three years' experience. It was hard to bear how many years, since Naples, but his circumstances would improve soon enough. He took up his glass and ascended the ladder to the quarterdeck.

The courses blocked his view down the deck, and he slung an arm through the mizzen's starboard ratlines, leaned out, and focused the American in his glass. Yes, it was a large brig, low and slow; they were gaining on him rapidly and he could not but have seen him. This should be a good day.

"What is your pleasure, m'lord? Shall you hail him?"

"Beat to quarters, Mr. Evans, ready your starboard bow chaser. At six hundred yards put a shot through his rigging. That will hail him well enough."

"Beat to quarters!" Evans barked to the bosun, and an instant later the ship leapt to life in response to the drum's tattoo. Both officers knew this was probably unnecessary when their quarry was an apparently unarmed merchant vessel, but both knew equally that an overawing display of firepower was the surest guarantor of a passive reception.

———//———

Aboard the *Althea*, Sam Bandy had been alerted to the approach of the British sloop and followed her through his glass, noting the deployment of starboard studding sails to increase her speed. He was studying her even as he saw the flash and smoke of her bow chaser; its booming report reached him almost simultaneously with the singing of a ball through his rigging. He started and shot his gaze upward at a loud pop, and beheld a rip in the main topsail, one edge flapping in the wind. He turned his head to the right, waiting for and then seeing the small splash a hundred yards out or more. Unarmed and laden too heavily to run, he had no choice but to furl his sails and wait for what fate should bring.

"She is bringing in her sails, m'lord," said Evans. "It looks as if she means no resistance."

"Good," said Kington. "Have the bosun swing out the cutter. You and I will go over with ten Marines for escort."

At the cutter's approach, Sam had a rope boarding ladder lowered. Eight Marines came smartly up in coats of brilliant scarlet, flanking the ladder, then two officers in blue frocks, and two more Marines.

Bandy faced them, arms akimbo, several paces in front of his curious and apprehensive crew.

"I am Captain Lord Arthur Kington, of His Majesty's sloop-of-war *Hound*. Are you the master of this vessel?"

"I am Samuel Bandy, captain of the brig *Althea*." Sam squared his shoulders against him. "By what right do you stop an American ship in international waters?" he demanded.

"By the authority of Orders in Council of His Majesty's government," he said highly. "We are at war with France, and we are charged to stop ships, search for deserters, and seize ships which are carrying contraband bound for French ports. What is your cargo?"

"Your orders are of no effect upon American ships."

"Mr. . . . Bandy, my broadside gives me all the authority I need. I ask you again, what is your cargo?"

"Salt fish, and kitchenware, and furniture."

"Where bound?"

"We are seven days out of Boston, bound for Charleston."

"I see. I require to see your manifest, and after that to inspect your hold. Take us down to your cabin."

Sam clattered down the ladder to his small cabin, followed by the two officers and behind them two of the Marines. From a shelf he pulled the log book and extracted the three pages of manifest, detailing his cargo to the last item.

He handed the papers over to Kington, who rattled the sheets as he barely glanced at them before folding them back along their existing creases and tucking them into his coat pocket. "Well, I say, you are a lively-looking fellow," said Kington.

Sam squinted and shook his head. "What?"

"We are searching for a Canadian deserter who bears the singularly appropriate name of Lively. Do you claim that the name means nothing to you?"

Sam was truculent. "Of course it means nothing to me. Why should it?"

"Because"—Kington looked Sam down and up and down again—"he stands about five feet nine inches, weight thirteen stone, very fair complected, reddish to blond hair." He looked more closely. "Blue eyes. Did you really believe we would never discover you?"

"Damn your eyes, I am Samuel Bandy of South Carolina, captain and part owner of this vessel!"

Kington crossed his arms doubtfully. "Well, your accent is plausible. Still, that can be affected. Let me see your protection."

"God damn it, I am the captain! I don't carry proof of my citizenship!"

Kington tossed his head lightly. "Well, then."

"Wait, I have my master's license. Wait." This was a document that he never expected that he would have to produce. He knew it was in a pouch of papers in his sea chest, and he dropped to his knees and flung open its lid.

"Hold!" barked Kington. The Marines who flanked him lowered their muskets at him. "Move very slowly."

"Bastard," muttered Sam. He rose again, unfolding his master's license and handing it to Kington, who glanced about the cabin.

"The light in here is very poor." He ambled over to the stern windows and opened one, sitting on its sill and leaning partly outside. "Now, let us see." He mumbled the lines as he read them. "Oh, dear!" He opened his fingers and the paper fluttered down to the rolling sea.

Sam swelled up but checked himself as the Marines took a half-step forward *en garde*.

Kington tapped his index finger against his chin. "Perhaps you are who you say you are, but perhaps not. You answer the wanted man's description too closely to dismiss the matter. Prudence dictates I shall bring you to Bermuda for more certain identification."

"Wait a minute, I know you!" Sam shook his head. "From where do I know you?"

Kington looked at him with his haughty expectation.

Sam's finger shot out at him. "Naples! After the war, the Barbary War, the American consulate, you had an altercation with Commodore Preble."

"Indeed? I cannot say that I remember you at all. I do remember one particularly impudent lieutenant, but it was not you. Mr. Evans?"

"M'lord?"

"We will select a prize crew to take this vessel to Bermuda. Poll the American crewmen. Those who carry protections and wish to go home we will put ashore when we reach Bermuda and they can catch a ship home as best they can. Naturally, any who wish to volunteer into His Majesty's service will be welcome to enlist." The two officers chuckled. Once carried to Bermuda, it could take months for some neutral ship to carry them home again.

"You're just a damned pirate," spat Sam. He knew that Kington would have no trouble finding enlistments among his crew. In the American merchant service, as in the Navy, a fair portion of his sailors went to sea to escape their problems on land. Among the men were surely some whose fortunes had sunk so low—wanted by the law, or in the shadow of debtors' prison—that a foreign ship seemed as viable an escape as walking into the Western wilderness, with the advantage that there were no bears or Indians. Given that they had no way home from Bermuda, it was tantamount to impressment just the same.

Kington smirked. "Damn fine chairs. Hepplewhite, by the make?"

"Fisk of Boston, damn you, and so stamped on the back of each." He swept an arm out grandly. "But please, have them. They will show very fine in a pirate's cabin."

"That remark," said Kington quietly, "will cost you six lashes, as the lightest of warnings. Provoke me further and you will regret it in proportion. Now, will you come quietly, or must we bind you? Before you answer, let me warn you that if you give me your parole to submit and then resist, I will surely hang you. I have no scruple about it."

"No, I have no doubt of that." He inclined his head toward a pine wardrobe. "Am I allowed to keep my clothes?"

"Certainly not. You will be fitted out in His Majesty's uniform for an able seaman." He glanced down. "You may keep your shoes, however. Shoes are in short supply."

"What of my clothes?"

"We will keep them safe. If your story proves out, they will be returned to you."

"Well, they are too large for you, at any rate. But perhaps your tailor can take them in for you."

"Six more lashes, and I urge you, do not build up a large account."

The swell on this morning was easy, as two Marines descended the boarding ladder to their cutter. Kington scanned about *Althea*'s deck and remembered that he had not inspected the hold. *Ah, well.* He had the manifest, and in this circumstance judged that sufficient. He had the ship; the nature of the cargo they could ascertain at leisure.

"Mr. Evans."

"Yes, m'lord?"

"Inspect the crew for their protections. I will send the cutter back with a prize crew. Those who wish to enlist with us send back across with the boat. With luck, it will be an even exchange and we will both have a full complement. Then you will follow me to Bermuda."

"Very good, m'lord." He made his respects as Kington and the remaining Marines, and Sam, descended to the cutter.

As they approached the sloop, Sam saw that she had turned a bit in the current, and he could make out the name HOUND freshly painted under her stern windows. Given his captivity, Sam debated whether he should open a conversation with this captain, try to reach at least a minimal respect between them, and weighed that against his visceral disgust with him, his almost visual desire to see him swinging on a noose.

"She is a handsome enough vessel," he ventured. "Twenty-two, by the look of her?"

Kington regarded him with some surprise. "You have a practiced eye, Mr. Lively. You have estimated her exactly."

"At fourteen I was a midshipman in the *Enterprise*, twelve, and then a lieutenant in the *Constitution*, forty-four," he stated quietly. "Some of that time we were in company with the *John Adams*, twenty-four, and your ship seems only the slightest degree smaller. And if you please, Captain, my name is Samuel Bandy, as you will discover upon a full investigation of the matter."

Kington perceived exactly what Sam was doing. "We shall see. On my ship, I am addressed as 'my lord,' and you will oblige me by adopting the custom."

Sam felt as though his jaw would break if he did so, but he swallowed his gorge and said, "Whatever you say, my lord." Those two words, from the mouth of any American, sounded ridiculous.

As soon as they tied up, Kington scaled the boarding ladder first, and Sam followed, finding the captain already engaged with his second officer, a smallish, auburn-haired man with freckles, named Crawford. Once the Marines were up, a well-armed prize crew descended and pulled away. It took half an hour to make the exchange on the *Althea*, and the cutter returned with Evans and five of Sam's crew who had determined to throw in with the English.

As soon as they came alongside, lines went tumbling down from the davits that curled out overhead. Crewmen made them fast to the eyebolts on the cutter's bow and stern, and as soon as the last of the men stood on deck the cutter came up after them by jerks. Sam marked which of his men had turned coat and determined not to speak to them, even as he admitted to himself that they were not entirely beyond his sympathy. As the cutter was made secure in the davits Sam heard the orders barked and saw the yards braced up as they tacked and settled on a course east-nor'east, under full sail, close hauled but not straining, running full-and-by. Kington may be a miserable wretch, he thought, but he knew how to use the wind. Sam peered astern and saw his *Althea* following suit. At least, he thought, they were on their way to somewhere.

"Well, Lively." It was Kington's voice, and Sam turned to face him. "I will say that your attempt at conversation was noted down in your favor, as perhaps indicating a quiescent bearing. We are bound for Bermuda, from where inquiries will be made. If you prove to be who you say you are, you will be set at liberty."

"And my ship?"

"That I cannot promise. But I tell you, if we find that you are who I think you are, you must hang. Not from my personal animus, understand, but because it is the law."

Sam's words were ready that when he was discovered to be a fellow officer, Kington would oblige him with satisfaction, but he barred the words from passing his lips, calculating that it would be his own death sentence.

"As it is," said Kington, "you have an account and we must square it. Mr. Crawford."

"Yes, m'lord."

"All hands on deck to witness punishment. Except"—he paused, considering—"except those five new enlistments; keep them below with the purser to get their uniforms." He looked at Sam. "I will spare you that. Bosun, do your duty."

"Aye, m'lord," replied a very deep voice. Sam regarded the bosun, middle-aged, gray and very curly hair, missing teeth, skin so salt-cured that he might well have been pulled from a cask in the meat stores. "Come along with ye," he said.

This shockingly grizzled man seized Sam tightly by an upper arm and led him across the thirty-foot beam of the ship. "Ordinarily," said the bosun so quietly that only Sam could hear, "ripping down your shirt is part of the show, but 'tis such a fine shirt, I will give you the opportunity to remove it yourself and lay it aside."

Glowering, Sam began pulling the shirttails out of his trousers.

"I have heard of an officer and gentleman, but never a bosun and gentleman. Thank you."

Four of the crew leaned a heavy hatch grate against the mainmast's starboard ratlines, at enough of an angle that he could not keep balance on his own feet, yet vertical enough that the crew could see the spectacle.

"Now lie you up against it," said the bosun. "Stretch up your arms." As soon as Sam extended his arms, crewmen seized his hands and bound them, threading the rope through the openings in the wooden mesh. From the corner of his eye Sam spied the bosun's mate shaking out a cat, running his fingers down its separate strands of twisted hemp to each end, picking off the bits of flesh from the tassels left from when it was last used, finally nodding to the bosun.

The bosun made his respects to the officers on the quarterdeck, calling out, "Ready to commence punishment."

The officers had been at their ease but followed Kington's lead in snugging his bicorne down on his head. "One dozen," he pronounced.

Sam steadied himself, concentrating at that instant on the lapping hiss of the water as it slid by, the creaking of the rigging, the warmth of the morning sun on his back. He knew that his life, or rather the way he regarded life, would never be the same after this morning. He was parsing how he would change, as he heard the cat's tails sing for an instant through the air before slapping across his back, searing like a great brand of fire laid across the flesh. He snapped taut against the ropes that spread his arms, but he made no sound. His teeth clenched, even as he determined that he would die before giving Kington the satisfaction of hearing him cry out.

"One," announced the bosun, as the bosun's mate shook out the tails behind him for a second strike.

He would withstand all dozen lashes, he would stand them by conjuring in his mind's eye himself, standing over Kington's broken body. Whatever it took and however long, he swore to himself that he would have his vengeance. There was a second quick whish of air and a second burning slap on his back, lower down. He clenched his teeth again but uttered nothing.

"Two," intoned the bosun.

Nor was it lost on him that he had been taken into slavery and whipped. He, who had grown up on a plantation and been wet-nursed and clothed and tended by slaves, and he who was now a master of dozens, had never in his life whipped a slave, nor seen one whipped. He knew that it happened, and he had seen the evidence of it in the scarred-over welts on the backs of others' slaves, mostly on those belonging to white trash who vented their own social envy upon the two or three hapless blacks in their power. Such drivers were not respected. Nevertheless, now he understood what it felt like. Whish, splat!

"Three," declared the bosun.

The Indians, he thought. He had heard of Indians beyond the woods who invent ceremonies and tortures and subject their young men to them, giving them the privilege of demonstrating their bravery, their disregard for pain. Those who passed this test became warriors; those who did not—such shame was not to be countenanced. If Indian boys could stand such, a Southern gentleman must surely be able to bear that, or more. Whish, splat!

"Four," called out the bosun.

After twelve lashes the strain had caused the sweat to pour down Sam's brow. As he was untied from the hatch grate he found himself unable to release the tension knotted in his back. Upon standing straight, he felt liquid trickle down his back, but he had no way of knowing if it was sweat or blood, and he was glad he could not see it. He had no desire to surmise how his broad white back was now scarred for life. He felt faint, and he summoned every ounce of rage and resolve not to fall; he would not give such pleasure to this horror of a human being who now held him in his power.

An officer in a blue coat, different, not a frock but a cutaway with gold buttons, stepped forward and touched Sam's back in several places with a white handkerchief, which came away streaked with crimson. "I am Dr. Kite," he said quietly, "ship's surgeon. You had best come with me, I will tend to your wounds."

Further civility was the last thing Sam had expected. "Yes. Yes, of course, thank you."

"Can you manage the ladder?"

"I think so."

The bosun handed Sam his shirt and whispered hoarsely, "Well done, Yankee lad. Keep up your courage, and for God's sake do nothing stupid. We will speak at a later time."

Sam held the shirt to his sweating chest and stomach as they went down. The sloop *Hound* was small enough that she mounted all her guns on the spar deck; the ladder descended to the single berth deck.

Kite led him forward of the galley to the sick bay and indicated a narrow berth along the curve of the hull. He pointed and said, "Lie on your belly."

Sam slipped off his shoes and did as he was bidden, watching the surgeon extract a bottle and a white cloth from a wooden chest.

"This will sting," said Kite. "It is an astringent." The pain was sharp and more localized than the lashes themselves had been, but not nearly as overwhelming. As the surgeon dabbed at the slices into his skin he said, "They tell me you served in the *Constitution*. Is that true?"

"Yes."

"Then you were acquainted with the surgeon on that vessel?"

"Dr. Cutbush, yes, very well."

"Did you know he is quite famous? What can you tell me about him?"

"Vastly skilled, but also very amiable." Sam started to turn onto his side to face Kite as he spoke, but a firm hand pressed him down to keep him on his stomach.

"Tell me about him, but lie still, I am not done."

Sam related his and Bliven's first day on the *Constitution*, Cutbush having met them on deck and seen to their comfort, of his fascination with ancient doctors and medicine, an element which he did not know personally but which Bliven had told him about.

"You have gratified my curiosity very well," Kite said at last. "Listen to me now. I want you to lie quietly on your belly until we know the bleeding has stopped. Do you feel like you could eat something?"

"Yes."

"There are things I must tend to, but I will have a meal brought to you. They tell me we are only two days from Bermuda. I am going to excuse you from duty until then; that will give you a chance to heal properly."

"When I get home," said Sam, not admitting to himself that he was unsure whether or when he would see home again, "and make a report to the Navy, I will mention your kindness prominently."

Kite departed, and Sam heard Evans the first officer accost him. "How is he, Bones?"

"As one might expect after a dozen lashes. Is the captain in his cabin?"

"I believe he is."

Kite strode the length of the berth deck, pausing to instruct the bosun to take Sam a meal when it was time to eat, before rapping on the door of the captain's cabin.

"Enter," the voice issued from within.

"M'lord, I have reason to believe that the captain of that American prize is indeed who he says he is."

Kington was seated at his desk. "Oh, and why is that?"

"Sir, I questioned him as I treated him. He claims to have served in the American frigate *Constitution*. The surgeon on that vessel, Dr. Cutbush, I know well from a call I made in Philadelphia many years ago. He knew the name, and he describes him so exactly, I have no doubt he is telling the truth. He would have been a very young lieutenant during the Barbary conflict, and cannot be the man you suspect."

"Thank you for telling me, Dr. Kite." When he didn't move, Kington asked, "Is there something more, Doctor?"

"M'lord, it occurs to me that when we reach port and an inquiry is opened, you will of course wish me to offer these facts into the record."

The next moment of tense silence freighted infinitely more conversation that what had orally passed to that point, that wonderful silence of polite exchange which indicates that the true message conveyed is other and greater than what was uttered. Both men recognized the impasse, that Kite had interposed himself in a matter not his concern, but to which Kington was vulnerable because he might have been treading at the very edge even of the freewheeling practice of impressment.

"You will be informed," said Kington at last. "You may return to your duties."

"M'lord." Kite made his respects but delayed withdrawing just long enough for Kington to look at him again, into his eyes, and realize that his intention was serious. Kite clattered up the ladder and sucked in the fresh salt air, recovering from his brazenness at challenging the captain in such a way, but also calm and satisfied that he had acted out of conscience, something that he was not sure he could still do.

—— // ——

Sam slept fitfully and had just opened his eyes when he counted the eight bells that signaled the onset of the first dog watch. Heavy steps approached, and he looked up to see the grizzled bosun standing over him, bearing a square wooden plate, a tin cup, a swatch of cloth, and a hammer. "Are ye hungry, Yankee lad?"

"I could eat, yes." He sat up, trying not to crack the new scabs on his back. "May I know your name?"

"You will know me as Mr. White." He set the square plate onto the thin mattress, and Sam beheld a shapeless mass of boiled beef, a small slather of peas, and a large rocklike biscuit.

Years had passed since Sam's last exposure to ship's biscuit. He looked up again, and White gave him a large mug of steaming tea and laid beside him a swatch of white cloth and the hammer. "I expect ye know of naval fare."

"When I was in the American Navy, it was not much different among our men. I was a lieutenant; the officers made out somewhat better."

"A word of advice, Yankee lad," he said quietly. "Do not follow that course. Protesting your identity will gain you nothing. On this vessel your name is Lively, a suspected Canadian deserter who will be used for duty pending your execution. Now, the Navy does inquire into such things, and if you can make your case, you will be set at liberty. But until then, do not provoke the captain's displeasure."

"I understand," said Sam.

"The surgeon has told me you are excused duty until we make port, so be guided by me, make yourself as little noticed as possible."

"Thank you for your consideration," Sam said, as White nodded curtly and disappeared. Left to regard his rations, Sam took a spoonful of peas, chewing them as he folded the biscuit into the white cloth. He pulled the thin mattress aside until the wood of the berth was exposed and hammered at the wrapping until the biscuit was broken up into small sherds, which he dumped into his tea to soften. He plunged a fork as deep as he could into the mass of beef, and he bit off a small chunk of it. It was hot and tasted of brine, and he knew it had not soaked long enough in the steep tub. He should eat it first, he thought, because it would make him devilish thirsty, and save the tea for last, for he did not know when he would be offered water.

Late in the next morning, Sam was roused from his bed by the bosun, who was accompanied by a brawny but dull-looking sailor. Motioned up the waist ladder, he found himself in a line, directly behind others whom he thought must be captives.

"We have raised Nelson Island off the starboard bow," White told him quietly. "It is the practice when coming into port to shackle the pressed men." Sam looked to the head of the line and saw the ship's armorer quickly and efficiently riveting irons to the ankles of each man. "You need not go back down," White continued. "You may stay on deck and take some air, if you feel up to it."

"Yes, I would like that," said Sam. "Thank you. Where are the other men from my ship?"

"Them? They enlisted, so they are not considered pressed men."

Sam nodded, calculating what a convenient policy that was to mask the true numbers of impressment, and turned his gaze aft to the unraised quarterdeck, where he saw Kington and a lieutenant quietly observing the armorer hammering the rivets of their shackles against a small anvil.

From this distance Sam and Kington made eye contact, with no sign of acknowledgment. Kington could readily admit that fitting chains to the pressed men was some inconvenience to them, but the sight of land, even such a hopelessly isolated island as Bermuda, might prove too great a temptation to impressed seamen to leap overboard and swim for it—despite the fact that there was no hiding in this tiny colony, separated from North America and safety by six hundred miles of open sea. Shackling them while in port decreased the incidence of desertions, and the subsequent odium of tracking the culprits down and hanging them.

As he waited his turn and then as the manacles were hammered about his ankles, Sam Bandy felt the ship enter a starboard turn, coming due east, and continuing until the sails were put over with the brief, confused snaps of the luffing canvas as she wore completely around, heading southwest. He could see land a half-mile off to port, and a half-mile to starboard the mole of the Royal Dockyard. He had never been here but had seen it a hundred times on the map as he shuttled up and down the coast in his trade and recognized Bermuda.

Kington leaned over to Evans. "You've been here before, you know the channel?"

"Yes, sir."

"Well, come around easy to starboard, you may take us into the anchorage." Kington strode a few paces forward and surveyed the length of the deck. He was fortunate, only a third of his crew had been pressed into service. Through the vastness of the Royal Navy the percentage was closer to half, and sometimes more.

"Mr. Evans," he said at length.

"Sir."

"Anchor us convenient to that frigate. I am going below; keep an eye on the armorer, make sure all the risky ones are chained."

The first officer made his respects. "Very good, sir."

At the top of the ladder Kington peered across the harbor to the much taller H.M.S. *Java*, gazing long enough to count fourteen large gunports down her gun deck, and saw the irregular black stubble of large carronades about her fo'c'sle and quarterdeck. That, he thought, is more like it; he could not wait to transfer over.

It is all Bonaparte's doing, he thought as he descended the ladder. For the English, the decade and more of war with the French had required a breathtaking inflation of the Navy, now more than one thousand ships—a thousand and one, he smirked briefly, with this fat American brig. What country on earth could deploy nine hundred vessels with all-volunteer crews? Impressment in the British Navy had been accepted for three centuries; now it was needed more than ever, and it was no time to question it. Of the one hundred forty thousand sailors presently in service, at least eight thousand made good an escape every year, but Kington was satisfied never to have lost one.

As he heard the *Hound*'s cable thunder from its tier and the anchor crash into the water, he opened a large red leather pouch and began assembling his papers—his commission, his orders, his personal correspondence.

Let no one doubt they were about the King's business. Well—the King's business after a fashion. The King himself was now famously imbecile, a raving, wigless waif wandering the corridors of Windsor Castle, or playing his organ, or holding imaginary conversations and, it was said, pissing purple water. The regency was now firmly in the hands of the Prince of Wales, who was a great friend of the Navy's—or at least he was when he wasn't paying more attention to his frills and laces and embroidered waistcoats. Luckily, he was under the influence of high and respectable men in the Admiralty.

The right half of Kington's mouth again screwed up into something like a smile. Sardonic irony was not his only emotion, but it was his favorite, and the closest to unaffected amusement as he was capable. One day these American upstarts must realize what kind of game the English were running there in Bermuda, that they were not just taking the odd American sailor while capturing "deserters" to round out deficient crews. Rather, they were harvesting them from America's growing merchant fleet, harvesting whole strings of them, like hops in August. Bermuda was their principal clearinghouse, from where they were distributed as needed to their undermanned men-o'-war.

When these Americans did realize how they were being used, great must be their rage, but greater still would be their impotence, for there was nothing they could do about it.

Lord Nelson himself, God rest his pickled soul, had endorsed the practice with all his heart. No admiral in the Navy had been so vocal in his disgust, his disdain for America and Americans. He respected those wonderfully designed heavy frigates of theirs well enough, and no doubt he would have approved the memorandum circulating within the Admiralty at this moment, a proposed instruction that British frigates not engage them with less than a two-to-one advantage. That was unduly alarmist, in Kington's opinion. Their ships might be well built, but their seamanship had nothing to offer against centuries of British tradition. And these United States, these Americans and their concept of a country and their vision of themselves as a people—no officer more than Nelson would have more stoutly advocated reducing them back to their proper station as colonial tributaries of the Empire.

Kington wondered, if it were not for the satisfaction he had derived from this business, whether he should have remained in the Navy. The duke his father was not without friends in the Admiralty; perhaps he had something to do with rescuing his fortunes, all very well if he did. At least now he was resuscitated to the point of commanding a frigate. That was a good step.

There came two sharp raps at the cabin door. "Enter."

It was First Officer Evans. "All the pressed men are secure, sir."

"Very well. Send a boat over to the frigate, alert them to pipe me aboard shortly."

"Very good, m'lord."

"Oh, and have that Canadian deserter, Lively, taken over as well. I think he is not who he says he is, but he is an experienced seaman and I can use him. Besides, he could raise a good deal of dust if we leave him here. I think we'll just keep him where he can cause no difficulties."

"Aye, m'lord, I will send him over with the boat and let them know the situation."

"Very well, I shall be ready to transfer by the time they get back."

The arrangements took only half an hour before Kington was in a boat, sitting with his back straight and his pouch upon his knees. As he approached the *Java* he could tell that she was but lightly constructed; she was French, a fifth-rate, captured at Madagascar with considerable damage only the previous May. He knew she had been refitted at Portsmouth before coming out to meet a seasoned captain. Kington noted darkly that on her stern below his cabin windows he could make out the shadow of her previous name, the *Renommée*, lurking beneath the golden letters JAVA.

Still, he was happy to have read in his briefing paper that she was only four years old, and he knew that her builders, Mathurin & Crucy of Nantes, turned out creditable vessels. Once they had tied up to the ladder, Kington looked up in surprise to see a bosun's chair being lowered to him.

"If you please, sir."

He had barely time to say "Oh" before he was being hoisted up and swung in.

"Welcome aboard, m'lord." Kington beheld a plump lieutenant with dark hair and eyes making his respects. "Lieutenant Freemantle, sir, first officer."

"Mr. Freemantle." He returned the salute and extended his hand, which the first officer took, but not in an overly familiar way. "Did you think I could not manage the ladder?"

"We saw that you were carrying a large pouch of papers, sir. The chair seemed indicated."

Kington inspected him. "Observation and initiative, eh? Very good. We'll get on."

"Will you inspect the ship, m'lord, or see your cabin first?"

"See the ship, yes, at once. I am pleased at what I see already." He gestured up to the fo'c'sle and down the spar deck. "How many carronades?"

"Eighteen, sir. Thirty-two-pounders."

"Excellent." Ordinarily, commanding officers were given a choice of what guns to mount, but *Java* had come out to Bermuda as a completed package. Still, this was exactly the secondary battery he would have chosen, for he preferred close action behind the raking power of carronades over mounting lighter long guns topside. Kington ran his hand lightly down one of the stumpy barrels. "They look new. Are they just from the factory?"

"Yes, m'lord. Each one came on board with its full kit just before leaving Portsmouth."

All knew what that meant. The Carron foundry in Scotland persuaded the Navy to contract for its carronades by delivering them as a complete firing system. Each gun came with twenty-five balls, fifteen double-headed shot, fifteen bar shot, ten charges of grape, and ten charges of canister. They delivered powder, too, premixed in woolen bags that eliminated the need for wadding. Carronades' low muzzle velocity did not overheat the barrels, thus there was no need to worm the barrels before reloading, which made them the most rapidly firing large guns in the world.

"Excellent," admired Kington, as he led the small clot of officers down the ladder to the gun deck. "How many crew?"

"Four hundred and two, m'lord."

"How many were pressed?"

"A hundred and eighty, sir."

"Mm." Kington considered this for a moment. "Round up your worst dozen and send them ashore for other duty. I just took some deserters and new recruits from that American brig. Bring them over from the *Hound*. I think it is better to keep them at sea. But separate them into different watches."

"I understand, m'lord," said Freemantle. He knew that that order embraced not merely understanding what he was to do but understanding that leaving American crewmen ashore could complicate any repercussions of having taken them in the first place. Better to have them safely incommunicado.

"How are your provisions?"

"The stores are full, m'lord. We can sail at your order. We can lay in fresh perishables if there is time."

On the gun deck, Kington paced with authority down the neatly tied-up rows of eighteen-pounders, buckets, garlands, and quoins neatly arranged, screws and swabs hung overhead, ropes coiled precisely. Kington had not felt so powerful in years; in such a ship he might take on anyone. In his mind he began calculating circumstances in which he might even gain an advantage over one of those vaunted American heavy frigates.

"There will be time. I want you to repaint the stern. I don't feel right sailing with her old name showing through. Bad omen, you know. And go see Mr. Evans on the *Hound*, get those other Americans over here. Em—" He waved a hand vapidly. "The deserters, I should mean."

Freemantle smiled. "Yes, m'lord. Right away."

———//———

After being shackled, Sam was left to himself, observing the *Hound* and his captive *Althea* gliding to an anchorage distantly abeam a trim and apparently new frigate. Watching a boat shuttle men and officers to and from the frigate, he had felt himself unnoticed until a seaman and a Marine stood on either side of him and ordered him down into a boat with several other pressed men.

As Sam descended the ladder he noted that the chains on his feet were exactly the length needed between the steps down . . . *Clever,* he thought. *Someone planned ahead.*

# — 1 —

*Dangerous Trade*

My Dear Putnam,

We dropped anchor in this place known so well to yourself on the day before yesterday. Being my first visit here since our salad days as midshipmen, and being a fresh autumn day, it did set me in mind of my time spent in Litchfield with you and your excellent parents, who I pray are still with you and in good health.

Rebecca bade me send you her fond regards straightaway as I made port. I tell you, Putnam, making her my wife was the best and wisest thing I shall ever do. At managing our plantation she has proved herself so capable I have considered dismissing our *foreman as a redundancy. I have not done so, for with two lively boys tearing about, and I do not believe we are yet quitted of that enterprise of going forth and multiplying, she must one day be more occupied in being a mother than in running the place. I do confess, however, that to this date she shows no sign of being overwhelmed. Indeed, sometimes to amuse the boys, she repairs to her old trunk in the attic and dons some of the exotic-looking clothes that she purloined from that pirate vessel in which you rescued her.*

*What a queer feeling it is, to see her playing at pirates with the boys, with no sign of what terrible memories that must arouse in her. She does tell them freely that she was once captured by pirates, and spent many months held prisoner in a castle by the sea, also that she was an honored captive, awaiting ransom and eating dates off a silver platter. And Bliven! Nothing do, but the boys asked, what are dates, and they would not rest until we procured some for them! When she is out of sight, they ask me if her stories can be true, and I am bound to tell them that they are, and that you and I saw her there, veiled and peering out from a window. Ha! It only deepens the adventure for them, and they are not old enough to have inquired into its darker nature.*

*I am bound to say also, that I marvel at her strength in this, for I did learn just how terrible is her memory of it. I have never written you of this—when we married I discovered that she was, let us say, not unknown to man. When put to the question, she admitted with evident unease that when she was a prisoner she was outraged by one of the bastard pirates.*

*She sank to her knees and prayed that this shame should not
come between us.*

*O, Putnam! I have never before felt so ashamed, that my pride
could cause this courageous woman to relive such an anguish.
I took her in my arms and vowed that I should never broach the
subject again, that her will to survive only deepened my affection
and respect for her.*

The very beginning of crow's-feet wrinkled the corners of Bliven's eyes as he broke into a smile. Good Rebecca, he had judged her rightly. Well done, once again. Their private duet during the opera in Naples would remain their secret.

"What is it, son? What has amused you? Who is the letter from?"

"From Mr. Bandy, Father. You remember him, he came to visit us when we were lieutenants on the *Enterprise*."

"Ah, yes. A well-seeming boy, for a Carolinian."

"Do you need help?"

"No, I thank you." Benjamin Putnam had entered from the hall with evident pain. "I give you I walk on sticks," then his eyes suddenly flew open. "But walk I still can, and as long as the good Lord vouchsafe me any use of my legs, I shall do so."

"Did you rest well?" It was close on two o'clock, a nap rather longer than usual.

"Yes."

When his father had become partly infirm, the result of a serious and warning apoplexy, Bliven had pulled a great heavy parson's bench into the keeping room and positioned it near the fireplace, lining it well with cushions. It was large enough that the elder Putnam could recline against one arm and stretch out his legs to the other arm, well tucked under a blanket. Thus he could pass time amid family activity and not feel himself an invalid. It was necessary to elevate his feet during the day, for with too much walking his feet and ankles swelled like bladders by evening. "Where is your mother?"

"Gone hunting."

"What? Ha!"

"Well, she bade me tell you she has gone hunting."

Benjamin Putnam beheld the family's two rifled muskets and fowling piece resting in their brackets above the mantel. "For what has she gone a-hunting?"

"Cloves and cinnamon, and ginger. I told her I had a mind to take a wagon out to the back field and cut pumpkins today. The first thing she thought of was spices, and that she is almost run out."

"Hmph! I hope she is able to find some. One hears that such nice commodities have become very dear for trying to race them past the British cruisers."

"How timely that you mention it. Mr. Bandy was just writing of this. Shall I read you what he sends?"

The elder Putnam touched a brand to his Dutch pipe and nodded "aye" between puffs.

"Bandy is no longer in the Navy but commands a merchant ship, and he has just dropped anchor in Boston—here it is."

*My good ship Althea is a tight handsome brig, as smart as any you have seen, and passing large for her species, near three*

*hundred tons and of great burthen, which makes her operation the*
*more profitable for her owners, among whom I am happy to*
*number myself, although claiming but a minor share.*

Old Putnam settled himself on the parson's bench and stretched
out. "Mercy! He writes a majestic great sentence, does he not?"
"He does, yes." Bliven continued.

*We loaded off a full cargo and received very good prices, for*
*being part owner of the vessel I partly pay myself. Is it not so, that*
*in the hearts and spades of commerce, one must take care not to*
*miss a trick?*
*You may find it of interest that in taking on a return cargo of*
*Fisk furniture, I heard it emphatically expressed that any progress*
*in local manufacturing that spoils the business for British goods*
*occasions great satisfaction here.*

"Hmph!" puffed Benjamin Putnam again. "I shouldn't wonder."
"Indeed," said Bliven, "he goes on in the same vein."

*Among these men of business, all the talk is of the endless*
*war betwixt the British and the French, and of their never-ending*
*wars with each other, and of the utter, utter disregard of our*
*own American rights by both sides. Our own veering and yawing*
*policy over the years has cost us hundreds—and I say, hundreds!—*
*of our trading vessels being seized by both England and France,*
*and converted by them into warships, and of millions of dollars of*
*cargo confiscated and never paid for. And worst of all has been—*

Bliven noticed that Bandy's hand changed as he had written this, more angular and almost slashing.

—*the impressment of American sailors, seized even upon American ships on the high seas, put in irons and forced to crew foreign men-o'-war. So prevalent has this become, that I marvel we have not felled every tree from Boston to Savannah, and built such a Navy, and taught them such a lesson, that they must leave off such damnable molestations. Mr. Madison, now he is President, seems to know not what policy to pursue—yet all here can see a terrible storm gathering.*

*For my own part I have little at hazard, for my partners and I limit our trade to our own coastal waters. You may likely judge the adventure I have had in procuring you the little gift that accompanies this letter, a sack of the most excellent Martinique coffee.*

The elder Putnam puffed on his pipe. "That would be what I smelled when I awakened."

"Yes, Mother roasted some while you slept, and I just ground and brewed it. Shall I pour you a cup?" He asked this even as he got to his feet, for his father's look of expectation gave a full answer. "Milk?"

"Just a little. Where is that strong-minded wife of yours?"

Bliven smiled as he stirred the coffee. "She is gone into town to have tea with her mother. She will be back before supper."

"Did you take her?"

"No, she hitched Cassius to the carriage and drove herself."

"Where was Frederick?"

"Hauling furniture for a customer."

"So she drove herself alone?" Bliven's father sucked some air audibly between his teeth in disapproval. "Well, that will give our village busybodies something new to talk about."

Bliven handed him the cup of coffee. "I needn't tell you how she declines to be fussed over and waited upon." He lowered his gaze and his voice. "Traits not unknown to yourself."

"Ha! Says he who stirs my coffee for me. Thank you." The elder Putnam relished a first sip. "Tell me truly, does it not . . . discomfit you at all that she spends so much time about her old life instead of here with you?"

"My word, no. I have to cut pumpkins the rest of the afternoon."

"No, son, I mean it generally. Her former life sported so much luxury, she cannot but find our circumstances too humble altogether."

Bliven shrugged. "Can you complain that she has neglected any of her duties here?"

"I cannot."

"Her mother is alone now, and not well. I do not begrudge them what time they have together."

"You will inherit better from her mother than you will from us, that is certain. You married well from that aspect."

"We married in no wise from that aspect, Father." It was telling that Benjamin phrased his observation in the manner that he did, for by their marriage, all of Clarity's property, including what she would inherit from her mother, would belong to him. Not without reason, however, had the Marsh family befriended Tapping Reeve, the proprietor of their famous law school, and obtained his advice on what he called Clarity's pending disability of coverture. As long as she remained single, she was heir to the Marsh fortune, but the instant she married, that was lost. They had been to see old Mr. Reeve in his comfortable manse that abutted his school, and to emphasize the point, Reeve had pulled the appropriate volume of Blackstone off the shelf and traced his finger along the lines for them: *By marriage, a husband and wife are one person in the law; that is, the very being or legal existence of the woman is suspended during the marriage, or at least is incorporated or consolidated into that of the husband, under whose wing, protection, and cover, she performs every thing.*

"I love you dearly," Clarity had said, and even as she smiled added, "but I think I shall not be looking to you as my master when it comes to my family's property." Nor did he wish her to. He might be lost at sea and his fate unknown for months, or years, and her life must continue and be paid for. Theirs was a case in which the law failed in its social purpose, and readily he signed deeds of trust to preserve her interest. The act made old Marsh and his wife trust him all the more, and intensified Clarity's devotion to him. There were still things she could not do—she could not incur debt nor make a contract, but with her unfettered access to money, she should not need to.

Together Bliven and Clarity agreed that there was no need to make his parents aware of their arrangement. Like all parents, they must regard a son's marriage into wealth as additional security for themselves should he die. Even in the Navy he was more likely to survive them than not, so the trust deeds, and Clarity's agreement to provide for his parents should he die, reposed with Mr. Reeve against that unlikely event.

"Besides, Father," Bliven added, "I must go back to sea one day, and we decided together that she should maintain lively interests of her own, and not just sit here and pine for me to come home."

"And that would include interests such as Reverend Beecher and that too-loud church of his?"

Bliven rolled his eyes. "Well, you have me there, I cannot disagree with that." Until the previous year, Lyman Beecher's visits to Litchfield had been confined to six a year as he crossed the Sound from his home church on Long Island. But now he had relocated to Litchfield itself, with its celebrated intellectual life and prosperous means. Especially, Bliven thought, for its prosperous means. At least Beecher had married and begun fathering children left, right, and center, so his former concern that Beecher's energy might be directed toward Clarity was allayed. He returned to happier thoughts and the last page of Sam's letter.

*We will stay here and make our presence known, until our hold is full of goods for which we will realize a good return back in Charleston. Providence alone knows when you might be recalled to active service, or when we shall meet again, but until we do, this missive travels with the esteem and affection of—as you remember we were once compelled to swear to each other—*

> *Yr. friend,*
> *Samuel Bandy*
> *Cmdg. Brig Althea*

*Bliven Putnam, Lieut.*
*Comdt., USN*
*So. Road, Litchfield,*
*Connecticut*

— // —

A chill gust curled through the keeping room as the door opened and Dorothea Putnam swept in, well shawled against the cold, clutching a small basket, a scattering of orange and brown leaves blowing in at her feet.

"Welcome and hail!" exclaimed Benjamin. "Diana home from the hunt."

Quickly she removed small packets from her basket and set them on the great pine table. Bliven held each to his nose and inhaled deeply, enjoying the treat of ginger and cinnamon not yet shaved, and cloves not yet ground. "Oh, I sense a pumpkin pie coming tonight."

"Bliven," she said, "may I ask you something?"

His face slackened with surprise. "Yes, certainly."

She seated herself but not comfortably. "Forgive my bluntness, but it is on my mind. I chanced across Mrs. Overton at the mercantile."

Bliven's heart fell as he guessed her meaning.

"You are acquainted with her son, I believe, who was lately second lieutenant in the *John Adams*. She said he has received a letter ordering him back to active service. Were you aware of this?"

"I was, yes."

Dorothea folded her hands in her lap, failing to disguise her anxiety. "And have you also received such a letter?"

"I have, yes."

Her voice rose despite herself. "And was there some point in time at which you were going to inform us of this?"

"Yes, but not yet. Soon, not yet."

"But how can you—"

"Mother." Bliven raised his hands in defense. "I am not ordered to report to the fleet. I am only to go to Washington City."

"Why ever?"

"I have no idea."

"When?"

"End of next week. Come, warm yourself by the fire." He handed her a cup of the fresh coffee.

She seated herself, both cold hands wrapped around the crockery cup for its warmth, her eyes sad and distant. "You are only nine months back from the West Indies and that awful business with those French pirates, those—"

"Buccaneers, Mother."

"Those buccaneers, as you so lightly call them. We nearly lost you there. I should think the Navy could give you more time to rest from that."

From his parson's bench Putnam guided his feet from their pillow down to the floor. "My dear, our son is a grown man, and a naval officer with a sworn duty to perform. And the times grow more perilous by the day. If we do not begin putting more ships to sea, a new war will find us defenseless."

"Men and wars," she muttered. "Men and wars. Things might be different if women had more say about things."

In his spare time Bliven had been reading a volume of the plays of Aristophanes borrowed from old Mr. Marsh's library, and he thought of his *Lysistrata* and the way that the Greek women had forced a war to a conclusion. Just as quickly he decided not to mention it because it would be well not to give either Clarity or his mother any ideas. "Now," he said, "I shall hitch up the wagon and see to those pumpkins."

Benjamin pushed himself to his feet with some effort. "I'll go with you."

It was a moment for Bliven to pause. He hated to see his father working in pain, but dreaded even more his father's reaction to being eased aside and denied his usefulness. "That will be very well. I will fetch the pumpkins if you could spread some fresh hay on the racks in the cellar."

Benjamin understood his calculation, exactly and appreciatively. "Up and doing," he said, "up and doing. What have you in mind for supper, my dear?"

Dorothea reined in her flash of temper as she understood that both her older and younger men had sensed a tempest coming and determined to seek the greater shelter of the open field. She took a more moderate tone. "We have yesterday's turkey," she assessed. "The crib is full of corn, and beans in the pantry. Perhaps some of that Brunswick soup you are so fond of?"

"Ah, yes!" His enthusiasm surfaced in the instant. "It was one of General Washington's favorites, as I hear. Something to look forward to, indeed." A measure of freshly ground ginger in the turkey soup, and fresh brown bread, and pumpkin pie, and a tankard of their own good hard cider before bed. *God is good*, he thought.

They walked slowly, at the older man's pace, to the barn. "So," Bliven began, "what is your thinking, Father? Who should we fight, the British or the French?"

Benjamin had no hesitation. "I grant you it is a close question for many people, but fight the Redcoats, for my part. The French have not such an all-powerful navy, mind, and if we join the British against them, victory would be swift and certain. But the high and mighty damned English would not thank us for our help, and as soon as the French be defeated, mark my words, they will directly resume the outrages upon us that they practice now. And if our Navy suffer losses in such a war, the more likely the English will turn on us afterward, and if they conquer us, we will be colonies again, and never under such a yoke before. But look now, if we and the French together can best the British again, we may gain a lasting alliance with France and force the British into a more respectful relation with us."

Bliven hitched their new shire mare to the wagon and heaved a bale of hay into it. Benjamin eased himself onto the tail of its bed, easier than clambering up onto the seat. They rolled slowly back toward the house, as far as the root cellar, where Bliven tumbled the bale of hay down into it and steadied his father to the top of the cellar stairs. "Do you want help down?"

"No, I thank you." Benjamin gathered himself. "Down I can manage. I may need help back up."

"That is a fair bargain. When I come back I will hand the pumpkins down to you."

"Right. Except take the best one in to your mother first, so she can set it to cooking. Every moment that pie is delayed is a moment lost!"

## — 2 —

*Mr. President Madison*

The day that Bliven left for Washington, he was up early in the snug suite that he had built for himself and Clarity onto the back of the Putnams' keeping room. As he dressed he faced away from her, as he habitually did, shielding her from the livid white scar that, after six years, still slashed across his lower belly. His souvenir of Naples reminded her every time she saw it how close she had come to losing him, and how she might yet.

When he returned from the Barbary War and he was furloughed on half-pay, her family saw no need for haste in their marriage. In fact they insisted on a lengthy courtship—for the first reason that they wanted to be sure that Clarity was certain of her affections, despite her two years of protest that she knew her mind very well; and for the second reason that they wanted to be certain that she understood she was marrying beneath her station, and beneath their expectations. She would be marrying honesty and enterprise, to be sure, but they needed her to accept that her social deposition would be noticed by all in their circle. It was true enough, once they were dead and gone, that her husband would rise inestimably in wealth, but that would not equal social acceptance, at least not without their friends noting how luckily he had married. They did not need to articulate a third argument, that the members of their church must be certain that there was no need for speed in the ceremonies—and all knew what that meant. Bliven took it as an affront that his honorable intentions should be to any degree suspect, and also as a commentary on the nature of the Reverend Beecher's church. Their faith was zealous, that was certain, but he doubted the need for it to extend to speculating, leave alone snooping, into one another's lives—never mind that many of them were the descendants of Pilgrims conceived by defeating the bundling board.

To Bliven's surprise, his parents sided with hers in the contest. Where the Marshes cited respectability, his parents relied on the platitude that they would have a lifetime together and there was no harm in letting their love mature and season before taking that irrevocable step. He and Clarity could not fight them all. After weighty discussion they made up their minds to regard this as a halcyon time that they could look back on with nostalgia, and he utilized the months of courtly calling and carefully governed privacy to improve the circumstances on their farm to such a degree that she could not feel she had descended to too low a perch. In fact, he took to calling it New Putnam Farm, to both connect it to and distinguish it from his great-uncle Israel's original Putnam Farm, near the town named for their family, in the very east of the state just across the Massachusetts line. That place was still worked by his cousins, still harvesting Vermont russet apples from the now-gnarled trees which were the first of their breed in the state, brought by their famous grandfather. Nor did it escape his design that tightening his identity with the celebrated General Putnam let Clarity's more rarified circle know that however fine their fortunes were now, it was his family that purchased their prosperity on the battlefield, and that he did not feel in the least their inferior. His dress uniform, which he habitually wore to church throughout the months of being furloughed on half-pay, did the rest.

As his father withdrew into a distant but supervisory consent, Bliven hired a man to run the livery and drayage, a young Pennsylvania man, Frederick Meriden, eager and amiable, keen to work his way up in the world. Bliven hired him at the farrier's wage of eighty cents per day, at which his father balked and pointed out that the youth had few expenses, for he had taken up residence with an aunt and uncle in Litchfield. With some application of logic Bliven brought him around to see that laborers were hired for their skills and services, not for their needs. Indeed, he pointed out, had the Navy taken himself on based on his material wants, they would not be paying him anything at all. It was true, he allowed, that eighty cents shaded to the generous side of the median, but that modest generosity was recompensed in young Fred's willingness to drive him and Clarity, and his parents when they chose to go, to church on Sundays.

Bliven also used a small inheritance from his mother's family to buy into Captain Bull's Tavern, of which they eventually assumed full ownership. Once certain of the tavern's earnings, Bliven hired another man to operate it. A Boston man and formerly a sailor named Peters, ruddy and strapping, he was possessed of a streak of amiable kindness that seemed to distinguish so many who had known the familiarity of life on a ship. Bliven hired him at sixty-six and two-thirds cents per day—not on the generous side of the median, but they provided him a room to live in upstairs and board from the tavern's larder, which left him content.

Bliven himself expended his energies on the farm, which allowed him to work off his frustrations both with the courtship and with the Navy, in a salutary way. While his parents occupied the main house, he built the extension onto the back of the keeping room, a large chamber partitioned first into a sitting area so Clarity might import some of her well-appointed previous life, and then a bedroom, enough removed from the main house to insure their privacy.

When they finally married, the transition was smooth, but it was apparent that Clarity had much to learn in the kitchen. Furnishings that were of everyday utility to Bliven's mother seemed curious artifacts to her. It had been many years, for instance, since Benjamin Putnam had left off raising sheep, so the spinning wheel in the corner was kept for the memories it brought, though his mother remembered well how to use it and still occasionally purchased a parcel of raw wool and eased her nerves by carding and spinning it. Using it defeated Clarity at first but she sensed an opportunity, in requesting lessons from her mother-in-law, to spin not only passable wool, but an affectionate bond between them.

———— // ————

Bliven knew how much his mother disliked leaving tasks undone, and as the day neared for his journey to Washington City, he concluded stages of work so as to leave her with the satisfaction that things were well paused until he should return: apples were harvested and cider pressed, Fred had been dispatched in the wagon to their Dutch accounts in the Hudson Valley, and he would return with ample cash for the winter. The farm now had entered its winter dormancy, and all that needed daily tending now were the pigs and chickens, well within his parents' and Clarity's capacity, and Fred when he returned would oversee the larger stock. A glance at the woodpile revealed less than a cord stacked, and he would have to see to that when he returned.

Bliven packed his sea bag—the same he had used since first shipping out on the *Enterprise*—though now as a lieutenant commandant when he went to sea he commonly took three trunks with it as well, one for more clothes, one for his books, and one that his mother always packed solid with a variety of preserved meats and treats. In exchange, he returned it to her packed with whatever exotic foodstuffs would survive the journey home. When he returned from the West Indies, most of the oranges he brought were spoiled, but the candied fruits and molasses had delighted her almost as much as the rum boiled from sugar cane had awakened his father to a new taste.

"I shall return and be back in harness in eight or ten days' time," Bliven told her as he hugged her and climbed into the carriage to go meet the stage at Bull's Tavern. "You will hardly have time to miss me."

She embraced him, longer than usual. "I shall try not to fear the news you will bring." There was no need to don his dress uniform yet; it was some days to Washington by the coach, but he was at his best when he materialized at the reception desk in the Navy Department four days later. Having been so long on furlough, it surprised him that the young adjutant rose and saluted him, which Bliven returned even as he realized this was in order. He had not felt much like a naval officer when he was so lately hauling pumpkins on the farm.

It surprised him even more that he seemed to be expected. The adjutant opened a door and disappeared within an interior warren of rooms, and when he returned he was in the wake of James Barron, who strode in with his hand extended. "By God, Putnam," he exclaimed. "By God, it has been a long time."

"Too long, Commodore. How have you been, sir?" He remembered to salute before taking his hand.

"Tolerable well, thank you." He was older and plumper but still bore his essential features, his balding dome poorly concealed by combing his curly hair forward, his nose now ending in a more prominent reddish bulb, his coat habitually unbuttoned because his growing stomach prevented it. It was now four years since that sad matter with the *Leopard* and Barron's court-martial. Everyone with whom Bliven had corresponded from the remoteness of his furlough felt that the whole business had made Barron a scapegoat, when the correct response would have been a declaration of war on Britain. But at least the Navy had seen sense in the end; they had reinstated him to rank and command, and all agreed to let the incident pass into history. "You remember Captain Hull?" Barron held his arm out to keep the door open as he entered.

Bliven saluted again. He and Hull had been friendly before, but now there was a matter of rank between them. "I remember him very well," he said. "Captain, your promotion was very welcome news. They could not have chosen better."

"Thank you, Mr. Putnam, thank you." Hull was now almost forty, gray showing at the temples of his black, curly hair. His form was settling into the greater heaviness of middle age, but his blue eyes were the same, sly and sleepy.

"Well." Barron smoothed his coat, trying not to be obvious in glancing over Hull's and Bliven's uniforms. "I am told our coach is ready. Are we prepared to meet the President?"

Bliven felt underdressed, with only his single epaulette of a lieutenant commandant, but he followed outside. Barron mounted first up into a black barouche with *vis-à-vis* double seats. Hull stepped up next and sat next to him; they faced forward, leaving Bliven to enter last and take the rear-facing seat; he must take care not to appear too much the peasant by turning around to take in the approaching sights of the capital city. The day was crisp but sunny; the top remained folded down. "You may walk on," Barron said to the sailor on the driver's seat, who gave a light snap of the reins to the matched grays who pulled them.

"Mr. Putnam," said Hull, "I was not aware until reviewing your dossier that you are from Litchfield."

*My dossier?* wondered Bliven. "Yes, sir, and my wife also." He was not married at the last time he was in nautical company, and he took some pride in being able to broach it.

"Ah. I wonder that we were not acquainted in earlier life," said Hull, "for I am from Huntington."

"I know the town," said Bliven. "I see the cut-off from Mr. Strait's coach as it leaves New Haven." It was only twenty-five or thirty miles south of Litchfield, an old town cut from the dense forest along the lower Housatonic. It was no mystery that Hull would have gone to sea; Huntington's first industry was building ships from its ancient oak and hickory trees.

Hull laughed. "You know Mr. Strait?"

"Yes, very well."

"Damn fine head for business, that one." Hull grew wistful. "I miss Connecticut. I miss it very much."

"I shouldn't wonder, sir," said Bliven. He missed it after four days. How could he cope with such homesickness if he were ordered back to sea? Perhaps he should have insisted on at least one more tour of duty before so much time had passed. Since returning from the Mediterranean with Preble in 1805, he had been recalled only once, to engage pirates in the West Indies. Since then he had become accustomed to marriage and home life. He took in some of the streets of the national capital as they slipped by. Some of the houses and commercial buildings were fine enough, but the town itself seemed unkempt and unclean. Natural enough, he supposed, for the untidiness of a democracy.

It was only a short ride before they turned into the grounds of the President's House. Bliven was disciplined not to remark upon its size, but he was taken aback at its expanse of cream-colored sandstone, its dry moat down to a ground floor that was not visible from the avenue, and the vast height of the portico into which the barouche pulled with the slowing clatter of hooves. He did allow his gaze to wander up to the angled *quatre-face* Ionic volutes, straight out of the Scamozzi pattern book. Suddenly it struck him how much he had absorbed from old Marsh's library in the preceding years, and how terribly he would miss those cultured books if he went back to sea.

A black servant in livery saw them down and held the door open as they passed inside. Bliven regarded the fawn-and-white diamond pattern of the foyer floor, of marble, and the height of the ceilings supported by paired Doric columns. In Naples he had supposed that marble floors and columns were limited to titled Europeans, but now he realized that he was wrong, and he was not sure how he should feel that the American President lived in similar state. But it was not quite right; there was something ignorant and imitative in it. The Doric order was meant to be stocky and bear weight; the pattern books he had seen showed that columns of this airy proportion should also have been Ionic, like those outside.

The doorman handed them off to a butler, also black and liveried, who showed them from the foyer, through a cross-hall, and then into a spacious round room with bow windows, dark parquet flooring, and white-painted wainscoting beneath a blue patterned paper.

"The President will be with you in a few moments," said the butler, and he closed the door after him as he withdrew.

There was ample seating among the fine mahogany sofas and chairs. "I wonder if we should sit," Hull said.

"Do we dare?" Bliven answered.

There was no time to consider it before there entered from an adjoining drawing room perhaps the most striking woman Bliven had ever seen. She wore pink silk with a white lace overdress, cut to the latest Parisian fashion with an Empire bustline, a matching pink turban with a large puff of teased feathers above that. Two things startled him: The first was her height. She was taller than any of the men present except Bliven himself, and in this assemblage she was quite his equal even before calculating her headgear. Second was her evident cheer. The raven-black curls that peeked from beneath her turban framed the merriest, most brilliant blue eyes he thought he had ever seen, her rouged cheeks raised like a well-formed apple in good humor that seemed completely without affectation. She looked as though she knew the funniest story in the room and was awaiting the right moment to tell it.

This remarkable lady strode across the room with no shyness and extended her hand to full arm's length. "Commodore Barron, welcome, how delightful to see you again."

"Ma'am, the pleasure is ours. May I present—"

"Lieutenant Commandant Putnam," she interrupted. "Am I correct? I am so pleased, I was told you would be coming." She extended her hand to him and took his with a grip perfectly balanced between heartiness and femininity.

"Lieutenant," said Barron, "may I present Mrs. President Madison?"

Bliven had the presence of mind to bow even as he took her hand. "A great honor, ma'am." He wished with all his might that Clarity were with him. He was certain that she and the Mrs. President would have become instant friends, and more than that, Clarity would have taken the lesson of how proper and pleasing it was for women to be so at ease in the company of men. At home most of her society was in Lyman Beecher's church, where women were supposed to fold up like daylilies when men held the floor.

"And Captain Hull, ma'am," added Barron.

She took his hand also. "Captain Hull, I believe we have only met once. You are most welcome. Please, gentlemen, pray be seated, and tell me all the Navy news. Commodore?"

"Well, ma'am," said Barron, "perhaps you have heard that Captain Hull is shortly to have command of the *Constitution*."

"I have indeed heard," she said. "Congratulations, Captain."

"Thank you, ma'am. She is a fine ship, and I shall try to be worthy of her."

"Oh, that appointment is well made," said Bliven. "She is a great ship, a splendid ship, and you will do her full justice, I doubt not."

"Thank you, Putnam. You served in her at Tripoli, did you not?"

"I had that honor, yes, sir, before being sent ashore with General Eaton at Alexandria."

"You were close to Commodore Preble, were you not?" asked Barron.

"I was, sir, yes. I was his aide for some time," Bliven answered.

"Damn shame when he passed away. He was much too young. Ulcer finally got him, did it not?"

"Yes, sir." Bliven had not thought of him in a while; it hardly seemed four years since he died. "Well, at least he had the satisfaction of knowing that Congress struck a gold medal for him. And he was offered the Navy Department, but of course he was too ill to accept."

The room had just fallen silent at his memory when the tall mahogany door to the hall clicked open and the liveried usher reappeared. "Gentlemen, the President will see you now."

Dolley Madison was the first to stand. "Thank you, Titus, I will show them up myself. Gentlemen, if you please?"

She led them through the cross-hall to a flight of stairs that seemed interminable. Bliven found himself curious to count the steps, but it occurred to him too late for they were already halfway up. On the second floor they turned left from the stairs; the hall ended at another door, which opened as they were ten feet from it, and two somberly suited gentlemen emerged. "Commodore Barron," said the first one.

"Mr. Secretary," Barron answered, as they shook hands, "you know Captain Hull, and may I introduce Lieutenant Commandant Putnam? Mr. Putnam, this is our Secretary of the Navy, Mr. Hamilton."

"Mr. Putnam"—Hamilton took his hand—"I am pleased to meet you. We have heard very good things about you."

Bliven had no time to wonder at this before being introduced to the other, much older, man. "This is Mr. Smith," said Hamilton, "our Secretary of State. We will visit again soon, Robert."

"Right," said Smith. "Good day to you." The elder gentleman nodded and walked toward the stairs, in deep and evident thought.

"Gentlemen," said Secretary Hamilton, "if you will come with me?"

Hamilton led them into a large study brightly lit by the morning sun. They beheld the President framed by the central arch of a Palladian window, his hands clasped tightly behind his back. "Mr.

President, Commodore Barron, Captain Hull, Lieutenant Commandant Putnam."

James Madison advanced two steps and gestured to a row of armchairs. "I pray you all, be seated." Bliven was shocked at the sight of him. Having already met Mrs. Madison, he had assumed that the President would be taller than she. Instead he beheld a tiny bird of a man, trim-waisted, certainly less than a hundred pounds. He could not stand more than five-feet-three without the heels of his shoes. He was past sixty, and as he settled behind his desk looked like a wrinkled little bewigged child, or changeling, poaching a perch in the President's chair.

"So, you are the famous Lieutenant Commandant Putnam."

"Yes, sir."

Madison leaned his head back and to the side, and tightened his lip with a dreamy look, almost visibly changing from the President to the aging revolutionary, the author of *The Federalist Papers*, turning over his memories. "You are related to Israel Putnam, of Massachusetts, as I understand."

"My great-uncle, yes, sir."

Madison rubbed a finger across his lips. Bliven half expected a reminiscence, a war story of Madison's highly regarded colleague. "Good stock" was all he said.

"We are happy to believe so, yes, sir."

Madison came back to the present and looked very sour for a moment. "Gentlemen, I will come straight to the point. For some long time we have been requesting the British to rescind their Orders in Council, which they claim gives them the right to stop and seize our ships, impound our cargoes unless we pay their tolls, and enslave our sailors. Mr. Smith has just informed me that our latest remonstrance has been rebuffed with even less consideration than usual. Gentlemen, I am after three years being cornered into a war that I have tried and tried to avert." Madison thought for a moment. "If we're going to get into a shooting war with the British, we're going to need men like Israel Putnam again. Smart. Brave. Resourceful. Do I remember that you were in the Barbary War, Lieutenant Commandant?"

"As a midshipman, Mr. President," interjected Barron, "Mr. Putnam was commended for gallantry when the *Enterprise* captured the *Tripoli*, and was promoted thereafter. He also accompanied General Eaton through Libya and commanded the artillery at the capture of Derna."

Madison smiled broadly. "Bombarded them with ramrods, yes, I remember now."

They all laughed. *God,* thought Bliven, *will I never live that down? Those damned Greeks.*

Barron continued, "He was cited again for gallantry in liberating American captives from the Dey's fortress in Algiers."

"Ah," said Madison, "yes, that was well done. But Eaton. Dear me, he raised quite a commotion when he got home, because we did not continue the war to utter conquest. Probably the sharpest thorn in my side when I was Secretary of State. How did you find serving with him, Mr. Putnam?"

Bliven found himself glad to offer some vindication, although it felt odd for one of such modest rank to be included in this moment. "He was fair and just to all he came in contact with, so far as my observation extended. His valor at Derna was exemplary; he led the assault and was wounded. He did feel humiliated at our betrayal of Hamet Pasha."

Madison held up his hands. "He was not without reason, but it couldn't be helped. We had to make peace because the Sicilians were about to cut off our ammunition and recall their ships."

"Yes, sir." Bliven nodded. "That is what I have since learned. They were afraid that Napoleon was going to come back at them again."

"Well." Madison pressed his hands together. "And I know you had rather a lively time down in the Indies since then. How have you found being laid up on furlough?"

Bliven smiled with a faint blanch, glancing nervously at Barron, unsure what was the most politic answer. "Sir, if there were action, I would prefer to be at sea of course. But, there is no action for the present."

"Well, there may be soon enough." Madison rose from his chair and walked over again to the great Palladian window that looked up Pennsylvania Avenue toward the Capitol. As he did so, the officers rose together in courtesy. Looking down at him accentuated what a spare, tiny man Madison was.

Madison turned at the rustle of uniforms and saw the officers standing. "Oh, for heaven's sake," he sighed. He strode over and returned to his desk. "Pray, sit, sit, sit," he said, and they arranged themselves again.

Once seated, Madison peered at Bliven impassively for what seemed an eternity.

Eventually Bliven wilted and could stand it no longer. "Mr. President," he ventured, struck even as he said them that those were two words that he never imagined he would utter in his lifetime, "I am finding myself in heady company. I have the profoundest respect for all here, in position and responsibility. But I am a junior officer from a past war who was furloughed home to plow. Forgive me, but, why am I here?"

"Because I wanted to have a look at you," said the President. "Putnam, we will shortly have, down in Charleston, a new, let us say, acquisition, a prize that we are refitting as a sloop-of-war."

Bliven's eyes widened, as Madison continued rubbing his lips before pointing at him suddenly. "I am curious, Mr. Putnam, perhaps you can tell me the truth of it. I have heard that your distinguished forebear General Putnam, in his youth, slew the last wolf known to live in Connecticut. Is that true?"

"Yes, Mr. President, it is true. The beast had been taking livestock, and my great-uncle tracked it to its lair, which was a small cave in a hillside. He crawled in after it, a torch in one hand and a musket in the other. The others with him had tied ropes around his feet, should they have to pull him out. They heard the most fearful snarling and snapping, and finally they heard the gun discharge, and they waited several minutes before it was my great-uncle who emerged alive, dragging the wolf out behind him. The cave is now something of a local landmark."

"Ha! Never had a lick of sense, that one," harrumphed Madison, though his admiration was evident. "I wish we had known that back then. Perhaps in the war we should have called him the Old Wolf instead of Old Put." Their laughter echoed in the large room. "He was old enough to have been my father; I was hero-struck right through. Have you any memory of him?"

"Bare memory of him, sir. I was three when he died. Others of my family have said that he foretold I should be the greatest of my family, but I only remember bouncing on his knee."

"Well," continued Madison, "the story you relate is substantially as I heard it. Our new ship in Charleston we are going to call the *Tempest*. The United States Ship *Tempest*. What do you think of that?"

"It sounds like she could fight, sir," he answered, daring to let his hopes rise.

"They tell me she's a Jamaica-man, she's built of cedar. Below-decks she probably smells like a coat closet."

"Doesn't matter, sir. Jamaica-built ships are known for their re-siliency. It is the resin in the wood, you see? It doesn't splinter as readily as oak, and it—"

Madison waved off the explanation. "Yes, yes, that is all very well. I have you in mind to command her." Madison saw Hamilton shoot a dubious look at Barron. "Now, some in my administration believe that you are too junior for such a command, and that you have been too long ashore between your cruises. And they believe that we mustn't damage the morale of older officers who feel themselves more deserving." There were at least twenty men in the service to whom such a pointed observation could apply, and they all knew it. "But look, I must put it to you plainly. The pressure to declare war on Great Britain is becoming more than I can resist any longer. I cannot be pestered with complaints of who thinks he deserves a command. Against the odds we face, I must have men who can fight! Men who I have confidence can fight. Preble advanced you for a command even while you were at home on your farm; Commodore Dale also, as he confirms in recent correspondence, attests that you are a man for action."

"Oh?" said Bliven. "I have lost touch with Commodore Dale. Where is he?" It pleased him beyond expression that Dale should remember him so.

Madison chewed angrily for a moment. "He is in Philadelphia, running an . . . insurance company. I would much rather he were here in this room and still in uniform."

"Well, as you know, sir," said Secretary Hamilton, "he was never one to forgive an insult. I have asked him twice, but he won't come back."

"Prickly damned porcupine of a man," said Madison. "But look here, Putnam, with those two holding you forward, I have a mind to put you in a place where you can show us what you can do. Well, what do you say? Do you want to come back?"

Bliven beheld all eyes on him. "Oh, sir, you have no idea."

Madison erupted in a volcanic laugh so out of character that every man of them started. "Well, by heaven, that is how we will have it. But now we come down to the hardest facts of it. Just within the past month alone, the British have taken another seventeen American merchant vessels; we cannot ascertain the whereabouts of many of their crews."

Madison nodded at Hamilton, who handed a memo to Barron, who handed it to Hull, who started to return it to Hamilton, but Bliven reached for it. "May I?"

No one forbade him, and he read quickly down the list of captured merchantmen—two-thirds down his blood froze as he saw the curt listing, "Brig *Althea*, Charleston, Captain Bandy."

"Oh my God. Mr. President, do you know anything of this ship, the *Althea*? Captain Bandy was in the Navy and we served together in the Mediterranean." He began breathing harder and could not stop it. "He wrote me a letter from Boston only a couple of weeks ago. How can we know so soon that the ship was taken? Do we know what has happened to him?"

"I am sorry for your alarm," said Hamilton. "Some of the crew with protection papers were put ashore in Bermuda. As it happened, a Swedish vessel passed through immediately thereafter, heading for Baltimore, and brought them home. Damned lucky, they might have been stuck there for months. Bandy was taken onto a British frigate as a pressed sailor. We don't know what one, but they have him out there somewhere."

"Oh my God," he almost whispered. "Oh, Sam."

"Forgive me, Mr. President," said Hull, "but—seizing ships, enslaving crews, stealing cargoes—are these not the reasons, the very reasons, for which we went to war against the Barbary pirates?"

"They are." Madison swelled in his chair. "But war was feasible then, with them. The Barbary pirates did not deploy, as the British do"—he grabbed and surveyed a small swatch of paper—"one hundred and twelve ships of the line, one hundred and forty-five frigates, and something over three hundred sloops, schooners, gunboats, and bomb scows, plus transports and armed merchantmen, to an aggregate total of one thousand and sixty ships. Gentlemen, forgive *me*, but what do you propose we do against *a thousand and sixty ships*?"

"Mr. President," said Secretary Hamilton, "let us remember that only a portion of those ships can be directed against us. The British have a global empire to defend—the Pacific, the Indian Ocean, the Mediterranean, the African coast. Now, the French do not have nearly so many ships, let us say a third of the British Navy, but enough to tie down the majority of their strength in other theatres."

"Until the British defeat the French," said Hull. "Then our goose will be cooked quick enough."

Madison looked darkly at Hamilton. "That is true. What about that?"

"Mr. President, I believe that our greatest ally is the ruinous expense that it will cost the British to prosecute a war against us. We need not defeat them entirely, we need only defeat them enough times that an opposition grows in Parliament to force a settlement."

"And our second ally," said Barron, "is the superiority of our ships, which can still take theirs two to one. And we can recover many of our merchant losses by practicing the same predation upon theirs. If Parliament can't force an end to such a war, Lloyd's of London would soon enough, I'll warrant."

Laughter rippled around the room. "And then," said Madison, "our Army commanders think very favorably upon an invasion of the Canadas before the British have a chance to reinforce those garrisons. If that goes well at all, it will enhance our bargaining position formidably. My mind is not set completely at rest. But I feel better than I did an hour ago, at least about the English. But now we come to the problems closer to home, and the first one is finding Mr. Putnam a crew. Let us ring for tea." He yanked twice on a velvet cord suspended behind his desk. "But first—" He fished through his cluttered desk to extract a large document filled with copperplate script, and blanks filled in with heavier ink. Quickly he dipped a quill in a crystal inkwell and applied his signature, small, studious, crabbed, and precise, to the bottom of the paper. "Mr. Putnam, you will sail in the rank of master commandant. Commodore Barron will hand you orders before you go home to arrange your affairs."

The door opened suddenly and the liveried Negro reappeared. "Titus," said the President, "we will take tea in the oval drawing room. Ask Mrs. Madison to join us, if you please."

"Very good, Mr. President."

Madison stood. "Very well, gentlemen, now you can stand up." He came from behind his desk, and in a very practiced way handed Bliven his commission with his left hand while extending his right. "Congratulations, Commander."

They passed down the central corridor until they turned into a room with an oval bay window mirroring the shape of the one beneath it where they had met Mrs. Madison. Bliven reflected that he had passed from one interim rank, which served a need but no one knew exactly how to address him, to another. Officially he would be master commandant, roughly equivalent to the Royal Navy's master and commander, ostensibly entitled to command a larger ship than a lieutenant commandant. That was an awkwardly long rank to be addressed by; informally he could be called Commander, although not everyone would, as that fashion had not firmly taken, and the men on his own ship would address him as Captain. No bad thing—he smiled to himself—to be prepared to answer to any rank that sounded appropriately dignified.

"Tell me, Putnam." Madison reached up and placed a hand familiarly on Bliven's shoulder as he pointed him to a chair. "Where shall we find men for your ship?"

*Sufficient crew*, thought Bliven darkly. *The same old obstacle.* "Can I not recruit enough men after I get to Charleston?"

"Well"—Madison extended the word in doubt—"Carolinians can show a fighting spirit, that is true enough. But they tend to come from the militia tradition. They fight when they want to, but then feel privileged to go home when they want to. I would not want to rely upon them on a long and hazardous voyage."

All rose as Dolley Madison entered the room, trailed by a maid bearing a large chased silver service which she set with a tiny clatter on a mahogany sideboard. "Sit, gentlemen," exclaimed Mrs. Madison, "sit, sit. I shan't interrupt you." Efficiently she placed milk and sugar on a low table among them and poured tea at the sideboard, distributing the cups, and each officer took milk and sugar as he pleased.

"Equally so," continued Madison, "I have my doubts about our New England Federalists. They represent the commercial interests of that region, and their hostility to any thought of war borders on apoplexy."

"Damn 'em," spat Hull. "Dying party, they won't last."

"Yes," acknowledged Madison, "but they are not dead yet. They are a minority, but they still wield enough power in the Congress to be troublesome, and the merchants they represent are willing to consider the loss of some ships, and the impressment of sailors, as a bearable cost of doing business."

"Forgive me, sir!" cried Bliven. "That is several thousands of our seamen, enslaved for as long as the British choose to keep them so! That is no cost of doing business."

Madison looked at him so long and so intensely that Bliven feared he had breached the etiquette in speaking out of turn. "I agree with you," said Madison at last, "and for that very reason I am as wary of recruiting all our seamen from New England as I am of the Carolinas."

"What is your solution, sir?" asked Hull.

"Mr. Hamilton?" Madison gestured. "You have the floor."

"Gentlemen," said Hamilton over his tea, "I need not tell you that we face a situation in which we hold few advantages. But one of our advantages is the British do not know how close we are to declaring war upon them. They merely count their thousand ships against our seventeen and assume that we will submit to whatever they require of us."

*And well they might,* thought Bliven.

"You know also in recent years we have built or acquired gunboats to protect our harbors, to the number of about one hundred and seventy, sufficient to ward off light molestations."

*Gunboats,* thought Bliven, *which proved at Tripoli how useless they are against a real naval force.*

"It will be some months before the British can deploy their naval strength against us, which gives us time to damage their merchant fleet considerably before they can respond. At this moment, our greatest concentration is in New York, where Commodore Rodgers has the *President* and the *Hornet. Essex* is with them but she needs repairs before she will be seaworthy. Presently they will be joined by the *United States*, the *Congress*, and the *Argus*. That is a considerable squadron—even more so, Captain Hull, when you leave here and join them with the *Constitution*."

Hull nodded in agreement.

"Mr. Putnam," Hamilton went on, "you will go with Captain Hull to New York. There you will undertake a recruitment effort. Post handbills, confer with local politicians to arrange patriotic gatherings. We will burnish some of that heroic luster you bore home from the Barbary War, and see if you can relieve us of the worry of manning these ships."

Bliven smiled, more in doubt than in pleasure. "Yes, sir."

"You will need about a hundred and thirty men for the *Tempest*, and Commodore Rodgers will make his needs known to you when you reach New York. The combined squadron of five sail, plus *Essex* if she's ready, will sortie into the shipping lanes and work the maximum destruction you can, take as many prizes as you can, before the British can reply in force."

*And God help us when they do,* thought Bliven. "And the *Tempest*, sir? What is our assignment?"

"Rodgers necessarily will have the only large squadron. All our remaining vessels will operate independently, or briefly in tandem as circumstances permit, to disrupt their shipping, take prizes, and avoid being forced into action against superior firepower."

Bliven nodded soberly. "Yes, sir."

"And of course," said Hamilton, "we are working diligently to issue letters of marque to as many privateers as we can enroll."

"Have you thoughts to offer, Commander Putnam?" asked Madison suddenly.

"Let us grant that the odds are unfavorable," said Bliven slowly, "but they are not impossible. Your generation won the Revolution, Mr. President, by declining to fight by their rules. Your squirrel hunters hid behind trees, when necessary, and decimated those marching red columns. We may be able to do the same at sea."

"And so, Commander, do you believe you have bravery equal to your uncle's? Would you follow a wolf into its dark den with aught but a torch and a musket?"

Bliven considered it for a moment. "Yes, sir, if I had no alternative. I do believe I would have first tried to trick the animal into revealing itself and dispatched it in greater safety. But failing that, yes, sir, I believe I should have done what was required for the safety of others."

"Well spoken, young man. Yes. Brains, and then bravery. That is what is needed." Bliven caught Madison searching deep into his eyes. "Brains and bravery," he continued softly. "And before my God, you shall have need of both."

## — 3 —

### *To War, Slowly*

The carriage ride back to the Navy Yard was somber, until at last Commodore Barron remarked upon it. "Putnam, you do not have the air about you of a man who has just been promoted and given a command."

The day had turned chilly, so that all three officers had their fore-and-aft bicornes tugged down almost to their ears. "I'm sorry, sir, I was thinking. If I am to go to South Carolina, I should try to call on Mr. Bandy's wife and see if there is anything I can do for her. We are old friends."

"Who?" asked Hull.

Bliven felt a wash of displeasure that Hull did not remember him. "That was Mr. Putnam's fellow lieutenant," said Barron, "who was lately pressed and taken from that commercial vessel."

"Has anyone written to inform her of this, sir, do you think?"

Barron shook his head. "I doubt it, the news was just received. The government might well post it in the *Intelligencer*, but as he is no longer in the Navy, there is no official channel through which she would be informed. Perhaps you should write her a letter."

"Yes, I will. I will."

"Where are you staying, Putnam?" Hull asked suddenly.

"I have no idea," said Bliven. "I left my sea bag at the Navy Yard, intending to inquire. Can you recommend a place?"

"Indeed I can, King's Tavern on Ninth Street, quite nearby. It is substantial and comfortable, although mind you the board is not so fine as when Mr. Tunnicliff was the proprietor. I reside there myself when in town, as now, and I know they have a room that is available."

At the Navy Yard they returned to the building from where they had started. "Gentlemen," said Barron, "I believe this will adjourn us for the day, but pray do tarry a moment. We do not have your sailing orders yet, Putnam, but I do have something for you that we are anxious for you to give attention."

Barron descended slowly, then turned and straightened himself to receive and return their salutes. "My aide will come out in a moment."

That young officer handed Bliven a thick sheaf of collected documents, all wrapped in a heavy sheet of paper, watermarked and very white, folded over and sealed with wax, which was impressed with an anchor. Bliven shot a quizzical look at Hull, who looked away as Bliven poked the bundle with some resistance down into his coat pocket.

"Walk on," Hull said to the driver, "to the receiving station. Putnam, you can pick up your kit. Then on to King's Tavern at Pennsylvania Avenue and Ninth Street."

"Captain, when do we expect this war to commence?"

Hull shrugged. "Oh, there will be no great hurry to it. Nothing but preparation can occur without a declaration of war, and that must await the next session of Congress. Now, mind you, preparations will keep us well occupied."

"When will you require me aboard the *Constitution*?"

"Oh, Lord." Hull rolled his eyes. "Not soon. You will have plenty of time to go home and arrange your affairs as you need." He laughed suddenly. "Believe me, the Navy does not wish to bring officers back to full-time pay until it is necessary."

"Oh." Bliven's eyebrows rose. "I had not thought of that."

"No, you would not think of that. There is something else this day that you did not think of, although it does you credit."

Bliven searched his mind. "In good faith, sir, I don't know what you mean."

"Exactly my point. You are the first man I ever saw promoted whose first thought was not to find the nearest purser and obtain the insignias of his new rank." Hull dug around in his coat pocket.

Bliven observed him closely, astonished, until Hull looked up and their eyes met, and Hull roared in laughter. "My God, Putnam, you are still so *earnest!*"

Bliven smiled broadly and looked away, shaking his head. In the moment he had forgotten that there indeed was no difference in the insignias between lieutenants commandant and masters commandant. "Very well, Captain," he sighed. "You have caught me in your witticism. I own it. Well done."

Hull was still wheezing in mirth as the barouche pulled to a stop at a massive but squat masonry structure, one central door and a window on either side, but nevertheless quite wide, a building of two stories, with two additional windows in the gable end, which faced the street. The multiple tall chimneys gave Bliven hope that he might obtain a room with a fireplace, for the cold damp promised frost in the morning. They descended, and inside the ground floor had a low ceiling thickly ribbed with massive joists, testifying to the weight of the building above.

At the sound of the door a weary-looking middle-aged man appeared from a store room.

"Good day to you, Mr. King!" boomed Hull. "This gentleman is Master Commandant Putnam, who requires a room for the night. I made bold to tell him you had one available, which I hope you have not filled in my absence."

"Indeed not, Captain, I thank you for the reference. I will happily accommodate the gentleman."

They found themselves at one end of a dim public room, and Hull slapped a silver half-dollar onto the desk. Bliven glanced down at it, always amused to see the same fat-busted female Liberty as on the silver dollar that Cutbush had him bite on in Naples. "We shall warm ourselves by the fire," said Hull, "with two tankards of your ale, if you please, sir."

"Right away, Captain, I shall draw your ale and then prepare the gentleman's room."

They took no notice of the three other men scattered about the room and they settled into two Windsor chairs near a broad, low-arching fireplace. Presently King set before them a wooden platter with two tankards of pewter, filled with dark foamy brew. "And what shall be your fare on this evening, King?"

"A fine Virginia ham, Captain, if that will please you. With potatoes cooked in milk, and peas."

"That will serve." Hull nodded emphatically. "That will serve."

"I find no defect in that bill of fare," said Bliven, after King had left.

"No, indeed I may have spoken too critically." Hull leaned back, obviously enjoying the fire and the ale. "Although, old Tunnicliff, my God, he had a conscience about food. He had a way with young cod, he served it in the Dutch way, split down the back and boned, broiled with butter—young cod, mind you, the most delicate flavor you can imagine. What is it?"

Hull had caught Bliven smiling broadly at him. "I'm sorry, sir. I was just thinking, upon this subject, how much you remind me of Commodore Preble."

Hull threw his head back. "Ah, Preble. God, I miss Preble. Now, that man knew how to dine. No captain ever set a finer table."

"No, indeed," Bliven agreed. "And what other officer would have ever dared sail with his own chef?" They laughed. "The more cruel the irony, it was his stomach that killed him. Well, here is to him." Bliven lifted his tankard.

Hull joined him. "The commodore."

"How are things with the *Constitution*?" asked Bliven.

"Better," answered Hull flatly. "Rodgers had her in Europe for four years. Four years! Can you imagine? The crew nearly mutinied, he brought her home nearly played out. They spent a hundred thousand refitting her before turning her over to me, and would you believe it? I took command and discovered no one had so much as looked at her bottom! She was a floating forest of weed and barnacles, they must have taken three knots off her speed. So I hove her down and had her scraped; they took off ten wagonloads!" Hull paused for a swig of ale. "First cruise I took her to Holland to make our specie payment to the Dutch. By God, I never sailed a vessel that handled so slick. Just got back in September. She's ready, she will take on any assignment, but for one thing that does concern me."

"Captain?"

"The crew's enlistments are up. I must ship out with all new men."

"No! It was not mentioned today." That was a potentially crippling impediment.

"No, well, that's why they are sending you to New York with me to find a crew for yourself; I must scour Washington and Baltimore for enough derelicts and farm boys to man the *Constitution*." Hull caught himself. "I mean you no offense about the farm boys."

"No offense taken, I assure you. We are in the same boat, as it were."

Hull shook his head. "At least the Navy has put seven hundred more Marines in uniform, that more than doubles the service. Spread among us, we can at least maintain discipline."

"True, but that does not change the odds of the contest. We have not a single line-of-battle ship; the British have more than a hundred. And even if they withhold them all and send only half their frigates, that is still their seventy against our ten."

"Seven," said Hull sourly.

Bliven paused. "Sir?"

"*New York* and *Boston* are not seaworthy; don't breathe a word of that to anyone. *Adams* needs heavy repair, as I have said. If we go to war, it will be with seven frigates and eight sloops and schooners. It is all laid out in that great packet of papers bulging in your pocket there."

"Indeed, sir? Will you, at last, tell me what is expected of me? I am still completely at sea concerning why I was even included in such a lofty gathering as today."

Hull drew a long breath. "Putnam, I don't know what you did to win such favor, but Preble, before he died, and Dale have urged it upon the Department—" He did not know how to finish the thought. "Brains and bravery, as Madison said, those are the words they used about you."

"Oh, I see. Truly, sir, I had no hand in promoting myself to—"

Hull waved it off. "No, no, we know you didn't. Eaton, too, he was in on it. But the war, if it comes, will be desperate. They want all the advice they can gather. The generals and commodores all have experience, maybe they think you will have a fresh look at things, see something new, or something they missed."

"I see."

"What you have in your pocket are the sum of our naval dispositions, harbor defenses, previous recommendations. When you get home to Connecticut and wait for orders, you are to devise plans, contingencies, everything you can think of. Approach it like a school problem, like on your lieutenant's examination."

"That will be an almighty serious undertaking on which to apply myself."

"Most serious," agreed Hull.

"Which I am to perform while I am furloughed on half-pay?"

Hull turned his palms up helplessly.

Bliven felt a wave of impatience come over him—not disgust altogether, for he was not without sympathy for the country's financial straits. "Is this not a remarkable circumstance? We are all but ready to empty the prisons to find common sailors, but to have too many officers to pay, well, now, that is a different matter entirely."

Hull stared into the fire. "When you write a report, don't send it to Hamilton at the Navy Department. We fear he is not long for the job."

"I understand," said Bliven.

"No, you don't, really. I might as well tell you, we don't trust him."

"Sir?"

Hull chewed uncomfortably on his thoughts for a moment. "When all this British piracy first reached a crisis, Madison convened a cabinet meeting and asked their advice. Their advice, Putnam? Their official recommendation was that the entire Navy be laid up in ordinary, taken off the sea. That, they said, would prove our peaceful intentions to the British, and we could confide in their magnanimity to cease their depredations upon our merchant vessels."

Bliven swallowed hard. "Good God, sir, you don't mean it."

"They went so far as to send orders to Rodgers not to sail from New York pending further orders. Well, Bainbridge and Stewart heard about it, and they came to Washington hot as boiling oil. They obtained an audience with Mr. President Madison, and they gave him such a broadside as he will never forget. I expect they believed that their careers were not worth a copper penny anyway. Well, sir, they carried the day, Madison agreed with them and overruled his cabinet, so we still have a Navy."

"Hamilton?" asked Bliven. "Nothing that he said today indicated such an opinion."

"No, indeed he did not. The President has stated his policy, and Hamilton is obeying and implementing it. And we suppose it is possible, that his previous advocacy to dispense with us was for the sake of argument only, to be certain that the entire range of options was discussed. But we cannot be sure. We must remain alive to the chance that he would sell us out in a snap."

Bliven shook his head. "I had no idea."

Hull gestured with his emptying mug at the bulge in Bliven's pocket. "So you will understand that your report is not for Mr. Hamilton. Do not trust it to the mails, bring it down to Barron, if you do not hear otherwise, and a copy for me."

———※———

It was four days by stages back to Connecticut; evening had deepened by the time Mr. Strait deposited Bliven at his door on the South Road. He could see candles burning behind curtains and smoke curling from the keeping room chimney, but not heavily. His father had always prided himself on making efficient fires. A smoking fire, he'd always said, is a wasteful fire. A glance across the yard reminded him straightaway, upon seeing the shrinking wood cache, to lay in sufficient firewood to see them through the winter, and, not knowing the outcome of the impending war, he would prefer wood for two winters. The countryside for many miles around had been so extensively improved into farmland that people remarked on the scarcity of remaining mature forest with a portion of large hardwoods from which to split and age logs. The winter after he and Clarity married, the woodcutters had done such a profitable trade, and firewood was so dear, that Bliven feared his father would endanger his and his mother's health by flapping around in a constant frost before consenting to pay their rate.

Benjamin Putnam greeted him in the hall, taking both his walking sticks in one hand and grasping him by the arm with the other. "Ah, my son, home at last. How was your trip?"

"Very full," said Bliven, "very, we can say, substantive." Suddenly he noticed that new slim, translucent tapers rose from the mirrored sconces on the hall wall. "Well, now, these are very fine."

"Do you see, do you see what that wife of yours has done? We had need of candles, and we sent her to the butcher for tallow. Your mother dips perfectly fine candles, as I need not tell you. Do you know what she did? She went not to the butcher but to the chandler—and came back with an entire parcel of beeswax tapers. Beeswax! When have we ever afforded beeswax?"

Bliven regarded again the elegant candles in their sconces. "I confess my surprise, Father." He well knew that beeswax candles were had at six to eight times the price of tallow. "I am certain she must have been thinking of your and Mother's comfort."

"Comfort? How comfortable shall I find debtors' prison when I am taken hence?"

Bliven patted Benjamin on the arm. "I will speak to her. Meantime, you have our permission to enjoy them. Ah, Mother."

"Welcome home, dear boy." They kissed on both cheeks and she led them into the keeping room. "There is warm cider. Would you like some?"

"Oh, yes. Where is my wife?"

Benjamin worked his way over to his pillowed parson's bench. "Dining with her mother. I will have a cup of cider, too, my dear, if you will be so kind."

"Oh, what is that?" Bliven pointed across the room to a piece of furniture abutting the large pine sideboard where food was prepared. "A new acquisition?" It was a stout cabinet on eight-inch legs, with doors of pierced metal.

"Yes, my dear. When Frederick took the wagon of cider to the Dutch towns on the Hudson, he filled the accounts and had several jugs remaining. There was a carpenter who desired them, but he had not the money to buy them. Frederick agreed to take this pie cabinet in exchange."

"Perhaps hard currency would have been better," mumbled Benjamin.

She harrumphed back at him. "You will not say so after your pie cools, I'll wager."

"Ha!"

"It is well made," she affirmed, "and I am glad to have it. And look, Bliv dear, he put new tin in the doors, punched with anchors and dolphins, especially for you. What nice thinking that was. Clarity will be back any moment. The post rider brought us your letter yesterday that you would be home today. Are you hungry?"

"I am, in fact. Mr. Strait was behind his time and did not stop in Watertown as he is wont to do, so I have not eaten. I feel I could eat a whole deer."

"Funny you should say so, you needn't eat the whole animal, but you may have as much as you like. Frederick went hunting and was favored with a fine large buck which he has shared most generously." She loaded a plate with roast venison, sweet potatoes, and fresh yellow bread made from Indian meal. She poured cups of warm cider, took one to Benjamin, and set Bliven's supper before him, then drew up a chair beside him. "Well, now, we have been waiting most patiently. What news do you bring us?"

"You would have me speak with my mouth full?"

"Yes. You are excused from manners for the evening."

"I am promoted, to the rank of master commandant. I am to have my own command, a twenty-gun sloop-of-war. She is on her way from Jamaica and will start fitting out for me in Charleston. That will take some time, however."

"Well, good," she said. "One hopes a great deal of time, not to sound unpatriotic."

"Don't get too hopeful. If there is a war, I am to sail with Hull on the *Constitution* until my own ship is ready."

"Well," said Dorothea, "better on her than on a lesser ship."

"And what is the name of your ship, son?" inquired the elder Putnam.

"The *Tempest*," he said with evident pride.

"Really?" His mother registered surprise. "Why *Tempest*?"

"Well, I suppose after wasps and hornets they ran out of stinging insects."

"Yes," she said, "the U.S.S. *Honey Bee* would not sound very ominous."

"Father," said Bliven, "you will be pleased to know that the President inquired after your Uncle Israel and his famous exploit at the wolf den."

Dorothea gasped. "The President?"

"Yes."

"What have you to do with the President?"

"Well, there was a conference of sorts. Believe me, I was the least one present. For the time being they want me to study our defenses and recommend improvements."

They heard the carriage approach and stop outside the keeping room's side door; Bliven excused himself and hurried outside in time to help Clarity down. It had begun to snow lightly, and flakes were sticking in the fur trim of her hooded cape. "Oh, my love," she almost squealed, and jumped down into his arms.

They clasped tightly before she looked back up to the carriage. "Thank you, Freddy."

"Hello, Freddy." Bliven reached up and they shook hands.

"Welcome home, Lieutenant. I trust you had a pleasant journey."

Bliven held Clarity about the shoulders, swinging her lightly forward and back. "Pleasant enough to have left a lieutenant and come home a commander, thank you."

"Well, Commander, then, congratulations."

"Thank you, and thank you for looking after everything so ably in my absence."

"Of course." He tapped the horse lightly with the reins. "Home, Cassius." And the carriage started forward into a tight turn.

Inside, Clarity shed her cloak and warmed herself by the fire. While Bliven was outside, his mother had begun preparing coffee and had placed cups in their saucers around the table. "If I were a gambling woman," she said, "I would wager that we all would like some pie before we retire. My dear, do you feel like joining us at the table?"

"Ha! Yes, yes." Benjamin pushed himself up from his parson's bench and made his way over, taking some satisfaction in once again heading his table. As Clarity poured the coffee, Dorothea busied herself at the sideboard and returned with two dessert plates in each hand, seating herself after they were served.

Putnam leaned back in his chair. "Well, here, now, what is this?" On his plate he regarded a wedge of custard, dark orange brown, underlain by a pastry crust.

Dorothea's and Clarity's eyes met, merry.

"Why," said Clarity, "pumpkin pie, Father Putnam."

He turned his plate as though expecting the wedge to change its shape. "No, 'tisn't."

"Try it, my dear," said Dorothea. "It is the new fashion of pumpkin pie. This is the way the best families have it now."

Putnam sank his fork through the custard and placed the piece dubiously in his mouth. He pressed it against his palate with his tongue. "'Tis well enough for taste, I grant you." He worked his way rapidly through two-thirds of his slice. "Yes, I will concede its qualities, but I confess, it is not the real pumpkin pie that I had my heart set on."

"Well, I suspected as much." Dorothea pushed herself back from the table and crossed to the fireplace, from which she removed a cast-iron Dutch oven. Onto the counter she turned out a roasted whole pumpkin, and from it she cut a wedge through to the center, revealing as she removed it a center of pale spiced custard, and within it the pale sheen of cooked apple slices.

She returned and set it before him, kissing him on top of the head. "You are a creature of habit, my dear."

"Oh, oh, you are good." Carefully he carved out a portion of the custard with a slice of apple, and added to it a peel of the spiced pumpkin meat. He let the whole assemblage of flavors roll around in his mouth. "Oh, incomparable," he said at last. Putnam placed his hands flat upon the edge of the table with a satisfied demeanor. "There, now, my son, do you see how it works? Remember this for your future. Just the tiniest and most delicate of complaint, well timed, will gain you two desserts instead of one!"

"Well done," Bliven agreed. He pushed himself up from the table and kissed his mother on the top of her head. "I give you the pumpkin pie was new-fangled, but I pronounce it delicious. I"— from a hook by the door to his and Clarity's room he took and donned a dark greatcoat, and settled his bicorne upon his head— "will just go make sure our menagerie is bedded down well before I turn in." From the mantel he took and lit a lantern and exited.

"You cut a fine figure, my son," said his mother after him, "but we really must find you a less ornamental hat for everyday use."

In the hen yard immediately behind the house he found their dozen chickens warm in their coop, and beyond them the pigs content in their sty shed. From the barnyard the cow had entered the barn of her own accord. He checked on her and closed up the barn; a cold pale moon had risen, and beyond the barn he surveyed their orchard of dormant apple trees. There was no need to walk to the edge of the orchard and peer down its rows, but he did so anyway, realizing as he did that he was surveying this dearly loved life because he must leave it once more. It made him want to weep. Warmth, good food, convivial family—his need to experience the world had led him to sea, his passage paid by serving the country as a naval officer. It was a post at which he acknowledged he had acquired skills that the nation now had sore use of, but to leave this hearth and these people was a heavy cost.

"Belay that," he muttered. Back out at the road he looked up and across to their livery establishment. It would have been superfluous to walk up and check on the horses, for Freddy always groomed and bedded them down with the most admirable attention.

Once he ascertained that everything outdoors was in order, Bliven passed through the keeping room, his lamp a moving small yellow circle of illumination. At the fireplace he set the lamp on the mantel, picked up the shovel, and scattered coals into a warming pan before entering their suite and latching the door behind him.

Clarity sat at her writing desk, at her elbow a silver candelabrum holding five of the new beeswax tapers amply lighting the papers before her. She leaned over the desk, perusing a small book, her hand over her mouth, shaking with mirth.

"What is it, my love? What are you reading?"

"One of your mother's cookbooks; she gave it to me this afternoon. I protested, but she insisted that it was time to pass it down to the new generation. Her reason was that she had long since committed to memory everything that your father would eat, and the rest she did not need to know."

"May I see?"

Clarity handed it up, and he read aloud, "'*American Cookery*, by Amelia Simmons, an American Orphan.' Why, I remember this from before I joined the Navy!"

"Here." She took it back. "Let me read it to you." Her voice took on a tone of knowledgeable and somewhat condescending explanation.

*The world, and the fashion thereof, is so variable, that old people cannot accommodate themselves to the various changes and fashions which daily occur. They will adhere to the fashions of their day, and will not surrender their attachments to the good old way—while the young and the gay, bend and conform readily to the taste of the times, and fancy of the hour.*

She pealed in laughter. "There. Does that not sound like anyone we know?"

"Surely it does. Which reminds me, that that one particular old person bids me protest to you the extravagance of beeswax candles. He is quite alarmed at such an expense."

Clarity stood beside her writing table. "Dearest." She squared herself. "Tallow candles burn ill and smoke. I have designs to work harder to finish my novel, and I cannot be forever fighting head-aches caused by the candles. Nor could I very well provide bees-wax for my work and then consign your parents to smoky tallow in the rest of the house. If your father thinks that I have spent too lavishly on them, you must let him understand that beeswax is now well within our means and I am quite happy to provide them. Do you not agree?"

"Yes, yes, when you pair generosity with common sense, you do overcome all obstacles. I will have a talk with him."

He held her briefly and released her, folded down the quilts from their pillows, and began pushing and pulling the warming pan between the sheets. Clarity watched him with amusement. "I rather thought we might be making our own heat this night."

He smiled as she blew out the candles and removed her layers of clothing by degrees, eventually slipping a nightgown over her head, as he exchanged his uniform for a night shirt. Beneath the covers he drew her close. "Are you not apprehensive at perhaps being left with a child when I must go back to sea?"

The palms of her hands framed his face. "Is that not what sail-ors do?"

He kissed her. "Not those with a conscience about such things."

"Well, never mind your conscience." Her fingers combed through his hair. "My dearest heart, what, what do you think would give me the greatest pleasure in this world than to have a little son or daughter to present you when you return? To give your parents a grandchild while they are still here to savor that experience? Would that not complete our family, our joy?"

He nestled her head to his chest. "Yes, it would. But childbearing is a dangerous undertaking. I would wish to be here."

She pulled back, her eyes finding his in the dark. "So would I, but you can't be. I knew this when I agreed to marry you." She kissed his throat. "The risks are the same whether you are here or no. I can face it. Your mother and mine are strong women, they will look after me, and this locale is hardly wanting for the medical attention. So fear not, and do your duty."

He kissed her more deeply, exploring with his hands as though it were their first time, discovering her anew. *God,* he thought. *God, I don't want to leave here. God, never let me take this woman for granted.*

Bliven awakened before it was light, and realized that neither he nor Clarity had moved a muscle from the moment they had expended their passion. She was sleeping soundly, and he could not disentangle from her without waking her, but he was content to study her features at rest in the warmth of the bed. He thought to doze back off but was no longer sleepy. At length in her sleep she shifted away from him, and quickly he slipped out of bed before his leaving would disturb her.

He slid into slippers and tiptoed into the dark keeping room. The fire had died down to where it could not be built up from surviving coals. He knew by feel in the dark where the tinderbox reposed on the mantel, but, having felt it, moved his fingers a few inches to the right for the implement he had come to prefer, a fire syringe he had purchased in Martinique the year before, along with a quantity of amadou—that tree fungus, pounded flat and impregnated with nitre. The fire had burnt down to where new kindling would not catch, so he placed a quantity of dried wool and straw on the ashes, and small kindling atop that.

Working quickly and by feel, he removed the plunger from the syringe and placed a generous pinch of the amadou into the notch at the end of the plunger and blessed whatever ancient alchemist first concocted it. He knelt upon the hearth, inserted the plunger into its cylinder, and struck it down forcefully. There was an explosion of light and fire in the bottom of the apparatus, and withdrawing the cylinder revealed the amadou in a burning flame. This he touched to the wool and straw, which in only a few moments he parlayed into a fire over which he swung a kettle of water. Why anyone would continue to fiddle with old-fashioned tinderboxes when a new wonder like this existed was beyond him. But then, fire syringes were not widely available and were considered exotic, even French. And old people do prefer to hew to the old ways—he smiled at the memory of the night's pumpkin-pie adventure. He opened the new pie cabinet, noting with appreciation the dolphins and anchors punched in the tin panels of the doors, and as the coffee brewed he cut himself a slice of the newly fashionable custard.

With coffee and candle in hand, Bliven quietly pushed open the door to their room and saw Clarity still fast asleep. Seating himself at her desk, he lit the five beeswax tapers in their candelabrum and broke the wax anchor seal on the thick sheaf of papers given him to labor over until he was recalled. He started and paused, raised partly out of his chair, leaned to one side, and sniffed at the beeswax. It was faint, but there was the definite scent of honey. *Of course,* he thought. *What else should beeswax smell of?* But it was pleasant, a luxury unknown through his youth in this house—and Clarity was right, the beeswax did burn brighter and more evenly.

He surveyed the papers once quickly, determining from the identical hand in which they were written that they were not original documents, but copies prepared for him: reports on the locations and state of readiness of their vessels, the existing disposition of the harbor defenses, the stocks and value of materiel laid up in the armories, and the cost of bringing them up to anything like a war footing. The great population of Americans, he realized, had no idea the expense, the sheer dollar burden, of maintaining a navy. Before the Barbary War, the largest item in the United States' national budget was the tribute annually handed over to the Moorish pirates; now the greatest expense was maintenance of the navy. Well, if an expense had to be borne, it was surely better spent on ships and sailors that could protect our shores from all manner of foes than in bribes to brigands. But Jesus on the Throne, the sum spent on it was astonishing—and ours, he realized, is a tiny navy. How in the world did the British maintain their thousand ships, what engine of economy must be required to float such a force? The answer was self-evident: to command an empire that bestrode the entire world and its resources and, of course, to capture and enslave the seamen of other nations, to the number of a third or more of their entire strength. And if they indeed had mastered the world, what chance did a small, freedom-loving country, which had no desire or design for empire, have to oppose them?

First at the top of the pile was Commodore Rodgers's recommendation for an overall strategy, which as he read he realized was the same plan that was imparted to him at Washington City and had started into effect: to assemble one respectable battle squadron at New York, perhaps four frigates and two brigs or sloops, to meet the threat of the most likely first squadron that the British could be expected to deploy against them. Then, when there was opportunity, to carry the operation to England's own shores, disrupt their commerce, capture prizes, and be gone before an overwhelming battle fleet could assemble. The remaining few frigates and smaller vessels would be dispatched to operate independently, according to their commanders' best instincts, to capture merchant prizes and make the conflict uncomfortably expensive for the British merchant class, and to battle and one hoped capture several of the swarm of smaller British warships that were ubiquitous upon the seas.

Bliven considered it. In important ways it made sense. America's swift, stout forty-fours could best any English frigate of their class and outrun any battle-line ship that might come against them. It was audacious but risky, for it left the home coast disastrously underdefended and subject to blockade at the English whim. He smiled wryly at Rodgers's conclusion:

*Permit me, Sir, to say, that in the event of a war it would be particularly gratifying to me to command such a squadron as I have mentioned. I may with propriety pledge myself to make that arrogant nation feel its effects to the very quick, to have such an opportunity, as I have mentioned, of affording them a more bitter subject for their still more bitter & illiberal animadversions.*

Of course, what else would Rodgers do than nominate himself to command our one real squadron? Personal glory was not incompatible with the national defense, and Rodgers was a capable and experienced commander, as he had proved in the Mediterranean. Yet, an overwhelming British response was certain, though it would not come quickly. When an English fleet materialized off Boston, or New York, or the Chesapeake, a sea of sail as far as the eye could see, carrying not just enormous guns but the troops of an army of occupation, what then? Rodgers's scheme entrusted defense of the harbors to the hundred and seventy gunboats whose construction had been the largest naval expenditure for the past several years. The sheer number of them gave one pause and presented the illusion of providing safety, yet the American Navy had shown at Tripoli that gunboats were all but hopeless in opposing real warships. Only once that Bliven could recall in recent history had gunboats mounted an effective defense.

Immediately below Rodgers's recommendation lay a similar report from Stephen Decatur, himself now raised to commodore, submitted in answer to the same interrogatories posed to Rodgers, and which disagreed with Rodgers on almost every fundamental principal. To Decatur, the entire navy, all seventeen ships, should be dispersed for independent operation, striking opportunistically, but most staying close enough to provide some measure of safety from any transitory British marauding of coastal towns. To Decatur this seemed the greater threat, in the near term, than the assembling of a massive strike force that would come in time.

It was apparent that Rodgers and Decatur had responded to the same questions independently, each not knowing how the other had declared. Now, how might he write his own recommendation without taking sides and necessarily alienating one or the other?

"Dearest, what are you reading?" Clarity was out of bed and on her way over to the desk even as she arranged the nightgown around her. Without asking, she lifted the top few sheets from the stack and began reading, her face not registering concern at their gravity, but indeed something like relief.

"The Navy let me stay home for a time longer, my love, but not without obligation to work at papers."

Her posture relaxed. "Oh, Bliv, I was afraid that your curiosity had gotten the better of you and you had decided to read a sample of my book. That would never do." On the other side of her desk she saw the loose binder of her manuscript, its ribbon undisturbed.

He stood, wrapped her in his arms, and kissed her. "And good morning to you, too."

Softly she banged her forehead against his chest. "Dearest, I am so sorry, I was not awake yet."

"Then let me bring you some coffee." He released her and passed into the keeping room to fetch it.

He returned to find her back in bed, sitting up, and gave her the steaming cup. "Thank you, dearest. You know, since we both have our work to do, perhaps we could find you a place where you can apply yourself to it undisturbed."

He sat by her quietly for a moment, holding her hand, assimilating that this was one of those moments when they must understand each other as much by what they did not say as by the words that did pass between them. He recognized the ferocity with which she meant to protect her privacy, and appreciated her diplomacy in expressing it as a matter not of her privacy but his. And Clarity appreciated, once she spoke, that he accepted the characterization of her novel as her work, and not some hobby or affectation. "Well," he said at last, "there is my old room upstairs. I could use that as a study."

"Yes." He felt her enthusiasm rise. "My father had a slant-top desk that is now sitting disused; it is not too large to move upstairs. I am having tea with my mother today. Shall I ask her if we may have it?"

"Certainly. And while you're about it, that property she owns out at the pond where your father took me hunting has some dead trees on it. I would like to take Freddy out and cut one down, if they haven't all been poached already. Firewood is going to get very expensive before spring comes."

"Oh, she won't care. I'll just tell her I told you to go ahead. You might divert some to her for the favor."

"Done and done." He kissed her hand. "It is a pleasure doing business with you."

That Sunday Fred drove Bliven and Clarity to church. Old Putnam proclaimed himself not feeling up to leaving the house, and Dorothea stayed home to tend him. This explanation was accepted, for it politely avoided the necessity of declaring their antipathy toward Reverend Beecher. The more that the doctrine of Unitarianism spread outward from Boston, the more Beecher railed and thundered against it, and Bliven's mother declined to conceal her opinion that she found its precepts sound and sensible. She felt still less inclined to silence after it was told her that Beecher once laid her heresy to the weakness of her sex, and that she needed the guidance of a learned man. This Sunday, however, the sermon was on his other staple, the need for the abolition of slavery, which always found Clarity's ready approbation.

As they left church, Beecher took Bliven by the hand at the door and held fast, which was unusual. Bliven tried not to study his features at close quarters, for the years seemed to have started melting the wax of his face, turning down the corners of his mouth even more, and, seen from the wrong angle, his eyes seemed to be sliding off sideways. "Well, then, Master Commandant Putnam. From following the newspapers, one suspects that one day soon you are again to carry our country's honor out upon the oceans."

"Yes, sir, it would seem likely."

"And you are to have your own command now, one hears."

"Yes, sir, that is true."

Beecher finally released him. "I hope you will forgive my familiarity, but I brought you a little something to take with you." He reached into the breast pocket of his coat and produced an awkwardly sized dark brown binding, too small to be a book, too large for a tract or pamphlet. "Some few years ago I had occasion to preach a closely reasoned sermon against the practice of dueling. Despite my natural modesty and disinclination to do so, many persons remonstrated with me to allow it to be printed for distribution. As I was mindful of that, well, singularly unfortunate experience of yours last year in the West Indies—"

Bliven stiffened.

"—I would like to give this to you. If you read it carefully you will find yourself logically and spiritually prepared to dissuade any under your command who feel inclined to again indulge in that hellish practice."

Bliven accepted it and allowed Beecher to shake his hand again. "Thank you, Reverend. I shall indeed read it, and should I find any of my officers or men engaged in a duel, let me assure you that I will make them very familiar with its precepts." He smiled. "Before I have them flogged."

Clarity took Bliven's arm as they walked toward their carriage. "Have them flogged? Tell me," she said, "somewhere in my letter-box, I have the most earnest missive from a callow young lieutenant decrying the violence with which captains rule their crews. Do you recall him? I was wondering what became of him."

Bliven placed his hand on hers as he nodded to acknowledge the other churchgoers who nodded to them. "He grew up, I imagine. He acquired responsibility. He came to realize what kind of men often join the Navy. He learned that he would be held responsible for their behavior."

Fred had waited in the carriage, for he was not a churchgoer and minded not who knew. Barely out of the churchyard, Clarity observed Bliven reading the pamphlet that Beecher had given him, and she leaned across his shoulder to observe. "How do you find his little book?"

Bliven flipped to the end. "Sixty pages of close-set type; allowing three handwritten pages for each, is one hundred and eighty pages in hand. I would judge that about average for one of his sermons."

She shrugged and looked away. "Pooh. He's not that bad."

"Ha! Well, in truth, I do not disagree with anything I see to denounce dueling, he is just so almighty long-winded about it."

Her smile was so patronizing that Bliven leapt to his feet in the carriage and turned, facing her, steadying himself by bracing his butt against Fred's back. Holding Beecher's book in his right hand, he read, loud, in a declamatory voice while gesturing with his left hand, mimicking Beecher's oratorical flourishes.

*Civil government is a divine ordinance. The particular form is left to the discretion of men, but the character of rulers God has himself prescribed. They must be* just men. *Such as* fear God—a terror to evil doers, and a praise to them that do well. *Do duelists answer this description? Are they just men? Do they fear God? Look at their law. It constitutes the party, judge in his own cause, and executor of his own sentence. Its precepts, like those of Draco, are written in blood. Death, or exposure to it, is its lightest punishment, perhaps upon the innocent as upon the guilty!*

"Oh, very well," Clarity sighed. "Perhaps he is that bad." A carriage in the lane passed in the opposite direction, whose staring occupants Clarity acknowledged with a smile and nod as though nothing unusual was transpiring.

Bliven plopped next to her, rocking the carriage briefly back and forth. "Sixty pages of this! My God Almighty, if I had to listen to all of it I'd shoot him myself."

Clarity laughed despite herself. "Thou shalt not forswear thyself."

"A worthy commandment, but it does not apply to sailors."

## 4

### *For the Commodore's Eyes Only*

What a queer feeling it was for Bliven to rediscover the attic bedroom of his youth, where he had lain in bed with borrowed books, dreaming what the rest of the world might be like, the room he had shared with Sam Bandy during his visit after the Barbary War—Bandy, who was now enslaved as a pressed sailor on a British vessel somewhere off their Atlantic shore, a thought that made him sick at his stomach. Sam might not be far distant; British cruisers maintained their posts for months at a time, like wolves patrolling their marked hunting circuits. If the United States could launch this war, spring their surprise, and conclude it swiftly, the repatriation of captured sailors must be part of the treaty. But if it dragged on, if Sam were on a ship that was transferred to the Indian Ocean, or Australia, his imprisonment might extend to years.

Bliven also felt keenly the spur of personal motivation. He was a United States naval officer. He wore the uniform and accepted the token retainer of pay, and the Navy needed no greater claim on him than that, to receive his best efforts at his duty. But his knowing that Sam was taken, and that he must be somewhere suffering, added such an incalculable personal animus that he knew he would, himself, have been at war even if the country were not.

Closed off from the rest of the house and with no fireplace, his old bedroom was fiercely cold, but he remembered a lesson from the *Enterprise*, of the heated shot in the bucket of sand. On the floor by his desk he deposited a shallow box which he filled with stream pebbles, there being no sand nearby. The first time he placed a quantity of live coals from the keeping room's fireplace in a small old iron kettle and set it on the tray of pebbles, he was satisfied to judge that it worked at least as well as the hot cannonball—actually better, for both the kettle and the pebbles absorbed and retained the heat better than sand.

The stairs up to his bedroom were steep and narrow, not just because that was the New England custom, but because it was dictated by the dimensions of their hall. When Fred Meriden brought up the wagon with old Mr. Marsh's writing desk well padded in its bed, it would have proven difficult to maneuver upstairs, had not its long, elegant ball-footed legs made it possible to carry up with half of it hanging outside the banister.

It was a well-made piece, of walnut, its slant top folding down to provide a spacious writing surface and reveal compartments within for the segregation of different manner of papers. Marsh had pasted small paper tags at their openings to indicate the papers of which of his many enterprises were folded into each. Bliven knew when he began courting Clarity that her family was comfortably situated, but he'd had no sense of the diversity of their wealth, extending, not uncommonly for New Englanders of their class, into speculation in western lands and into shipping. It was impossible not to wonder whether, had he lived, her father would have supported the coming war and its cost to American commerce or whether he would have joined with the great majority of his fellow magnates in regarding the forced capture of American seamen a regrettable cost of doing business. Perhaps, Bliven thought, it was fortunate that he would never know.

Left alone at last to his packet of documents, his first thought was not of naval defense but, surprisingly, of his future here, on the farm. He regarded the comfortable but common bed of his boyhood and the other solid, yeomanlike furniture of his youth, contrasted now with the elegant walnut writing desk, the fine utensils, and realized that he was suddenly closeted with his past, his present, and his future all at once. He had been a farm boy, was now a naval officer, and apparently one day must be a gentleman of society. He realized that he and Clarity had not discussed where they would live when her mother and his parents were gone.

He might safely guess from the amount of time Clarity still spent with her mother that she missed her former luxuries. When her mother finally died, to dismiss the servants and sell the great house would be impossible to ask. Yet he was no less fond of his life and its virtues, closer to the land. Perhaps there would be no need to choose, or perhaps as he did now he must endlessly choose, but they must navigate that discussion one day.

Over the following weeks he learned his packet of documents

intimately. He undertook subscriptions to the newspapers in Boston, New Haven, and Hartford, each issue perused for political and naval news and shared with his family before depositing them in what they still called Captain Bull's Tavern for the enjoyment of its patrons. He corresponded regularly with Hull and occasionally with Barron, to learn the latest of what the Navy knew of British strengths in its different anchorages, and of America's own preparedness. This last was an easy matter to assimilate: what the Navy could do to maintain and supply its ships, it did do faithfully. That which required heavy expenditures of money—repairs to the *New York*, the *Boston*, and the *Adams*, and the conversion and fitting out of new vessels, including his own *Tempest* in Charleston, as he was dismayed to discover—was regularly deferred until Congress should make the money available.

The winter was as cold as any could remember, and he and Freddy did drive the wagon out to Marsh's Pond—since he was to eventually own it, he took to calling it Marsh Pond, amused that people one day would think it so named for a reedy wetland around it, which did not exist, and would not know the connection to the family. They dismembered two dead trees, a maple and a chestnut, which they sawed into lengths that fit into the wagon bed. Bliven used their time together to question Freddy about Pennsylvania and his Quaker faith—Freddy still referred to them as Friends—and learned that a century before the Revolution, when the Puritans from whom the Congregationalists descended still enjoyed the power of state compulsion, the Quakers were run out of the area. Four who kept returning to Boston to preach their faith were publicly hanged. That was a generation even before the hysteria about witches in Salem, but the Quakers became keenly aware of where they were not wanted, and to this day there was no meeting of Friends in western Connecticut.

Hauling the dead wood required five trips, which, coming back through town, was a hard pull even for their two shire mares, and they piled the wood behind the barn where passers-by could not see it. The widely shared opinion that firewood would reach record prices came to pass, leaving the poorer families searching for ways to become ever more thrifty with their wood, and their money. Keeping the heavy, long-dead logs hidden from public view was only prudent. Through the winter Bliven read and wrote until he thought he would go mad without fresh air, and then he would exercise himself productively on the woodpile.

He brought himself abreast of the politics of the dispute with Great Britain, learning that the United States had again petitioned the British to lift their Orders in Council and leave off seizing American ships and sailors. In Parliament, the Tory government of Spencer Perceval was preoccupied with the madness of the King, and managing a transfer of the monarchical powers to a regency under the Prince of Wales, a man who was as silly and preoccupied with fashion and his mistresses as the old King had been dedicated to duty before he lost his mind. The drift—irrevocably, it seemed—was toward war.

With the first signs of spring it was time to prepare for planting, which, as war talk increased, Bliven determined to diversify, to give his parents as much independence as possible when he should be called back to sea: wheat, oats, corn, root vegetables, and table garden. He gave Freddy a raise and made certain of his contentment to manage the farm until Bliven should return. When the spring session of Congress met, the political content of the newspapers increased sufficiently to give him a near enough idea of the state of things.

The greatest vexation was why such an assignment should have been given to him. Perhaps Dale and Eaton, and others, had told the Department of his fascination with history, or perhaps he merely flattered himself that they should esteem him so highly. Sometimes policies already decided upon needed various viewpoints to aid in politically defending them, this he knew, but surely the desired voice would speak with greater gravitas than he could. There was no way to divine it, but he needed to send them something before becoming occupied with planting. Thus when he organized his pages of notes and memoranda, and set pen to paper, he could only assume that his superior officers had their own reasons for tasking him with it, and he must write the most cogent summary and recommendation that he could.

LITCHFIELD, CONNECTICUT
10TH MARCH 1812

*Dear Sir:*

*Conformably to instructions given me in Washington City in October last, I have the honor to report my impressions of the intelligence supplied me at that time, relative to our harbor defenses and naval disposition, with my recommendations for how they might most effectively be utilized in the defense of the country.*

*The disparities of the coming conflict are well known, yet it is useful to have the exact numbers freshly stated, lest the imbalance of the contest ever be forgotten for a moment. The sum of our resources as of this date are as follows: three heavy frigates of a forty-four-gun rating, the* Constitution, President, *and* United States; *four medium frigates of thirty-eight or thirty-six guns,* Congress, Constellation, Chesapeake, *and* New York; *four light frigates of twenty-eight or thirty-two guns,* Essex, Boston, Adams, *and* John Adams; *four sloops-of-war of sixteen or eighteen guns,* Wasp, Hornet, Argus, *and* Siren *(omitting the* Oneida, *sixteen, which was built and serves upon Lake Ontario); and four brigs of twelve or fourteen guns,* Vixen, Nautilus, Enterprise, *and* Viper. *Our harbors are guarded by divisions of a flotilla of one hundred and seventy numbered gunboats, mounting in aggregate one large and one or two small guns each.*

*With these resources, we face the most powerful navy the world has ever seen. Of figures cited by the President, the English possess in total 112 ships of the battle line, 145 frigates, and smaller vessels to a total—the exact estimates vary depending upon what classes of smaller vessels may be discounted—of from 900 to 1,060 sail.*

*This report will assume the willingness of the government, recognizing the gravity of a new war with Britain, to spend whatever is necessary to place all nineteen cruising vessels in preparedness to sail. Thus, the* New York, *the* Boston, *and the* Adams, *while each requires extensive repairs before putting to sea, will be assumed for our purposes to be ready to report to the fleet by the time hostilities commence.*

*It may be proper, by way of general introduction, to note that throughout history, select nations have become wealthy on maritime commerce: the British, and before them the Dutch, and before them the Hanseatic League, and before them the Venetians, and in ancient times the Phoenicians. The United States has aspired to join this elite of commercial history, for we have built and deployed a fleet of merchant ships that aggregates not less than one million tons, or round about two thousand five hundred several ships of varying sizes. However, to defend this mighty engine of commerce, we have provided the above-enumerated Navy of nineteen vessels. That is, we have one effective warship for the protection of every (approximately) one hundred fifty commercial ships. Truly never, in the history of the world, has a country been so derelict in protecting such a vital source of its wealth, and future generations will be justified in looking back with censure, not to say wonder.*

*In the present emergency, however, this liability may possibly be turned to advantage by looking upon the merchant fleet as a source of privateers, which will be considered in more detail hereinafter.*

## *Of Gunboats*

*Let us consider first the matter of the gunboats. Over recent years, the greatest investment in our Navy has been in the construction of gunboats, to the remarkable number of approximately one hundred and seventy. No doubt, this has been because they can be built quickly and inexpensively, and their* construction gives the illusion that something meaningful is being accomplished for the national defense. It seems certain that these appropriations were easier to pass through the Congress, because the prospect of gaining one hundred and seventy vessels built for the one and a quarter million dollars that they cost, sounds more persuasive than the mere four heavy frigates that could have been built for the same amount of money.

As a class, our gunboats average fifty feet in length, are powered by eight or ten oarsmen, some with the aid of a sail, and each one mounts a single eighteen- or twenty-four-pounder long gun in the bow, and perhaps one or two small carronades or swivel guns in the waist. These latter are of limited utility, as their recoil sets the boats to rocking uncontrollably. Few of the gunboats have a covered deck, and they are exceptionally miserable for their crews in bad weather.

Historically, the greatest effectiveness of gunboats lies in waterborne assault against a shore battery or fortification. They are small and mobile, and from a distance of some hundreds of yards present an almost impossible target for shore guns, yet a squadron of eight or ten of them can equal the broadside of a large sloop-of-war, which would present an infinitely more vulnerable target during such a bombardment.

This circumstance, however, of a naval attack upon a land fortification is not likely ever to present itself in the defense of our shores in a war with England. If we have allowed ourselves to believe that gunboats would be effective in defending against invasion, or even a raid in strength, we have deceived none but *ourselves. Indeed, history affords us one example only of a successful encounter of a number of gunboats with a large warship. This was at the late battle at Alvøen, outlying the city of Bergen, where a Dano-Norwegian schooner and about five gunboats (the accounts differ in the exact number) overmatched and forced the withdrawal of the frigate H.M.S. Tartar, thirty-two, with the loss of her captain and a dozen of her crew.*

*Even in this successful action, however, it is to be noted that the Norwegians enjoyed the advantage of a dead calm, in which the Tartar could not maneuver, which allowed them to take up positions of relative safety, and also of a dense fog, which further prevented effective fire from the frigate. To think that such circumstances will ever align to aid American gunboats in defending against an English attack is to grasp at a straw.*

*One other aspect of the action at Alvøen is worthy of note. The Tartar's business at Bergen was to enter the port and take as prizes the merchant vessels she found there. This was prevented by the Norwegians having erected a chain barrier across the entrance of the harbor. As a possibility of providing safe refuges for our merchant vessels, this plan might be considered for small harbors such as Newport, where the existence of Fort Adams, and the presence of rocky islets on which such a chain could be anchored and defended, make it feasible. Most of our harbors, such as Charleston, which is of similar size, lack fortifications, or such as New York, are too large for a chain to extend across.*

*We must also anticipate that if the English mobilize such a fleet as can press the war home to us, the invasion of unfortified* harbor towns must take place at their pleasure, which would render harbor defense moot, whether by a chain guard or with gunboats. Equally, our large estuaries, such as the Chesapeake Bay, whose entrance is some seventeen miles across, are indefensible and must be conceded whenever the enemy shall choose to enter them, if they arrive in force.

Before such a great enemy fleet can assemble, we may expect harassment of our coastal towns by the many smaller enemy vessels cruising singly off our shores. Against these, if one venture into a harbor, gunboats may be of some utility, if they separate themselves to divide the enemy's fire.

Of our coast on the Gulf of Mexico, and of defending New Orleans, little can be said except to advise assembling a large local militia, amply reinforced and guided by experienced officers commanding regiments of regular troops, capable of resisting any British attempt at invasion. Events in the Atlantic will likely make it all but impossible to thwart a blockade of its shipping with our larger vessels, for the British naval bases in the West Indies, once brought to strength, can easily overmatch anything we can do in opposition. In other words, we must concede them their blockade but deny them the city. That much is feasible, by stationing numerous gunboats and privateers in such a way as to support the guns of Fort St. Philip, which may be proof against an assault upon the city from the Mississippi River. Less certain of an outcome would be an attack from the east, for without any fortifications, the only defense of Lake Pontchartrain would be by an assemblage of gunboats.

## Of British Preparedness

*Of what, then, among this depressing disparity of resources, can any advantage be taken? Foremost, it is to be observed that British disdain for us, and arrogance, has led them to so discount the possibility of our ever resisting their aggressions that they have not planned for it. They have so disregarded us that, at the last report, there was but one British ship of the battle line anywhere close to our theatre of action, and that one the quite old H.M.S. Africa, sixty-four, at Halifax. Their number of frigates cruising from that place seems to be four, the* Aeolus, Belvidera, Shannon, *and* Guerriere. *Of these, the most dangerously successful at raiding our commerce has been the last-named* Guerriere, *a captured French thirty-eight, commanded by an exceedingly audacious and very young captain, James Dacres, who is said to be from a naval family and is keen to distinguish himself.*

*The ships operating from Bermuda are less known, for intelligence from that remote tiny island, six hundred miles off the Carolina coast, is difficult to come by. Considering, however, that most of the harassment of our merchant fleet near our shores has been carried out by smaller vessels of from twelve to twenty-two guns, whose number may be estimated at from forty to sixty ships, and most are not known to frequent the anchorage in Halifax, we must conclude that Bermuda is an exceedingly active station—so much so that if it were possible to capture the island in the surprise commencement of the war, and deny that anchorage to the enemy for a time, this would leave their smaller warships at sea and forced either to Halifax or the West Indies for supply. If we commence hostilities precipitously, and send out our frigate strength casting as wide a net as possible, there is a chance of capturing a number of these brigs and sloops-of-war and bringing them into our own service before the English know what is on them. This could double or even treble our force of available auxiliary vessels before the enemy can effectively respond.*

*How long that may be cannot be known. It must necessarily require four to six weeks from the time war is declared for them to learn of it, and an additional four to six weeks for reinforcing ships to be positioned there from the bases in their West Indies islands or for a larger force to sortie from their bases in England. This latter may not even be possible, for it would leave their home coast open to attack by the French, and it must take many months for ships that can be spared to be recalled from the Pacific and Indian Oceans. Swift and sure action on our part is therefore most urgently to the case.*

### *Of Privateers*

*It would not be responsible to venture into a war without taking sober prospect of the political sentiments at home, as indeed the President discussed in the October meeting. As he expressed, the hostility to the notion of defending our national rights upon the sea, on the part of our Northern states, whose commerce is so reliant upon seafaring trade, is greatly to be wondered at. That the wealthiest of ship-owning concerns are willing to accept British seizure of some certain number of our merchant ships, and impressment of sailors from among their*

*crews, as an annoying but acceptable cost of doing business, truly
cannot be seen as either patriotic or even humane.*

*The hard fact is, however, that for the duration of hostilities
there will be little trade to be gotten up with anyone, without great
hazard to their ships, crews, and cargoes. What patriotism will
not motivate, let greed supply. Let Letters of Marque be issued
with liberality, to enroll them as privateers upon the most generous
terms, to keep all or the greatest part of whatever British
shipping they can capture. If, say, only one in five of our
merchant vessels takes up our cause, the loosing of five hundred
American privateers upon the sea lanes, preying upon British
merchant vessels for the value of their cargoes and as prizes, must
bring enormous pressure upon their Parliament to end the conflict.
One may also expect our American sea captains to be able to
acquit themselves against smaller British cruisers, and this will go
a long way to even the disparity we now face in the naval conflict.
The issuance of Letters of Marque, therefore, must be pursued
with the greatest diligence. Thought should also be given to
establishing new foundries or enlarging existing ones, for the need
for five thousand or more guns of various sizes from six to twenty-
four pounds is more than the present supply, and more than
private enterprise should be tasked to find for themselves.*

### Of Strategies Now Advanced

*To date, two different general strategies have been put forward
to guide the President and the Secretary in making a policy. One,*

from Commodore Rodgers, recommends the maintenance of one
formidable battle squadron of four frigates and perhaps two
ancillary vessels, to overtake and damage British commercial
convoys en route from the West Indies, and to carry the war to
British shores themselves. The other, from Commodore Decatur,
recommends dispatching each of our ships to independent action,
to scatter, each to engage when it is opportune, and to avoid action
when safety requires it.

Each plan presents dangers and opportunities. Of the first, we
know that Commodore Rodgers is a brave and able commander.
The squadron that he envisions would very likely be the victor, if
the enemy squadron at Halifax could be brought to battle. His
primary objective, however, is to prey upon the very rich British
West Indies convoys that carry the produce of those colonial
islands across the Atlantic, and those convoys at this time are but
lightly escorted. He then proposes to raid coastal towns of the
British homeland, and get away before an overwhelming force can
be sent out against them. A single successful raid upon such a
convoy would create a huge economic loss for the enemy as to bring
pressure in Parliament to make peace with us. It might be borne in
mind, however, that forays against undefended points of the
British coast, while certainly giving vent to our well-founded
indignation, as the commodore expresses in his proposal, and
which may avenge some of the wrongs we have suffered, may be
seen by neutral nations as merely piratical, and could perhaps
damage us in diplomatic standing.

It must also be recognized that this plan contains risks. If we *concentrate such a large proportion of our entire fleet strength in one squadron, and it be defeated, there would hardly be any way to recover from it. It is, as it were, to risk our whole fate, not just upon a single throw of the dice but upon every throw. We should also consider that the English officers have decades of experience in planning and executing fleet actions, where our entire history, in the Revolution, in the Quasi-War with the French, and in the Mediterranean, has been in individual ship-to-ship contests. At these we have excelled, but the tactics of fleet engagement is a level of complexity at which we are yet untried. It does not question the valor of our ablest commander to question the wisdom of risking so much with a fight on the enemy's terms.*

*Commodore Decatur's plan capitalizes on the strengths we have—that is, the superior construction of our ships and the craftiness and initiative of our officers, to dispatch all our vessels to individual operations, for combat when it is advantageous, capturing merchant prizes at every opportunity, and also amenable to operate in concert when two or more ships find themselves in proximity, or when news of a West Indies convoy putting to sea is received in time to organize a force.*

*With all matters under consideration, I would place my endorsement upon the Decatur plan of deployment, if it can take place quickly, with a mind to capture British vessels at the very commencement of hostilities, and accompanied, as I have recommended, with an active recruitment of privateers.*

*I have, sir, the honor to be*
*yr. obedient servant,*

*Bliven Putnam*
*Master Comdt., USN*

*Isaac Hull, Capt., USN*
*Cmdg. U.S. Frigate*
Constitution
*Annapolis, Maryland*

*Saml. Barron, Commodore*
*Washington Navy Yard*

———— // ————

Bliven's errand to deliver his report was accomplished quickly. He made two copies in a fair hand, packed enough clothes and a couple of books for the journey, and arranged himself in the coach. The *Constitution* now was moored in Annapolis, fully supplied and ready for sea, except for want of a crew, which left her not entirely a ghost ship, but which did leave Isaac Hull glaring with covetousness at the *Adams*, a hundred yards distant, unseaworthy but with nearly a full complement of seamen. If war came, he settled it in his mind that he would raid her like a hungry man would break into a bakery, take the men he needed, and leave the *Adams* to look after her own needs.

Hull received him cordially but only briefly, accepted both copies with the assurance that he would see that Barron received his, and excused himself to return to the myriad details of preparing his ship for sea. It was their parting that contained the important news, that Bliven would receive his orders to return to active service within a few weeks, but exactly what his assignment would be was still to be determined.

His family received the news as he anticipated: his father stoic, his mother glum, Clarity quiet and contemplative. The morning after telling them, he ascended to his bedroom study as had become his habit, and found displayed on his desk one of the most elegant curiosities he had ever beheld. It was a dressing box, just greater than a foot and a half in width, about ten inches in depth and perhaps eight inches high, the whole of deeply colored mahogany, edged in brass. There was a lid that did not cut straight across but had a lock higher on the back and hinged on the front, but lower down. He turned the key and opened the lid, revealing the padded slanting leather surface of a portable writing desk. He removed it, and beheld such an array of comb, brush, scissors, razor, snips, and some implements that he puzzled over what they must be.

"Do you like it?" He jumped a little at the sound of Clarity's voice, as he had not heard her come up the stairs.

"Why, it is the finest dressing box I have ever seen."

"No, dearest, indeed it is more than a dressing box. It is a captain's box. Look." She edged Bliven aside, and removed the first layer of grooming aids to reveal a puzzle of trays and compartments packed with implements to explore later. These trays she also removed until she had burrowed to the bottom of the box, where she slid aside tiny slats of wood to reveal the tops of screws. "It fastens to the table top that you place it on, do you see? Then it won't slide off when you are in rough seas."

"Good heavens, that is very fine." Bliven studied it closely, noting a small brass plate in the bottom that read GIBBS & LEWIS, 137 BOND STREET, LONDON. As a midshipman he had known Preble to possess a similar dressing box, but it never occurred to him why it never moved from the commodore's bureau until Preble took it with him when he left the ship. It was screwed down.

"It is marvelous," he added. "Was it your father's?"

"No, dearest, I ordered it for you. I thought since you are going to be a captain I should help you look the part. See there? They have thought of everything." She had begun replacing the velvet-lined trays in the reverse order that she had removed them. "Every conceivable grooming commodity and implement, and it will be as useful to you at home as when you are at sea."

Bliven also noted that the implements appeared to be silver, with ivory handles, and he was not certain how he felt about owning something so extraordinary. He circled behind and wrapped his arms around her. "What is this, are you exiling me from our hidey-hole?"

"Mercy, no!" She held on to his arms. "But in future years, when I am confined while with child and perhaps not feeling well, you will have this sanctum where you will still be in command." She smiled wryly. "Or at least believe that you are."

## 5

*Chasing Men, Chasing Ships*

It was in the afternoon of June 3 that Bliven was checking on
affairs at Captain Bull's Tavern, when that morning's number
of the Hartford newspaper caught his eye. It was the shortest
word, WAR, that snagged him like a fishhook, and he snatched it up.
PRESIDENT SEEKS WAR. Madison had finally delivered his message to
the Congress seeking a declaration of war against Great Britain
and, as the article expounded, the subject was expected to be hotly
debated in those halls.

He knew, almost to a certainty, before he strode with purpose
into the postal office, that his orders would be waiting for him
there. He accepted the folded and sealed paper grimly, paying the
twelve cents to the postmaster, not opening it until he was well
outside and beyond any well-intended questions. "Report immediately," it read, "to Captain Hull on the *Constitution*, at Annapolis."

In a way, this was merciful. No long vigil for his mother to endure. No long, clumsy searches for the right words of comfort or encouragement. Yet it was clear from the moment he entered the house and he saw her, working doggedly at the table; it was the presence of molasses, and raisins, and chopped apples, that betrayed the matter. She was making a plum pudding, and he understood she knew all. It had become a running witticism between them. When he returned from the Mediterranean, he described in full the horrors of shipboard plum duff, nothing but grease and flour and raisins, with a little salt. The next day she prepared a rich, succulent, real plum pudding, the kind that the Puritans had once banned for being sinful in its luxury. That was his welcome home. Then when he shipped out for the West Indies she made another, to remind him of what he would be missing, and let him take it with him. It was kind, but pointed, as indeed she was when cornered into voicing any opinion about politics and especially war.

"You know?" was all he could say.

She did not look up. "We learned about the newspaper. The rest I guessed. You must leave on the morrow?"

"I fear so, yes."

"Is your ship ready?"

"No, I am to report to Captain Hull in the *Constitution*. Where is Clarity?"

"Mrs. Beecher is ill. She went up to see if she was in need of anything." Bliven knew the house, on a lane just off the green, but had thus far managed to avoid calling there. It was a large old house and severe, with small windows and small dormers, as though whoever dwelt there feared to admit the joy of sunlight. It was enough to listen to Beecher in church, he thought, without calling on the lion in his den.

Benjamin entered from the hall, leaning heavily on his sticks. "I was resting and heard you come in." He eased himself onto his cushioned parson's bench. "So, there is to be a war?"

"Almost certainly, yes."

He shook his head. "Oh, I fear it will not at all be what they expect it will. May I ask you one question?"

"What is it, Father?"

"Do you still have that great, wide-bladed, terrifying dagger that you brought back from Africa?"

"My jambia? Yes."

"Are you taking it with you? I mean to say, has it now become some charm of good luck to you?"

"No, not particularly."

"Can you do me the favor to leave it here? I wish to be able to look upon it when you are in my mind."

"Well, yes, of course." Bliven excused himself and mounted the stairs to his study. He kept the dagger now in the broad lower compartment of old Marsh's writing desk, for it was too large for the cubbyholes above it. He liked to admire it from time to time, the brilliant steel of its blade, the iridescent handle, which he had since learned was carved from the horn of a rhinoceros—a creature that he'd had to discover in a bestiary from the Marsh library.

"Here we are." Bliven handed the jambia to his father, who withdrew it from its tooled leather sheath and turned it over in his hands. "Ha. From an Arab chieftain to our Connecticut mantelpiece." He grew wistful. "It was never my fate to travel very far from home, you know." He handed it back.

"I never knew you wanted to." Bliven set the dagger upon the mantel beneath their muskets, pulling it a third of the way out of the scabbard so the steel would reflect the lamplight.

"Oh, it was a youthful folly, I suppose."

"Yet you allowed me to go out and find the world."

"Yes. Well, I imagine you inherited the desire from me. Better to have inherited that than to have inherited my legs."

"Ha! If I have inherited your character, I shall be happy. I have spoken to Freddy; he has agreed to do everything necessary in tending to the farm. You can rely on him. And I would remind you there is no need to fear for my safety at any near time."

"What?" His mother had finished mixing the pudding and came around the table, sitting on the parson's bench beside her husband.

"Nothing in the Navy is certain," he began, "but at present, before I go to Charleston, I am to go to New York and participate in a recruiting drive. At least, that is the present plan. I have no idea how long I will be there."

"Well." She relaxed visibly. "That is good hearing." She rose, patting him on the shoulder as she passed by. "But you're still getting your plum pudding. Come help me." After she poured the pudding mix into its cloth he tied it tightly with a cord whose other end he made fast to an iron hook, and then lowered the heavy bundle into a boiling kettle at the edge of the fireplace.

They heard the front door open and close, and Clarity entered the keeping room, exchanging a quick kiss with Bliven. "Hello, dearest."

"How is poor Mrs. Beecher?" asked Dorothea.

Clarity tried the coffeepot, and finding it not empty poured herself half a cup. "Weak," she answered. "She is not at all well. Her last child"—she shook her head—"was almost too much for her. They had to engage a wet nurse for her entire infancy, and now that she is weaned, Mrs. Beecher tries to be cheerful, but I fear she is spent, and I fear she knows it. And all the talk was of the newspaper. Will it be war, dearest?"

"I think so, yes."

She noticed the post lying on the table. "Are those your orders?"

"Yes, they came today."

"Don't worry, my dear," said Dorothea. "He's not headed for battle, but to New York to be a recruiter."

"At least," said Bliven, "that was the last plan I heard. I will know more definitely after I report."

Clarity assimilated all the fragments and announced, "Well, good. So we won't need to make a big emotional scene."

When next he entered their room, she quietly followed him and closed the door behind her. A yard from him she folded her hands in front of her. "I know when we married I said I could pay this price. I am trying to be as strong as your mother. But do not leave this house thinking it is easy for me." She sobbed once but stifled it, and only when he drew her to him did she allow her emotions to cleanse themselves.

———*//*———

Bliven had not seen Annapolis, for it lay many miles removed from the Baltimore–Washington road. Baltimore lay at the head of the

Patapsco River estuary, and Annapolis at the mouth of the Severn. Both lay far up the indefensible Chesapeake, and while Baltimore itself might be adequately defended by the combination of Fort McHenry and a picket of gunboats, it must surely be judged of signal importance not to let any of their ships become bottled up in the Chesapeake once the war started.

Annapolis itself he found a tidy white town of fewer than two thousand people—surprisingly small for a place that had once served as the temporary capital of the United States. It would have become greater, had not Baltimore with its deeper harbor been declared the port of entry. Bliven found the Navy Yard little to speak of, but the captain's gig of the *Constitution* he found tied up at the quay, ready to row him out to the great frigate which lay at anchor farther out in the tide than the smaller *Adams*, which reposed halfway across to the southern shore of the Severn.

In old Marsh's bestiary Bliven had read of African lizards that can change their color depending upon what surface they stand on, and that was much on his mind as the gig made fast to the *Constitution*'s convenience ladder. As he stepped up to its lowest plank he felt himself a farmer, still wary of what he was letting himself in for, and by the time twenty feet higher he stepped onto the frigate's pine weather deck, kept fresh and yellow with regular holystoning, he had gone far to transform once more into a naval officer. He could not recall the name of those African lizards, but he suspected that he was not unrelated.

Nevertheless, it took a moment topside for the familiarities to fill him again, for him to acclimate himself. He remembered to salute and ask permission of the officer of the deck to come aboard. Much was the same, the masts and then topmasts more than two hundred feet tall, the forest of rigging. But much was different. The eighteen-pounders that he remembered lining the spar deck were gone, replaced with stubby, large-bore carronades, thirty-six-pounders, for close action. Briefly he wondered if they had been imported, or whether the United States now had gained the capacity to manufacture their own. The ship also carried more boats than he remembered, two longboats and two cutters, plus small craft to a total, as he glanced around, of eight.

He descended the after ladder and entered the wardroom, finding the purser working at a desk outside the captain's cabin, and handed him his orders. "Master Commandant Putnam reporting as ordered."

"Good. Very good." The purser stood and offered his hand. "My name is Cooper, glad to have you aboard."

Bliven took it. "Thank you, Mr. Cooper."

"One moment." Cooper announced him and returned at once, motioning for him to come into the cabin, where Bliven found it impossible not to see in his mind's eye Edward Preble still sitting, grouchy, at his table. Hull rose, they traded salutes as the captain advanced, and they shook hands, but his greeting was not what Bliven expected. "Alvin?" he boomed. "The God damn Battle of Alvin? What in hell put you in mind to cite such a thing as a course of action? Come sit down."

Bliven finally understood what Hull was trying to say, and made himself comfortable in a chair. "Forgive me, sir, it is pronounced *Alverrin*, that *o* with the line through it."

"Call it Moses if you like! Where did you dig that up? Putnam, you cannot help but have been aware that your government some years past made a decision to divert its limited funds for naval construction to a great many gunboats, as opposed to a few large ships. You have not made us any friends on the naval committees, who by the way control our budget, by telling them they were wrong, and then for good measure showing them by means of an exquisite historical example just how they were wrong. Good God, man!"

"I'm sorry, sir, but they *were* wrong."

"Of course they were wrong, but that isn't the point! Our job is to think up a way to win this war within the limits they set, even if they have made it harder for us. And another thing. You endorsed Decatur's plan of deployment over Rodgers's, for Barron to read. Were you not aware of the bad blood between Decatur and Barron? Decatur sat on the court-martial that gave Barron five years suspension over the *Leopard* attack."

Bliven was flustering under the ambush. "So did Rodgers, as I understand."

"That is true," Hull conceded.

"So." Bliven straightened himself in the chair. "No matter what I wrote, I was certain to make an enemy somewhere."

"Perhaps."

"And 'perhaps' that is a reason why the assignment was given to me. A written report would issue, and, being written down, it would have the force of the matter having been studied at length, stating conclusions that one might think should seem obvious, and any unpleasant repercussions would fall upon me and not some higher officer who would have been a more appropriate author, say, a senior captain?"

Hull narrowed his sloe eyes. "Take care, Commander."

"Captain Hull." Bliven folded his hands in his lap. "I do not wish to shock you, but I actually do endeavor to be an honest man. I was raised to be this way."

"Oh, there is no doubt of that, Putnam."

"But because I try to be honest, do others regard me as a simpleton?" He paused for a reply but received none. "Captain, I am in the Navy to serve my country. And I am simple—simple enough to believe that in the coming times I may be useful. But let me assure you, I have no need of my own to be here seeking glory, or fame, as do some others, or fleeing some personal demon. I have a life ashore"—he heard his own voice rising in volume, and he spoke with a rapidity hitherto unknown to himself—"a wonderful and blessed life that half of me feels I betray every time I put on this uniform and leave it. Let me assure you most earnestly that if ever I am given to believe that my utility to the Navy lies in being the sport of cynical, scheming old bastards, I am capable, entirely and serenely capable, of resigning my commission, in a heartbeat, without a second's regret."

"Be silent!" Hull softened almost at once. "Oh, Putnam, do shut up before you say too much." After a moment his belly began shaking in an avuncular chuckle. "By God, I'm damned if you haven't just told off the entire Navy, and named not a single officer who could call you out to a duel. Well done."

"Yes, there is an art to that, as I have learned."

"Ha! Well, we understand each other."

Bliven was at the point of adding that suddenly Commodore Dale's resignation was put in a new light of understanding, but

Hull's readiness to end the topic offered a truce that was better to accept. "I do have one question, Captain, which I would appreciate if you could gratify me."

"What is that?"

"If I am supposed to go to New York and enroll new seamen, why bring me all the way down here, only to go back? Why not just send me to New York and let me get on with it?"

"Ah." Hull leaned his head to one side and closed his eyes for a moment. "If only it were so easy. There was a time when we could depend upon patriotism to fill our want of seamen. Nowadays? People take their freedom for granted. All want to get out there and chase their dreams, and never think that we are not yet finished paying for the right to pursue all that happiness. The Secretary believes that your efforts will be crowned with greater success if they are accompanied by a bit of theatre. We can't just send you quietly to New York to sit at a desk in the Navy Yard and sign up one and two. You are going to make an entrance, with the squadron at your back, ships dressed overall, guns firing salutes. People will make speeches. They'll be ladling out whiskey." Hull waved a hand rhythmically in the air. "A band will play patriotic airs."

"Oh, God, no," Bliven mumbled.

"Now, the Secretary believes that if it works, you may recruit your entire company at the outset, and what you accomplish in two or three weeks will help the Navy a great deal."

"Well." Bliven recovered himself. "At least I know my fate, and I can prepare for it. What about you? Will you be dispatched to an individual patrol?"

"Hardly. After we top off our provisions in New York, we will stand out with Rodgers and his squadron."

Bliven sagged a little at the recognition. "So, they did adopt Rodgers's plan over Decatur's?"

"Yes, they did. That was their initial inclination, as you know."

In the back of his mind Bliven registered that it could prove useful one day to know exactly how little his best advice was worth, but he thought it well to see the other side of it. "In a way, it makes sense. Rodgers is senior, his desires would have more weight. Add to that the mental image of an American battle squadron, booming it out with the British and winning, would have a certain attraction in exciting public support for the war."

"Why, Putnam!" Hull was grinning. "Are you thinking like a politician?"

Bliven shook his head. "A weak moment, sir, I apologize."

"Ha! Well, in truth, events are overtaking us. We have reason to believe that Admiral Sawyer in Halifax has learned of Rodgers's design to attack a large convoy now coming north from Jamaica. If Sawyer sends out the *Africa* and his frigates to defend it, at the same time Rodgers gets there to attack it, we'll have a battle whether we seek it or no. Adding *Constitution* to Rodgers's squadron will make it our five against their five."

"And I must be left in New York?"

They rose and Hull walked him to the door, patting him on the back. "Well, thank God you are not in it for the glory, eh?"

"When do we sail?"

"We have been still bringing the crew up to strength," answered Hull. "Are you surprised?"

"Oh, for heaven's sake."

"Take heart, that is changing. Our need was not urgent, because the President had yet to submit a war message to the Congress. Now that has changed, and I aim to sail with the tide on the day after tomorrow. Cooper will be occupied in logging in stores, so in the morning you will accompany me over to the *Adams* and we will take off what we need."

"I wonder how her captain will feel about that."

"Oh, you don't know, do you? They have decided to strike the *Adams* for now; they're going to saw her in half across the waist and rebuild her as a corvette. If they work like dervishes it will take at least a year."

"What, now? We need every ship we've got!"

"No, believe me, bringing her back on line as a frigate would take longer, and she would still be a lousy slow sailer. She had a defective design from the beginning. Her men have nowhere to go, so we can have our choice."

Bliven brightened. "Then why not let me have the rest and I can get down to Charleston right now!"

Hull chuckled. "Your eagerness does you credit, but I'm afraid you will have to stand in line. Your sloop is not yet ready and we cannot have a hundred and twenty men sitting on their backsides waiting."

Cooper rose from his desk as they exited the cabin. "Cooper here will assign you a berth. I am glad to have you aboard, Commander. Let us hope for a swift passage up to New York. You will have no fixed duties, except as I have need of you. Turn out for breakfast in the morning and we will fill out our crew."

"Aye, sir." They saluted and shook hands again. "Mr. Cooper." Bliven turned his attention to the purser. "As you may know, my final destination is Charleston to assume my own command, so I am laden with greater baggage than otherwise. I hope that will not present a difficulty."

Cooper pursed his lips and shrugged. "Not for me. If you have many trunks you will have to sleep on them." He strode across the wardroom and opened one of the long file of doors. "You may take the second stateroom port side. Will it suffice?"

Bliven kept it to himself that it was the same compartment that Sam Bandy had occupied in earlier days. Cooper stood outside as Bliven entered. Just to the right of the door reposed the smallest of chairs and writing table; to the left at the far end were hooks to hang clothing. Separating them, a hammock was hung diagonally, bolted on the near left to the bulkhead that separated the compartment from the wardroom, and on the far right to one of the ship's massive knees that supported the spar deck. "Excellent, veritable luxury, Mr. Cooper. Will anyone mind if I commandeer the captain's gig back over to the yard for my trunks?"

"Not at all, make yourself at home."

"One other thing, Mr. Cooper." He motioned down the quiet of the gun deck, past the cook and steward quietly working at the camboose. "I have seen no evidence that we have a surgeon on board. Surely we will not sail without one."

"Ah," Cooper nodded. "Yes, that has been noted. They are sending us one down express from Philadelphia. Said to be one of the very best, he will arrive this evening or in the morning."

———— // ————

Standing his sea bag in the corner beyond the hammock and lining his three trunks beneath it, accessible but unobtrusive, took almost none of the otherwise usable space in the stateroom. His most important task was to remove the mahogany dressing box that Clarity had gifted him, but he was chagrined to discover that it was wider than the table provided him. It occurred to him to bore but one of the screws into the table, and that would secure it sufficiently for the short voyage to New York. When he opened it he saw to his surprise a thin box, stenciled WM MONROE, CONCORD, and a note from Clarity, which he unfolded.

> *Dearest—Pen and ink at sea can create such a mess in a mischance. If you will forgive me the liberty, I purchased of Mr. Monroe a small box of these new writing implements. Each is a thin dowel of wood, into which a filling of soft graphite has been inserted. You whittle one end to a point and write with the graphite lead as you would the nib of a pen. There is nothing to spill or stain, and the visual result you see from this little note in your hand, as I have prepared the first one for you. They are called pencils. Is not the progress of mankind wonderful? Come safe home to me, my dearest heart. C.*

He slept so soundly that he awoke early and entered the wardroom just as the steward filled the urn with coffee and arranged milk, sugar, butter, and a tray of muffins on the sideboard. "Half an hour until breakfast, sir," he said as he withdrew, and overhead he could hear the orders being barked and the squeaking and rumbling of boats being lowered.

Bliven regarded with a kind of grateful contemplation the eggs and ham and toasted bread that the steward set before the officers. Good food, even excellent food, they could expect when in port, and it was not so far to New York that the meat would turn green or the flour would go rancid. It was impossible not to look ahead to Charleston and wonder what kind of cook he could capture for his own ship when he was sent out on a long patrol. Many times had Sam Bandy extolled the wizardry of the slaves who cooked for his family, enhancing the standard fare of the Piedmont with exotic touches of their own invention, no doubt rooted in their African origins. He knew from Sam that not all the blacks in the South were slaves, that in any given city there was a community of free Negroes, and certainly none should be more resourceful in managing a diminishing or spoiling food supply. The first necessary errand when he arrived there would be to visit Rebecca in Abbeville; perhaps she could offer some guidance on finding a cook.

He smiled suddenly. Would food really be the most substantive topic of their conversation? Would their tryst in Naples really remain an unspoken memory of their history? Ought he to thank her for her discretion in having never spoken of it to Sam? Of one thing he must be certain: If she ambushed him again, he must refuse, and he must refuse with a delicacy that conveyed his very fond regard for her, yet be plain that his love as well as his duty was fully engaged elsewhere now.

Isaac Hull ate alone in his cabin, poring over dispatches that had been brought out early from the yard office. He allowed time for his officers to finish their breakfast before emerging in his dress uniform, and Bliven realized with a wave of embarrassment that he had not yet procured a pair of the new high boots that the dress code now mandated. He must find time during the day to get back ashore and find some. "Gentlemen," Hull announced when he appeared, "it is done. The President signed the declaration yesterday, and it will be published today. We are at war with Great Britain."

The murmur around the table was approving in tone but muted. Every man of them knew what a near-suicidal step the country was taking. It was a step mandated by the honor of the country, but one that some of them, perhaps many of them, would not survive. Bliven had been sitting opposite the lieutenant of Marines, a young fellow named Bush, who wiped jam from his lips with his napkin. "Well," he said, "now we're in for it, but when they tangle with us, they will feel it."

At the end of the table, nearest the screen that separated them from the gun deck, sat the ship's chaplain, old and bald, named Wright, who even in their very short acquaintance Bliven had marked as sanctimonious and annoying. Indeed his first thought upon meeting him was that he would like to have locked him and Beecher in the same room together and see who emerged alive after such a duel of self-righteousness. And Wright was so large that he left Bliven wondering how one could grow so fat on Navy fare. "Gentlemen," intoned this chaplain with a solemnity that left Bliven dreading to be led in a long-winded prayer, "the die is cast. Let no one of us fail to daily approach the Almighty for courage and guidance in doing our duty."

Amens circled the table quietly, to which Bliven had just added his own when Hull, passing behind him, leaned down and whispered, "Come, let us away."

Just outside the wardroom Cooper gave him a wide, flat roll book and showed him how to enter the names of the men they took off. "Pen and ink they will have on the *Adams*."

Bliven remembered suddenly. "Oh! Your pardon one moment." He handed the register back to Cooper, ducked into his stateroom, plucked up the new wooden writing tool, and showed it to Cooper. "It is called a pencil. There is no ink to spill."

Cooper turned it over and marveled, "Really! Oh, that is wondrous. I should think there is a military contract in it for the one who thinks quickly enough."

Topside, Bliven saw their four large boats tied in a string one behind the other. Eight rowers waited in the first one with their sweeps raised. Of course, he realized, the men they took would row themselves back over. Hull first descended the convenience ladder, and Bliven followed. He descended awkwardly down the flaring tumble home, aware of and hating the sight he must present, one hand fast on the rope as the other clutched the oversized register.

The captain of the *Adams*, a sharp-featured man named John Herbert Dent, came up to meet them but excused himself again straightaway, descended to his gig, and was rowed ashore, leaving his clerk to transfer one hundred thirty-two seamen, about half able and half ordinary. The process went smoothly until they came to a wiry, ginger-haired tar who saluted with his knuckles bent in the British fashion of making respects, and he spoke in an unmistakable Irish brogue. "Your pardon, sirs," he said. "I have been debarred from speaking until now, but I take this moment to inform Your Honors that I am a British subject, wrongly taken and pressed into service in your Navy. I claim the right of repatriation."

Hull had been standing behind Bliven as he wrote down their names, ages, places of birth, and skills, but now he stepped forward in evident fury. "What!"

"Yes, sir, it is true, sir."

"What is your name?"

"Davis, sir. Charles Davis."

"Where and when were you pressed, as you claim?"

"In Charleston, sir, two months short of two year' ago."

"From what ship were you taken?"

"The merchant brig *Margaret*, sir."

"In what circumstance?"

"I and four mates went ashore to a tavern, sir. It is true, I imbibed too liberally, and when I came to at sea, I was on your sloop-of-war *Wasp*, sixteen, Master Commandant Jones."

The more Davis could give account of himself, the angrier Hull became, partly at having the enrollment impeded, partly that this man's fate had fallen into his lap, and partly, Bliven hoped, in shame that the United States could be caught in the same wretched, indefensible trade that the British had engaged in for years. He had heard and suspected that there were such cases as this, but nothing had been so severely impeached within his hearing until this moment.

"How shall we know you are telling the truth?"

"In good faith, sir, there must be ample records. I escaped the

*Wasp* after three months, when she was back in Charleston. I swam ashore and walked over a hundred miles to Savannah. There I was retaken, confined in double irons seventy-two days, tried, and brought here for flogging, seventy-eight lashes for desertion. Now, really, sir, in fairness, ought I to suffer such an extreme and perhaps fatal punishment, when I was wrongly taken to begin with?"

Bliven turned in his chair and saw Hull's face flushing as red as a tomato. "Well, Captain," he ventured, "no wonder Mr. Dent ducked away on us."

"That bilious bastard! All right! Well, Davis, we are at war with your country. Our Navy needs men and must have them. You, I don't care if you are English or Chinese or from stinking Fiji, I shall take you. I put you a choice, Davis! You may stay here and face your flogging, or you may sign on with me, and I will forgive your flogging."

"Oh, but, sir!"

"Make your choice, man!"

"Well," he despaired, "I have never been flogged and do not wish to begin now."

He nodded at Bliven, who entered his name. He felt, even as Clarity's pencil glided across the faintly ruled register, that he was signing his own name into the book of damnation, for participating in the same odious injustice they were supposed to be fighting against. But with Hull looming over him and in such a temper, this could not be the time to voice his reservations.

It was into the afternoon when they returned to the *Constitution* with the very full longboats and cutters behind them. Hull was first up the ladder, with Bliven following, and Bliven saw a table had been set up by the mainmast, with a doctor's case upon it, and who he saw standing by it made his heart leap. "Dr. Cutbush!"

"Why, Mr. Putnam, how very good to see you." He advanced and they shook hands warmly. Cutbush was seven years older than he was when Bliven last saw him, and it showed, but his essential features were unchanged and he was as immaculately kept as ever.

"The purser told me last evening that we would have a surgeon coming down from Philadelphia, but I had no mind it would be you. I am so happy to see you."

"You two know each other, I see," Hull joined in.

Cutbush laughed. "Yes, very well. I stitched up this lad's belly when he caught the business edge of a British sabre in Naples. I am happy to see my handiwork walking about in such good condition."

"Where have you been?" asked Bliven. "What have you been doing?"

"In Philadelphia, as you heard, directing the hospital in the Navy Yard there. They felt with hostilities coming I would be more useful again at sea, a conclusion with which I do not disagree. Now, we shall have opportunity to visit soon, I am sure, but at this moment your new men are coming up the ladder, and I wish to look them over one by one as they do so."

———— // ————

They sailed with the ebb of the morning tide, the *Constitution* loaded to her full twenty-three-foot draught, wearing laboriously down the Chesapeake against a breeze so oblique that it almost forced them to stay in port, also working the pilot so hard in the boat leading them through the shallows that he barely saw them safe past Fisherman Island off Cape Charles before putting his helm hard over and racing back up the bay, speaking them as he splashed by to wish them fair sailing and good hunting.

Once she made the open sea, setting her heading north-north-east to gradually wear away from land, the wind was favorable and stout behind them, but the coastal current so strong against them that they found themselves sailing hard only, it seemed, to barely crawl in forward progress. Worse, the wind fell off continuously, by degrees, until by early evening of their fifth day, July 17, there was only a slight breeze. They remained under easy sail, but Hull began worrying whether their forward speed into the current had stalled altogether. "Carpenter, what is your sounding?"

"Twenty fathoms, Captain!"

Hull frowned. "A very shallow sea, Mr. Putnam."

"Indeed yes, Captain." Instinctively, Bliven glanced to westward. They were well out of sight of land, and the Atlantic here only twenty fathoms. In his mind's eye he saw, if they were bested and sunk in this damnable calm, their topgallants and royals would still rise above the water, straining to catch a breeze.

"Keep sounding," shouted Hull. "Sing out if it comes up to fifteen."

"Aye, Captain!"

Charles Morris came on deck and saluted. "Captain, according to my navigating, we are just about abreast of Egg Harbor."

That put them forty miles up the New Jersey coast. "It's about time. Very well, bring your helm northeast, we'll keep well clear of the shore until we can turn north off Sandy Hook."

"Your pardon, Captain, I find myself uncomfortably indisposed. If I may be excused, perhaps Mr. Putnam can stand in for me this watch?"

"It's the same to me. Mr. Putnam, you heard?"

"Yes, sir." Bliven saluted. "I am most willing to take over for Mr. Morris."

"All right, Morris, go below and see if Cutbush can give you something, then go lie down." Hull glanced up and regarded the set. "Brace up, now, Mr. Putnam, will you? We don't want to lose what little wind we have."

Bliven made a quick salute and said, "Aye, sir" before peering down the spar deck and barking, "Bosun!"

Shipping an entirely new crew, he doubted that even the captain knew which man he was yet, but one who was occupying himself about the waist ladder faced the quarterdeck at attention, and Bliven recognized his rank by his hard top hat. "Sir!"

"Brace up, now!"

"Aye, sir!" The order given, there was no need to direct him in greater detail how close to haul the yards; the bosun could read the wind as well as they could.

"Deck!" At two in the afternoon the call came down from the masthead. "Deck, there!"

Bliven cupped his hands to his mouth. "Lookout, what do you see?"

"Four sail, north of us, heading west!"

"What do you make of them?"

"Hulls are down, sir, too far to see!"

Bliven sent a midshipman down to inform the captain, and Hull was on deck in an instant. He raised his glass but saw nothing from the deck. "Well, good, must be Rodgers, left New York early, came south to meet us. I wonder why?"

Bliven also descried nothing through his glass yet. "Perhaps he was fearful of being blockaded, trapped in port." He felt a spark of excitement rise in his breast. If Rodgers had come out to meet them, perhaps now they would not call in New York at all.

Hull glanced at the canvas. "Set your staysails, come to the windward tack, I don't want to lose them." He stayed on deck, pacing impatiently.

It seemed like the next hour would never pass.

"Deck! Deck, there!"

"Lookout, what do you see?" shouted Bliven.

"Those four ships are under easy sail! Three big ships, maybe frigates. One smaller, looks like a brig. Deck there! I see a fifth sail, north by east, four miles, she's a frigate, sir, under full sail."

"It must be Rodgers," said Hull, "but we can't take any chances. Beat to quarters."

"Beat to quarters!" shouted Bliven, and the Marine standing duty at the waist ladder began rapping out a loud tattoo on his drum. In the back of his mind Bliven thought of Andrew Sterett and his mania for preparedness drills. In five days Hull, after allowing the men to divide their watches, had held only a couple. His crew was newly assembled, but most were experienced seamen. It seemed that the entire ship groaned as the gun crews strained to roll in the fifty-seven-hundred-pound twenty-fours and pull out their tompions, as boys deposited extra balls and powder in the garlands behind them. One innovation that Bliven noted was that the powder now came up from the handling room prepared not in woven cloth bags but in thin shells of sheet lead slightly smaller than the guns' bores—safer, easier to load, and more certain of firing. He also noticed the guns fitted with sights and firing locks; no more linstock matches or accounting for the timing of the fuse when deciding when to fire. With such improvements, if he were still pointing guns he felt sure he could put a ball through an open window at six hundred yards.

The guns were run back out and there was mostly silence until a quarter past six. "Deck! Deck there!"

"What do you see?"

"Fifth ship now bears east-northeast; she is closing."

The officers on the quarterdeck had been observing exactly this. "Well, let us see if we can speak her. Wear ship, come to the east, set your light stuns'ls. We will stay to her windward, just in case."

Bliven was glad that in these latitudes, the summer light lasted until very late. By eight the ships were clearly visible to one another; the stranger flew no pennant, and she began standing off, evincing a wary curiosity, which continued until it was well dark by ten. "Raise the private signal of the day," said Hull. "If she is with Rodgers, she will answer."

The array of lanterns was raised to the main topmast, where they remained for an hour without answer. Hull called his lieutenants around him. "Gentlemen, I am now inclined to believe that she is English. We will maintain our position with a sharp lookout until dawn, and if I am confirmed in my suspicion, we will have us a fight."

"The men must be getting very hungry by now," said Morris, back on deck.

"Yes," Hull answered. "Yes." It was Friday, the one meatless day in the week of prescribed Navy rations. Today they must subsist on bread and butter, and rice and cheese, and he would have preferred the men have more fuel in their bellies. "Pass the word among the men, they must remain ready for instant action, at any moment. They must eat and sleep by their guns. Is that understood? Go and tell your gun crews. I want two officers up here at all times; change the lookouts every hour to make sure they are fresh and alert."

Hull made a final assay of the enemy ships, determining that there seemed to be a kind of agreement to hold their relative positions until all once more enjoyed the benefit of daylight. He lowered his glass and sighed. "Well, no sense starving ourselves to death before the damned English can finish us off. Why don't you go below, Putnam, arouse a steward to bring us some supper before we sleep just a little?"

"Aye, sir." Bliven scanned the quarterdeck, thick with eager young officers. Some of the lieutenants and the midshipmen were betraying their lack of experience, as though they expected some dramatic turn at any moment. Those who were coming off watch, and those not on duty but tired, leaned against the netting and napped. A sea battle, Bliven had come to learn, develops over many hours, or perhaps days, before ripening into action. It could be maddening, not knowing whether each meal might be one's last before events began to accelerate, or deciding when to go to the head, so one did not have to fight with a full bladder. Bliven watched them tolerantly, straining their sight into the night for any sign of change from the stranger, but decided not to wear himself down with them.

He joined Hull in his great cabin, and the steward set them plates of rice and cheese, and bread and butter, but with strips of fried beef between them. When Hull was finished he retired to his cabin, and Bliven went down to fetch a book from his stateroom, returned and tiptoed down the gun deck as quietly as his boots would allow, passing along the gun crews asleep virtually in piles at their stations, fully clothed, some few with small pillows, others using a mate's shoulder or belly to rest their heads on, or doing without. Bliven crept forward and was startled to discover no curtain divider or sick bay beyond the galley.

Nonplussed, he descended the forward ladder, and there discovered the divider and the lamp lit in the sick bay beyond. "Dr. Cutbush?"

"Mr. Putnam!" he whispered hoarsely. "Delighted! You have found me, I was not certain that you would. Come sit down."

"Excuse me, Doctor, but did you not used to be—" He pointed to the planking overhead.

Cutbush nodded emphatically. "Indeed I did, but after you left the ship in, what was it, aught five? I became increasingly unsettled about locating the sick so near where the food was prepared. I spoke with the captain, and he agreed to move the sick bay forward in the berth deck—more quiet, less chance of infecting the food. I do know that sick bays are located in different places in different ships, but this suits me the best. But tell me your news!"

"You may not know, I am supposed to be destined for my own command, she is being fitted out in Charleston. She's a sloop-of-war, twenty guns, she's Jamaica-built of cedar."

"That is very fine, congratulations."

"Thank you, but I wish particularly to solicit your advice on a point. As commands go, it will be relatively minor, enough so that I cannot expect to be assigned a surgeon on board, likely only a surgeon's mate."

"I see." Cutbush was giving him full attention.

"Anticipating, therefore, that my medical officer may not be experienced or even, God forbid, qualified for the post, I recently took the trouble to acquire a medical text I had learned of, to provide him if he seems out of his depth."

"I see, good, that is prudent."

"Of course, I know nothing of such matters, and I wonder if you would be so kind as to provide me your estimation of the work?" He handed Cutbush a fat little brown volume.

Cutbush lit up. "Ha! My book! Well, yes, I believe I can recommend it in general terms. Wherever did you come across it?"

"I know a dealer in New Haven, who procured it for me."

"Well, at least you see I was not idle during my years ashore. While I directed the hospital at the Navy Yard in Philadelphia, I gathered the sources and wrote most of it there in my spare time. Would you like some tea?"

"Most surely, yes. Do you still use lemon?"

"What a memory you have."

A steaming pot was already on Cutbush's desk, and as he poured tea and halved a lemon, Bliven continued, "In your book you advocate most earnestly the provision of fresh air for the men, even to the point of recommending that timber for ships be felled when the sap is low, so that the space belowdecks is not noxious."

"Yes, most certainly."

"You know how cedar smells. It is the very oils in the wood, not a question of sap. What would you recommend?"

"Well, let us apply ourselves. It is a sloop-of-war, you say?"

"Yes."

"So all the guns will be on the weather deck, and the berth deck below is the only full deck above the hold?"

"I've not seen her yet, but I would expect so."

"Well, if you keep your hatches uncovered at night and admit as much fresh air as possible, it should be well. I am not overly famil- iar with ships built of cedar, but I have read nothing of greater sickness on them owing to that."

Bliven accepted his tea with the half-lemon in it. "I am glad to hear that. By the way, those seemed to be quite thorough inspec- tions you were giving these new crewmen from the *Adams* since they came aboard."

"And not in prime condition, many of them. Skin eruptions, vermin, not immediately dangerous to health, but surely indicative of a drift down toward sickness."

"Mm." Bliven swallowed some tea. "In your book you spend considerable length extolling the virtues of hygiene. That was quite prominent."

"What do you do when you take over a ship that has been worn down by sailing in unknown waters? You scrub her from stem to stern, do you not? You heave her down and scrape her bottom. I'd like to do the same with most of these new men!"

Bliven's hand shot to his mouth to keep from laughing loudly. "Oh, I think you did not mean to say that you would scrape their bottoms!"

"Oh, would I not, now, Mr. Putnam? If you read my book, you know that pests and vermin are the cause of most of the disease and discomfort at sea. These men join the Navy and march on board with the fleas and ticks from their woods, lice from a woman in some dockside stew. No, I tell you, if I thought they would survive it, I would strip them naked, burn their clothes, shave them bare, and boil them in lye."

Bliven was shaking in silent laughter.

"And"—Cutbush raised a finger—"that would advance us only to the physical examination. Those with bad lungs or weak constitutions, and especially those who exhibit any evidence of tropical or communicable disease, I would thank for their interest and send them right back ashore. You may laugh now, Mr. Putnam, but you take this to heart, New Orleans and Charleston are the last two ports in the United States where I would want to ship a crew."

Bliven grew more serious. "I do understand, Doctor, and I will follow your advice."

"Good. Have you ever seen a ship quarantined for pestilence? Can you imagine, in the close confines of a ship, a crew being ravaged by typhus or yellow fever? I tell you, simple cleanliness is the greatest preventative."

Bliven reached into his pocket and produced his pencil. "Would you sign your book for me as a memento, please?"

Cutbush took it. "Ah, a pencil. They are becoming quite the rage, are they not? I saw my first one three months ago."

Bliven returned to his tiny stateroom but did not undress, and left the door ajar to alert him to any sound. He napped only fitfully, and returned to the quarterdeck long before it was light. The morning watch had just been called, indeed the ringing of the bell had hardly faded, when the northeast was lit up by a spray of sparks as a rocket shot up from the strange ship.

"Deck! Deck there!"

"What do you see?" shouted Morris.

"She has worn around completely and is bearing up."

Morris pushed a midshipman toward the ladder. "Go get the captain, hurry!"

Bliven thought it best to visit the head before events could get any more interesting, and clattered down the ladder. Just as Hull emerged, two small guns banged from the stranger, their little muzzle flashes making bright pinpoints in the gray. Bliven heard their small reports from within the officers' privy. He heard shouting between the officers and the lookouts, but heard it only indistinctly.

He finished and returned to the deck, standing close to Hull, but having no duties, not interrupting.

"Well, Mr. Putnam, are you well refreshed?"

"Yes, sir," he answered, a little embarrassed.

"Good. Tell me, Mr. Putnam, how long has it been since you sat for your lieutenant's examination?"

"Why, it was in Gibraltar, sir, during the Barbary War."

Hull nodded. "Well, I have a new examination question for you. I am interested to hear how you would solve it."

"Very well, sir." It was always good to come topside and find the captain jovial.

"I put it to you, your ship is in a near calm on a clear morning, the sea smooth as glass." Bliven glanced around and up and noted that those were the conditions exactly. "As the light clears, your lookouts inform you that two enemy frigates are approaching on your lee quarter. Astern of you approach two more enemy frigates, a ship of the line, a brig, and a schooner. What is your course of action?"

Hull looked at him, so impassively bemused that Bliven felt his stomach drop to the very bottom of his belly. Instantly he raised his glass, and after only a few degrees' sweep he beheld five sail, fully set including stuns'ls, maybe three miles astern, and a mile closer off their lee quarter, two clearly visible frigates bearing up. "God damn!" he wheezed.

"Ha! Why, Mr. Putnam, in all the time I have known you, that is the first time I have heard you utter such an imprecation."

"Then, sir, it bears repeating: God damn!" He looked again. They could see them distantly, but clearly. Rodgers's *President* was a big vessel, sister of the *Constitution*, but still there was a vast, an unmistakable, difference in the expanse of her hull, versus a tall third-rate like the *Africa*. There was no question that that massive ship of the line was in the squadron closing in on them.

"Well, Putnam, what would you do?"

"Well! Well, we mount in total fifty-six guns." He spoke as fast as he thought. "We should expect them to attack from both sides. The *Africa* mounts sixty-four guns, five frigates at, say, thirty-six each is, five times forty is two hundred, less twenty is a hundred and eighty, plus sixty-four makes two hundred and forty-four, plus two smaller makes it about two hundred and seventy guns to our fifty-six. In short, sir, we don't stand a chance in hell, and I would get out of here, sir!"

"Mr. Putnam, there is no wind."

"Then I would put my boats down and row!"

"A very good answer, Mr. Putnam. If you would be so kind, tell the bosun to get the longboats and a cutter into the water and start sweeping us out of here."

"Aye-aye, sir!" His sword swinging at his side, Bliven ran to the waist ladder and gave the orders, letting the bosun pick men who were not needed at the guns, while he took it upon himself to direct a midshipman into each boat to exhort and encourage the men as they rowed.

Hull strode ten paces forward on the starboard side. "Carpenter," he called, "what is your sounding?"

"Now eighteen fathoms, Captain."

"Very well. Now, listen to me. I want you to put a detail together. Remove the windows from my cabin. Move your aft twenty-fours into my cabin, point them through the windows. We'll use them for heavier stern chasers."

The bosun saluted. "Right away, Captain!"

"And move our eighteen here to the stern. Cut a space in the taffrail and we'll use it as well. At the double, now!"

Bliven rejoined him on the quarterdeck. "That rocket, and the signal guns, she was telling them to come up?"

Hull nodded. "That's right. She was signaling her position to the others."

Only a moment passed before below them they could hear the carpenter setting to his work. The stern windows that made the captain's cabin the most brilliant and airy compartment in the ship were not built to be removed. The turned-lathe divider that separated the wardroom from the length of the gun deck must have a section cut out; equally so, the bulkhead between the wardroom and the captain's cabin must have a space cut out. There was not time to saw them neatly, and they could hear axes biting into the wood.

And moving the guns—they knew the herculean effort this would require. A twenty-four-pounder, with its iron barrel nine feet, six inches long, weighed two and three-quarter tons; its wooden carriage another half-ton. It was lucky the coming squadron could not overhaul them quickly, for they must be in the same near-dead air, but they did have the current working with them and not against them.

Three boats, manned with sailors who could see their fate approaching even as they pulled their oars, laid into their work and began to turn the *Constitution*'s head around. Eventually those on the quarterdeck could hear the thick wooden wheels of the twenty-fours squeaking into position in the captain's cabin, lurch by lurch as the men heaved on the ropes.

"Deck there!"

Bliven was the first to answer. "What do you see?"

"All ships flying English ensigns. And, sir, the brig, I'm sure it's the *Nautilus*!"

It was now past six in the morning, sunny, cloudless. All the glasses on the quarterdeck were trained on the larger spread of ships, studying the smallest but one. Any doubt that the *Nautilus* had been captured was removed when a slight shift in their course revealed the American flag hanging lifeless beneath the British ensign.

All looked at one another mutely. Discourse was unnecessary, for they all had the same questions: Had Rodgers left New York without waiting for them? Was the *Nautilus* with him or was she taken singly? Had there been a battle beyond their hearing, and what was the result? What of Rodgers and the *President*, the *New York*, and the *United States*, the fighting heart of the American Navy? Were they lost? With the *Nautilus* captured, her crew must be prisoners aboard one of the other vessels in their sight, but which one? If they engaged, they ran the risk of firing upon their own men.

At length Hull lowered his glass. "Damn."

Slowly, by degrees, they saw the compass rose turn until they were on a southerly heading.

"Deck there!"

"What do you see?"

"The enemy vessels are lowering boats, they're making to sweep just as we are!"

They raised their glasses and saw the truth of the lookout's conclusion. "What original thinking," groused Bliven as he lowered his glass and collapsed it. "They must have confounded their teachers with their brilliance in school."

"Mr. Putnam?" Hull spoke after a moment without having lowered his glass.

"Captain?"

"Did I hear you complaining just now that you wish the British would show some initiative and do something original, and not just imitate our maneuver?"

"I did, sir, yes."

"Well, kindly do not say it so loudly next time, it seems they were listening to you. Look again."

Bliven strode almost to the taffrail and raised his glass. Of the three leading ships, two had cut loose the boats towing them, which all were now rigging lines to the central largest frigate, an apparent thirty-eight, which would now have nine boats pulling her, and she must gain on them rapidly. He lowered his glass. "Oh my God."

Hull braced his glass on his hip. "What d'you think?"

"Well," said Bliven, "they are game for a fight right enough, so I salute them for that."

"But?"

"Did they not just hand the advantage to us? If they catch us, they are no match for us. And before they catch us, we can rake their boats with the carronades until there are none left to row."

"Not very sporting of you, Mr. Putnam."

"Not sporting of me? They must be wagering that that one frigate by engaging us can slow us enough for the others to come within range and overwhelm us. They are willing to sacrifice those men and perhaps that ship on the chance of cornering us with the others. It seems to me the lack of sportsmanship is theirs, not ours."

"Ha!"

"They look to delay us, and if we make but two or three tacks while engaging her, they will have calculated correctly."

"Tack?" Hull laughed. "Mr. Putnam, there is no wind! With nine boats pulling her, she can lay off wherever we can't bear on her and reduce us at her pleasure. Well, I say, almost no wind."

That was well spoken, for they felt the very slightest of zephyrs from the northwest. If it would only freshen, it would be a great advantage on this heading.

The morning's stillness was split by the double boom of the following frigate's bow chasers. All heads turned to see twin splashes several hundred yards astern of them. "Well," said Hull, "that was pretty pointless."

"Keen to show us how eager he is, I'll bet," offered Bliven.

"I still don't like the look of it," said Hull. "See, those other two frigates have caught a wind, they have worn to windward and are gaining on us. We had better warn the gun crews, the ship may have to fight both sides."

"Captain?"

"Mr. Morris?"

"I would not wish to state the obvious, but whether we could tack or not, if that lead ship can do anything to us, anything at all, even grape through our sails, it will cost us the margin of our escape. To say nothing of those other two bearing up on us."

"Yes," said Hull warily. "Go on."

"You know, I was rather scrappy when I was a lad, and I remember my father once advising that when I was in a situation in which I could not possibly prevail, only a coward would run, but a gentleman might well extricate himself if he but excused himself politely and slowly walked away."

"Speak plainly, man! What do you mean?"

"Kedge anchors, Captain. We are still in only twenty fathoms of water. Let us send out kedge anchors as far as we can and drop them. Stick the bars in the capstan, pull ourselves along as we wind them in, and just . . . walk away."

"By God." Hull looked at him, blasted. "By God. Bring the boats in! Leave one down, put fresh men in it. You go down and lead them, stay under the bow until we can get a kedge down to you. Putnam?"

"Sir?"

"Have the bosun splice all the line we have left on board, a thousand yards if he can. Splice them well, our lives depend on it. Have him rig both kedge anchors. You know what to do, one end in the capstan, lower the kedge to Mr. Morris."

"Right away, sir!" he returned directly. "Captain Hull, the bosun says we should have enough line to manage whatever we need. They are getting lines on the kedge anchors. He recommends that you send one out as you reel us forward with the other. We may look a bit like a drunken man crawling down the lane, but it should work. The last sounding was twenty-six fathoms, still plenty shallow."

Bliven observed the kedge being lowered to Morris from the starboard cathead, and felt a wash of apprehension spread through his belly. Its six foot shank of wrought iron was alarmingly slender, as was its curved four-foot crown. When this device hit the muddy ocean floor, would its flukes gain the purchase to pull the fifteen-hundred-ton frigate forward, or by turning the capstan would they merely dig a furrow in the mud as they dragged the kedge back toward the ship? If the flukes did catch hold, might not the weight of the ship snap the crown from the spindly shank? Or it might work, all were possibilities. Morris's boat pulled out the full thousand yards before letting it fall into the glass-calm sea with a hiss of bubbles. He saw the kedge fall and waited a few seconds for it to strike the bottom. He ran to and descended the waist ladder, for the capstan was located midships on the gun deck, and with the bars inserted spread nearly the whole width of the deck, from the breeches of the port guns to those starboard. He ordered the ladders raised. "Now, boys, push for it!" As they overcame the initial inertia the capstan turned grudgingly, but steadily, and up on the spar deck the line they pulled in became wet. Chips dropped overboard began to show greater forward progress than they had made by sweeping.

"Come on men," he exhorted, "put your backs into it! Every yard wound up is another yard toward safety!" Their motivation was increased by more booming reports from the bow chasers of the nearest frigate. The balls continued to fall short but served the *Constitution* well, for each concussion that rolled over them gave the men at the capstan a fresh burst of energy. At the outer end of one of the bars Bliven saw a middle-aged tar, black hair gray at the temples, underweight but hardened by life at sea, whom he had seen stagger out of a longboat, exhausted from rowing. Bliven urged him out of the way. "Your sense of duty is admirable, but you are spent. Rest yourself, I will do this. Come on, boys! For your lives, now!"

His boots did not give him enough purchase on the deck, but his presence had a good effect, and as they turned the capstan the momentum of the ship began to help them. Morris came back for the second kedge, lowered from the port cathead. They rowed ahead with it as Morris looked back, dropping it when he saw the first kedge rising from the water.

Hull on the quarterdeck could feel their forward increase, and he strode down the spar deck to observe the labor at the capstan, looking down through the hatch. "Boys, this is capital, this is excellent. We are opening a distance from them, keep at it. You, bear a hand there, if you please, take over for Commander Putnam. Mr. Putnam, come up here with me."

They had just gained the quarterdeck when Hull stopped in his tracks. "Lord God, did you feel that?"

The same puff of wind lifted Bliven's hair below the rim of his hat. "Yes, sir, I most surely and gratefully did." He pulled off his bicorne, facing different points, looking up to their pennants to see what direction they pointed, trying to judge whether this hope of a wind was errant or whether it would come steady. The canvas above them ruffled as the sails began to fill, the rippling pennants curling south-southwest.

Hull was reading the wind, too, and with wind to work with, he was confident of his and his ship's ability to outsail anything of similar size. "Bring your boats in! Get your boats in! Trim your sails, now, larboard tack! Mark it for the log," he exulted. "It is nine minutes past nine."

Exhausted but grateful, the men in the longboats came under their davits and tied on before shinnying up the nets cast down to them. The men at the capstans continued turning until both kedges dangled from the catheads, not fully secured in case they should be needed again. The boats were hoisted clear of the water but also not secured, for none knew when they might have to be lowered again.

Hull came forward again from the quarterdeck. "Well done, lads, by God. There is grog for those who want it, get something to eat, and rest. Well done, I think you have gotten us out of this."

For an hour Hull paced the quarterdeck, watching the two closest enemy vessels, the one astern of him and one off his lee quarter, fall slowly behind. And then shortly after ten the wind died, completely, the sails falling slack. "Damn," Hull sighed. "All right, Mr. Morris, let us try towing again; get your longboats into the water, try to select some fresh men to man the sweeps."

"Well," he said tiredly to Bliven, "at least by the time we're done our new boys will know how to lower and raise boats, if nothing else. Oh, now what?"

The slightest puff of wind came over their port quarter, then died, and then another straight over their stern. "Bosun!"

"Sir?"

"It appears that we will continue with a light and baffling wind. Make this your task, read the water and mind the cat's paws. Trim your sails instantly whichever way they point. Do you understand?"

"Yes, sir."

"Can you do this?"

"Aye, sir, I have followed cat's paws before."

"Very well, get to it. And wet the sails. By all means, wet the sails." Such an order increased the labor by a great factor. All knew that wet sails captured more of the wind than dry, but buckets of sea water had to be hauled to the yards and poured down, and not merely hauled but hauled continuously, for even in a slight and humid wind, the thinly spread water would evaporate almost before the next bucket arrived.

"Deck! Deck there!"

"What do you see?" called Bliven through cupped hands.

"Four frigates off the lee quarter, approaching. Ship of the line and two small ships off the lee beam, approaching. They've found us again!"

Hull raised his glass and saw the truth of it. "Oh, this is iniquitous. They have managed to catch a wind that has eluded us. Mr. Putnam, would you not agree that it is time to lighten ship?"

"Yes, sir, absolutely."

"Nothing too extreme," said Hull.

"Yes, sir." Bliven remembered Bainbridge at Tripoli, who had rolled the *Philadelphia*'s guns overboard and chopped down the foremast to try and free himself from the reef that held him fast.

"Take a few men, rid us of some of the fresh water, say ten tons to start; we will see how much that helps us."

"Right away, sir." He was calculating even as he strode forward to the waist ladder. After five days at sea in no extreme heat, they must still carry about a hundred and forty tons of water, so ten tons would be no great danger to lose. He clattered down the waist ladder and roused the crew of the closest starboard twenty-four. "Men, come bear a hand here, quick, quick! Bring hammers!"

He descended farther with the gun crew following to the orlop deck and a few steps farther to the hold, where they stood next to and were dwarfed by a solid mass of nested water casks. "Boys, we are going to lighten ship and see if we can open some distance between us and them that's after us, and we're going to start with some of the fresh water."

"You mean us to carry casks up on deck and throw them overboard?" The sailor looked apprehensive, for each ten-gallon cask weighed more than eighty pounds.

"No, no," answered Bliven. "That would take forever." Not to mention waste the barrels and make weeks of work for the cooper. "Just open the bungholes and let the water run down into the kentledge." They made their way in the dim light of battle lanterns to where the curve of the bottom told them they were at the deepest part of the *Constitution*'s vast round belly. Bliven looked up and found where six pipes of joined wood sections punched through from the berth deck above; he traced them down to where they disappeared into the ballast, where he knew their ends opened next to the keelson. "Start with these here."

"How many?"

"Count out two hundred fifty."

"Two hundred fifty!"

Bliven spun and glared at him.

"Yes, sir, drain two hundred fifty water casks."

No sooner had Bliven set his foot on the ladder than he saw one of the crew knock the plug from a cask at the very bottom, and a stream of water shoot out from it. "No!" he roared. "Start with the uppermost or it will become top-heavy, come down, and crush you. Do you hear? Move the empty casks forward and aft to get them out of the way and expose the next layer. Do you understand?"

It was the gun crew's chief who was accustomed to take responsibility. "Yes, sir, we will manage it for you."

As he ascended, Bliven heard the hammers knocking away the bungs as loud splashing commenced, and one of the men spluttered, "We're going to get mighty wet by the time we're done."

"Are we not lucky?" barked the chief. "Others on this vessel would give a month's wages to have a nice bath."

Bliven bounded back up the ladder to the gun deck, where between the ladder and the mainmast the bilge pipes terminated in six onion-shaped bulbs of beaten copper, each a foot across, topped with tightly sealed leather from which yard-long rods extended up to pump arms, and an open mouth that poured the water pumped up to run out onto the deck. They were set in three pairs, each pair connected to reciprocating ends of the arms so that one piston drew up as the other discharged down. He hailed the crew of the port gun opposite that whose crew he had taken down. "Boys, bear a hand. Break out the bars and pump until it runs dry. You fellows there," he addressed another gun crew, "take up some mops. Come, now, hop to it!"

By the time he regained the spar deck and rejoined Hull, they could hear the racing splatter of water as it ran out of the gun deck's scuppers, down the tumble home, and into the sea. "Sir, you have resumed kedging as well as towing?"

"Yes. We have barely enough left on board to work the sails and the guns, if we have to. It's a hell of a deal. We can't catch a breath of wind."

Once again their discussion was ended by the double boom from the bow chasers of the frigate dead astern of them. "Oh, I am getting tired of this. Observe now, observe!" shouted Hull. The balls made two great splashes two hundred yards astern of them. "What do you make of that?"

"I'm with you, Captain. Most British frigates mount eighteens. If that is their maximum range, if we answer with our twenty-fours, we might do some damage."

"Mr. Walker!"

"Sir!" Hull was answered by a midshipman of perhaps twelve,

standing at attention at the head of the after ladder. He was not large for his age, his voice had not yet changed, and Bliven wondered if he had looked similarly ludicrous when he was a boy doing his best to mimic the dress and manner of the officers. He quickly concluded that he had not, for he didn't join the Navy until he was fourteen—very late, by the standard of the day.

"The guns in my cabin, are they ready?" demanded Hull.

Midshipman Walker cupped his hands beside his mouth and shouted down the ladder, "Are you ready?"

Bliven heard the question relayed to another, unseen, midshipman at the bottom of the ladder, who shouted through the wardroom into the cabin.

"Guns are pointed and ready, Captain."

"At my command, Mr. Walker—fire!"

There came deafening simultaneous explosions, and they felt the quarterdeck lift beneath them—not from sea swell nor the shock of the concussion, the deck was dislodged, the planks separating just enough that jets of smoke erupted from between them. Hull was thrown from his feet and landed hard on his right hip, pushing himself up to a sitting position. "My God," he was saying, "my God, a gun has blown up!"

Bliven was standing at the very stern of the starboard side and was thrown against the taffrail but saw the muzzle blasts shoot out fifty feet before dispersing. "No, sir, I don't think so!" He waited a couple of seconds before responding further, looking for splashes but seeing none, and thought they might have hit her. He saw Hull struggling to his feet and rushed to help him. "The discharges appeared quite normal. Here, are you hurt?"

"No, no, thank you." He spun around to little Walker. "Cease your firing! Cease fire!" They heard the urgent, squeaky voices relaying the order. "What in bloody hell?"

"Sir, come see, look." Bliven helped him take his first couple of steps before Hull found his balance again; they leaned over the taffrail and peered down. "It is the stern rake, I think, it is too severe. The way the guns sit in their carriages, they cannot protrude enough beyond the windows to discharge safely. Much of the blast remained in the cabin."

"Oh!" Hull groaned. He shook his head violently to clear his brain. "I see. Well, it seemed like a good idea, what? Ha! Have the carpenter inspect the deck planking and secure it if any of it pulled loose."

"Yes, sir, I'll go below at once." Bliven excused himself by Midshipman Walker, slightly amused at what a little boy he yet was but what a career he might make for himself, in time, as he himself was doing. He clattered down the ladder.

"Have you orders for us, sir?" In the commotion the gun crews of the eighteen that had been pulled aft, and a section of taffrail cut out to point it, felt forgotten. "We are ready."

Hull's head was still spinning. "I thank you for your eagerness, boys, but no, they are beyond your range. We will not waste the shot, just stand ready."

In the captain's cabin thick with powder smoke Bliven found the carpenter already inspecting for damage. "What do you make of it?" he asked.

"No real damage in here," he replied. "It will just stink for a good while. I will inspect the decking when I can."

Topside, Bliven relayed it to Hull. "Captain, the carpenter says he can find no serious damage. Your cabin will smell like smoke for a while."

"Ha! Just what I need. When I can finally get some sleep I will dream of brimstone and the devil."

"Deck! Deck there!"

"What do you see?"

"Frigates on the lee quarter have resumed towing!"

"Well, good," muttered Hull. "At least they have run out of wind, too." At a thousand yards distant, it was none too soon.

Again the lookout called down. "One of them, her boats are turning her." Bliven and Hull looked through their glasses in time to see the frigate come broadside to them and her entire side erupt in a flaming salvo whose staccato boom-boom-boom reached them several seconds later, about the time they saw the splashes several hundred yards short.

Hull smiled derisively. "Well, that was kind of him to show us his maximum range."

"Sir," said Bliven, "the men in the boats must be about to collapse. May I recommend we get some fresh men out?"

"Yes, yes, see to it. And take a walk down the gun deck. The men have been at their stations for the better part of two days. Make sure they are all right."

"Yes, sir."

———— # ————

He napped only fitfully again that night; he never imagined that war could be fought so slowly, that their game of cat-and-mouse could be sustained for so long, with their destruction all but assured if they failed for a moment in their elusiveness.

First light of the third day revealed the remarkable sight of four frigates chasing one, all of them sweeping and kedging, their full-set sails hanging limp as wet bedsheets. The ship of the line, the brig, and the schooner had fallen off. Bliven came on deck apprehensive, but found Hull ebullient. "We shall have a wind, Mr. Putnam, the wind is rising with the sun. Do you feel it?"

"Indeed, sir, yes."

"This changes the game!" All the ships were pulling in their boats and setting more canvas.

"The small frigate there." Bliven pointed. "She is within range, why does she not fire?"

"A ship that size?" answered Hull. "She probably only mounts twelve-pounders. It is probably his aversion to suicide that makes him hold his fire."

Of greater concern at that moment was the frigate that had gotten ahead of them and was tacking, forcing *Constitution* to tack also or be crossed. But surely, doggedly, hour by hour, Hull gained the advantage, slowly pulling ahead until by late afternoon the closest British vessel was two and a half miles distant.

"Captain Hull?"

"Mr. Putnam."

"May I say, sir, that watching you handle this vessel has been an education that could never be got in any classroom?"

"Thank you, Mr. Putnam, but you haven't seen anything yet. Do you regard those clouds over there?"

"Aye, sir."

"By seven this evening we will be in a raging squall. Those boys are going to shorten sail to ride out the storm. They will think we shall do the same, but we are going to ride it hard and get the hell out of here."

His forecast was prescient, and as the first large raindrops thudded on the deck shortly after seven, Hull ordered the bosun to come under short sail. The light canvas was taken in, a second reef taken in the mizzen topsail, the mainsails clewed up. "Now watch!" Hull pointed to the nearest British ships.

Bliven raised his glass and saw them do exactly the same. "The storm will hit us first; they assume that we will ride it out, as they will."

No sooner had he said this than the rain hit them like a wet wall, with great exultant blasts of wind. "Sheet her home!" roared Hull.

Fore and main topgallant yards jerked aloft and the sails filled, and canvas added by degrees. The hard rain lasted twenty minutes, shielding them from British scrutiny. The wind remained after the rain, shooting *Constitution* ahead at eleven knots on an easy bowline.

"Ha!" boomed Hull. "They will be confused for a while, then they will guess what we have done and chase us but will not catch us. Let us see what morning brings."

Hull gave Bliven confidence to sleep a little deeper that night, less unnerved at war fought at the pace of angry snails. The hail from the lookout he heard at first light, washed his face to gain alertness and went up, where Morris had the deck. "What do you see?"

"British squadron six miles to the northeast, bearing east!"

"They're giving it up." If pure satisfaction give a voice timbre, Hull uttered it. "They are giving up." Hull lifted his bicorne high in salute at the disappearing enemy squadron as their masts disappeared over the horizon. "Fare thee well, ye God damn sons of bitches," he shouted across the ocean. "Rot in hell, the lot of ye! Ha!" He turned around. "Mr. Morris, lay us a course for Boston, if you please."

———— // ————

They put into Boston on July 27, but Hull could learn next to nothing of affairs. Rodgers and his squadron had sailed from New York on June 21, within an hour of learning that war had been declared. Nothing had been heard of them since. There were no orders for Hull or the *Constitution*, which should have been annoying, but Hull welcomed it as merely giving him the discretion to sail without orders, which he determined to do as soon as his stores were topped off.

"Have you orders for me?" Bliven asked the yard commandant.

"Ah, yes, you are supposed to have a ship being made ready for you in Charleston, aren't you?"

"Yes, sir. I am getting most anxious to get to it, as you may imagine."

"Well, I am sorry, I have nothing for you. If Captain Hull finds you useful, you should go back out with him."

Bliven considered this with no outward emotion. He desired his own command, but it would be in a small ship with an unproven crew. Here, he was sailing in perhaps the strongest, fastest frigate in the world. Nowhere in the American Navy could he have a better chance of returning home in one piece. He could raise a dust about going to Charleston, but for now he liked his chances better in the *Constitution*. "As you wish, sir."

"You say you are Master Commandant Putnam?"

"I am."

"It is fortunate that you are here. We have received a letter, enclosing a letter to you and asking us to direct it on to a station where it might find you." He offered the small fold of sheets, sealed with wax.

Bliven looked down, recognized his mother's hand, and was filled with foreboding. "Thank you. Thank you very much."

There was no reason short of bad news for his mother to have written him so soon after his departing. He returned to the ship, where he could be distracted by activity in the event it told of disaster.

LITCHFIELD
24TH JUNE, 1812

*My Own Dearly Beloved Son,*

*I must tell you straightaway that your father has taken ill, although it does not appear from this distance, some two days since his attack, that he is dangerously so.*

*If you are reading this letter, it must have been given you in a naval station, therefore you will have heard, perhaps long ago, what we learned two days since, that war is declared upon Great Britain.*

*Your father did first read it in the newspaper, and he celebrated that the decision was to the policy that he favored. But then, as he read how many in the Congress opposed the measure, he grew indignant. The poll, you may have read, was only 19 to 13 in the Senate, and 79 to 49 in the lower chamber of representatives.*

*Surely, leading our nation into war is a step so momentous, so fraught, and so irrevocable that it should require greater consensus than the barest majority. Indeed, your father read it to me twice over that not one member of the Congress from New England voted in favor, and he vented his temper most dangerously. When he exhausted his known invective to have called them knaves, scoundrels, and rogues, he was compelled to make an expedition into the jungle, and he enumerated apes, baboons, jackals, and diverse other unpleasant species.*

*What caused him most particular anguish was the talk racing all about of invading the Canadas and annexing their territory to our own. How, he said, will we propose to do this, when so many of the northern states that border on the Canadas are united in opposition to this war and doubtless will prevent their militia forces from participating, and can otherwise obstruct this design? And against its advocates, he likewise pronounced it the greatest tom foolery to argue, as they have, that the Canadians will welcome us as liberators and join our forces, when large sections of those colonies were settled by our own people who were driven out for not supporting our Revolution. What love have they for us?*

*However great the valor of our Navy, your father apprehends a terrible disaster awaiting in the contest on land.*

*After a long exposition he was seized with coughing, until he could not draw breath and was taken with a kind of seizure. The doctor pronounced it another apoplexy. Your father did not speak the rest of that day, which alarmed us greatly, lest the attack have left him mute. He slept very soundly, and in the morning he asked for porridge, speaking slowly but distinctly. We also were encouraged that he seemed to know that he might not sustain a heavy meal, and thus his mind was likely intact. While I sat with him your angel wife made a wonderful pot of oats with cream and butter and raisins. She came to the bedside to feed him, but thanking her, he took the bowl himself, which rejoiced us greatly.*

*Our practice shall be to keep him quiet, to keep news from him except what shall give him comfort, and to let him repair by degrees. This, my son, is the first reason that I write you.*

*The second is I am certain that your father's honest opinion of this war is as he has expressed it. He also knows my feelings against war in general, and I believe that he thinks that this is because I am a woman, and as men imagine, we have not the stomach for contest.*

*My son, let us keep this confidence between ourselves, but I do not yield to this notion for an instant. I need not tell you that I am not of Pennsylvania stock, my scruple against war is not religiously impelled as among the Quakers of that place. Rather, every thing I have seen of war is that it derives in its past from greed, or pride, or envy, or simple malice, or other of the Seven Deadly Sins—war from the party that seeks ill gain comes of evil.*

*They that are placed in the position of either submitting to wrong or resisting it, must resort to reason in determining their path.*

*Therefore my dearly loved son, understand your mother rightly. Though I abhor war and killing, I know well that your part in this is carried on in the full day light of honor, that you fight to defend our country from again suffering what your father and I did in Boston many years ago.*

*Never doubt my pride in you, never doubt that you are the object of my daily prayer on bended knee, that you will come home safe to me—and, yes, that you will come home victorious.*

*Your loving mother,*
*Doro. Putnam*

Bliven set the letter down, quiet in thought, before removing a sheet from his own writing kit and trimming it to match hers, and dipping his quill in the inkpot.

BOSTON
JULY 28TH, 1812

*Dear Mother,*

*I have no doubt you were expecting your letter to reach me months hence, in some distant quarter of the globe, yet here it is, scarce a month gone and I as close as Boston. The command that awaits me in Charleston was so far from ready that I was sent out on the Constitution under Captain Hull, happily so, for he is a fine officer, to see what we might effect. We set a course for New York, he to join a squadron under Commodore Rodgers, I to recruit new men into the Navy, but instead we encountered a British squadron of five sail, then seven, and at one point, eleven. They chased us the better part of three days, and Capt. Hull led a most wonderful escape. You need not be anxious for me, for I tell you, if I had known that war could be fought at so slow a pace, I would have brought more books with me.*

*I am heartily glad to learn of Father's recovery, and hope that you will take the lesson to be watchful for your own health as well.*

*You will see that I am returning your letter, not because anything within displeases me, but because I wish it kept safe. Should any ill thing befall me, I want the future to know that my mother would have been as courageous a sailor, or as wise a statesman, as any man in her day.*

*Your loving son,*
*Bliven Putnam*
*Master Cmdt., USN*

*P.S.—We set sail again within the day, as soon as we can replace provisions. There are no orders for me here, so I am going back out with Hull. The British gave us such a merry chase that we were compelled to pump out several thousand gallons of fresh water to lighten ship, although upon reaching this place we were only a little thirsty. BP*

## The Warrior

The *Constitution* lay in Boston for a week, not just replenishing stores but ascertaining that there was no damage to the stern plate, rebuilding the bulkhead between the captain's cabin and the gun deck, and freshly painting Hull's quarters, which still smelled of powder smoke. Hull paced his deck as long as he could stand it, until the arrival of August, when he announced to the Yard that he was leaving before he could be blockaded, and waited upon no argument.

Stores were still stacked on the spar deck when Morris approached and saluted. "Captain, the master at arms reports that there is a missing man. It is the Irishman Davis who came aboard at Annapolis."

Bliven's attention sharpened to hear how Hull would answer. "Oh, I remember him, he had seventy-eight lashes coming to him for desertion, said he was British and wanted to be repatriated."

"Shall we send a party ashore, sir?" asked Morris.

Hull considered it and shook his head slowly. "No."

"An Irishman would not be hard to find in Boston, sir. He will give himself away every time he speaks."

Hull thought on it further. The Navy took a dim view of desertion, and to not chase him down and flog him within an inch of his life—or flog him to death—might inspire others to attempt the same. "No," said Hull at last. "I was perhaps wrong to take him. He said he had been pressed, but I was busy and angry. We'll just let him go." He thought for one more moment. "How many more English do we have in our crew?"

"About twenty, sir."

"Were they all willing volunteers?"

"Yes, sir—as far as we know."

"Naturalized citizens?"

"Mostly."

"Well, spread the word among them, I have let Davis go because he was wrongly pressed. They, on the contrary, volunteered to join the Navy, and if any man among them have a mind to join him in desertion, he will bear Davis's lashes in addition to his own. Make sure they understand."

"Yes, sir." Morris saluted and left.

Owing to the *Constitution*'s deep draught they had to be particularly mindful of following the pilot through the trickery of Boston's shallows, but Bliven thought he had never seen Hull happier than when they approached the open reaches of Massachusetts Bay. Once past the Harbor Islands and Halftide Rocks, Hull craned his neck upward. "Masthead there!"

"Sir!"

"What do you see?"

"Clear horizon, sir!"

"Ha. Well, Putnam, I am glad you decided to come back out with me, when you could be sitting in Boston waiting for orders."

"If I may speak frankly, sir?"

"By all means."

"Your handling of the ship during the late chase was the best advanced education I could receive. I rather think I am better preparing myself for command by shipping out with you again."

Hull dropped his head in apparent self-deprecation. "Well, I am glad to have you aboard once more."

Bliven looked eagerly out to sea. "Where bound, Captain?"

"Well," Hull began slowly, "let us review. Rodgers has flown the coop from New York to chase down British convoys and, according to his plan, sail as far as the British coast to pull the lion's tail. Admiral Sawyer has sent his squadron out after him, but they lost three days trying to run us to ground. Now they must be back after him. What, do you think, does all that leave undefended?"

Bliven scanned his mental Atlantic and it hit him like a thunderbolt. "Halifax!"

"Won't old Sawyer be surprised when we show up for breakfast some morning?"

Bliven had his doubts. "I don't know, sir. I saw a chart, that harbor is a very devil, the entrance is narrow as a hallway, turns twice, certainly lined with guns down both sides. We don't know how deep it is."

"Now, now. We have no need to enter the harbor. We need only pounce on their ships as they arrive, and do to them what the British have been doing to us for years. We'll see how they like it."

They ran north and then northeast, near land, within distant sight of Portsmouth in New Hampshire and the long, rocky desolation of Massachusetts's northern territory, until navigation told them they were at the wide mouth of the Bay of Fundy, and they had seen nothing. They turned east until within sight of Nova Scotia, then southeast. They rounded the colony's southern tip at Cape Sable Island, standing northeast toward Halifax, ready to intercept any vessels making for a port, challenging any to come out and fight, but the frigid waters of the Labrador Current in which they found themselves remained devoid of a single other vessel. When they found nothing doing outside Halifax itself, they stood east by south, near two hundred miles to the Isle of Sables, found no one, and turned north for the broad entrance of the Gulf of St. Lawrence.

"Where in hell is everybody?" blustered Hull at last.

"Cowed by our naval might to stay in port?" Charles Morris smiled wryly.

"Perhaps," said Bliven, "if we continue on to the North Pole we might find someone."

They were twelve days out of Boston, midway between Cape Breton Island and the French fishing enclave at St. Pierre, when the cry came down. "Deck! Deck there!"

Bliven rejoiced that he had the deck. "What do you see?"

"Sail, on the lee beam."

"What do you make of her?"

"A trading vessel, sir, small and slovenly."

*Constitution* ran down upon her in full panoply and did not even have to fire a shot across her bows before the small trader took in every stitch of canvas. Her master was a gray and fleshy old sailor of sixty named Fouts, who admitted with a grudge that he knew Great Britain was at war with America, and was sorry for it, for it had nothing to do with him. Bliven then had the sour experience of hearing a captain plead for the life of his ship.

"Where were you bound?" questioned Hull.

"Five days out of St. John's, bound for Ship's Harbour. Do you know it? It is on the channel between—"

"I know it," said Hull. "Mr. Fouts, I am sorry to make you a casualty of war, but it is a maritime war, whose success is measured principally in the seizure of ships. We can keep you and your crew here until we can land you someplace. Or if you prefer, if you have a boat on board, you may take your boat west; you should make Cape Breton Island in a day or a little more."

"May we take food and water?"

"Of course."

"Then that is how we shall have it."

The men of the *Constitution* watched Fouts and his crew of nine hoist a sail and diminish to westward in the small chop. When the report came back that the ship was not worth taking as a prize, Hull ordered her burned, a command that he plainly disliked to give. When the whole experience was repeated with a second small merchantman on the next day, Hull had had enough, and turned south.

"Deck! Deck there!"

"What do you see?"

"Five sail, on the weather bow."

Hull strode quickly to the port railing. "Oh, hell, not again!"

Hull tapped his glass into his open hand, as Bliven came near. "What are your orders, Captain?"

"Small ships," the lookout called down without being asked. "A sloop-of-war, maybe his prizes."

"Well, that's different," said Hull. "Come to full sail and make for 'em. Let's see what they are up to."

As soon as their increased canvas and changed heading was made out, the apparent sloop-of-war before them to windward made all sail to get away, and a moment later they saw flames on one of the vessels in her train, a fire that quickly rose from rails to mastheads. Hull lowered his glass. "Well, damn me if that was not a craven thing to do. The coward."

Bliven pointed. "The others are scattering, sir, like quail out of a bush. They know we can only take one."

"Well," answered Hull, "let's see if we can run down that closest one. No one would mistake her for a greyhound." This prey was more fortunate, an American privateer that had been bested and captured, and her master and crew now happy to be recaptured.

"Gentlemen?" The officers gathered around Hull, emphasizing to a somewhat embarrassing degree how much the shorter he was of all of them. None would have dared call him fat, but his shape was equally obvious. "I do not often play at cards, but when I do I will not play for pennies. I am tired of this. Take us south again, into the sea lanes, and for God's sake find us somebody worth fighting."

It was at two in the afternoon on August 19, two hundred

miles south of Nova Scotia, that the call came down. "Deck! Deck there!"

"What do you see?"

"Sail off the lee bow, bearing east-sou'east!"

The officers gathered at the starboard railing, glasses raised.

"What do you make of her?"

"Seems a large vessel, sir, can't see more than that!"

"Very well!"

Hull lowered his glass and hardly had to say it out loud. "Gentlemen, if she were ours, she would probably be with Rodgers, and Rodgers should not be in these waters. I believe we have a fair chance at a fight this afternoon. Mr. Morris, beat to quarters; Mr. Bush, get your Marines into the tops, well supplied, keep a platoon handy down here in case we come to a boarding."

The *Constitution* leapt to life with the drum's tattoo as her thirty boys skittered down the ladders to the magazine and powder room in the deepest bowels of the ship where grown men could move only in a crouch. They emerged struggling under the weight of thirty twenty-four-pound solid shot for the main battery, an eighteen for the bow chaser, twenty charges of grape for the carronades, and sheet-lead canisters of powder, eight pounds each for the twenty-fours, and less for the smaller guns. Crew chiefs barked their orders as the three-ton long guns were rolled in with rhythmic heaves, tompions removed, they were quoined level for loading, the quoins removed for elevation and run back out. In three minutes the ship fell into an eerie silence.

The next hour crawled by as the unknown ship grew larger by tiny degrees, surely a large vessel, but her details still a mystery.

"Deck there!"

"What is it?"

"She is a frigate, sir! Close hauled under easy sail, on the starboard tack."

The other officers could almost see Hull making his mental triangulations, working out how to play his advantages, the weather gage, the heavy rolling swell that was keeping them all alert on their sea legs. His third and fourth lieutenants were at their gun crews, he was happy to have Morris with him to relay his commands, and it was well to have Bliven standing by, who could take over if any of them fell.

"Gentlemen, let us run down freely upon her, time enough to shorten sail when we get closer."

"Deck there!"

"What do you see?"

"She is shortening sail, sir! Taken in her courses!"

"Very well!"

One league from her, all could see that she had backed her topsails and was waiting on them. She ran up no fewer than three British naval ensigns, one at the head of each mast. "Well, by God," said Hull, "if ever I have been challenged to a fight! Well, we'll show him. Mr. Morris, let's run up four."

"Yes, sir." Morris grinned but, having once turned to go, stopped. "Sir, where shall we fly the fourth flag?"

"Why, right up here, from the driver, Mr. Morris! That will give a nice symmetry overall, don't you think? Go!" They could see the challenger's gunports snap open and the guns run out. "Bosun!"

"Sir!"

"Bring in your flying jib and stays'ls, bring down your royal yards."

"Aye, sir!"

The two great vessels approached each other elegantly, with a kind of chivalry, like medieval knights on horse at a joust. The British captain had invited a single combat with traditional good manners, and Hull determined to oblige him. The British ship turned alternately port and starboard to present her two broadsides, opening fire, but the balls fell well short. Hull also yawed port and starboard to prevent their being raked, allowing ranging shots from his bow chasers to ascertain an advantageous time to begin firing in earnest.

As they closed the range, the Americans could read their enemy's name, ornately gilded beneath her stern windows, *Guerriere*, and surmised that she must be one of the many French prizes taken and assimilated into the Royal Navy. But that did not alter her history, and, being French, she must be but lightly built, and capable of inflicting more damage than she could sustain.

*Guerriere*, thought Bliven. *Warrior. Well, we shall see.* Seconds after her next broadside they heard a popping rip in the canvas overhead as a ball flew through, and hammerblows of balls beginning to strike the hull. Clearly this showy Englishman was now within their own range.

Morris was about to jump out of his skin. "Sir, shall we not open fire?"

"On my order, sir." Hull's growl issued from the very depth of his throat. "Not before, do you hear?" When Hull had turned to answer, Bliven saw that look in his eyes. He had seen it before, in

Stephen Decatur's eyes when they fired the *Philadelphia* in Tripoli harbor—wild, predatory, eager, fully engaged and, if anything, in his own world, and somehow, deeply happy. Bliven could not help but wonder if this was a trait necessary for a successful career. Whether he desired it for himself he set aside for later examination.

The carpenter came up and reported that though the hull had been hit, they had not been holed anywhere; there was no evidence of penetration or even splinters. The next British salvo went high and cut up some rigging but did no damage. "Do you see, Captain?" said Bliven. "She fires on the uproll to disable us; she means to take us, not sink us."

Hull's emotion intensified by the second. "Well, we won't be returning the favor."

They closed to within a hundred yards, and Bliven thought it well to keep moving about, to give the British Marines at least a moving target to try to hit, and perhaps discreetly keep some solid object such as the wheel between himself and the marksmen in their tops. Hull, he noted, stood as squat and foursquare as Napoleon, all but daring the British Marines to strike him down if they could. "We will fire a rolling broadside, on the downroll," he shouted down the spar deck, and command was relayed below to the main battery.

*Brilliant*, thought Bliven. A rolling broadside, firing the guns sequentially from fore to aft, accounting for their relative speed in passing each other, would concentrate their fury, and the damage, upon a shorter span of the enemy's hull.

At seventy-five yards Hull bellowed, "Set your courses! Set your topsails!" With the added canvas, the ship began picking up speed.

It seemed as though their yardarms must foul their enemy's as the *Constitution* glided up in eerie silence, until she was a scant twenty-five yards away. *Guerriere's* guns continued to boom as they were loaded, the balls continuing to strike the hull with no effect.

The next swell pushed up *Constitution's* starboard side, the sea itself aiming her main battery low into the enemy's hull, the carronades pointing down upon their spar deck. Hull sprinted forward to make sure he was heard, hardly noticing that as he did so he split his too-tight trousers along the entire length of the crotch seam. "Fire!" roared Hull at last. "Open fire!" In a split second the side of the *Constitution* erupted in a fusillade—deafening, crushing, a concussive, staccato rolling broadside from bow back to stern that must have lasted fifteen seconds, obscuring sight of their point-blank target behind a wall of smoke but not stifling the screams and the crunching of wood being splintered. The grape from the carronades worked dreadful execution upon the enemy's spar deck at the same instant as the solid shot from their twenty-fours grievously wounded the ship herself. As the smoke rose they saw numerous holes in her hull, a couple between wind and water, many around her gunports, each hole representing a lethal shower of splinters within that preceded the ball itself, mowing down the helpless gun crews.

"Keep firing!" bellowed Hull. "Reload! Reload, fast as you can, now! Let them have it! Pour it on 'em!"

Although firing at will, the crews were trained enough that they were all reloaded and the guns run back out almost together, and they got off a second full broadside before the *Constitution* ran past her.

One of *Guerriere*'s shots took effect, a spray of grape from a carronade mowing down three of its opposing gun crew, a port-side carronade on the *Constitution*. The wounded were bundled below before it could be seen how badly they were hit, and within seconds the crew of the starboard carronade took over operation of the port gun. A couple more gunners on the spar deck were felled by muskets from *Guerriere*'s Marines in her fighting tops, whose heads were mostly kept low by their own Marines shooting at what was, for them, point-blank range.

Bliven knew that Cutbush would be ready for the wounded in his cockpit, deep within the orlop. He would be grim and efficient in his leather apron, not unaffected by the writhing agonies laid before him, but aware that a swift and determined application of his skills was their best hope. His empathy, and his animated and erudite affability, he would resume when the emergency was passed, but for now, Bliven knew he was an automaton of surgical precision.

*Constitution* with her sudden extra canvas, which *Guerriere* did not match, pulled ahead after delivering this lethal stroke. Once well clear, Hull cupped his hands and shouted, "Port guns reload, hold your fire! Port your helm! Rake her bow as we cross! At my command!"

The American frigate answered the helm with a tight turn to port, her full broadside pointed at the oncoming Englishman's bow, where she could not answer. "As you bear, fire!" A second rolling broadside, slower than the first, each gun chief sighting on *Guerriere*'s foremast, narrowly missing, but that was no matter, for the British suffered the full, withering slaughter of a bow rake.

Again clear, Hull roared, "Hard a-starboard! Wear ship! Come about, starboard broadside ready! Give it to them again!"

The wind no longer behind them, *Constitution* was slower to answer the steering. "Wear ship!" bellowed Hull. "Wear ship!"

From *Guerriere* they heard a dreadful explosive popping and snapping, and watched as her one-hundred-fifty-foot mizzenmast went over the starboard rail, its descent slowed by the web of lines that had to break or pull free. Her vast spanker now partly covered the quarterdeck in canvas, leaving men to crawl out from under it, and it partly trailed in the water, acting as a giant rudder that spun her to starboard.

Thus as the *Constitution* finally began her turn, *Guerriere* turned toward her, out of control. *Constitution* was half again heavier, but as *Guerriere* came upon their stern she was still a looming mighty presence. Hull spun around to see her eighty-foot bowsprit glide above them and spear into their spanker rigging, deeper and deeper until that spar's lower thickness crunched through their taffrail. So far from seeing this as a threat, and with a boarding party at the ready, eager young men sensed the opportunity to burnish their careers.

Lieutenant Morris seized a cut line from the *Guerriere*'s rigging that hung from the bowsprit and attempted to lash the two ships together. It was a futile show of bravado, for the irresistible swell made the British bow and American stern sweep up and down past each other by as much as eight feet. With one ship of a thousand tons and the other of fifteen hundred, no rope could have bound them together, but for young officers on the rise, to be seen in valiant conduct was the avenue of promotion. For Morris it was a demonstration of personal bravery that he paid for with a British musket ball high in his right chest that blew him back several yards to fall almost at Bliven's feet.

Instantly, Bliven knelt by him. "Mr. Morris!"

"Oh, God," he groaned. "I fear I am killed."

"No, I don't think so, it does not look mortal." He had no idea whether it was mortal, but he knew the value of encouragement. "Let me get you below."

Morris was able to get himself into a crouch, but shrieked when Bliven got under him and stood, with Morris slung over his shoulder. Bliven managed the after ladder down to the gun deck and hollered for surgeon's mates, who took Morris down to the cockpit. On his way back up the ladder, Bliven noticed his right shoulder smeared with Morris's blood and damned the spoilage of his coat.

In Morris's absence, the lieutenant of the *Constitution*'s Marines leapt upon the taffrail; his sword was sheathed in its scabbard, but he gripped a slender iron boarding pike held *en garde*. "Captain! Shall we board her?" There was no time to answer until all saw his bicorne spin off his head, for a musket ball had entered his left cheek and come out the back of his head. He fell like timber back onto the quarterdeck, the grip on his pike still tight, his eyes wide, his cheeks florid as dislodged parts of his brain oozed through the exit wound.

"Mr. Bush!" roared Hull. "Mr. Bush! Damn! Mr. Contee, you are now in command of the Marines. You shall not board, but prepare to repel boarders!" The order made perfect sense, for the two ships' bow and stern passed each other on the same plane for only an instant every several seconds as one rose and the other fell. Boarding in such conditions was madness, and then the two ships must soon begin to pull apart. If any of the British were that eager and foolish, as Bush had been, let them come and let them be lost instead. Contee was only seventeen and in his first action; he was far less likely to attempt more than he was ordered.

The Marines on their quarterdeck formed up, but Bliven saw where the fire was coming from that felled Bush and Morris. In a crouch, he ran to a spot next to the ship's great double wheel, craned his neck upward, and cupped his hands beside his mouth. "Mizzentop! Mizzentop, there!"

A corporal who could not have been more than twenty peered over the railing.

"Do you want to see us all killed? Shoot at their foretop! Engage their foretop!"

The corporal nodded with a faint salute and disappeared, and Bliven knew his order had been obeyed when twenty seconds later a musket volley boomed in unison, the jets of powder smoke pointing like accusing fingers to the *Guerriere's* foretop.

With *Guerriere* being the smaller by some five hundred tons, her bow rode several feet lower than the *Constitution's* stern, giving her fourth lieutenant in command of her eighteen-pounder bow chasers as close a view through Isaac Hull's cabin windows as any Peeping Tom would have. There was no need to lay the guns with any more care; he simply yanked the lanyard of the first one, then sprinted to the second one and yanked it also.

Hull's cabin windows shattered with the concussion even before the balls crashed through them invisible, the first one demolishing his quarter gallery and head, the second one shattering through a mahogany cabinet, through the bulkhead into the gun deck, and spending itself in knocking the cascabel from the breech of a twenty-four-pounder. Spinning crazily, it rolled until it stopped with a thud at the wooden base of the camboose mounting. After the balls came the expanding yellow balloons of flame, licking into every last crevice of Hull's cabin, setting papers and bedding afire, which quickly ignited the new paint and varnish. In a moment Hull beheld a voluminous billow of smoke rising from below the taffrail and knew the circumstance exactly. "God damn ye!" he bellowed. "That's my cabin!"

With *Guerriere*'s bowsprit trapped in *Constitution*'s spanker rigging, the latter in her starboard turn and the former trailing the greater part of her spanker like a giant tiller, the two ships spun together in the current like two great dogs who had each other by the tail. The *Constitution* began to twist back on her opponent until most of her starboard guns once more came to bear, the range closing to point-blank, so that the muzzle blasts themselves could start fires on the deck. "Fire!" screamed Hull. "Don't let up, keep it on 'em!"

In the pummeling that followed, *Guerriere* suffered terribly, her gun crews cut down and unable to respond. "Pour it on 'em," gesticulated Hull, taking no notice that his white underclothes were still peeking through the rent in his tight trousers.

Further expression was arrested by wrenching creaks and snaps as *Guerriere*'s bowsprit began to back away; their counterclockwise spin while locked together had brought *Constitution* once more into the wind, and her filling courses and topsails began to pull her away. No sooner were they safely separated than the officers on the quarterdeck heard an almost living groan from the *Guerriere* as her stays popped and the foremast tottered drunkenly backward until it fell into the mainmast, which popped like a stick, and both masts crashed down over the starboard rail.

"Gentlemen, the day is ours!" exulted Hull. "Let us stand off and repair our rigging. She won't be going anywhere." Within seconds the bosun and his mates, studded with marlinspikes, began reweaving the web of lines that made the *Constitution* the modern wonder of war that she was. From the safety of two hundred yards they watched their enemy roll helpless in the swell, watched her smoke and smolder, the dead canvas chopped from the downed masts sliding into the deep.

After an hour, they saw and heard a heavy gun discharge and saw the smoke shoot directly away from them—the accepted gesture of surrender when there are no colors to lower. But one could never be sure; it might simply have gone off or been carelessly fired. "Mr. Putnam," said Hull, "Mr. Morris is wounded. Are you willing to take a boat over under a flag of truce and ascertain their intentions?"

"Certainly, sir."

"Can't go myself, I've split my trousers."

——*//*——

The captain's gig was lowered, with rowers, and Bliven felt himself uneasy at being in such a small boat in such a swell. They came upon *Guerriere*'s lee beam. The sea was too dangerous to use her convenience ladder, and Bliven sent a Marine up the netting first, so that the first thing visible over the rail would be their white flag of truce. The ship's roll was heavy but easy, and Bliven climbed the netting after him.

Stepping into *Guerriere*'s open waist, his first sight of the butchery was so overwhelming that he would have vomited had he not instantly raised his sight back to the quarterdeck. "Come on." He pulled the Marine by the sleeve and walked quickly aft, stepping around the blood where they could. He observed the carnage only out of the corners of his eyes, as though that made it somehow less real—bodiless legs, opened rib cages, one man lying on his back, his face seeming flush with the deck planking, or formed of it, and Bliven realized that was because the back of his head had been carried away. It was one tiny blessing amid the gore, that the sheer volume of blood made individual body parts impossible to recognize, and he could take less mental note of what he could not identify. Yet he knew they were striding through hell.

Upon gaining the quarterdeck, Bliven was astonished to behold a man no older than himself, short, slender, pale, and gracile, with large and intensely expressive eyes. "Captain Dacres?" Bliven asked uncertainly.

The young man raised his head to give Bliven his attention.

Bliven saluted. "Captain, my captain's compliments, we observed that you fired a lee gun. Were you signaling your intention to surrender your ship?"

Dacres placed one hand on his hip, fingers down, leaning obliquely to one side, as though he were assessing the condition of his rigging, but in a manner that seemed altogether effete and disagreeable.

"Sir, do you wish to surrender your vessel?" he repeated.

"Well, I don't know," he said at last.

Bliven was confounded. "Sir?"

"My mizzenmast is gone. My fore and main masts are gone. My berth deck is coming awash." Dacres erupted suddenly, "What in bloody hell do you think!" The very force of his exclamation caused him to stumble, and he caught himself on the wheel. Bliven saw a wet stain of purple spreading on the back of his blue coat and realized that Dacres's hand was on his hip to support himself. "Sir, you have been wounded!" he exclaimed, and reached out to steady him.

"I think, on the whole, you may say that we have struck our flag."

"Help here!" Bliven shouted.

Two British sailors stepped forward and supported Dacres under his arms. "No, let us end this. Take me across to your ship."

"You cannot manage the ladder, sir."

"It is not as bad as that. Come, they can swing out a bosun's chair."

They made their way along the waist of the ship. "What are your casualties, Captain, do you know?"

"Seventy when they last told me, but still counting."

As a bosun's chair was rigged, Bliven was surprised to see another boat being lowered, *Guerriere*'s only intact one, and a dozen men not in uniform rowing it over, under a similar white flag.

While being pulled across, the occasional shocking splash of the Labrador Current's freezing water snapped all to alertness. "You will understand," said Dacres, "it is awkward to lower one's colors when one has no mast left. You rather lowered them for us."

"Yes, sir, I suppose we did."

Hull was equally surprised to see a second boat lowered by civilian-looking men under no officer, and ordered its leader brought to him as soon as he came aboard. "What is your name, sir?" inquired Hull.

"Orne, sir, William B. Orne, master of the trading ship *Bessie Anne*, until captured by that smoking hulk over there and taken captive with my crew." He spoke in the piercing, drawn-out accent that was developing in vast and nearly vacant upper Massachusetts, separated from Boston and the main population by New Hampshire's toehold coastline.

"You are all well and accounted for?"

"Yes, sir, and rejoicing to be back on an American ship. May they come aboard?"

"Bring them up!" ordered Hull. "See to their needs."

"Captain, it will interest you to know that I was on the quarter-deck with the British captain at the commencement of the action. Had me spot you through the glass and say what I made of you. At first he did not want to agree that you were an American. Said you came on too boldly for an American, but he hoped you were. Said he would be made for life by being the first British captain to take an American frigate."

"Ha!" shouted Hull. "Did he, now?"

"Yes, sir, and once it became certain that you meant to fight, he encouraged his officers, said that the better you behaved, the more honor they should gain by capturing you."

"Ha! I wonder what he will have to say now."

"Well"—Orne pointed—"you may ask him yourself directly; they are bringing him across now."

Hull grew more serious. "Are you aware whether there were any pressed Americans serving in his crew?"

"Yes, sir, there are ten, but Dacres sent them below so they would not have to fire upon their countrymen."

Hull's mood altered completely. "Did he? Well, damn me."

"He is a gentleman, Captain," said Orne, "as fine a one as I've ever seen, especially seeing he is so young."

"Bosun's chair here," Bliven shouted from the base of the ladder. Such an order was not expected, and it took a moment to rig one. Dacres bore his pain stoically as he was hoisted aboard. The swell was still too great to trust his footing on the ladder steps, and Bliven climbed the netting with the men who had rowed across.

As Dacres was helped from the chair, Bliven reported to the quarterdeck and saluted. Bliven explained to Hull his interview with Dacres on the *Guerriere*'s quarterdeck, and what he had said about not knowing whether he would surrender. Hull wanted to burst out laughing, but out of respect did not, for Dacres was now waiting in the background to meet him. "One other thing, too, Captain. He says there are ten Americans on board, pressed men. He sent them below so they would not have to take part."

"Yes, I have heard already. Bring him over to me." Dacres was led over, leaning on a Marine's arm. "Captain Dacres, you are hurt," said Hull. "We will get you attention."

"Captain Hull, I thank you, I am all right for the moment."

"It is my understanding that you are surrendering your vessel."

Dacres freed himself from the Marine and fumbled at unbuckling his belt. "My sword, sir."

"No, by God, sir." Hull stepped forward and placed his hand over Dacres's. "I will not take the sword of a man who fought as gallantly as you."

Tears welled up in Dacres's eyes, not for his pain, but all recognized the manly tears of relief that he had heard it admitted, he had fought his best.

"Get him below to Cutbush. Make him comfortable. Captain Dacres, I would berth you in my cabin, but that would be no great courtesy, for you have burnt it out like a pottery kiln."

"I am sorry for that, Captain Hull."

"Well, never mind, fortunes of war, what? We will do our best for you. Putnam, take a detail back over, go through his cabin, remove his papers and his personal effects, give them to the purser until we can figure something out. He has been a gentleman and, by God, we are going to treat him as one."

"Aye, sir."

"And one other thing, Mr. Putnam." Hull pointed at the smoldering *Guerriere* with his glass. "I do not want that ship to sink. While you are over there, assess her condition. Then tell me what we must do to lead her in as a prize. I want all of Boston to see her. If you can save her, you shall command the prize crew. If you can't save her, burn her."

"Very good, Captain." Bliven saluted and excused himself to carry out this instruction before the fires on the stricken *Guerriere* could make much more progress. It was apparent from his first moment back aboard her, however, that her case was hopeless. Even with twelve men manning her pumps, they informed Bliven that two of the holes punched between wind and water were now underwater and could not be mended nor even reached. They were going down by the head, slowly but hopelessly. The forward hold was already flooded and the forward berth deck coming awash.

"Well, stay by your pumps," Bliven said. "We will start with your wounded, but we will take you all off as quickly as we can."

It took two hours, with all of *Constitution*'s longboats and cutters shuttling back and forth, for the ship to be evacuated, and when the hulk was empty, Bliven set a fire on the rising stern; the paint stores which would have spread the fire quickly were forward and flooded, but there was enough shredded canvas on deck and a fire in the galley to do the job. He was at least grateful that the British sailors had cast the dead and parts of the dead overboard, so he did not have to see them again.

Into the darkness the officers on the *Constitution*'s quarterdeck watched the fire rise as they slowly opened distance between them, and saw the fire blown down for an instant by the shock wave of a ripping explosion that boomed over them several seconds later.

With Morris wounded, it was the second lieutenant who came on deck and saluted Hull. "Captain, sir, the carpenter and the bosun have completed their inspections. The ship is undamaged, despite several hits. There are several balls embedded in the hull, but they have penetrated only into the outer layer. We have expended only a third of our ammunition. Shall we continue to Bermuda?"

Hull chewed on this for a moment. "Not with two hundred prisoners aboard, no. We'll make for Boston, put them ashore, replenish the water, and top off with powder and shot. Besides, this victory is news that will burst like a bomb upon the public. Let us not forget how controversial this war is, and nothing shores up popularity like a victory."

Bliven took this in silently, amazed that Hull included such thoughts in his calculus.

"Moreover," added Hull, "I fear that the Army is not going to make such a good show of it. Won't be a bad thing to let the Congress know that of their two services upon whom they have lavished money, it is the Navy that is returning on their investment."

"Yes, sir."

Bliven did not disapprove, but he was noting down, as he would a lesson in a schoolroom, how a comprehensive view of the Navy's affairs could never omit events' impacts upon the politicians.

In the galley Bliven poured a cup of tea, then descended the after ladder to the wardroom, where he spooned some sugar into a folded paper pouch, then went forward to the sick bay, where he found the British commander lying on his stomach, his hands beneath the pillow, a large fresh bandage over his upper back. "Captain Dacres? How are you feeling?"

Dacres was awake and had observed him approach. "Much better, I am surprised to say. Your ship's surgeon is very skilled."

"Yes, we value him highly. I brought you some tea. Do you feel up to it?"

"Oh my God, you are a gentleman. Thank'ee." Dacres removed his right hand from beneath the pillow, although with evident pain, and let the cup rest on the edge of the mattress as he sipped some of it. "I heard a tremendous explosion."

"That was your ship, I'm afraid. We tried, but when we couldn't save her the captain order her burned."

"Well"—Dacres nodded sadly—"I cannot say I am sorry that she won't be a prize."

"I understand."

"Do you know?" said Dacres. "No, you wouldn't know. My uncle is a rear admiral in the Royal Navy. My cousin is a post captain. And here . . . am I."

Bliven smiled. "I am the very first of my family to go to sea."

"I shall be court-martialed."

"Surely not. But if you are, I can assure you, every officer on board this vessel will swear affidavits that you fought your ship to the utter extent that circumstances allowed."

"That is kind of you, thank you, but there is always a court-martial when a ship is lost. Someone or something must bear the blame. Often it works to absolve the captain. For my family's sake, if nothing else, they will probably rule that the ship was lost owing to the masts being defective, or some such silliness. Besides"—he toasted Bliven with the tea—"that would deny you the credit for having shot them down. The Admiralty is clever that way. How are my men?"

"We have made them as comfortable as we can in the cable tier, below. The captain has determined to put back into Boston rather than continue our cruise, so they will be ashore in a few days. No doubt you will be exchanged in short order."

"Where is your surgeon?"

"He is still in the cockpit, doing what he can. And by the way, your surgeon is with him. They have set up a second table to operate on, they are side by side."

Dacres smiled wanly and nodded. "Ha. Our doctors seem to cooperate well enough, what a pity that our governments could not."

BOSTON HARBOR
30TH AUGUST, 1812

*My Own Dear Wife,*

*If the news papers reach you before this letter does, you will have learned that our ship has achieved a most signal victory in defeating the British frigate* Guerriere *in single combat. Our casualties were seven killed and seven wounded, the ship only slightly damaged, and I, unscathed.*

*The British lost several times that number. On paper it was a nearly even match, our forty-four guns against their thirty-eight, but what I imagine the news papers will not report is that our opponent was severely undermanned, our broadside threw at least half a ton more weight of shot than hers, and the* Guerriere, *being French-built (and captured and put into English service), was too light in its construction.*

*Nonetheless, Capt. Hull fought our ship brilliantly. I am glad now that I did not go to Charleston straightaway and wait to assume my own command, for I feel I have learned much from him, and the officers and crew were inspired. A few short weeks ago our crew were all new to one another, and many new to the sea, yet from the way they worked the ship and the guns, no one would have suspected that to be the case.*

*And the ship herself—oh, my love!—to say that she is magnificent in battle does her but little justice. At one point when the fight was at its hottest, a crewman looked down and actually saw a ball from the Guerriere bounce off our hull. "Look there, boys," he says. "It's like she's made of iron!" And so the crew have taken it up and now refer to her as "Old Ironsides."*

*It is quite curious, really. It seems that with every ship and crew, there must come some moment when all its pieces, all its men with all its spars and guns and all its component parts, fuse into a unit. My moment with the Enterprise came when we defeated the Tripolitans without a single casualty, and our men's fear of Sterett changed to devotion. With Preble on the Constitution it came off Cape St. Vincent, when the Commodore swore out a British ship of the line that he would be damn'd before he would send a boat over, and was roundly cheered by the men. And now, for our crew, they feel themselves part of a truly extraordinary and perhaps impregnable vessel.*

*That is the good of the report. Now must come the other. Once returned to port, I have heard news that has come close to making me resign my commission, come home, and take up farming, never to leave again, nor care for the fates of governments. Though this occurred months ago, the sequence of events is only now becoming clear, and, my love, it is almost enough to make a moral man lunatic. As you well know, one of the principal causes of our going to war was the British insistence upon their Orders in Council, by which they claimed the right to stop neutral vessels—including ours—on the high seas, which opportunities they then parlayed into absconding with innocent American seamen. The chief proponent of this pernicious policy has been the Tory prime minister, Mr. Perceval. The policy has had many enemies within Parliament, while Perceval himself has not been perceived as heading a strong government. The weakness of his majority I never knew before.*

*Perhaps you have read of this already, but on May 11 last, Perceval was assassinated in the very lobby of the House of Commons. The man who shot him through the heart did so for reasons totally unrelated to us, so it seems that Perceval's injustices extended into still wider spheres. Lord Liverpool is now the prime minister, a man who has long advocated a more moderate policy toward the United States.*

*Indeed, Liverpool canceled the hated Orders in Council, and a ship was dispatched carrying that intelligence to our government. That ship westbound crossed paths with our ship eastbound, carrying news of our declaration of war. And so, my love, none of this bloodshed might have been necessary. A little more patience, a little more forbearance, a little more statecraft on our part to gain the favor of friends in foreign governments, and war with all its horrors and expense might have been averted.*

*On the deck of a defeated enemy one sees sights too terrible to relate, and the thought that such carnage, such butchery, might not have been necessary calls forth in me no feeling more than despair. The likelihood now is that, battle having been joined, both* sides will pour themselves into vindicating their national honor, but let us pray that somewhere above the sight of those who do the fighting, cooler heads may prevail.

Until then, I leave tomorrow for Charleston by coach. My ship the Tempest is nearly ready, and the recruiting difficulties of which everyone made such a fuss have been resolved. It seems that news of Rodgers putting to sea with a squadron has brought English warships racing in pursuit, which drew them away from their previous occupation of hunting down American merchantmen. This has had the unintended result that numerous American commercial vessels have safely put into the various Atlantic ports and interned themselves for the duration. It seems that at least for a short time Charleston is awash in seamen who have nowhere else to go, and I must hasten to harvest my share.

Be not anxious for my welfare, my love. I am in robust health, and, God willing, this war will soon be behind us. For just one moment I will hold this letter as close to my heart as ever I held you, and when you do the same I know I shall feel it.

> Your devoted husband,
> Bliven Putnam
> Master Cmdt., USN

Mrs. Clarity Putnam
New Putnam Farm
So. Road
Litchfield, Connectient

## — 7 —

### *The Shaded Bower*

Bidding farewell to a ship is a hard business, there are so many things of which to let go: the associations built up with shipmates, the knowledge of her eccentricities and intimacy with her nether spaces, the emotion expended in seeing men killed. And there must be the last gaze, perhaps over one's shoulder but better if one turns to frame the final picture, while understanding that the vessel herself no canvas could capture: the proud angle of her hundred-foot bowsprit, the beetling vastness of her hull beneath the two-hundred-foot masts.

Bliven turned twice as the drayman's wagon carried him and his trunks down the Long Wharf toward Faneuil Hall, and he turned a third time as they rounded the corner, wondering if he would ever serve in such a monarch of a ship again. At the depot he arranged his passage for New York, feeling stung anew at the requirement to pay extra to carry more than one article of baggage. Perhaps with more competition, he thought, the common carriers would be forced to a more reasonable posture.

It was unsettling to rumble along the familiar pike from Boston to Providence, and on to New Haven—and then not to obey the very habit of his limbs to change coaches and head north, to Litchfield and home. There would have been no point to write ahead and see if Clarity could meet him in New Haven, for his coach was the one carrying the mail.

The bustle and hurry of New York he found disagreeable to the point of not even wanting to stay to see its famous places. He paid a different stage company his passage to Philadelphia, which he found equally busy, albeit more friendly, and he arranged passage to Baltimore, and so on. There was no single company to carry him the whole distance, and he found himself grateful now to be a wealthy man; travel was not for the poor.

His uniform gained him deference, and occasionally polite conversation, but what occupied his most intense interest was the way the forest changed, by degrees, becoming more temperate, better watered. Traveling constantly enough, he assessed, he could see the apparent way of life change, too, the fieldstone fences of New England transforming through the stage windows into the tobacco barns of Virginia.

Beyond Virginia he began to feel uncomfortably warm, at a time of year when New England would be preparing for the first cool breaths of autumn, and he knew his apples would be growing fat in his orchard. The creeks, when they forded them, began to feature thickets of the most exotic-looking strange tree, or rather not a tree, but not a bush, either. Their spreading leaves were as broad as a small dining table and composed of a fan of fibrous green strips interlocking like a hand of cards. A whole spray of such leaves erupted from the top of a trunk, of sorts, that was not solid but seemed to be a rising succession of the material of the remains of leaves' stems that had lived their span, and died and hardened. The whole effect was one of a kind of unapproachable spikiness—not unlike the Carolinas' own reputation.

Their second night in South Carolina, where they were told they would reach Charleston the next day, was spent at an inn in a tiny settlement they called Wappetaw, which in Bliven awakened an ancient association. He was certain that he remembered the name, for it was settled by people who determined to leave Salem, Massachusetts, because they could not stomach the insanity of the witch trials of 1692. Most people did not know that there were some people in Salem who'd had a conscience against that madness, but there were.

Charleston when he reached it proved to be the most water-bound city he had ever seen, more so than Boston or even New York. It lay at the confluence or environ of five wide, sluggish, tepid, snaky rivers, which made him understand the city's reputation for miasma and the yellow jack that had claimed Sam's father. The city occupied a peninsula between two of those rivers, its approximate northern boundary being a broad avenue marking the line of a former city wall, which the British had assaulted during the Revolution, and had since been dismantled.

The city was larger, much larger, than Bliven imagined it would be. Though there were neighborhoods of apparent poverty, some thickly inhabited by families of free Africans who lived on their own without belonging to anybody, his overall impression was that it was a city of commercial importance, with fine, large homes and well-fed-looking people. He had contracted with the driver to deliver him to the Navy Yard itself, and discovering it was a shock, for it was all but indiscernible within the commercial stretch of the waterfront. Bounded by alleys on the left and right, and by masts of what he took to be his *Tempest* at the wharf beyond a scatter of smallish nondescript structures, the only identifying feature was the American flag fluttering from a pole before what must be the receiving office.

When Bliven entered a small front room, a lieutenant working at a table stood and saluted. Bliven returned it. "I am Master Commandant Putnam, reporting to take command of the United States Ship *Tempest*."

"Welcome to Charleston, Commander. Captain Dent is in command here. I will let him know you have arrived."

"Captain John Dent?"

"Yes, sir."

*How fallen are the mighty,* thought Bliven.

The lieutenant entered a rear chamber and returned. "The captain will receive you."

John Herbert Dent was tall and well made, darkly complected, with a large aquiline nose, his dark hair swept forward like Hull's and most men's in the ubiquitous Brutus crop. They traded salutes and Dent extended his hand. "Welcome to the end of the world."

Bliven took it. "Is it, truly? I am sorry we have never met. By reputation you are one of the most widely experienced officers in the service, it seems we should have crossed paths at some point."

"We almost did, once. Do sit and be comfortable."

"Really, where?"

Dent folded his arms and grinned. "I was a midshipman in the *President* when you and that other fellow got into a sword fight in, was it Algiers? During the Barbary War."

"Oh my goodness! Yes, that was Sam Bandy, my fellow midshipman. Your lieutenants on the *President* were bored and decided to amuse themselves by goading him into fighting me. You must have been at the back of the cheering crowd."

"I was! I went on to serve in the *Essex*, the *Constellation*, and the *John Adams*, and I commanded the *Scourge* and the *Nautilus*. I must have made an enemy somewhere, for here I am in this . . . place."

The double window of this back office afforded a prospect of the wharf, at which a ship-sloop was moored, seeming a hundred and twenty feet or so between perpendiculars. Dent's voice trailed off as he noticed Bliven's study of the vessel.

"That is she?" Bliven asked reflectively.

"Such as she is. We are working on her. You look as though you are dreaming of your future glory."

Bliven rose and walked over to the window. "No, actually I was thinking of Mr. Bandy. He became a merchant captain, and some months ago he was taken at sea and pressed into British service. He is out there somewhere, under lash and chains; he is never out of my mind."

"He and thousands of others," said Dent. "That's why we are having a war."

"I don't know them, I know him. I just hope there is some justice at the end of it all. Well, your installation seems it may be too small for a mess. Where does one eat around here?"

"Do you wish to eat, or would you see your ship first?"

"Just at this moment, my hunger outweighs my apprehension."

"I could eat as well," said Dent. "Come, I'll show you." They exited into the front room. "Lieutenant, we will be lunching at Mrs. Finklea's, if you need me."

"Yes, sir."

From the waterfront they walked leisurely two blocks into the commercial district, which struck Bliven as having been exceedingly prosperous, but at that moment was capable of sustaining greater bustle than it was. Certainly the activity did not equal what he had seen in New York or Philadelphia or Baltimore, although it apparently might have done so.

They entered a tavern whose sign in front was simple and to the point: GOOD FOOD.

The proprietress was a blond woman of middle age, who seemed as though she had not shared much of the surrounding prosperity. "Good day, Captain. Who is your friend?"

"Good day, Mrs. Finklea. This is Commander Putnam, who has come down to take command of the sloop we have been rebuilding."

"Commander." She nodded.

"Captain Dent speaks highly of your fare. What would you recommend?"

"Beef stew and bread, and beer, twenty-five cents a head."

"You must allow me," Bliven said aside to Dent. He produced and proffered a silver half-dollar.

"Have you no Carolina money?" she said with no expression whatever.

"Carolina money?"

The proprietress removed from a pocket in her apron two small pieces of paper, about one-eighth the size of a sheet of writing paper. They were crudely typeset with the name of the Bank of South Carolina, and denominations, with some copperplate gewgaws.

"Ma'am," said Bliven, "I have seen a good deal of the East Coast, and in every place federal coin was the standard by which local currencies were measured. Is silver not always to be preferred to local paper?"

"In South Carolina, sir, we have learned to trust our own."

"Well, is there a bank nearby where I could change the coin for your local bills of exchange? That will make it more convenient for you when I come back next time."

"In town, Bank of South Carolina, you will see it." Her manner eased. "But if you will have your lunch, your silver will do for now." He gave over the coin and she left.

"If I come back," he muttered to Captain Dent. Although, he thought, that must be good business for the bank. They must be eager enough to take in good government silver coin and exchange it for this worthless scrip that was supported by nothing beyond their own conceit. He wondered for a moment how many years it had taken for the local population to be talked into such a vaunted imagining.

"If you find her attitude objectionable," warned Dent, "you may not be giving much business to anyone else hereabouts. Her view is the prevailing one. You know, I am from Maryland, so I have some sympathy for Southern opinions, but I tell you, Carolinians are a stiff-necked bunch."

The stew was thick and flavored with herbs that Bliven determined that he should inquire after, the bread warm and fresh.

Dent broke his bread and stirred it into his bowl. "Still, we might consider, Commander Putnam, that South Carolina began its association with the Union in good faith. Let us not forget, before the Revolution Charleston was the most heavily defended city in the country, not just harbor forts but city walls, and a moat across the neck of the peninsula. And after the war they demilitarized, completely. They demolished the fortifications and used the materials for other construction, developed the harbor, and built up a huge profitable commerce from exporting their cotton and rice and all the rest of it. To be sure, they got on well enough at the beginning. Then what did we do? The Embargo Act of 1807 deprived them of more than half their markets, for they have always sold much more to Europe than to the North. So they said, very well, this hurts us, but as long as England and Napoleon are fighting and both are taking our ships, we can recognize the need to restrict trade, and they bore it. And then what did we do? The very next year we outlawed the importation of new slaves from Africa, and it became harder for them to find workers for their fields. I think we might forgive them if they begin to feel picked upon."

Bliven nodded slowly. This was the juncture, he thought, where

Clarity would have raised the immorality of slavery and declared that any economy that depended upon it deserved to collapse. Indeed, owing to the ferocity of the history classes that she had survived in Miss Pierce's School for Girls, Clarity was even able to stake out the position that Rome herself, with all her marble temples and forum, and her gigantic empire, never deserved her greatness, for all was built on the backs of slaves. With Rome it was imperial greatness, with Charleston—as he observed through the tavern's windows—it was gracious ease, a comfortable life that wanted for little, but equally built on the toil of others who could not share in it.

In justice, he told himself, it made him question how a nation of the size and diversity of the United States could ever find a true unity when its widely flung sections had such divergent economies, and societies, and ways of living. *E pluribus unum,* they had declared, but how would that ever be possible?

"You will be wanting to see your ship now."

"Oh, yes." Bliven's eye engaged the hostess. "Ma'am, your stew was delicious, and of a flavoring I have never encountered. May I ask how you achieved it?"

"Well, I thank you for that pretty compliment." The hostess seemed to relax somewhat. "The truth is, I have never inquired. That is the way our cook has prepared it ever since I was little. Kitchen is out back; you are welcome to ask her, if you like."

He and Dent exited the rear door and saw the kitchen—three walls, a capacious high fireplace, and an open front, well supplied with all manner of pots and utensils, and busy among them a black woman, elderly and large, her hair tied in a red bandana, her dress a swaying bell of cream-gray calico, printed with a fading pattern of tiny red and blue flowers.

"Good afternoon," said Bliven as he and Dent approached.

She looked up with tiny black eyes. "Good day, suh." She was as toothless as a baby.

"May I ask how you flavored your stew? It was very tasty."

"Oh, suh, dat's my secret!" she played with him.

"Well." Bliven affected a kind of coyness. "I am from very far away; do you think you might tell me your secret, please?"

The slave cook emitted a high cackle. "Suh, I will make you a bargain. You don't ask me my secret, and I won't tell you no lie."

"Ah. Well, I suppose I must just come back and eat again."

She waved her ladle at him. "Well, now, you come back anytime."

———  #  ———

In the Yard once more, Captain Dent unlocked the door of a long, low warehouse with two windows in front. "The armory," he said as they entered.

Within, Bliven beheld two opposing files of new twelve-pounder long guns, about half mounted on carriages, the rest lying on the dirt floor amid the timbers that would become their carriages.

"You will mount twenty guns. Obviously, you would not want to take on a frigate with them, but they will be more than sufficient for raiding the enemy's commerce, which will be your principal occupation. They are new, you will see they have firing locks."

"I should hope so," Bliven replied. "I would not know where to even look for linstocks anymore."

"Ha! I rather imagine there are plenty still lying around a Navy Yard somewhere. I could probably even find you biscuit left over from the Revolution."

"Probably still edible, in the Navy's estimation."

"Probably. Balls? It is likely I can find you ample solid shot. I have no bar shot, nor chain. Grape, I can give you some, but you must use it sparingly. You should not need grape in taking merchantmen, you would only use it if you were attacked."

"It is mid-afternoon. Should there not be carpenters at work on these gun carriages?"

They exited, and Dent locked the door behind them. "He works in the morning. Afternoons he attends his other employment."

"Did I understand you to say 'he,' in the singular, and he works but half a day?"

"Yes, though he does have a helper." Bliven's look of astonishment prompted Dent to further explanation. "Commander, do you remember what I said when you first arrived?"

"I remember it very well. You said, 'Welcome to the end of the world.' I wondered what you meant by it."

"You must realize this sooner or later. In the supplying of naval stations, Charleston stands at the end of the line with an empty bowl. I would say that half my letters for requisitions are never even answered. In a way, I understand it, for the great ships sail from New York and Boston, or the Chesapeake. But Charleston is the rear door to the heart of the country. I do know that they realize its importance, for they have done well with rebuilding the city's fortifications, Fort Moultrie, and so on. But they feel that is enough, and of naval strength—pah!—I have two gunboats, and you."

"Well, you don't have me yet; my guns are lying in the armory."

"Here is the magazine." Dent unlocked the door of a squat stone building with walls more than two feet thick. There were no windows, the only light from the open door, but enough to see tall rows of stacked twenty-five-pound wooden quarter-casks fastened with copper hoops.

Bliven ran his hand over the nearest one. "How old is the powder?"

"I've no idea," admitted Dent. "I asked the same question of the previous commandant, and it had been here throughout his tenure. He did not know where it came from."

"That is not good hearing. How often is it turned?"

"Not since I've been here, frankly."

"Well, I'm sure you will agree that it must be thoroughly tested before we put it aboard."

"Yes." Dent seemed disappointed that questioning the state of the powder would even have occurred to him. "Yes, of course."

Bliven lifted one quarter-cask and listened to the rustle of the powder shifting within. As he expected, it was not completely full but had an air space to allow the powder to mix when the barrels were turned. Each twelve-pounder required four pounds of powder for each shot. A full discharge of twenty guns on board would require four casks of powder; carrying ten rounds per gun would be forty casks; twenty rounds, eighty casks. Quickly Bliven concluded that he would not sail with fewer than a hundred sixty casks, and that at a minimum. "Well, let us have a look at my vessel."

She grew larger in their sight as they approached, and Bliven's heart grew with the hope that she would be in better preparedness than the guns or the powder.

"As you see," said Dent, "we have fashioned her into a sloop-of-war, one hundred twelve feet long, thirty-two feet in the beam, four hundred twenty tons. Ship rigged."

"What does she draw?"

"Fourteen feet."

"Really?" Bliven was surprised. "That is rather deep for a ship this size." He pointed down at her waterline. "I don't suppose there is any chance of copper sheathing down there."

"Ha! No, no. That's why the Jamaicans build their ships out of cedar. The resin resists the seaworms for a while, and by the time they do burrow in, the ship is paid off without having the expense of the copper."

"Ah, yes." Of course, Jamaica was British, and would follow the British custom of expensing out their ships, like bookkeepers, rather than keeping them serviceable as long as they could.

"How old is she?"

"No one has any idea. We hove her down briefly, the hull is still in good shape."

They ascended a gangplank to her open waist, and Bliven's first thought upon hearing the hollow thump of his boots on the weather deck was of its apparent thinness.

"Only one ladder," noted Bliven. "That could be a hindrance, if we get into a fight." His gaze ascended, and he saw she was rigged for three courses of sail. They walked aft along the open hatch, the grate having been removed for the rebuilding. Bliven turned the wheel idly and it offered no resistance, for the tiller was not engaged. "How many crew have you signed so far?"

"None."

Bliven shot him an angry look.

"By order of the Department," added Dent in defensive haste. "The monthly outlay for the crew of this vessel is calculated at about one thousand four hundred dollars per month. Knowing now that there is an abundance of beached sailors in Charleston trapped here owing to the war, the Department is interested not to have to start spending that money before they are wanted."

"Oh, for heaven's sake!"

"Let me show you your cabin," said Dent, and he led the way down the ladder. The berth deck terminated forward at the galley, with a smaller camboose than Bliven remembered from the *Constitution*, and they would arrange a sick bay in the bow. There was no proper wardroom, but there were two tiny staterooms on either side of a sort of vestibule, then a door to the captain's cabin, which they entered.

"I took the liberty," said Dent. "I did not think you would want to stay ashore once you got here, so we have made up your cabin— food, linens, and so on." Three large stern windows amply lit the compartment. "Your privy just there." It was a tiny enclosed closet, to which he did not object. The captain's privy on the *Constitution* was open to the quarter gallery, and while no one could intrude on the moment, Bliven always wondered if it did not feel a bit queer to relieve oneself in front of God and all the seagulls.

"That is very kind, thank you, you guessed correctly. Let us go below."

Lacking an orlop, the ladder descended all the way to the bottom of the hold, lit somewhat by the smaller hatch to the berth deck. "How much ballast did she carry?"

"We removed about six tons," answered Dent.

Bliven sighted as carefully down her keelson as the light permitted, searching for any sign of hogging, although he well knew that by the time such a distension became visible, it had also become dangerous. "Well, I'll bet she's never carried forty tons of guns topside. I will feel better if we put in about ten tons."

"Yes, I agree," said Dent.

He looked fore-and-aft and back again. "Why, the entire hold is open," he said in astonishment, "from forepeak to afterpeak."

"Yes," answered Dent.

The footings for the masts seemed well enough, and two pipes of joined elm trees descended to open beside the keelson to suck up bilge water. A few vertical beams on the center line aided the knees in supporting the deck, but that was the entirety of interior strength. "It is like an eggshell! We must have a powder magazine that is closed off from the rest of the ship, and a handling room, and racks for the shot. We will need at least one compartment forward for a sail room and stores."

With each item Bliven listed, Dent appeared more and more exasperated. "Yes, yes, we will get to that, but you must appreciate the limits of my budget. I have been allocated only so much money to rebuild this vessel, and you must accept that you are no longer in the largest frigate in the world!"

For a moment they glared at each other. "Do you not find her seaworthy?" demanded Dent.

"She is seaworthy," he replied. "She is not battleworthy. I do not require a large ship, I fought quite well enough on the *Enterprise*, thank you. But I will not risk a hundred human lives in this vessel until she is something better than a Viking funeral waiting to happen."

"Well, we are both tired," said Dent. "I will have your trunks sent aboard. Get a good night's sleep, and tomorrow we will decide what priorities to tend first."

After sundown, Bliven removed his fire syringe from the sea bag and lit several candles. He was not unfamiliar with the operation of a camboose, and with some adjusting of its vents was able to quickly fry some eggs and ham, and brew coffee. Afterward he carried two candles back down into the hold. He sat down on the bottom rung and thought, *They are sending me to my death.*

CHARLESTON HARBOR
15TH SEPTEMBER, 1812

*My dear Mrs. Bandy,*

*I wish to let you know that I arrived in Charleston some days since, to assume command of my ship, the* Tempest. *She still wants interior construction before she will be suitable for service, and then she must be supplied, and a crew drawn in. Therefore, time does not press.*

*It would afford me great pleasure to call on you and ascertain for myself whether there is anything I can do for you during the hardship of our Sam's captivity, if there is a convenient time when I might come.*

*Be pleased to address your correspondence to me through the
Navy Yard, in Charleston. If you do so, I will hope to receive it.
The hostility toward the federal government on the part of many
people in this section is perceptible and their distemper extends
even to the Navy, which is here for their protection. This is a
mystery to me, and I hope does not extend to failing to deliver
our mail.*

> *Yrs. with great respect,*
> *Bliven Putnam*
> *Master Comdt., USN*

Mrs. Rebecca Bandy
Abbeville Plantation,
So. Carolina

———//———

It required a few days to test the stock of powder in the magazine,
but Bliven found Captain Dent attentive to it. In the safety of the
magazine, a team of three opened each of the twenty-five-pound
quarter-casks in turn, weighing out four pounds of powder and
stitching them into round linen sacks, careful to number each to
note the barrel it had come from. In a quarter of the casks, the
powder had caked and was useless. "It is as we feared," Dent said
to Bliven, quietly adding himself to Bliven's doubtfulness whether
the powder was viable, and ordered those casks discarded.

Their smaller gunboat had a twelve-pounder mounted upon

her bow, and Dent assembled a gun crew from among his yard crew of thirty, six men who had fired guns before. With Bliven and Dent aboard they rowed to the openness of Charleston's outer harbor and anchored in shallows, facing seaward.

Following the drill specified in the manual, the gun was leveled and loaded, the quoin removed to nest the gun in its standard elevation. Bliven turned to Dent. "Are you ready to begin, Captain?"

"Proceed."

"Fire," said Bliven quietly.

The morning stillness was rent, not by an exploding report but a loud, hissing *foom* that expelled the ball from the barrel. They saw it emerge, watched it fly, and observed its splash a hundred feet away.

"Well, Captain Dent," said Bliven. "Do you think we might mark that cask as suitable for very close engagement?"

"Damn," mumbled the captain.

Of the morning's test, three of the charges expelled a ball to a normal range of six hundred yards. Most shot between two and three hundred yards. "I see no course but to empty the magazine and begin again," said Dent sourly. "What powder we have that is still viable, we must assume could turn at any time. I will requisition new stores with the greatest urgency."

Bliven could not express his wash of relief without also revealing his doubt of Dent's sensibility. "Yes, I agree. Do you think they will tend to it promptly?"

"We shall see," Dent answered, "but now you are here, and you may begin sharing in my waiting games. Gentlemen," he said to those of his yard crew who had pulled them out into the bay, "you may row us back to the wharf."

Dent sat next to him as the men hauled in their anchor and began pulling their sweeps. "I am going to hire a second carpenter with helpers to begin making compartments in the hold of your ship. You will understand that we cannot transform her into some little ship of the line, but I agree that a magazine and handling room are essential, and racks for the shot. In the mean, I authorize you to engage not an entire crew but the essentials whom you will have to rely upon, first and second mates, sailing master, and bosun."

"Aye, sir." Bliven nodded. "A few have already approached me on this matter. In my head I had composed a handbill to post in the taverns, but now I think that will not be necessary. The men I have spoken to seem competent, have good experience, and have many acquaintances hereabouts. I am inclined to trust their judgments more than just issue a call to all and sundry."

———— // ————

It required only two days for the skeleton crew to assemble, eager enough to sign up for the Navy's twelve dollars per month, and it encouraged him to hear the sawing and hammering begin in the hold below his cabin. With work well in hand, Dent agreed that Bliven might take a few days to call upon the wife of his former shipmate and satisfy himself of her welfare, which was timely as he was called down the gangplank to speak with an elderly Negro who had descended from a carriage, and presented him with a letter.

ABBEVILLE, S.C.
20TH SEPT. 1812

*My Dear Commander Putnam,*

*This salutation seems to embrace a promotion since last you corresponded with my husband, therefore congratulations for recognition that is surely deserved.*

*Thank you for your favor of the 15th inst. Since receiving it I have engaged, and acted upon, some basic arithmetic. You state that time does not press while your ship is being finished out, and you ask when it might be convenient for me to receive you. The partial sum is that I am anxious to receive you at your first opportunity. As my own driver can move as fast as the mail, and you seem free to come, the full sum is that I am sending a carriage for you. This letter will be handed to you by our driver, Mose. He is plausible and capable, and entirely to be trusted with whatever you require. You need take no trouble for him, for, if you cannot come at once, he has people in Charleston with whom he can stay until you are free.*

*My hope is that you can come straightaway, for we are all most keen to have you visit us. I gather from your letter that you have no more recent news of our poor Sam, whose fate has me in knots of anxiety, but surely, even the English would not harm such a useful and capable sailor—as long as he can keep his temper in check. Do come!*

> *Yr. sincere friend,*
> *Rebecca Bandy*

*Bliven Putnam, Master*
*Comdt., U.S.N.*
*Charleston Navy Yard*

Bliven had to smile. Rebecca had not changed, still direct and practical. He regarded the man still before him, surely past sixty but straight, silver stubble on his face. "You are Mose, then."

"Yes, suh."

"Well, let me just clear this with the commandant, and I should join you presently." He started to leave but turned back. "Have you ever been on a ship before?"

"No, suh."

"Would you like to see one?"

"Oh, thank you, no, suh, I's jes' fine with good ol' dirt under my feet."

It took only moments to pack clothes and Clarity's captain's box in a trunk and arrange himself in the carriage beside the driver. "Is it a difficult journey?"

"Oh, no, suh. We jes' follow the main road up the river and the canal to Columbia, then west another day. Got nice places for you to stop nights. Walk on, hosses." He flicked the reins lightly on their backs.

"Well, then, shall I call you Mr. Mose?"

He chuckled. "Oh, no, suh. That would never do. The white folk would think I am puttin' on airs. Now, further out, we get among them free colored folk, you want to call me Mr. Mose, that would be fine."

"Are there many free coloreds around Charleston?"

"Oh, yes, suh, hundreds of 'em. We don't have to go by that way, though. Some of them I don't care fo'."

"Oh? Why not?"

"'Cause lots of them own slaves of they own."

"What! I had no idea. Do they really?"

"Oh, I'm here to tell you, ain't no nation so hard a masta as them free coloreds. You'd think they have some pity on others, but Law have mercy!"

Bliven wondered how freely he might converse with this servant. He seemed genial and intelligent. "How long have you—" He hesitated. He did not want to say "worked for" the Bandy family, as it seemed to avoid acknowledging his servitude, but his own inclination balked at saying "belonged to" to another human being. Yet he must not say anything to arouse discontent. "How long have you been with the Bandy family? Were you born here or brought from Africa?"

"Heh. I was born and raised on the very place. I served Masta Sam's father and grandfather."

"Did you, indeed?"

After a silence Mose said, "Masta Putnam, may I speak up?"

Those were two words that Bliven had never imagined he would hear together, and their effect on him approached alarm, but he could not sort out everything about this strange place at once. "Of course."

"My mistress done tol' me you have never been at the South

befo'. She said you would be uncertain 'bout how to talk and behave 'round slaves. Well, suh, my mistress said, you are free to ask
me whatever you like."

"Well!" Bliven thought he should have known Rebecca would
anticipate this. "This is not my part of the country, that is true.
And certainly no one made me judge over Israel."

Mose chuckled. "Yes, suh. Exodus, chapter two."

Bliven stared at him, blasted.

"Yes, suh, we goes to church. Sometimes we even believe what
they preach."

"Ha! Well! So you are . . . well looked-after, then?"

Mose shrugged. "I ain't never been naked, ain't never been hongry. That's mo' than I can say for some free folks. Law, Masta Putnam, askin' me 'bout freedom be like askin' a man who never drink
whether he prefer rum or whiskey. I can't imagine."

"Yes, I think I can see that."

"Where would I go?"

Bliven wondered whether the affection he had begun feeling for
this old Negro might be like the moss that covered the jaggedness
of the rocks, that it obscured the brutality of his condition, and it
had overgrown the South and prevented them from recognizing
the inhumanity of what they were doing.

Their road followed north and west along the Cooper River,
and then the Congaree, and then the Santee Canal, which Bliven
had always been curious to see. The South had always been vocal
in desiring internal improvements, and the Santee was one of the
very first canals in the United States. For all that, it was a modest
affair, thirty-five feet wide and only four feet deep, but there were

modern locks to raise and lower the flatboats laden with rice and cotton. With a city the size and heft of Charleston on the coast, some in the North had thought it extravagant of the Carolinians to desire a new capital city deep in the interior, but at least construction of the canal made it plain that the region was not as neglected as they perennially claimed.

As soon as they reached the open lowlands the road passed slaves laboring in cotton fields and rice paddies, stooped and silent. Mose caught Bliven looking at them with unutterable sadness. "Is that your life, then, Mose?"

"Oh, no, suh. I's the blacksmith and the ferrier. I keep the hosses shod and the hoes sharp, fix wagon wheels. Law, you give me a hammer and the anvil, I can fix jes' about anything."

Bliven nodded. "I am glad to hear it."

"Thank you, though"—Mose inclined his head toward the side of the road—"for feelin' sorry for them po' folk."

Early afternoon on the fourth day they turned up a road that followed a strong, tumbling stream. "That's the Lone Cane," said Mose. "Won't be long now."

Much of the country was rolling, even rugged, with dense forests falling away into rocky defiles. "I am surprised," said Bliven. "How can you farm in such rocky country?"

"Oh, there's plenty of level places. You'll see. But you are right, clearin' this land took a lot of work."

The Bandy house fairly struck him when he saw it on a low rise, of two stories, with deep dim verandas behind a thick file of Doric columns, and behind it the outbuildings of a working plantation.

So this was what gave rise to Sam Bandy. To the south the lawn descended to a stream that had been dammed into a pond edged with reeds. Just above it a terrace had been paved in a grove of great arching trees. If the great Capability Brown had worked in the tropics, thought Bliven, this is what he would have wrought. Within the shaded grove were a table and chairs, and from the shade Rebecca emerged to greet him as Mose stopped the carriage.

"Commander Putnam, how very good of you to come all this way to visit us. Hello, Mose."

Bliven leapt from the carriage and took both her hands. "Well, Mrs. Bandy, it has been far too long."

"Mose, will you send Dicey down with some lemonade?"

"Yes'm. Masta Putnam, it has been a pleasure, thank you for your kind attentions."

"And thank you, Mose, for such a pleasant journey."

Mose started the horses up the rise to the house and its out-buildings.

"Oh, Bliven, if you aren't a sight for sore eyes. Come sit down. Do you have any news of Sam?"

"No, I am so sorry. We only know that he was pressed and taken off his ship, and his ship was seized and is probably in the British Navy by now."

"Damn the ship," she said quickly. "I can do without the ship, but I want my husband back."

"Well, we can be reasonably certain that he will be taken care of; he possesses valuable skills."

"Yes, I pray that may be the case."

"Look at you, you have hardly changed!" He spoke truly; her body still filled an ample frame, but she was slimmer than he remembered, tan and fit.

"Thank you. You know, there are two ways a woman can live this life. Some never leave the house and wait to be worshipped, and become these magnolia flowers that will spoil if you touch them. Others pitch in and take part, and I enjoy to be useful. We are a minority, to be sure, and in the very richest families this would be taken as a sign of poor breeding. I think they are full of themselves."

Bliven gazed at her with admiration; he might have predicted this is how she would mature. "So, like England, you have your aristocracy here."

"Ironic, is it not? South Carolina has perhaps a hundred families that control most of the land and the wealth. Despite what you see looking around you, Sam's family is not among them. They are considered on the cusp, aspiring to the golden circle. Sam's mother, you will meet her, she very much acts the part. I am afraid I have not enhanced their prospect for social advancement, but I'll wager I have helped put this place on a better footing than ever it was before. Why are you smiling?"

"Because I am guessing that Sam would not have you any other way."

She smiled at their good beginning. "Do you ever think of us, in Naples?"

She was as direct as ever, which put him off his guard, but he knew that it was her directness only, and that she intended nothing more. "Yes," he said, "I have thought of you often, in wishing that you have made a happy life for yourself." He raised his brow at the end of the sentence, making it a gentle question.

"Yes, I have. More than I imagined that I could. I was unhappy when I was a girl, but now? Sam is—" She shook her head wistfully. "He is everything a woman could wish for. Ah, here comes some lemonade, the fruit grown in our very own greenhouse, thank you."

"Dr. Cutbush would be very proud of you."

"Who?"

"Dr. Cutbush, he is the ship's surgeon in the *Constitution*. Brilliant and famous doctor, he's written a book about medical care of soldiers and sailors, and he is manic about lemons and their benefits to health."

"Really? I am glad to hear it. Thank you, Dicey, just set it on the table. Dicey, would you say good afternoon to Commander Putnam?"

She curtsied shyly, a thin, light-skinned mulatto girl who seemed barely big enough to carry the silver platter with its pitcher and glasses. "Good afternoon, suh."

"Dicey," repeated Bliven. "What an interesting name. How did you come by it?"

The girl twisted bashfully from the waist without moving her feet, after the fashion of her class. "Law, Masta Putnam, Masta Sam won me rollin' *crapaud*, and that's a fact."

"What? Oh my goodness!" he stammered for something to say. "Well! Well, he must have liked you very much to have gambled to have you."

"Yes, sir, I specks he did, m-hm."

"Dicey," Rebecca broke in, "why don't you go up to the house now, see if you can find my boys and send them down to me, and then see if your Aunt Liza needs some help with the dinner?"

"Yes'm." She departed in no particular hurry, humming.

Bliven and Rebecca looked at each other a long time, their eyes fond and merry. "He won her shooting dice?" he asked at last.

She smiled gently. "No. That is what we have told her." She sipped some lemonade and drew his attention to his own glass. "Try it, an extra measure of sugar performs miracles. Children are much in demand now," she explained. "Since the African trade was banned four years ago, we must depend upon their natural increase. Six years ago that was not the case at all. Sam and I were in Charleston on business, and we happened by the slave market when an auction was in progress. A young woman and her child of about two were on the block; the man who bid on her did not want the baby. They were separated, the child was old enough to scream and cling. The woman was too frightened to make any demonstration, but one look was enough—her heart was broken."

"Heaven have mercy," whispered Bliven.

"I did not need to speak a word to Sam. He said he would buy the child, and we took her away. Poor thing, she wept and shrieked till I thought her heart would stop. We bought her a candy and some ribbons to tie in her hair. That calmed her somewhat. As soon as we got home I gave her to our cook and our maid to care for; they had no children of their own." Rebecca paused for breath, taken aback by her own story. "Dicey has no memory now of any of this, mercifully. Yet I cannot help but think the pain remains deep in her somewhere, for her nature is often melancholy."

"I see."

Liza and Betsy, she is our maid, could not be more tender with her, and old Tessie, she is the cook for the field hands, has become a sort of grandmother to her. It is the best we could do for her."

"Yes."

Before the silence could lengthen, Rebecca sat up straighter. "Bliven, I know that you are from a part of the country that, well, lives a very different life. Sam has told me about meeting the girl who became your wife, how virulently she disapproves."

He smiled wryly. "Clarity, yes. She tried not to let it show, but she is not one to conceal an honest opinion. She is an abolitionist, there are no two ways about it."

"And you?"

He took a long sip of the lemonade. "Oh, that is good. Shall we be honest with each other?"

"That is where we parted." She smiled. "That would be an excellent place to resume."

"I tell you, sailing with Sam, and my memories of North Africa, made me well aware that right and wrong are seldom absolute."

"How do you mean?"

"Sam was most definite in pointing out that the cotton raised by your slaves is sold to our mills in New England, which make a handsome profit for our Yankee owners. And in North Africa, the chamberlain of the Algerine king—Jonah, you must remember him?"

"I remember him very well, he was a perfect gentleman in tending to my needs."

"He was the one who pointed out to me that the ships that—

until as you say four years ago—transported the slaves from Africa were mostly from our northern ports. So it seems to me that if slavery is a sin, and I do tend to believe it is, no one's hands are clean."

Rebecca nodded. "Fair and just—even as I remember you."

"There was something else that I learned when I was in the West Indies last year, that I can tell you."

"Yes?"

"Of all the blacks in Africa who were captured, and chained, and loaded onto ships and brought to the Americas, maybe only about one in twenty came to our shores. Nineteen in twenty went to Brazil, or Hispaniola, or Jamaica, or Cuba, or New Spain. Now, that does not in any measure excuse our part in it, but I regarded our Southern states somewhat differently after I learned what a small part of it we truly are."

"Indeed, I was not aware of that. What became of Jonah, do you know?"

"Oh, carry me back, let me see. Commodore Preble docked in Boston after the Barbary War. He contacted one of the African churches in the city and put Jonah in their care. In very short order he found employment as a teacher, and his company was much sought among those people. He adapted readily. Of course, any man would who could go from the coast of Africa to a Virginia plantation, recross the ocean to become chamberlain to a Moorish king, and cross back to a free life in Boston. Last I heard, he was doing very well."

"I am glad of it. I can picture him there. And old Commodore Preble, he was an interesting sort. What became of him?"

"Oh, poor man, his ulcer finally killed him a few years ago. I always felt badly for him. His dismissal from command after reducing Tripoli was thoroughly unjust. He was held responsible for losing the *Philadelphia*, even though that was plainly Bainbridge's fault. But he did live long enough to be vindicated, and the Congress awarded him a gold medal."

"Good, so there is some justice in the world. Oh, how I hope that if Someone up there does dispense justice, it may protect my Sam. You have no idea how I miss him and worry about him."

"I know. Is there anything you need, anything I can do for you?"

She shook her head. "You are so good to ask, but unless you can get out there on that ocean and find him, no. Plantations are rather self-sustaining entities, life here will go on regardless, but my anxiety for him is rather consuming. I was always an independent girl, but now I find I need my husband, and my children need their father. Oh, look up at the house! Those two little specks you see on the porch are my two sons. Boys!" she called out. "Come down!

"Quick," she added to Bliven, "put your hat on, they love uniforms."

Her sudden command shook from him a thought that had begun forming, whether Clarity, when left on her own, was really as strong as she seemed to be when he was home. What did she really feel in his absence? he started to wonder, but then rose and assumed his most military bearing.

Two little boys came tumbling down the slope from the house; they were Sam in small, round, and blond, and giggling.

"Boys, boys! Straighten up! This is Commander Putnam, who you have heard us speak of as a particular friend of your father's.

"Commander, the one you see slightly the larger is Sam Junior, who is six; the only slightly smaller is David, who is just turned five."

"What was your name again, young man?" Bliven said to the younger.

"David, sir."

"David! Why, that is my own second name!"

"Yes," Rebecca said from behind him. "We did have you in mind, but 'Bliven' was a bit too unusual, and would have excited comment."

"Oh, oh, I can't tell you how that pleases me!" It nearly raised a tear from him that they had named a son for him.

"Sir," asked the older, "is it true you fought pirates with our father?"

"Yes, very true. We were in a ship called the *Enterprise*. The captain trusted your father with the wheel, to keep us on course, and he fought, one hand with a sword and the other steering the ship."

"And boys," interjected Rebecca, "when your father was almost overwhelmed, the commander shot the pirate who was about to strike him down."

"We knew it," they cried. "We knew it! Will you tell us more about it?"

"He will over dinner, boys. Now run up and tell Grandmama that we will be up to visit her soon."

"We're going to fight pirates!" They departed at a dead run.

"Lively lads."

"You have no idea," she laughed.

"What a pleasant bower you have here. I have never seen the like. I have never seen such enormous trees."

"Our live oaks, yes."

"Wait! These are live oak?"

"Of course. What did you think?"

"I have never seen one," he exclaimed. "They are the heart of our frigates. May I look?"

She was confused by his burst of enthusiasm, but before she could remark on it he was on his feet, trotting to the nearest one. "God in heaven," he breathed as he laid his hands flat against it. Its umber brown trunk was five feet in diameter and began its arching spread fifteen feet above his head, shading an area more than a hundred feet across.

She rose and followed him, confused. "What on earth has gotten into you?"

"Magnificent. No wonder they can't be sunk. Look, there is a limb that has fallen!" Indeed it had not just fallen, but lain there so long that the bark had peeled away, exposing the naked wood and its tiny, whorled grain. Bliven knelt and ran his hand across it. "Look at this, how each layer ties into the next. I've never—my God, no wonder."

"I declare, Commander, you are frightening me a little. What is this about?"

The section of fallen limb was about seven feet long, and at its thickest was as large around as his thigh. He crouched, scooping his hands into the cool grass under it, and lifted but could not dislodge it. "Incredible," he said. "I have never seen wood so heavy."

"Of course it is." Rebecca had joined him. "It makes the best fires in winter; it burns forever and the coals keep all night."

"You should understand." He straddled the limb and sat upon it. "The hulls of our frigates are built in three layers, white oak inside and out, with live oak in the middle. When we fought the *Guerriere*, her cannonballs either bounced off or stuck in the outer layer because they could not penetrate the live oak. Now I see why. God in heaven, I am glad to have seen such trees."

"That," she said, "is the prettiest compliment I have heard paid to South Carolina in a very long time."

"And look up there." He pointed suddenly into its canopy. "See the shape of the limbs, how they bend and twist? They are perfect to be fashioned into the knees and scantling and odd shapes you need in building a ship. There is almost no need to work them, it is as though nature made them exactly for what is needed."

"Well, now, don't you go getting a design on *our* trees, these are not for sale!"

"Ha! I appreciate your feeling. Did you know it takes more than a thousand of these trees to build one frigate?"

"Well, then, you surely won't mind leaving a few for us. Why don't we walk up to the house, Sam's mother will be waiting to meet you."

———//———

Mrs. Bandy was precisely what Bliven had expected—reserved, polite, gracious, bearing her burdens, her widowhood, and her anxiety over Sam, with such fortitude that others were pricked every moment by the weight of her cares. There was a distinct Southern character to the art of it. After dinner Mrs. Bandy led them to a kind of conservatory at the rear of the house, where they were served brandy.

Their house, he discovered, was quite simple in its design but cavernous in scale, which he also took for a Southern metaphor. Mrs. Bandy took up work on a cross-stitch as he kept the boys entertained with stories of the *Enterprise* and the *Constitution*, of the apes at Gibraltar and meeting the Sicilian king, of the recent chase by an entire British squadron, and their desperate fight with the *Guerriere*. And during this time, until he saw them up and held the covers for them to climb into the double bed that they shared, Bliven thought he would have given anything to have had such a brother to pass his childhood with. And as he came back downstairs he thought what a strange feeling, what a queer flavor of pain, to have been so lonely and not to have realized it until now.

Rebecca had Mose drive him back to Charleston, as Bliven witnessed the scenery reverse itself, from rugged to flat and fertile piedmont. He had Mose stop the carriage in front of the Bank of South Carolina, which he entered briefly before resuming his seat in the carriage. "Now, Mose, I didn't mention this at the house, but I don't know your rules down here, and I didn't know whether this was proper. But just between us, I want you to have this." He handed over a small cloth purse tied with a drawstring, obviously containing a quantity of coins.

"Oh, now, Masta Putnam! You got no call—"

"No arguing. Where I come from, when somebody goes out of his way to do more favors for you than his job calls for, it is customary to pay him a little something. People call it a tip. Now, I am guessing that some here might find it suspicious for a black man to possess a large coin."

"Yes, suh, that's true."

"So I had it broken down into smaller coins that nobody will question."

"Why, that is so good. Thank you, Masta Putnam. When I go back through the colored town, I's gonna buy some sweeties fo' my missus an' chilluns."

"You have a family!"

"Oh, yes, suh! I started late, but the old masta, he said if we had chilluns, he wouldn' never sell them. So we have fo'."

"That is wonderful, I am happy for you."

"Well, them chilluns—mhm! They is a handful, but they keeps us laughin'."

———  //  ———

Back in the Charleston Navy Yard, the lieutenant in the receiving office fairly leapt out of his chair when Bliven entered. "Commander, at last! The most extraordinary things have happened. Please, come with me, we must show you some things."

They strode quickly to the back of the building. "There in the harbor"—the lieutenant pointed—"you see two new vessels. The larger one is the *Castor*, an American privateer who came in the day after you left. There behind him—"

"Why, that is an American flag flying above a British jack. Is that his prize?"

"Exactly." A captive schooner of perhaps ten guns lay in shame at his stern.

Bliven felt a surge of pride to see the name TEMPEST emblazoned in yellow beneath his stern windows. He had nearly to run to keep up with the lieutenant, up the gangplank, down the ladder all the way to the hold. "What do you think, Commander?"

Bliven's jaw slacked open. Planking laid to almost cover tons of iron kentledge, water casks stacked to the overhead decking, racks of twelve-pounder shot next to a small hatch into a dark compartment that must be for powder handling. Forward, more shelves held canvas sailcloth by the hundredweight, a bench with a fully equipped carpenter's shop. "I am astonished. I am undone, how did this happen?"

"The ship that the *Castor* captured was fresh from Bermuda, come to prowl about Charleston harbor, and was freshly provisioned. Captain Dent requisitioned her stores and gave a draught to the *Castor*'s captain, who was satisfied with the reward. Come, the captain is in your cabin with your surgeon, who is newly arrived."

"What? That is excellent." They clattered at a trot up the ladder to the berth deck and into the cabin, where they interrupted Captain Dent, whose shouting they heard even before they entered.

"Commander," said Dent, "I would like you to meet Dr. Gabriel, who will be surgeon's mate on your ship. Doctor, this is Bliven Putnam, Master Commandant."

Bliven advanced and shook hands, regarding the man, as short as Captain Hull, and barrel-chested, but not as fat. He had an olive complexion, curly black hair, and a prominent nose.

"Gabriel, an unusual name. Might you be of the Jewish faith?"

The stocky man drew himself up. "I am. I hope that will not present a problem."

"Not in the least. I only inquire because I once served with a Jew, in the Barbary War. He was the bravest man I have ever known, only he was killed before I had a chance to tell him so. That is a regret I have borne ever since."

"Oh. Heh! That is not the conversational direction I am accustomed to."

"No, I gather not. Now, I may not always be able to avoid a fight on a Saturday," Bliven said lightly. "If we get into one, you will have to do your work, Sabbath or no."

"Well, performing medical miracles on the Sabbath would put me in rather heady company, would it not?"

They all laughed loudly, and Bliven found himself charmed. "He will do, Captain Dent. He will do very well. Tell me, Doctor, where did you study?"

"In Providence, Commander."

"Ah! When I lately served in the *Constitution*, our surgeon was the great Dr. Cutbush. Do you know him?"

"After graduating, I worked a year in the Philadelphia Navy Yard, training under Dr. Cutbush. I know him very well."

"Oh, excellent. Do you have his book? I have one if you lack it."

"No, no, I have it in my trunk."

"Tell me," said Bliven, "when I entered you were discussing something in great animation. May I know what that was about?"

"Oh, for—" Dent shifted his weight. "Dr. Gabriel went to a local apothecary to obtain the supplies necessary for getting you to sea.

He went with a draught on the United States Navy for the supplies, but the druggist would not receive it without a twenty percent depreciation. Poor Gabriel here had to come back here and get permission. He wants me to go down and present it in person."

"What? Tell me, Doctor." Bliven examined him closely. "Do you think he declined this payment because it was a draught on the Navy, or perhaps it had something to do with you being who you are?"

"Indeed, I do not know," said Gabriel. "He did say he wanted some proof that I did represent the Navy on this business."

"Let me ask you, did you inventory the medical supplies in the sick bay of the prize just brought in and subtract them from your list of what you need?"

"I did not think to, no."

"Please do so at once. Reduce your wants by as much as you can, without endangering the well-being of the men. I will go with you back to the apothecary, and by God we will see what he thinks of Navy business with a uniform present."

The whole way there Bliven tried to visualize Commodore Preble, and how he would have dealt with the coming meeting.

They entered the apothecary, which was as tidy and well stocked as any in New England, and found an owlish but plucky little proprietor behind the counter. "I asked for the commandant of your station to call on me and verify this draught," he snapped to Gabriel. "Where is he?"

Bliven did not remove his bicorne. "Captain Dent has more pressing matters to require his attention than your pompous airs, sir. I am the commander of the vessel you have seen being fitted out, for which my surgeon, here, is tasked with laying in medical supplies. What in screeching hell do you mean to decline a draught from the United States Navy?"

His shot struck but did not disable. "It is not me, sir, it is the bank. They will only receive federal draughts at depreciation. I cannot bear that loss, the margin of my profit is too small."

"Indeed? Well, I wonder how concerned you will be for your business if we all sail out of here and leave you to the British!"

The proprietor made no reply but gave no ground.

"Well, by valor of arms a prize has been brought into harbor, whose medical supplies have provided many of our needs. However, these items are still wanted, and I have brought Carolina bills to pay for them." He handed over the new list and brandished the scrip. "Will you supply them, sir, or will you not?"

The druggist's face fell. "There is not ten dollars in merchandise here."

"Well," said Bliven slowly, "if you had not been such a—that is, if you had accepted the original draught, you would have made your next several months' profit, wouldn't you? Well, that is a shame, but that is on your watch. Still, we will take these all the same."

The druggist prepared a packet of the items and added the sum sourly. "This amounts to eight dollars and fifty cents."

"Very well." Bliven withdrew a ten-dollar South Carolina note and handed it over.

The druggist took it with thanks, and at once produced one dollar and fifty cents, also in state scrip.

Bliven made no move to receive it. "Have you no silver?"

"What!"

"I am so sorry, the Navy discounts state paper twenty percent. If I accept this as payment, I will have to ask another thirty cents."

"What!"

Somewhere in his travels Bliven had heard of puffers, a fish that when threatened inflates to several times its normal size until it becomes a tight, round, spiky, inedible ball; the druggist now put him in mind of them. Bliven relented and he took the dollar fifty in paper. "Oh, never mind, the amount is so trivial. Good day to you, sir."

Dr. Gabriel did not speak until they were halfway back to the Navy Yard. "Mr. Putnam, in my time I have paid good money to attend famous theatres and not seen so fine a performance. I am in some awe."

"Thank you, Doctor. I confess, I found that satisfying."

CHARLESTON HARBOR
23RD OCTOBER, 1812

*My Dearest Love,*

*We are this date making preparation to sail upon the morning's tide, therefore I avail myself of the chance to write you, for I know not when I shall next be proximate to a postal dispatch. Our orders are to stand to the South, even so far as equatorial waters, and even beyond, to interdict British shipping in a locale where they believe their vessels safe, and have thus deployed few warships to protect them. Captain Dent is of the opinion that other ships, the* Hornet *and even the* Constitution *herself, will be sent to that region, so we shall not be entirely alone in that desolate part of the world.*

*As badly as I miss your company, I confess I am glad you are not here, for Charleston is a place that would not please you. It is a city of no fewer than twenty-five thousand persons, the largest in the country south of Philadelphia. The shops have every thing for sale that you could find in Boston. But, O! A more ignorant and suspicious set of people I never saw, excepting perhaps in the Egyptian desert. Federal money is despised even more than the currencies of other states, and only the bills of local banks are wanted. Federal coin is accepted, for the value of its silver is not to be denied, but those who accept it act as though they are doing something that is vaguely disloyal, or immoral.*

*Being here has brought me to a right understanding of some things. For instance, I know now why, when our federal Constitution was adopted, the South Carolinians insisted that their slave population be counted, for census purposes, at three-fifths of a white person. The white people hereabouts would never accord a black the dignity of being counted as a whole person, but not to count them at all—noting that there are far more blacks here than whites—would have left them showing such a small population that they might not have even qualified for statehood!*

*Despite this concession, Carolinians feel only the most tenuous connection to their sister states, and if anything view the federal government as little less than a hostile power. They view the outlawing of the African slave trade four years ago as a personal affront, the most shocking betrayal, and a dagger aimed at their commercial heart. With its advent, they seem to have abandoned any expectation of harmony or satisfaction in the Union of States. It seems settled in their own minds that they shall go their own way, avoiding conflict with the federal authority when they can and defying it when put to the test.*

*And what is this way of life that they defend so ardently, that they turn their backs on the rest of the states? You would be amazed, my love, that of a modestly prosperous merchant class there are almost none. The great preponderance of the wealth is controlled by a very few families—I was told fewer than a hundred in the whole state, who also own the vast majority of the slaves.*

*In justice it must be stated that in some ways, as in the Embargo Act, this state's well-being has been plowed under by federal policy with little more consideration than we would plow under last year's straw. Yet her own view of the public good is so pinched and so primitive that she damages her credibility in the eyes of the more enlightened reaches of the country. Public education such as we know it in New England is almost unknown here. Our Sam's children are schooled at home by their mother, and by a tutor who calls regularly. Rebecca tells me that the notion that all should be taxed for the education of all children is anathema. The most wealthy send their children to private academies. Support for educating the poor would be viewed as dangerous to the existing social order, for it would give ambition to the poor and deprive the rich of a large pool of cheap labor and tradesmen. This thinking has become so entrenched and accepted that even the slaves in their cabins make free to mock those they have started calling "poor white trash." At least two great ironies* arise from this. The first is that the teachers who tutor the children of the wealthy are, themselves, accorded little respect and are treated little better than servants. The second is that as new lands are opened in the west, in Tennessee or Kentucky, or Louisiana, the poor move away to do better for themselves, and this loss of white population, in many places ten percent or even more, has made worse the racial imbalance that afflicts those who remain.

All told, I can safely say that if at this moment an angel of Providence were to appear before me and say, "Behold, you shall never see Charleston again," I would leap from my chair and kiss her for joy. (The foregoing assumes, of course, that angels can be kissed, which based upon my own earthly experience I believe must be true, for you have never seemed to raise objection to being so approached.)

And so, my love, farewell. My intention is to sail from here and do my duty, whate'er befall. If I come home victorious, may it be for the good of the country, but whatever the disposition of battle, do I but come home to you again, I shall have reason for contentment.

> Yr. true husband,
> Bliven Putnam
> Master Comdt., USN

Mrs. Clarity Putnam
New Putnam Farm
So. Road
Litchfield, Connectcut

# 8

## Two Sailors, One Sea

"Now, look'ye here, Yankee lad." White, the *Java*'s bosun, lowered himself by Sam's pallet on the berth deck. "What's this I hear of ye complainin' about the biscuits has gone wormy?"

"All I said was that if I caught one of my sons in South Carolina eating worms, I would so spank him that he would remember not to do it again."

"Aye, well, it is nearly a year now you have been aboard this vessel. Has your complainin' brought ye one footfall closer to your liberty?"

Sam sat up wearily. "It should have. We resupplied in Bermuda months ago. I should have been granted a hearing, but instead I was put in irons and kept out of sight. My fear now is that the captain must eventually design to kill me to hide his crime, for if my case were ever laid before a fair tribunal, he would come in for a terrible censure."

"Aha, don't you bet on it. Look'ye, lad, my country is fighting for its life, its very survival, do you understand? Do you think that Napoleon has given up for one minute on his plan to invade England? The Royal Navy is the only thing that keeps him out, and the Navy must have men. Neither your life nor mine matters a damn against the life of the nation."

"Against which one might argue that a nation which depends for its existence on the capture and servitude of others may not deserve to survive." While that statement served his need for the moment, it also continued to ring with a distinctly disquieting echo deep in his psyche, and he knew that if someone else had uttered it to him about his own life, and his own slaves, he would have taken offense.

"Haha!" Bosun White shook his head. "You have given me pleasure these past months to listen to your arguments. But now look'ye here—there is a simple way to deal with worms in the biscuit. When you break it up, just put it in your tea right away. The hot tea kills the worms and they float to the top. Just rake them off, they don't affect the flavor none. You'll be none the wiser if you just don't think about it."

"A metaphor of life, that." Sam got to his feet, and the bosun rose with him. "But I thank you for the kindness you have shown me."

"Remember, the doctor and the chaplain are aware of your claims. They may act for you if they get the chance."

Sam climbed two decks to the open air, where he noticed three sailors, off duty, fishing with rods and lines. The British Navy encouraged sailors to augment their rations with fresh fish when they could. In fact, English rations were not much different from the American: Every day each man received four biscuits weighing a quarter-pound each. Each week he received six pounds of salt meat, two pints of peas, six ounces of butter, and twelve ounces of cheese, and there was a pint of oatmeal for breakfast three mornings a week. But the most important ration was each man's daily gallon of beer. Few Englishmen ashore ever enjoyed a gallon a day. Sam reckoned it was enough to deaden the pain of their existence but little enough that they remained docile. Any more and they might stay drunk enough to mutiny. The Admiralty, he reasoned, probably arrived at the dosage scientifically. The daily tot of grog—half-rancid water made more palatable by half rum—seemed just a bonus.

Sam looked down into the water as it slid by; they were bearing south, in the densest part of the Sargasso Sea, that mighty Atlantic gyre that accumulated and circulated vast clumps of green-brown seaweed. If ever he was to throw himself overboard and end this misery, he concluded that it must not be in these nasty waters.

He could not claim that fate had singled him out, or that he had been uniquely victimized, for what he was suffering many thousands of other American seamen were suffering, some even in this vessel. The officers were careful to keep them separated into different messes and occupied at different duties, to minimize their chance to congregate and compare grievances. And beyond that, British ships hosted larger companies of Marines than typically did American ships. Seditious talk was difficult to spread when there always seemed to be an armed redcoat just within earshot to report what was said. It was no wonder that the common English tars loathed the Marines and swore and spat after them. What Sam did not understand about the British seamen was their acquiescence, their sullen acceptance, of their impressment. American pressed men felt themselves wronged; English pressed men viewed themselves merely as unlucky.

Seven and a half million people in the United States—where were they? Why could they not find him? Sam stared into the water and sargassum for long minutes before closing his eyes, trying to visualize his family. As long as there was hope to see them again, he would not end it, he would endure.

———#———

The sloop-of-war *Tempest*, twenty guns, was piloted out of Charleston harbor on the morning of October 24 and stood southeast under easy sail. Bliven had a table and chair moved onto the quarterdeck so he could study his maps in the fresh air and walk around. Summer lingered in the South, and it was annoying to be putting out just as the first cool puffs of autumn had eddied through that humid city—and then be ordered south, even to the tropics, where they would surely remain in sweat.

She was a very full ship, not just his own crew of a hundred, easily rounded up from stranded merchant sailors interned at Charleston, but thirty supernumeraries from whom to form prize crews, and forty Marines for close action if he engaged a warship. They would be useful if things came to boarding, but in any case they would have to fight from the deck because the *Tempest* lacked fighting tops. But it gave him seventy men more than his crew to start, which would be a very formidable boarding party, and below, next to the new-built magazine, Captain Dent had fully stocked a partition that served as a gun room with myriad small arms and ammunition. Bliven had to smile. Once he had abhorred Barbary pirates and their larcenous operation of overhauling merchantmen and frightening them into submission with their whooping and brandishing of weapons. Most vessels they captured without firing a shot, and now that was his own best prospect.

In the very center of the berth deck swung the hammocks of his seven boys, the powder monkeys to shuttle powder and shot to the guns. They ranged in age from eight to ten, and Bliven had been of two minds about accepting them at all. The magazine that Dent had had constructed was not of the traditional frigate's variety, accessible through a scuttle hole that only a boy could wriggle through. He concluded to take them, anyway, first because it was tradition, and many great officers had begun their careers as powder monkeys, and second because for boys to bring powder and shot freed more men for fighting, and in a close scrape, that could be the margin of a victory. It was usual in the Navy to hang the boys' hammocks in the very center of the berth deck, to minimize the chance of their being cornered and tormented or badly used by any of the men—Bliven did not understand it but could not deny that it happened. In his present case this had a second value, in keeping these Carolina orphans and incorrigibles in sight. Some had already learned to wrest their own terms from the world, were already hard and asked no quarter. They were capable of harsh mischief and best kept under observation, yet also when he was honest with himself Bliven could admit that they triggered his desire to parent them, that they filled a void in his life.

She was a very full ship, but at last, his own ship, done, at five-and-twenty. He took just a moment to be satisfied. He and Sam had begun late as midshipmen, to have been fourteen. They escaped the earlier drudgery as powder monkeys, many of whom Bliven noticed then and now were orphans who had no better prospects in life, and the Navy became their mother and father. He could not but be content with his own childhood, its memories and associations. It was his advantage over other Navy men that he had that alternative life which, as he had made perhaps too plain to Isaac Hull, he could return to quite happily if he felt his services were no longer wanted. But at this moment's balance, he had his own command, he had a wife and parents who were proud of him, and he had been set a task that was difficult but within his abilities. Nor was the prospect of prize money lost on him. Give him two heavily laden merchantmen to send home, and he would have the purse to match his growing reputation in Litchfield and give a different complexion to the gossip that he had married money. And always in the back of his mind was Sam, or a cloud in the shape of Sam, that hovered and gave him no peace.

A black man in a white apron emerged from the ladder and came aft, rocking with small extra steps against the ship's roll, trying not to spill the coffee he was bearing onto the white napkin. Bliven watched him approach with some amusement and nodded. "Well done, Gaston," he said as he set the coffee and napkin on the table. "We were able to find you some good coffee, now we must find you some sea legs." Bliven was pleased to have landed him: during his weeks in Charleston he had actually become friendly with Mrs. Finklea, and had returned for many samplings of her unique stew. When she learned that he was in search of a cook for his ship, it was she who had brought Gaston to him, a free Creole from New Orleans with a somewhat murky past and an anxiety to be clear of land. Gaston had cemented their relationship when he sampled Mrs. Finklea's stew, pronounced it delicious, and when they were clear of her hearing said, "Oregano, with a little Cajun filé. It works well."

Southerners in the crew of the *Tempest* whom Bliven had heard mutter about having a colored man aboard were silenced when he berthed the cook in one of the four small staterooms next to his own cabin, and then were won over with the first meal of stew prepared from the salt beef with which the hold was laden. Bliven did not know how long the flour would last, perhaps longer than on other ships, for Gaston professed a knowledge that a bay leaf laid in the top in a barrel of flour would retard the worms. They would see. Biscuit in plenty was stocked below, but also enough flour for stew and fresh bread for the time being.

With steaming coffee in hand, Bliven studied the chart before him, a general map of the Caribbean. Those who spent their lives on land had insufficient appreciation of what a complex body of water it was. The heart of British imperial wealth was Jamaica, which lay on the opposite side of the length of Cuba, and her commerce bound for the mother country must pass through the Windward Passage, between Spanish Cuba and newly independent but vexed Haiti. The closest fleet anchorage of warships to protect them was Nelson's Dockyard—it seemed that all British naval installations were now named for Nelson—at Antigua, four hundred miles to the east and at the end of the chain of Leeward Islands. The trick would be to intercept a commercial vessel before it could rendezvous with an escort or form into a convoy.

An escorted convoy he would have no play against in his twenty-gun sloop. Or merchantmen who sailed first to Antigua, skirting the south shore of Cuba and Hispaniola, he would have no play against. Indeed, that entire stretch of the Greater Antilles he must regard as British home waters and avoid at all costs. But there must be a weak spot, a point where British shipping must be vulnerable. *There,* he thought, and tapped his finger on the sixty-mile-wide outlet of the Windward Passage, between Great Inagua Island on the north and the Île de la Tortue on the south; he would first try his luck there. Of course, he must get by Grand Turk to reach it, but the British were not known to have placed any frigates there. Any vessel smaller than a frigate he would be content to play his hand against. Again, he had to smile. This must be why the Almighty had saddled him with his fascination with maps since his earliest childhood. This must be what he was born for, here with the morning wind in his hair and a ship at his command.

"Excuse me, Captain." Gaston had returned, and Bliven marked the instant, the first time that he had been addressed as captain. Master commandants were well recognized as captain upon their own vessel, a privilege that he suddenly approved of more than ever. "You will be wanting more coffee?"

"Yes, Gaston, thank you."

"Captain, in the British Navy, sailors are allowed to fish, to give themselves a variation in their diet. I had a friend once who was a cook in the French Navy, he said that every day he would throw scraps from the galley overboard, and he would always include some of the meat. Within a day or two, sharks began following the ship. Sharks are smart fish, they never take the trouble to hunt if they can snatch scraps for free. One day, one of those pieces of meat had a big hook in it, and he fed the crew for three days on that shark. Their flesh is very good. You see where I am going?"

"Yes, I see." Bliven was inclined to agree, but he had reservations. Before leaving Charleston word had come in that Rodgers had returned to Boston with the *President* and his squadron. They had succeeded in locating the convoy of Jamaica-men that they had gone out after, or rather, they never caught sight of the ships, but they followed the freshening trail of kitchen debris, orange peels and coconut husks, thrown overboard. "But might not leaving a trail of refuse risk leading a British man-o'-war right to us?"

"We throw only edible refuse over the side. Only bait. I will keep other scraps on board until we can weight it in sacks. How is that?"

"Well, that is how we will have it, then." And he had to admit he was curious, for he had never eaten shark. Gaston filled his cup and departed.

Alone again, Bliven turned his attention to a stout packet of papers that Dent had given him immediately before they sailed. He had read it before sailing and now read it again.

WASHINGTON

22 SEPTEMBER 1812

Dear Sir:

I have the honor to enclose a copy of the book of recognition signals and countersigns for the coming months, for use on your cruise from Charleston. You are instructed to act upon your own initiative, seizing British commercial vessels wherever you may encounter them, excepting neutral ports and waters, of course. You are further advised that the Constitution, accompanied by the Hornet, are being dispatched to this same area. If practicable, you will attempt to rendezvous with them in the waters about the Isle of Ascension on or about the first of the new year, and act as a squadron in coordination with them.

Yrs. respectfully,

Jas. Barron, Commodore,

USN

Bliven Putnam, Master

Comdt., USN

Charleston

P.S.—It has come to our hearing, from sailors returned home from Bermuda after the capture of an American merchantman, that the gentleman for whom you have been concerned, Mr. Bandy, was taken aboard a British frigate in Bermuda. We do not know the

*identity of this ship, but it is not among those who port in*
*Halifax, and as most American shipping have reached safe ports,*
*it is not beyond question that this frigate will also be dispatched to*
*southern waters to protect their commerce.*

Bliven pondered one other element. Rodgers, in pursuit of that convoy, did overhaul and engage robust fire with a British frigate. Indeed, Rodgers had pointed the first shot himself and hit her, only to have to break off the action when one of his guns exploded, killing fifteen men and breaking Rodgers's leg. Bliven determined to follow Andrew Sterett's lesson and become a tiger on the efficient operation of the guns. They mounted mere twelve-pounders, but he had begun his career with twelves and knew them very well. Following the captain's prerogative of deploying them as he chose, he ranged them eight guns down either broadside, with two bow and two stern chasers. One thing that life at sea had taught him was that chasers were used much more often than he would have imagined, and ships when caught up in pursuit had to suddenly move guns to chase positions to meet an emergency. This disposition made him feel reasonably prepared all around.

"Mr. Lewis!" he called forward, and his first lieutenant made his way aft and saluted.

"Captain?" Abel Lewis was not a man whom society belles would have sought out. He was short, his very curly blond hair prematurely balding, and he had a hooked nose and an annoying, nasal laugh. But he had ten years on a large civilian brig, could navigate, and if anything happened to their bosun, he could accomplish anything concerning the rigging.

"Pass the word among the crew, we will have a gun drill this afternoon. You are familiar with the standard exercise of the great guns?"

"Yes, sir."

"Well, have the men form up into gun crews of four, try to have at least one man in each who has fired a gun before. That may be a bit much to ask, but try. We will run through the drill twice dry, and once with live fire. This will also give us a chance to test the powder that was seized from that prize and brought aboard. And it will give the new men exposure to the noise of the guns so they will not flinch when it counts."

"I understand, sir, yes." Lewis saluted and went about it.

Bliven returned to his map. Ideally, he thought, he could sneak through that passage between Florida and the Bahamas, then run southeast down the coast of Cuba and approach the Windward Passage from the west. That would surprise the British right enough, but it also meant he must sail into the irresistible push of the Florida Current as it shot through that slot. Fighting the Antilles Current that flowed northwest up the outside of the Bahamas would be less arduous, but still better it might be to stand far enough out to sea to approach from the north. That might put him at risk of the British naval traffic in and out of Bermuda, but up to this point, that was mostly smaller vessels that he could contest with his own. On the other hand, the English had had five months now to respond to America's declaration of war. It would be madness not to assume that they were diverting a powerful portion of their naval strength to the western Atlantic.

Alone again on the quarterdeck, he took his coffee and walked slowly aft until he leaned against the taffrail, hypnotized by the quiet wake behind them, smooth for a time, until invaded by the ocean's chop and swell. "Sam," he whispered, "Sam, Sam, where are you?"

—— // ——

With November, the season for hurricanes was past, but the great pulses of heat that blew west from the African desert were not yet exhausted, and ten days out of Charleston they encountered a storm that baptized the ship into her name. Bliven was forced to shorten sail and run before it, even as he played down its danger to his men, and took the wheel himself, cold and soaked to the skin, the only dry part of his uniform his bicorne, which he had left in the cabin. Yet that was preferable to being on the berth deck, where his cabin door could not bar the foul odor of seasickness which spread its own contagion, and those afflicted dared not venture out to the head on the bow that plunged down into each heavy sea and shot geysers of cold sea water up through the toilet openings.

Bliven could not help but recall his first meeting with Clarity, when she had asked him whether he believed in God, and he asked if she had ever been in a storm at sea. It was still true: Nothing would lead one quicker to a fear of God. But after the storm came the sun, beaming onto the rolling sapphire swells, the sails bellied full out as they stood south and ran full-and-by on the last of the storm winds.

Abel Lewis had marked which men best withstood the tempest, and with the return of the sun and a horizon he sent the sturdiest of them to the masthead, which in the swell was cutting more than a twenty-foot arc back and forth above them. The conditions changed little as they ran down upon the Windward Passage.

Lewis also kept a strict eye on their boys, and was eventually moved to seize one of them by his arm and take him to Bliven's cabin. "Your pardon, sir, this boy was caught taking another's bread away from him."

The youth was so surly that Lewis stood by in case he was needed.

"What is your name, son?" asked Bliven.

"Turner," he answered with a sour face.

"Turner what?"

"Turner's m'last name. First one's Richard."

"Turner, on this vessel you will address the captain and all officers as 'sir.' Do you understand?"

Lewis thumped the boy smartly on the back of his head.

"Yes, sir," the boy replied, although there was a sarcastic emphasis on the *sir*.

"Turner, why did you try to steal that boy's bread?"

"'Cause I was hongry."

"Well, steal on this ship again and you will be whipped, do you understand? When you are hungry, ask Gaston for something and he will give you more bread."

The boy seemed downcast. "Yes, sir."

"How old are you?"

"Ten."

"Ten what?"

"Ten, sir."

"You are not very big for your age."

Turner swelled up. "Tougher'n I look, as that boy found out!"

"Tell me about your parents."

"Ain't got none."

"No relatives?"

"They ain't got no use for me. I raised myse'f."

"I see," said Bliven. He also saw, this was how the cycle began, of low-born men with no manners and a vicious streak, whom vindictive officers whipped into submission as he had seen on the *Enterprise* years before. This was where it began, with boys like this. "Well, Turner, it looks like it falls to the Navy to raise you. We will feed you and train you, and pay you, but for your part, you must be willing to learn and to get along with your shipmates. Many great captains began as ships' boys, did you know that?"

"No, sir."

"Turner, the United States has a use for you, even if your relatives do not, but you must do your part. Do we have a bargain?"

"You not gonna whip me, then?"

"Not this time, this is your warning and your offer. Behave well, and I will see that you are well treated and advanced. Defy me, and I promise you, you will go back to the street to live like an animal. Is it a deal?"

"Yes, sir."

"Then come and shake hands on it."

Decent treatment proved to have its effect on the boy. He left off his path toward criminality and indeed took an active interest in the ship and its running. Bliven gave Gaston access to his captain's box that he had screwed down to the table in his cabin, and also the responsibility to see that the boys were kept in trimmed hair and nails.

The matter was in hand by the time the sextant told them they were nearing the latitude of the Windward Passage. They knew they were approaching it only by navigation, however, for they could see no land when the call came down. "Deck! Deck!"

Abel Lewis had the deck. "What do you see?"

"Sail, bearing southeast, about three miles."

*Three miles?* thought Bliven as he heard the exchange through his open cabin windows. *Why would he not see it until only three miles away?* In a few seconds he had his hat on, grabbed up his speaking trumpet, and was up the ladder and back to the quarterdeck.

"What do you make of her?"

"Small brig, sir, Jamaica-man, just like us!"

"Ha! This sounds hopeful. Run up British colors, Mr. Lewis, let us not alarm him." It had not occurred to him until this moment that their sailing in a Jamaica-built cedar vessel would offer the best disguise they could want, better than the common ruse of the false flag.

Almost at once the vessel they were espying also broke out English colors and altered course toward them. "Apparently," said Bliven, "he wishes to speak us."

"Yes, sir, but this could get awkward if she is also an American trying to draw us in."

"Ha! It would, but I cannot imagine an American vessel coming through this passage."

The strangest thing about capturing his first prize was that it was not a battle, it was a transaction. Two hundred yards from the prize, Bliven wore ship and came to its heading, opened his gunports, raised his true colors, and spoke him to heave to. It was a sad business no doubt for the owners of the prize he was about to take, but Bliven imagined that the whole exchange might not have been ten words different from what the Moorish pirates had done for centuries. Only now he was the one doing it.

Her cargo proved to be mostly oranges and rum; she was in good condition and well worth selling as a prize, and her crew of twenty would not overcrowd his own hold when confined below. For years American sailors had evinced the preference for the whiskey now distilled in Kentucky and Virginia for their grog, but some of his Carolinians did acknowledge a fondness for rum. Bliven therefore diverted two barrels of the rum and had Gaston rig a second grog tub so that his seamen now could have their choice of daily spirits.

He selected a prize crew and warned them strictly that he had made, and had attested, the number of barrels of rum in the hold, and for their sakes they had better make port in Charleston with the same number on board. Seldom did a prize reach port whose cargo was more valuable than the vessel herself, but this was a rich and lucky find.

After dispatching his prize, Bliven and the *Tempest* stood back to the east, running along the coasts of Hispaniola and Puerto Rico, expecting several weeks of open sea, skirting well to the east as she ran south to the northeast coast of South America.

São Salvador da Bahia de Todos os Santos
Portuguese Brazil
16th December, 1812

*My Own Dear Wife,*

*I apprehend at this season what frigid blasts and snows you must be enduring at home, while here in the tropics the heat, even at night, is such that one can hardly sleep without first wetting the sheets. We dropped anchor at this place on yesterday midday, and I desire you to notice the exactness with which I copied out its full name—the Bay of the Savior of All the Saints. I do not know how it got its name (but how you must be rolling your eyes at the Popish sound of it)—except possibly that the bay is capacious enough to contain all of them. The entrance from the ocean is five miles wide but presently opens out into a vast inland sea of several hundreds of square miles. The roads are thickly crowded with ships of many nations, indeed whether to even use the word* roads, *for there is no inner harbor, yet all is sheltered from the ocean. Some of the vessels are English, but as we find ourselves in a neutral port I can make no act toward them. I wish that I could search them and discover if Sam was taken up in one of them, but that is so doubtful that the thought must grow only out of my anxiety for him. The information is that he was taken onto a frigate, from which he would be a much harder case to recover.*

*We have had a most eventful cruise. Having come safely down the colonial isles of the Caribbean, we were running southeast past the coast of Guiana, and took a second prize as she was standing out of Demerara, a British brig laden with tropical woods, no doubt intended for fine furniture or paneling in the great house of some lord or other. She surrendered quite tamely, yet I cannot say I am disappointed at having taken two prizes without firing a shot. (Perhaps I begin to understand why the Barbary Moors established a profession at it; it does seem such a leisure way to make a living!) I sent her home with a prize crew, and when she is sold off we will profit most handsome. The*

British crew are corked up in my hold, which I disliked for their
sakes as much as for my inconvenience, and I put them ashore
here, where they can get passage home.

My love, one "lark" I must tell you of. We were running down
close inshore, and as we crossed the equator, I re-created the act
of the Portuguese navigator who dipped a bucket into the sea and
was astonished to draw up fresh water. Do you know? It is true!
The great wash of the Rio Amazonas is so gigantic that it pushes
fresh water far out into the ocean. Well, then, having crossed the
equator, we had to have the proper ceremony about it. Being now
a "captain," all was under my command. I had Gaston our Negro
cook dress up as Neptune, strands of a mop for his hair, wielding a
trident which he had fashioned from cooking utensils. We raised
him a dais at the end of the galley. Knowing that we were safely
supplied with fresh water until we should reach here, I had Gaston
empty the brine from the steep tub and fill it with fresh water, well
heated. The whole area was decorated with sand, shells, and
seaweed from a party I had sent ashore. All the poor Griffins who
had never crossed the equator before were stripped and given a bath,
so as to make them "worthy" of attending Neptune in his court.
We had both rum and whiskey in plenty, so all was very merry.

And now I can hear you saying, "Wait, dearest, you yourself
have never crossed the equator before." That is quite true, and I
was presented as a prince before Neptune and given the first bath.
I confess very readily that it was a wonderful luxury, a hot bath,
and all the better for being first, because in good faith I should
have hated to bathe after some of those who followed me! The
great purpose of it all, which none actually suspected, was to get

*at least some of them clean, for Dr. Cutbush had been most emphatic in telling me he would hate to ship out with men recruited in Charleston. And fear not, I had Gaston give the steep tub a thorough cleansing before returning to its wonted use.*

*And now, my love, business presses. There is an American consul here who in former years has been engaged mostly in the repatriation of American sailors taken from American ships seized by the English, but who carried protection papers, and were put ashore, their ships being seized for British service. I will entrust this letter to the consul, with some hope that through him it will find its way to you in a more or less direct route, and not wander through Arabia, or Madagascar, or Tahiti, or make some similarly improbable detour.*

*My business here will not long detain us, I must disembark the prisoners I have taken from the British merchantmen. How they make their way home, I leave that to the diplomats. I care only that the consul procure us water and provisions and spring me loose at the first moment. It was my good fortune to find only one British man-o'-war here, a corvette called the* Bonne Citoyenne, *yet another French capture—sometimes I wonder that the English ever actually build ships of their own, they take so many from others. I sent her captain an invitation to single combat, for we are evenly matched, but he replied not, and I have since learned the reason, that she carries in cargo half a million pounds in specie which he dares not risk in battle.*

*Indeed, the consul informs me that there is an enemy thirty-eight expected here to escort her, and if a British merchantman leave here, chance across him, and speak him of our presence, it*

*could go very hard with us. Therefore, we shall "verschwinde,"
as the Germans say, while the going is good.*

*Ah, but my love, there is one other matter I must tell you—as
much as I miss you and desire you with me, I am even more than
at Charleston heartily glad that you are not here, for I fear the way
of life in Brazil would sear your sensibilities beyond recovery. The
issue is that great one that has occupied your conscience since I
have known you, that being slavery. It exists here on such a scale
that I could scarcely believe my eyes. I tell you in cold sobriety that
for every slave that was taken into our American South before the
trade was banned, at least fifteen were taken into Brazil. They tell
me that the Portuguese have been here upward of two hundred
and fifty years, and the broad avenues of the city are lined with
beautiful stone buildings of quaint and beautiful architecture
of a style I have never seen before. But, my love, it is the slaves
who quarry the stone and haul it, and grind the lime for mortar.
Of course they also are the labor for the very substantial
agriculture of the region—and, my love, it is slaves who carry
the wealthy around in sedan chairs! Never in even the most remote
parts of our backward South did I witness such depravity.*

*Slaves here were imported in such numbers, from diverse parts
of Africa, that unlike in our Southern states where they are
required to leave off their native customs, rather, here they live in
communities wherein they maintain their old languages and
customs, and the Portuguese do not mind so long as they perform
the labors required of them. At a glance this seems kind, yet it is
only occasioned by the sheer numbers of the poor wretches who are
grabbed in their homes and brought across the ocean in chains.*

*And there was a further surprise to me. In North Africa we saw white Christians held as slaves by the Moors—here there is a population of Moors who are the slaves! O, is not the world a vast place, with many ways to live life—and are we not damn'd lucky to live where we do?*

*My love, it is time to close. The lighter is coming alongside, and I shall send this letter back with its captain, along with my receipt for the filled barrels he brings. This departs with the kisses of*

> *Yr ever husband,*
> *Bliven Putnam*
> *Master Cmdt., USN*

From Salvador the *Tempest* stood to the east, with the intention of crossing the sea lanes of commercial ships heading for Britain with the produce of her Indian possessions. The winds opposed her, however, and three days' hard sailing bore them scarcely a hundred miles.

"Deck! Deck there!"

"What do you see?"

"Ship, bearing to the north, maybe five miles!"

*Five miles?* thought Bliven. Either the lookout's eyes had grown sharper or the day was really clear or it was a ship large enough, unlike his own, to be seen at that distance. "What do you make of her?"

"Hull's down, sir!"

"Keep us informed!"

Coming from the north, she would not be loaded with exotic

cargo. Perhaps she was bearing manufactured goods, bound for one of the South American ports. Two hours passed.

"Deck!"

"Masthead, what do you see?"

"She is a frigate, sir, coming on fast!"

*Yes, it could be the* Constitution, thought Bliven. The Navy had expressed its desire to attack British shipping in the Southern Hemisphere. Rodgers had his squadron, he'd heard that Decatur now had a squadron; she might have been the only large ship free to dispatch to this area. He realized he was the only one on board who would recognize her if he saw her; he disliked going aloft, but he slung his glass over his shoulder, grabbed hold of the ratlines, and began climbing. If what Barron had written him was accurate, he could well join up with the *Constitution* and the *Hornet*.

Bracing himself in the iron hoop of the masthead, he was reminded just how much greater circle of vision one had from up there. The ship was clearly visible, making toward them. He put the glass to his eye and realized in a flash it was not the *Constitution*. It was a lighter vessel, probably a thirty-eight, elegant, probably French built. She flew no pennant, but Bliven had to assume she was English. Solidifying that conclusion, he saw she had set stuns'ls and was coming on like a greyhound.

"Sing out, now, if she changes course," he said to the lookout, hoping to convey none of his own anxiety that he had perhaps an hour to prepare for an attack. By the time he was back on deck he was breathing hard. "It is indeed a frigate, Mr. Lewis, but I fear not ours. Beat to quarters."

Lewis shouted the order to the Marine standing ready at the

head of the ladder, and the ship leapt to life as he beat out the tattoo. Guns were hauled in and tompions pulled, crowed up and quoins inserted to level them for loading; the boys began running about, depositing powder and shot in the garlands behind the guns. They prepared well enough, he allowed, but could they fight? How would they react when a mate's intestines blew across their faces? For that matter, how would he himself react?

That his whole ship was untested, and he, in his first command, was unnerving and close to a cause for panic. What cruel witticism was God working upon him, to show him now how little he really knew and how ill prepared he was to command, how unready for battle? In his first days as a midshipman embarked for the Mediterranean, he had harbored the darkest apprehension of Lieutenant Sterett, for his fame in skewering one of his own gunners upon his sword for flinching from enemy fire. Now the guns of his own ship were manned by clots of terrified recruits, still civilian merchant sailors at heart, who were more petrified of the too-famous butchery of naval battle than they were of disobeying him. Should he not have made these men fear him?

During the Barbary War, officers had remarked endlessly on the lightly built Tripolitan ships, converted merchantmen who had no business mounting guns for they could not receive fire. Now here he was, in his cedar-built Jamaican eggshell that would take no punishment, and the only way to reinforce her inside, even just between wind and water, and even had he time and lumber and a carpenter to do so, would have added so much weight that he must lose any advantage of speed he might otherwise have had.

"Brains and bravery," President Madison had said. "Before my

God, you shall have need of both." Is this what they meant, that they were sending him to his likely death, that junior officers such as he were expendable? But then, who in their tiny Navy was not expendable?

No—battle and honorable defeat, perhaps honorable death, were all that were left him.

A new look through his glass revealed that the frigate bearing down on him had run up the British naval pennant, and signal flags, a code he had no hope of answering, and he knew even now that her guns were being run out. He cupped his hands at his mouth. "Mr. Lewis!"

"Captain!"

"Show our colors!"

"Aye, sir." Within seconds the Stars and Stripes curled from the spanker boom.

It was certain to his eye now that she was a thirty-eight, probably actually mounting forty guns or more, which would overmatch him two to one, the weight of broadside probably three to one. At a gaming table he would have folded his hand and awaited the next deal of cards, but here, to capitulate without resistance, even to save the lives of his crew, would be an unspeakable dishonor. He believed he knew his father well enough to know that he would prefer the grief of his death over the shame of his tame surrender. And likewise his mother, as she had made clear. And Clarity? The worst pang of all was the possibility of not seeing her again. If regaining her was the only question, he might indeed throw his honor overboard, and they could steal away to some place where he was not known and they could live out their days together. But that was not the only question, for to do that he would have to ask her to live with a coward, and no organ in his body could permit that.

Bliven snapped back to the present with the boom of the frigate's bow chaser, and then all heads snapped up as the ball popped through their mizzen topsail.

It was necessary to assess any advantages, however slight and few, that he might have. He might not be faster than a frigate, although in a stouter wind he might take his chances, but it seemed possible that he could be more maneuverable. If he could make a tighter turn, unexpectedly, he might perhaps wreak enough damage to level the odds. If something happened to him, it was imperative to let the lieutenant know his plan.

"Mr. Lewis, listen to me carefully. I am going to turn just enough to bring your stern chasers to bear. Take your shot now, reload with grape." He paused, as their attacker was a thousand yards distant, and only now shortened to fighting sail; he had never seen such an assault, he was coming on like a tiger in its spring. "You see he has the weather gauge. If he turns to rake us, we will match his turn. If he stays and comes upon our weather beam, I am going to shear away at the last possible instant before he can deliver a broadside. When I do, luff the sails and spill the wind so he will shoot ahead. Do you understand?"

"Yes, sir."

"Good. Now, listen. Your forward four guns stay elevated to cut his rigging. Level your after four guns and try to hit his rudder. Do you understand?"

"Exactly, sir, yes." Lewis ran forward and relayed the instruction to the eight port-side guns, and the after four began to be quoined up and leveled.

"Well, she'll find we have a stinger in our tail now. Helm, starboard ten degrees."

Lewis loped back to the stern chasers and knelt at the sights. "On my order, boys, fire." The second he shouted, twin explosions reported from their stern. At five hundred yards it would have been hard to miss. One ball crashed into the starboard cathead, sending the anchor dangling by its cable; the other flew higher, popping a hole in the jib.

"Well done, Mr. Lewis. Now come back to your course. Helm, be ready for a starboard turn on my order." He knew it must be an illusion, but the frigate seemed to fly at them. A ship approaching from an oblique course, shortened to fighting sail, could only close in a stately manner, but now with his own possible death in the balance, the hands of the clock seemed to spin. "Mr. Lewis, how much taller do you make her freeboard than ours?"

"Five feet, sir, more or less."

"As do I, Mr. Lewis. Elevate your chasers to just rake her deck, if you get the opportunity." She bore up only a hundred yards away. "Marines! Commence firing, keep their heads down in the tops! Mr. Lewis, this is your last opportunity with the chasers. Fire when you bear." Bliven took the wheel and edged the *Tempest* to starboard until the chasers boomed behind him, and he came back to course.

It was apparent that the Englishman was holding his fury until he was alongside, and he meant to do to the *Tempest* what Hull had done to the *Guerriere*. But, if he could turn just enough from her broadside, the tough elasticity of *Tempest*'s cedar hull might deflect the eighteen-pounder balls. He must not turn away completely, he realized urgently. If *Tempest* showed her full stern she would be raked; balls smashing through the undefended cabin would wreak havoc down the length of the ship belowdeck. But if he could present only an oblique target, they might just glance off his hull.

Bliven sighted until he saw her bowsprit just come even with himself, only a hundred feet away. "Hard a'starboard! Luff your sails!"

The fast *Tempest* answered with alacrity and the big frigate plowed ahead until Bliven could read the name on her stern: JAVA. His four after twelves took their shots at the frigate's rudder, one crashing into the quarter gallery, another smashing a hole in the afterpeak, a third, and he saw it clearly, striking the British mizzenmast and shivering it violently, shaking its topsail like a bedsheet in the laundry. The fourth ball must have passed through, or astern, for he descried no effect.

Then to Bliven's horror he saw her heel ponderously, matching his turn exactly, and come alongside him on his new heading. "Brace up! Brace up!" he bellowed, but before his words died away *Java* unleashed a hellish withering broadside. Eighteen-pound balls crushed into his hull timbers like she was a furniture crate; grape from her carronades mowed down Marines and sail handlers like they were standing before a firing squad.

He had never imagined such rapidity of fire from large guns. His own gunners were bowled over as twelves were knocked from their carriages. Starboard crews crossed the deck to replace them only to find the guns useless. Bliven's helmsman cried out as he was dropped by a musket ball, and Lewis quickly took the wheel.

Turner, the Charleston powder monkey, emerged from the ladder carrying ball and powder, running aft to find a gun that needed them. Bliven's eye met his for an instant. "What shall I do, Captain?"

"Leave them in the garland there and get below!"

Turner crouched to deposit his burden in the garland of the aftmost twelve, stood to stretch out the strain they had been on his back. "Captain, am I doing better?"—and then he was not there anymore. Bliven had seen the result of what cannonballs did to human flesh, seen it lying in heaps on decks slick with blood, but this was the first time he had seen it as it happened, with his own eyes, how it was over in an instant, and seen how far blood could spray and spot everything it touched, seen life itself ebb away and the soul be released, leaving only inanimate flesh and organs lying warm and pliable on the charnel house deck. Sentience was reduced to meat, in less than a second, and it bent him double in a scream: "Turner! No!"

As Bliven raised himself back up he heard the crushing rapid deep-booming staccato of another broadside, from the *Java*'s eighteens, now so close he could not see them beneath his rail. But he could feel the *Tempest* shudder under the pounding, no doubt each ball flying right through the cedar hull. One ball shot away the top of the rudder, severing its connection to the tiller, and suddenly the wheel spun into a blur as Lewis jumped back from it, praying that his hands had not been broken.

With *Tempest* now beyond control, his port guns wrecked or off their carriages, Bliven saw the *Java* begin to wear around to present her other broadside. Had he considered it he would have hesitated, for it was his nature to work at a problem until he found some way through, but that would have been a conceit now. It was without such thinking that he drew his sword and severed the line to the spanker boom and pulled down their flag.

*Java* was still so close he could hear the order to cease fire repeated to all her stations, followed by the most galling three cheers he could ever hear. But thank God, at least now it was over. Within a moment davits lowered a boat from the *Java*, which her sweeps began to pull over. *Tempest* had no boarding ladder. "Are you all right, Mr. Lewis?"

"I think so, sir, yes."

"Go have a net thrown down to them. Get to my cabin, throw the codebooks overboard. Then bring me a report on our casualties. If we are taking on water, get some able men working the pumps."

"Yes, sir."

As the boat neared, pulled by Marines, Bliven could scarce believe his eyes. Her captain, in a spanking clean uniform, stood erect, one hand bracing himself against the boat's spindle of a mast. He had last seen him in a powdered wig, and his hair was now swept forward in a Brutus crop, but there was no doubt it was he.

All came up the net, captain and Marines, and Lewis gestured them toward the quarterdeck.

The captain touched one of the Marines on the arm, pointed down at Turner's remains. Wreckage from the yards prevented them from walking around, and he said, "Throw that overboard."

Bliven could not bear to watch and turned away. What was left of Turner made small splashes when the pieces struck the water below, and the captain approached. "I am Captain Lord Sir Arthur Kington, commanding His Majesty's frigate *Java*." Bliven turned to face him and Kington's face went slack. "You!"

Bliven saluted. "Bliven Putnam, Master Commandant, United States sloop-of-war *Tempest*. You have beaten us, sir. My sword."

Kington took it. "I remember you, from Naples, you were with your commodore."

"Yes, sir."

Kington surveyed the quarterdeck, and then down the wreckage of the spar deck. "What kind of slapped-together, made-up tub of sticks did they send you out in?"

"Whatever they could find to fight you with, sir. Whatever would float."

"Hm! Well, she won't be floating for long, I'll warrant. I confess I respect your sand, Commander, I will give you that. What are your casualties?"

"My lieutenant is just coming with his report, sir. Mr. Lewis, what did you find?"

"Seventeen killed, sir, thirty-five wounded. Dr. Gabriel believes he can save most of them. Excuse me, sir." He saluted Kington. "Abel Lewis, first lieutenant."

Kington nodded at his good manners. "Lieutenant, speak to Mr. DeWest here, my lieutenant of Marines, about starting to transfer your wounded. Mr. DeWest?"

"Sir!"

"Follow this man."

"Yes, sir."

He turned his notice back to Bliven. "Well, Commander, did you take any prizes with this vessel?"

"Two, sir. One in the Windward Passage, and one off Demerara."

"Have you any prisoners aboard?"

"No, sir, I turned them over to the British consul at Salvador a few days ago."

"I see. Good. Well, you are the first vessel I have encountered since leaving Bermuda. Your officers and crew will be confined to my cable tier until I can get them ashore. You, as captain, I accord you a stateroom with my officers, if you will swear to me your parole that you will take no action against my men or my ship."

"You have it, sir, thank you."

"I remind you, your parole is upon your life. Break it and I will hang you."

"I have given it, I will not break it. You have shot our boat away, we will have to use yours to effect the transfer."

"Of course. Please report to Lieutenant Chads when you have got your men across. My men will salvage what of your stores we can use. We observed you hit several times between wind and water, and, to put it plainly, this vessel is not worth saving. We will let her sink when we are done."

The transfer required three hours; Dr. Gabriel saved his chest of medical implements, Gaston his cabinet of Creole spices, and each man was allowed a small clutch of personal items. Once the pumps went still the *Tempest* settled quickly and quietly, and Bliven could at least say that he was the last man off the ship. He carried with him sufficient clothes to change, and Clarity's dressing box, but he grieved the loss of his books, for he would have to start a new collection from the beginning. And if he came to sea again, he resolved to bring only the dearest volumes to keep him company, for he knew he could not bear to lose them all again.

On the *Java* he was given a tiny stateroom not at all unlike what he had known on the *Constitution*. Later he found no officer at hand to ask whether he might use their privy, and decided he was not too proud to make his way forward to use the common head.

Bliven made his way down the gun deck toward the forward ladder, followed by the impassive stares of the British tars, but then was hailed by a voice that shocked him like an electric wire. "Excuse me, Captain, sir? May I have a word?"

Bliven stopped in his tracks as Sam Bandy stood and faced him—wan, thinner than he had ever seen him, but the soul behind those clear blue eyes was not possible to mistake. Bliven gasped audibly, and Bandy held up his hands. "Excuse me, sir, you do not know me." It was Bandy's eyes that conveyed the further imperative that indeed they must not know each other, that Sam's life might depend upon their not knowing each other. "But I am an American, wrongly taken at sea and forced into impressment. As you are an officer and will be soon released, can you at least get word to my family that I am alive?"

Bliven swallowed and realized that he must play along. "What is your name?"

"Bandy, sir, Samuel Bandy, late captain of the brig *Althea*, taken at sea a year ago."

"Where are you from?"

"South Carolina, sir, the Abbeville District. My wife and two sons, and my mother, are there and must be in despair."

White came storming over in his bosun's hard hat. "Be silent, there! You have no right to address this officer. As you were!"

"Bosun," said Bliven, "are you acquainted with this man?"

White made his respects uncertainly, not sure whether he was called upon to salute an enemy officer, but he deferred to his rank. "He is a suspected Canadian deserter, being bound over for examination when we can get him ashore."

"Is your ship not based in Bermuda?"

"It is, sir."

"And he was taken a year ago? Have you been at sea for a year without an opportunity to give this man a hearing?"

"Our port calls there have been very brief, sir; there has been no opportunity, no, sir."

An officer came forward from the wardroom, having noticed the small commotion of their conversation. "Henry Chads, sir, first lieutenant. What is going on here?"

"Lieutenant Chads, sir," White made his respects, "this man has accosted the American captain and once again pled his case that he himself is an American and is trying to send word to his family in South Carolina, as he claims, sir."

"Mr. Lively, once again you are cruising in danger of a lashing. You have no right to address this officer."

"Lieutenant." Bliven saluted, obligating Chads to return it. "I am Bliven Putnam, master commandant of the vessel you have just taken. In considering the matter before us, may I recommend your tolerance of this man's interruption? He has not discommoded me at all, and further, I would like your permission to return to him when I can and take his information. If it turns out that he is who he says he is, why, the matter is concluded without further trouble. And if his information does not bear out, and he is still possibly a Canadian deserter, well, there will be your *habeas corpus* to dispose of him as it pleases your captain. I would be only too happy to assist in clearing the matter, if I may serve."

"Commander Putnam," said Chads, clearly taken aback and unsure of his ground, "your dispassion and good sense are very welcome. I can see no obstacle to your interviewing this man and, when you are released or exchanged, taking up his cause to the extent that you are able."

"That is kind of you, Lieutenant. If your purser can supply me with something from a writing kit, I believe I have enough pocket money to purchase it equitably."

"Oh, no! I can give you pen and paper," said Chads. "Call at my stateroom in a moment and we will attend to it."

"That will do very well," Bliven acknowledged with a shallow bow. "Now, if you will excuse me, I was bound for your head for a most important errand."

"Ha! Of course, go on. Mr. Lively, as you were, you may count yourself lucky to have encountered such an amiable officer."

"Yes, sir, Lieutenant." Bandy made his respects in the British fashion. "I do indeed."

As he departed, Bliven's eyes met Sam's. Facially Sam gave no hint of his thoughts, but deep in his eyes his satisfaction at having established their ruse shone clearly.

Returning from the head, Bliven entered the wardroom and

found Chads's door open, three sheets of paper, a pen, and an inkwell all reposing on a stiff tablet. "Are you certain you will not let me pay you for these?" he asked.

"No, not at all. You should just be able to take the man's statement—the captain believes him to be a Canadian named Lively, wanted for desertion, but his protests, and the circumstances of his having been taken, caused enough doubt to prevent his summary hanging—you should have time to do that and wash up for dinner in the captain's cabin."

"I will return your tablet and pen and ink as soon as I have done, thank you." Again Bliven saluted, prompting Chads to return it and become more accustomed to conversation with a prisoner given freedom of the ship on parole.

As he walked forward down the berth deck, Sam saw him and rose.

"Mr. Lively," said Bliven loudly, "will you speak with me now?"

Again Sam made his respects. "Yes, sir, thank you."

As he drew near, they were able to speak in a hush that no others could overhear. "Sam! Are you all right?"

The first inquiry into his welfare in a year caused Sam to choke, and he could not speak at first. "I am alive," he said at last.

"Oh, Sam. Do you want to go up on deck and get some air?"

"No! No, no, no! We must not risk the captain seeing us. I know where we can go." He led Bliven forward, past the galley and into the sick bay. "Dr. Kite?"

"Mr. Lively."

"May I introduce you to Master Commandant Putnam, of the ship lately taken?"

"Doctor." Bliven saluted and extended his hand.

"Commander." Kite took his hand. "Are you hurt?"

"No, sir, I thank you. I wish to take down some information from this man, as he claims to be an American and I may be able to do something for him when I am exchanged. May we borrow a corner of your space for our conversation?"

"Commander," said Sam, "Dr. Kite is one of the two sources of kindness that have been extended to me on this ship. The other is the bosun, whom you just met."

"I was just going to take a turn on deck," said Kite. "I will leave you gentlemen to your interview."

"That was good of him," said Bliven when he had gone.

"I suspect there is tension between him and the captain. The less he ever hears me say, the less the captain can compel from him. Bliv, that captain Lord Almighty What-Have-You is a monster, he is a murderer, he has the blackest heart I've ever seen. He knows very well who I am, I showed him my master's license and he dropped it into the sea. Coldly, looking right at me, dropped it out my window."

"Jesus!"

"He must not find out that we know each other, it might well mean my death."

"I understand. I have seen Rebecca."

"Oh!"

"She and the boys are well. Your mother is well."

"Ah!" He was starting to weep, but for their safety's sake bottled the emotion deep within him. "How did you—"

"My ship"—Bliven took up their wonted teasing attitude—"which you just sank, thank you very much—"

"Oh, I am sorry. I'm afraid it was my shot that took out your rudder, you know." Sam's eyes shone again when he saw he had nonplussed Bliven into an inability to reply.

"My ship was fitted out in Charleston. I wrote Rebecca, and she sent a carriage to fetch me."

"Was Mose driving?"

"He was."

"Oh, how is he?"

"He was well, and delightful company." It was obvious how starved Sam was for news of home, so famished that Bliven had never realized how strong are the bonds that tie one to home, for he had never had his severed. The terrible effect of such a wound he had never suspected.

"My boys?"

"My God, engines of perpetual motion. The night I stayed at your house, nothing do but I take them up and put them to bed. You have filled them with sea stories, I don't know how you will prevent them from sailing away the day they are old enough."

"My wife," he said tenderly.

"She is strong, capable, sensible, and for all that misses you terribly. I told her that you had been captured and pressed but were probably safe."

"Wait, how could you have known that?"

"We had word of your ship's capture before I left. Sam, how are we to manage this?"

"We must never let on that we know each other."

"Yes," said Bliven. "I guess we must play for time and watch for an opportunity. England and America have been fighting since early last summer. We declared war mostly over the capture and impressment of Americans just like you. However dear you are to your family and to me, I fear that to the government you are just one among thousands. Assuming we win the war, and that is doubtful as I need not explain, whatever disposition is arranged for the thousands will likely apply to you."

"Well, we will figure something out. Now, quick, before you have to leave, write down my essentials: name, residence, history, claims. You might need to produce something to show that lieutenant."

Bliven flipped open the inkwell and began writing.

"Is your family well?" asked Sam.

"Yes, very well. Did you tell the captain, and the others, of your service in the Navy, on the *Enterprise*?"

"Yes, I did," Sam answered.

"Good, maybe we can get the Navy particularly interested in your case." When he had covered a sheet and a half of paper, Bliven closed the inkwell and emptied the pen with a lengthy rubric and stood to leave. "Sam, do you need anything?"

"No, it is just so good to see you. Even if I do not live to get home, at least I know—"

"No, no, we will get through this somehow."

Sam glanced about, ascertaining that the draperies of the sick bay screened them from others' view, and he extended his hand. "Friends forever, still?"

Bliven made his own survey of their privacy, seized his hand, and held it tight to his chest. "You know we are."

———  #  ———

Captain's table was held promptly, and Bliven was provided a basin of water and a washcloth in his stateroom, and a fresh shirt to wear under his own coat and insignia. The first thing that struck him about the captain's cabin was that it bore signs of damage hurriedly repaired—a new wooden patch in the screen that separated this compartment from the length of the gun deck, a hole in the sideboard, a swatch of sailcloth tied over its mirror that was apparently broken, a table leg missing and replaced with two straight pine boards.

"You cut us up quite nasty," said Kington. "I've a mind not to feed you at all, but the custom is what it is."

"I regret the necessity of having done it, Captain," said Bliven. "I was hoping to work some damage to your gun deck further on. Or, if your stern was up, to hit your rudder."

"I see. Well, if it makes you feel any better, you did knock one eighteen off its carriage. Killed one of the crew, wounded two others."

"I am sorry to have caused any loss of life, even in performance of my duty."

Kington regarded him, penetrating him. "Yes, I believe you are."

Bliven waited for Kington to motion him to a chair to sit down, having been introduced again to the surgeon Dr. Kite, the chaplain Dr. Eskew, and three lieutenants. Lord Kington headed the table, and Bliven was seated at his right, leaving him to wonder whether this was a chair for a principal guest or, like in a Roman procession, he was the prize captive to exhibit. He also waited to see what the protocol was for the napkins, only to discover that there was none; some of the officers tucked them into the throats of their shirts, others laid them across their laps. As the steward poured wine, none of the men refused it, and Bliven allowed him to fill his own glass.

"Do you fancy Madeira, Commander Putnam?" asked Kington.

"I cannot say, my lord. In truth I was raised on a farm in Connecticut, with an apple orchard, so I know more about the respective merits of ciders than of wines."

"Ha!" triumphed Kington. "So in the Royal Navy we have the rank of master and commander. You, apparently, are a farmer and commander."

Bliven sensed the insult but determined on the best response. "That is more true than you know, my lord. If Britain would but leave us alone, I would resign my commission and go home to my farm in a heart's beat."

First Lieutenant Chads sensed a disagreeable exchange coming. "Damn convenient islands, the Madeiras," he boomed. "Make sou'sou'west from England to swing round the bulge of Africa, and there they are. Can't miss 'em. And considering the quality of the wine, it's far better to drop anchor and get some than have to navigate around. I am often surprised that we can even purchase any, for ninety-five bottles in a hundred they say are sold to you Americans. I wonder that you can find the time to drink anything else."

Bliven noticed that none partook of the wine, and then Kington scooted back his chair, rose, and raised his glass. "Gentlemen, the King."

Bliven felt no choice but to join in as the scraping of chairs on the deck became general and all toasted, "The King," before they resumed their seats. Perhaps the evening was intended to be an exercise in humiliation, he had no idea.

"Commander Putnam, you have no pause in drinking the health of our King?"

"Indeed, no, sir. I bear no ill will toward your King. All my country wants is to be left in peace and not have our ships and men seized." *Besides,* he kept to himself, *your King is a lunatic prisoner in his own castle. I do wish him well, and peace of mind.*

"A noble sentiment," said Eskew, "but for all the cry your people raise about impressment, nothing is ever said about your resorting to the same practice."

"Well, we have no equal to your naval might in enforcing the practice, do we? Your six or eight thousand captives as against our one here or there, I believe does not make an equivalency." Bliven sensed the protest coming and raised his hand. "But I will say this, that even if it is only one, it is still wrong. In fact, I myself witnessed one such incident, in recruiting men for the *Constitution.*"

"By God, sir, your candor does you credit," said one of the lieutenants.

"Both our services face great difficulties in manning our ships. I was with Captain Hull when he boarded another frigate, not his own, which could not sail immediately, to take off some of her crew. One man identified himself as Irish and said he wished to be repatriated. We had just learned of your capture of several merchant vessels and impressing many of their crewmen; Captain Hull was very angry and said he did not care, be the man English or Chinese or from Fiji, he would take him. I did not approve, but he was my superior and I could not speak out."

"Quite right," said Kington. "Do you remember his name?"

"I do not, sir, I am sorry."

Three stewards entered the wardroom, two bearing silver chafing dishes and a third a stack of dishes of white china.

"You set a fine table indeed, Captain," said Bliven. "But I thought the Royal Navy was famous for its square plates."

"It is, for them." Kington gestured beyond the bulkhead to the gun deck. "Not for gentlemen."

"Ah, I see." Bliven looked down in disbelief. On his plate reposed the hindquarter of a fowl on a bed of rice with a thick reddish-brown sauce next to peas sprinkled with melted cheese and a thick slice of bread—not fine bread, but of surprising quality for the length of time they must have been at sea. "Excuse me, Captain," he said, "is this chicken?"

"Of course. Is it so amazing?"

"Well, rather. At home in New England, chickens are wanted for their eggs. Only the most extravagant of people would ever actually serve the birds."

Dr. Kite laid his hand on Bliven's arm and gestured at his plate as though he were imparting a great confidence. "No one told her this is what happens if you stop laying."

Low laughter spread along the table. "Commander Putnam," said Kington, "I wonder if you would be so good as to gratify my curiosity on a couple of points."

"If I can."

"Is it not customary, when battle portends, to shorten your canvas to fighting sail, to see what you are doing, and keep them out of fire?"

"It is, yes."

"But you did not. May we know why?"

Bliven cocked his head, considering his answer. "Sir, I had no desire to engage you. I could see in an instant that we were overmatched, two to one or more. The *Tempest* was a cedar-built Jamaica-man, light and fast, and very quick to handle. I knew that you would shorten sail to prepare for battle, and if I did not, I might outrun you."

"Yet you did not set stuns'ls."

"We were not rigged for them, nor had room to stow the spars."

"I see."

"And, being a fast ship, she was more maneuverable at speed. Had I clewed up the courses I would have been no more nimble than you. So my design was to hold my course until right before I thought you would open fire, then shear off and luff the sails before you could react. Then if that worked, as you passed us by, I had some of the twelve-pounders elevated and loaded with grape to cut your sails and rigging, with the hope to slow your speed, and some loaded with solid shot and leveled to rake your stern into the gun deck, or, as I said, to hit your rudder. If I had managed in a few shots to render you unmaneuverable, the odds would have swung considerably to my side."

"Very creative. Indeed, I never heard the like. Why do you think it did not succeed?"

Biven drained his Madeira at the memory. It was a fortified wine and very strong. "Unfortunately, my plan depended upon my success at the first exchange. Your first broadside killed my bosun and four sail handlers. And then you matched my turn quicker than I thought you would, and I had to fire the twelves before enough range opened up to hole your tops'ls. After that, all you need do was maintain your fire and the conclusion was inevitable."

"Young man," said Dr. Kite, "seeing yourself overmatched, you could have struck your colors at the outset and saved your crew a terrible cutting up. I and my surgeon's mate have spent a frantic afternoon trying to patch them up."

Bliven laid his flatware upon the table. "Young as I am, Dr. Kite, I hope you will understand that I would die before I would dishonor my flag in such a way. My cause was not hopeless, only doubtful."

"Extremely doubtful."

"Yes, but not hopeless. No commander, certainly no American commander, would have struck without even firing a shot. With great sincerity, however, I thank you for your attentions to my crew. When I am set at liberty, I will credit your kindness in my report."

"And you will understand, Commander," said Kington, "that will be some time. We are newly provisioned, and have no thought of making port unless it is leading a string of prizes."

Bliven's mind raced. Kington had introduced the element of their long months at sea. If ever there was a time to broach the topic of Sam Bandy, this was it. The whole company of officers were present as witnesses; Kite and Eskew, Sam was inclined to believe, favored his cause. But would English officers dare contradict their captain? If he spoke up on Sam's behalf, and avowed that he knew him and had served with him, he might be cut off from any further contact with him. Indeed, Sam might have been correct that Kington would have him killed to cover the whole affair. But if he held his peace now, to preserve some means to continue communicating with Sam, and then in future he claimed to know him, his silence now might be taken as evidence that indeed he did not know him. There was no good course of action, and far safer to play their respective roles until circumstances presented them some chance to act. Adding this evening's dinner with what he remembered of Kington from Naples, Bliven resolved to make no further mention of Sam and to answer generally and noncommittally if he were asked about him. They would both be confined to this ship for perhaps months; to say too much now would probably end badly.

## 9

*Obookiah*

It was the week before Christmas, that occasion which the Congregationalists eschewed as a popish frippery, that Lyman and Roxana Beecher hosted a glittering convocation of the high and mighty of their denomination. As Boston, and even Harvard College, fell increasingly into such fashionable heresies as Unitarianism and even Deism, the pious, traditional Congregationalists had come to view more rural Connecticut as their refuge, and Litchfield as its high redoubt.

The snow lay solid but not deep, the night cold as iced crystal, the moon robust to illuminate the white landscape, as the carriages began arriving at their high solemn house off the green. Clarity and her mother were invited, and Mrs. Marsh had Fred Meriden hitch the Putnams' horses to her sleigh, though it was not more than six blocks between their houses.

It was Lyman Beecher who met them in the hall, who said after inquiring into their health, "Your driver brought you, I presume?"

"Freddy, yes," answered Clarity.

"Let us have him drive on around to the kitchen, where he can warm himself until you are ready to go home?"

"Yes. Yes, that would be very kind." They already knew that Freddy would drape blankets over their horses—uncommon care, but that was Freddy's way.

Beecher spoke quietly to a young man, who went out and relayed the message. Clarity was unsure whether to call him an usher or a butler or a footman, for they had never employed a man in such a capacity. "And now, Mrs. Putnam, there is someone whom you have not seen in a very long time." They exited the hall and entered the parlor, where a loose huddle of cordial people was gathered around an older couple by the fire. Beecher excused their way through them.

"Dr. Dwight, I wonder if you remember Miss Clarity Marsh, now Mrs. Putnam?" It did not escape Clarity's notice that she was presented to Dwight before he was introduced to her. In mere social protocol, he would be introduced to her because she was a lady; rather, she was introduced to him because, she presumed, he was ecclesiastical nobility.

She judged Dwight to be perhaps sixty and he looked all of it, although well kept. He was tall, and pasty as a scholar might be, certainly one who had been president of Yale College for sixteen years, and he bulged suitably in all those elderly places. He regarded the world through thick round spectacles heavily rimmed, and from the few and chosen steps that he took, Clarity judged that his feet must hurt. Even for such a brilliant man, the author of many books, he, like Saint Paul, must have a thorn in his flesh—or at least pain in his feet.

Dwight introduced his wife, who stood at his side, Mary née Woolsey, the daughter of New York money, backing Dwight's descent from Jonathan Edwards himself. Who had not read, and heard, his famous sermon describing "Sinners in the Hands of an Angry God"? And who could come away from it not feeling much like that insect that the Almighty held over the fire of hell, and might let fall at his pleasure?

She appeared to be her husband's equal in age and had a stern look about her, a steel that was concealed to the casual eye by her feminine features and dress. Clarity imagined that she would reach greatly advanced years. Inwardly, Clarity was pleased with herself, how the new persons she met she sized up as potential characters with their own peculiar stories, grist for novels that she would write.

"Mrs. Marsh." Dwight bowed ever so slightly, smiling tightly and without showing any teeth, likely a matter of declining dentition more than excessive rigidity of temper. "How very good to see you again, it has been quite some time."

Clarity's mother smiled and inclined her head to the equal degree but did not curtsey and did not extend her hand. "Dr. Dwight, it was very kind of you to invite us. Mrs. Dwight, you look well." It was the appropriate posture for a wealthy dowager who contributed materially to the well-being of the church. Indeed, all knew that Mrs. Marsh was if anything a caryatid without whose support their edifice might well not stand.

"Young lady," said Dwight to Clarity, "you probably do not re-member us. You were a very little girl when last we met."

Clarity did not often get to use the poise she had practiced in Miss Pierce's School for Girls. "Oh, perhaps I have a vague memory—something of learned discourse far above my under-standing."

The Dwights chuckled approvingly. Timothy Dwight was re-nowned for his intellectual prowess. It was widely known that he had been a prodigy who had learned his alphabet at one sitting, and who could discourse on the precepts of the Bible when he was but three years old. The brilliance of his theological career, his mastery of the biblical languages, was equaled only by his reputa-tion as an indefatigable traveler. There seemed to be no corner of New England which he had not visited, and preached, and spread his grace and common touch, even as he took voluminous notes, ferocious notes, on the resources of the countryside, on the char-acter of the towns and their people for the benefit of the pastors who would come after him to safeguard their spiritual welfare. Did this town lack a subscription for a cemetery? He could help. Did that town need improved harbor facilities? He could write a letter to their representative in the Congress. His decades of expe-rience had taught him that people could easier love the Bible who first loved its messengers.

"Well, Mrs. Putnam, they tell me that your husband is an officer in our Navy. I am sorry he could not be here."

"Thank you, he was lately serving with Captain Hull in the *Con-stitution*. He now has his own command, a sloop-of-war called the *Tempest*."

"Then we shall pray that he will be as safe in her as he was in that frigate. Let us hope cannonballs bounce off her as well."

How quickly that story has spread, thought Clarity, Old Ironsides.

"You have not met our special guest," said Dwight eagerly. "Reverend Beecher, you must introduce her, he is just over there."

"Yes," Beecher agreed. As he led Clarity and Mrs. Marsh across the room, Clarity thought how skillful Dwight was, to direct her to a new and important person to meet while keeping his own line of admirers moving.

They approached a slim young man, elegantly dressed, very dark with curling black hair. She had assumed that he was a Negro and a servant, except he did not bear a tray; indeed he sipped a glass of punch as he conversed among others with great animation, flashing a smile of bright white teeth. His eyes fixed on Clarity as they approached and he did not wait on an introduction but stepped forward, smiling. "What your name?"

"Clarity." She extended her hand. "Mrs. Clarity Putnam."

He took it, surprised that a woman would venture to touch him. That had not been his experience. "Clarity? Like, see far?"

"Yes, exactly."

He giggled unaffectedly. "A clear day. Miss Clear Day!"

"Henry," said Beecher, "you may address her as Mrs. Putnam."

"Yes, of course." The young man smiled. "Please excuse me. My name—" He uttered a brief tumble of syllables that used parts of the tongue and throat unknown to English. "They can't say it, they call me Henry Obookiah."

"Mr. Obookiah," repeated Clarity.

"Very good!"

"Mr. Obookiah, may I introduce you to my mother?"

He bowed somberly. "In my country, people give great honor to mothers."

"Do they indeed?" inquired Mrs. Marsh.

"Oh, yes. People fear kings, honor queens."

Mrs. Marsh cocked her head in perspicacity. "Well, then, I think I like your country very much."

"Thank you! Please, meet my friend, Mr. Edwin Dwight, young cousin of that great man over there."

They were interrupted as the same butler who had gone out to send Freddy to the kitchen entered the parlor to announce that dinner was served, and they began moving toward the dining room. Obookiah stayed by Clarity. "Is not funny? In your country, all people who look like me are slaves!"

"Oh, not slaves!" she exclaimed. "Many of them are servants, but not slaves."

"They have money? Go live where they want?"

"Well, not exactly."

"So, they kind of slaves?"

The company seated themselves, Clarity between Obookiah and her mother, until it was only the elder Dwight who remained standing, at the head of the table. "My dear friends, since as we know the Holy Scripture tells us that wherever even two are gathered in the name of our Lord, there is He also, does it not follow from the arithmetic that wherever"—Dwight tapped his finger quickly in the air, affecting to count the number at the table—

"wherever a dozen and a half are gathered in His name, His loving presence must be nine times greater?"

He paused for the appreciative chuckle to die away.

"Will you favor me by joining me in the first verse of 'Rock of Ages'?" He raised his hand to indicate when to begin.

*Rock of Ages, cleft for me,*
*Let me hide myself in Thee.*
*Let the water and the blood*
*From Thy riven side which flowed*
*Be of sin the double cure,*
*Cleanse me from its guilt and pow'r.*

"Oh, my friends, what a wonderful and instructive song was written by the Reverend Mr. Toplady, back when I was a young man. And while he did eventually fall from the Way, and became a Methodist, still the sentiment of his prayerful song was no less sincere."

Mrs. Marsh leaned halfway over to Clarity, who leaned halfway back. "Please let this not be a long sermon," she whispered, "for I am very hungry."

"Our own movement, whose passion is shared by those around this table, the passion to spread the gospel of our Lord to the heathens around the world, did not begin as it did for Reverend Mr. Toplady, by seeking shelter during a storm in the cleft of a rocky defile in Somerset in England. It began rather here, when five righteous young souls, who had met in a meadow by the Hoosic River six years ago to pray and debate the way of the Lord, sought shelter from a storm in a lowly haystack. And as they looked out upon that harvested field, they realized that the single greatest mission, for them and for all believers, was to bring the light of salvation to the darkest corners of the world. Forasmuch as our Savior gave the Great Commission unto His disciples, He gives it also unto us, to go and preach the Good News to all nations. Thus was born our American Board of Commissioners for Foreign Missions, which those around this table have supported so nobly. And I wish to tell you, as we approach the first anniversary of sending out our first evangelists, to benighted and mysterious India, we have received a letter from their leader, Brother Adoniram Judson. He rejoices to inform us that all of our dear friends who made the journey to India are well, but he is grieved to inform us that owing to the unfortunate state of affairs between the United States and England, the British East India Company have not welcomed them into Calcutta. In fact, they are being thrown out."

An audible groan rose from the company.

The group's corresponding secretary, Samuel Worcester, impossibly young and pretty and self-assured and well dressed, opened his hands to the air. "There, you see? This ill-advised and improvident war which we have launched upon the British thwarts the very will of God."

Before she could check herself, Clarity flashed, yet politely. "Forgive me, Brother Worcester, but if the British Empire were not run by fools like those in Calcutta, we would have no war. Nor would we have needed a revolution, I daresay."

"Keeping to the matter at hand," Dwight interjected with

friendly control, "our brethren report that some Burmese residents of Calcutta have informed them that they may expect a warmer reception among the Buddhists of Burma than they have received among the Hindus of India. Accordingly, they report their present intention to apply to the King of Burma, Bodawpaya, for permission to go there. And they have begun acquiring Burmese texts and have engaged a tutor to learn their language and customs."

"The work of the Lord is righteous," volunteered Lyman Beecher. "No one said it would be easy."

His wife, Roxana, was sitting by him, pale and tired but doggedly the hostess. "And they just spent two years learning the language of the Hindus."

"Oh, that effort is far from wasted," said Dwight with confidence. "They have already translated the most important books of the Bible into the Hindu language, and they will be gotten into the country. And then, when relations between us and the British improve and a permanent mission is established, the ground will be better prepared. Indeed, as we cast our eye about the world even as those first five under the haystack looked at that wet field, we are filled with awe at the sheer scope of the task before us. But we are not discouraged. God is pointing the way, for He has brought among us this remarkable young man who many of you have had the opportunity to meet."

Obookiah leaned over to Clarity and whispered, "He make me blush."

"He comes to us from the Sandwich Islands, on the very opposite side of the world, and totally unknown to civilization, until discovered by the famous Captain Cook, even within the lifetimes of many of us. As he imparts his story to us during our dinner, you will hear, I doubt not, the most remarkable story you have ever heard. And now, dear Lord"—his visage rose upward—"we pray that You will bless this nourishment to our bodies, that we may ever glorify Thee."

Amens murmured around the table as Dwight seated himself and added to Roxana Beecher next to him, "Especially the turtle soup, which I have not tasted these last two years, and which I am beside myself to dip a spoon into."

As the soup was served, Clarity was the first to prompt him. "Do tell us, Mr. Obookiah, how you came among us."

"In my country, you say Sandwich, we call it Hawai'i, there was a war." He was answering her question, but spoke loudly and clearly enough that all could hear. "Old king die, different chiefs have a war to see who be new king."

"That does not sound very sensible," said Clarity.

"True. But always been so." He spoke easily, albeit slowly, making certain the meaning of words before he uttered them. "Any king die, chiefs who want be king go to war. Biggest chief, name Kamehameha, want be king. My chief, Keouakuahuula, also want be king."

"Wait, please!" Clarity touched his hand lightly. She had never heard so many vowels in a row, and tried it herself. "Keoua? Not K-a-e-i-o-u-a?"

Laughter exploded around the table, from Obookiah most of all. "You make joke! Think maybe name got all vowels"—he pointed at her in merry accusation—"but got no *i* in it!"

"Ah, yes. No *i*."

"One day," he continued, "Kamehameha warriors come to my village. Burn houses, kill people. My parents run away. Take me, little brother, run up mountain, hide in cave." His mood began to quiet, and then darken. "Got no water, can't go out, warriors looking everywhere. After two days, my parents say to me, 'You stay here, hide, we go ask for mercy. We done nothing, maybe they not kill us.' They go down, warriors take 'em." His voice broke, but he recovered himself. "Kill 'em, cut 'em in pieces. Cut off heads, make sacrifice to war god."

Clarity had had no idea that his narrative would take such a horrifying turn, and the shock around the table was palpable.

"Thank you, Henry," interrupted Beecher. "We all feel for the pain that you have suffered; perhaps now we should speak of more pleasant things."

Clarity teetered for an instant, deciding whether to speak or not. "Forgive me, Reverend Beecher. We are the ones who compelled him to relive this memory. To cut him off now because it is difficult for us to hear must communicate to him that it is not important to us, and that is most surely not the case. Perhaps we should hear him out." From the silence around the table, Clarity could not divine whether it was because others agreed with her or they were nonplussed that she had contradicted a man, and a clergyman at that. She determined to continue before the others could further calculate her boldness. "Mr. Obookiah, of course you do not have to continue, if it is too painful for you. But we are most interested to hear the rest of your story. What would you prefer?"

"You are very kind, Mrs., I will tell you. Me crying," he said, and shrugged. "Me just little boy, crying. Warrior saw me, said, 'Look up there! Let's go get him!' I took baby brother, carry him across my back, start to run away. One warrior take a spear and throw it. Hawai'i spears." He looked around the room for a comparison. "Very big. Longer than table, maybe high as ceiling. Spear go through my brother, kill him, same spear I feel go in my back. I fall. Warriors come up with clubs and knives. They pull out spear, pull off my brother, I saw him dead. One says, 'Wait! Look! He nephew to Lono. Better not kill him, we take him there.'"

"How terrible," hushed Clarity. "Who was Lono? He must have been very important."

"Lono is god of storms, and harvest, and . . . and, how do you say?" he asked the younger Dwight, who put a napkin to his lips a little too long.

"Fertility," he mumbled.

A hush of "Oh, my" went around the table.

"Me not really nephew to god, my uncle his priest, we say his *kahuna*. They take me to uncle's temple, he raise me, teach me be priest to storm god. Teach me chants, teach me ceremonies, teach me sacrifice people."

"Human sacrifice?" gasped Clarity.

"Oh, yes."

"*You* have sacrificed people?"

"No, no, me just a child, still learning, but watch many times. Later, I visit my mother's sister, warriors come, say she break law. Say she ate banana. Not true." He shook his head. "She no eat banana. But they take her, throw her off cliff. She scream all way down, long way down, so long way. Cliffs at Kealakekua, thousand feet high."

Clarity saw the look in his eyes and realized that he was hearing her fading scream, over again, even at that moment.

"For eating a banana?" asked Mrs. Dwight with incredulity.

"Oh, yes. My country, woman eat banana is terrible sin." Obookiah shook his head again. "My people in such darkness." He gestured around the table. "Men, women, eat together, is terrible sin. In my country, Hawai'i, if we all eat dinner together, we all be taken to temple and killed. Many things like this. I make up my mind, get away! Go anywhere! One night, I jump in water, swim out to American ship. Brig *Triumph*, Captain Brintnall, New Haven." Obookiah was conscious that he had recited ship, master, and home port in the best American fashion, and allowed himself to look just a little proud. "Sailors kind to me. Teach me reading, teach me Bible, teach me Jesus. We go all over world. See China, see Africa, see England. Come to New Haven. I live with Captain Brintnall, he give me more learning."

"You really have come on quite a journey!" said Clarity.

"Yes, ma'am. One day, he show me Yale College. Oh! Young men everywhere, learning." He closed his eyes in rapture, but opened them in sadness. "But no one talk to me. I find library, see books and books and books full of learning, but no one talk to me. I go outside, sit down and cry."

Obookiah laid his hand on Edwin Dwight's arm. "Then this man find me, say, what is wrong? I say, no one will give me learning. He say, we will so give you learning. He take me to Mr. Timothy

Dwight." He nodded across the table to the elder Dwight. "They and others teach me so many things."

"I am so glad," Clarity said.

"They teach me more about Jesus." Obookiah paused, his earnestness profound almost beyond fathoming. "Hawai'i gods no good, you see? We take wood"—he held up his hands—"our hands make 'em. They no see, no hear, no do nothing. They not gods, we make 'em! Me wanna go home, put 'em in a pile, burn 'em up! Christian god," he whispered, "he make us. Send Jesus to love us. My people don't know this. Me wanna go home, teach 'em. But Mr. Dwight, Mr. Beecher, say me not ready."

"Perhaps you should be patient," Clarity suggested. "When you go home, your people will have many questions. If they ask you a question and you cannot answer it, they might not believe you, and that must damage your cause. Should you not be as thoroughly prepared as possible?"

"Yes, ma'am. Me know you are right, they are right, but me in a hurry. Every day, my people live and die in darkness, this hurts me."

There was a moment's quiet around the table. "I have never heard your language," said Clarity. "Will you say something?"

Obookiah thought for just a second, and said gently, *"E pili mau na pomaika'i ia 'oe."*

"And what does it mean?"

"That mean, may blessings be ever with thee."

Mrs. Dwight set down her spoon. "How lovely!"

*"Mahalo nui loa,"* said Obookiah. "That mean, thank you very much." In this fashion the dinner passed through its courses.

"It is a beautiful language," said Clarity, "but I cannot tell how the words are separated. Are there any books?"

"No, no writing in my language. But"—he brightened—"me read English, and speak my language. So me translate Bible for my people."

Mrs. Marsh grew more interested. "But that would require a very thorough knowledge of English. Do you feel you know it quite well enough?"

Obookiah grinned. "Don't need English. Hebrew more easy."

A murmur of "What?" echoed in the room, even from those who had not been taking part in the conversation.

"It is entirely true," said Dr. Dwight, "he is not exaggerating. This past term he has received excellent marks in the biblical languages. There seems to be something in the structure of written Hebrew that resonates in his native tongue. I have no idea what it is, but the connection is astonishing."

"And yet," interjected the younger Edwin Dwight, "there are parts of English that remain beyond him. Henry, try saying, 'The red rabbit ran down the road.'"

Obookiah laughed and dropped his head at having to repeat a parlor trick he had plainly attempted many times before. "The . . ." Then he cocked his head to one side, straining mightily within his mouth to shape his tongue to mimic the sound, but finally spat out "weddwabbit" and stopped in self-censure.

"Try!" encouraged the younger Dwight. "It is not hard. 'The red rabbit.'"

Obookiah tried again but threw up his hands helplessly, leading the others in self-deprecating laughter. "My language, we not make that sound."

"Yes," interjected Clarity. "From what you spoke, it sounds as though in your language, consonants are always followed by vowels, and you make much greater use of vowels than we do."

"Yes!" Obookiah beamed. "Everybody, listen to her, she understand!"

"So," said Mary Dwight, "from what you have told us, in your native religion, to break any commandment is death. There is no provision for forgiveness, or redemption?"

Obookiah held up a hand in correction. "No, that not right. We have place to forgive. Say somebody break kapu. Kahunas chase him, gonna kill him. He run and run, try to reach place to forgive. If he reach it, kahunas there purify him, forgive him. Then, nobody hurt him. This place, called *Pu'uhonua o Honaunau*. That mean City of Refuge."

Edwin Dwight leaned over. "What was that, again?"

"*Pu'uhonua o Honaunau.*" Obookiah's face lit up mischievously. "Can you say?"

"What?"

"You say!" he insisted.

Edwin Dwight hung his head, knowing he had been bested. "Puku," he began, "no, how, now—" and gave up.

"Try!" Obookiah poked him. "Is not hard!" The pointedness of his turning the joke back on Edwin Dwight caused the company to dissolve in laughter, none more so than the younger Dwight himself, nodding gamely, bowing in surrender.

This somber house, thought Clarity, these dour people, surely these sad walls needed many more evenings such as this. "Dr. Dwight," she ventured, "if it can be done, what all would be involved in opening a school for missionaries?"

The venerable president of Yale peeled his spectacles from his face, unmasking the pale and wrinkled thin skin about his eyes, and placed the glasses in a case which he tucked in a pocket. "Oh, my, it will be an effort of years. It would not suffice to send evangelists of the Bible. Missionary work in new lands requires doctors and teachers and farmers, who can elevate their lives, as well as ministers of the gospel. And then those laypeople must also be trained, and not just in the Bible, but in missionary techniques of how to transmit the Good News to the heathen."

"And we would need more native speakers," added Edwin Dwight.

"Got more natives!" enthused Obookiah. "My friend Hopu, came to America with me, he live in Bristol. And Kaumuali'i, he live in New Haven and he the son of a king!"

"And then," said Beecher, "we must provide for the safety of the missionary company. Let us not forget that there have been places in the South Pacific where the British have sent missionaries, who wound up not just feeding the hungry, they *were* the dinner."

"Have you considered this well, Henry?" asked the elder Dwight. "If you return home and attack your people's ancient religion, they may turn on you and kill you."

"I am ready," Obookiah said, a little defiantly. "That Bible says, 'He who lose his life for my sake shall find it.' Is it not so? If is God's will that I die telling people about Jesus, I am ready. Are you not ready?"

313

"We all commend your zeal, Henry," said Beecher, "but there is much more to consider, such as the safety of the women. And, certainly, we could only send married couples to undertake such an effort."

"Oh, yes, absolutely," Timothy Dwight said, and nodded in agreement.

That was an element Clarity had not expected. "What? Why?"

Beecher looked embarrassed. "My dear, the South Seas are home to, shall we say, a licentious culture, utterly lacking in shame-facedness. Their aggression and perverseness in this regard has been the downfall of Western sailors since the islands were discovered. The temptations have proven insuperable to the strongest Christian single men. We dare only send missionaries who are already well settled in the marital estate."

"And"—the elder Dwight raised one finger—"couples who can provide examples of godly, Christian marriage to the heathen."

When Clarity's mother dabbed her lips with her napkin and said, "Well, at least we're good for something," it raised a new din of laughter around the table.

A tiny figure appeared in the doorway, barefoot, in a nightgown, clutching a doll, noticed simultaneously by several of the company. "Well, good evening, young lady," said Mrs. Dwight.

Beecher's back was to the door and he turned in his chair. "Harriet! Child, why are you not in bed?"

The child of barely four rubbed her eyes. "I heard laughing. It sounded so gay."

"Still, my dear, you should be asleep."

Clarity sensed the situation and rose. "She was asleep, Reverend. It was our boisterousness that disturbed her rest." Her gaze caught that of Roxana Beecher; she was pale, able to sit and eat but she had said little, and it was obvious that mounting the stairs would exhaust her. "With your permission, I will take her back up and put her to bed."

"We would be most obliged," said Beecher.

Clarity rose and walked over to the door. "Would you like that, Harriet?"

"Yes, please, Mrs. Putnam." She extended her hand, but rather than take it Clarity reached under her arm and hefted her up, and Harriet wrapped her arm around Clarity's neck. "Oh my goodness," Clarity groaned. "You are getting to be a big girl!"

"Good night, Father."

"Good night, Harriet. Off you go, now."

In the hall Clarity found a single candlestick, which she lit from the sconce on the wall. "Hang on tight!" She felt Harriet tighten her grip as with her free hand Clarity gathered her dress before her and she mounted the New England stairs, steep and narrow as a ship's ladder. When she reached the top, Harriet whispered, "You should put me down now, Mrs. Putnam. I don't want you to strain yourself."

Clarity set her down noiselessly. "Do you want me to come bundle you back into bed?"

"Oh, yes, please. My sisters sleep very deeply, we will not wake them."

"Do you have a warming pan?"

"Oh, it is still warm from before."

"All right." The mattress was of deep down, still bearing the impress of Harriet's body from when she left. Clarity pulled the covers up to her chin.

"Will you tell me a story?"

Clarity betrayed no outer hint of it, but inside she felt a wash of panic. She had never told a story before in her life, and now suddenly she was confronted by her own incongruity. What kind of author must she ever be if she could not tell a story to satisfy a four-year-old? She stalled. "Does Papa tell you stories?" she whispered.

"Sometimes."

"What are they about?"

"Bad people who go to hell and burn up forever."

"Oh, my!" She hardly knew what to think of what struck her as appalling parental ineptitude, to terrorize toddlers with the flames of hell. "Well! Well, do you have any of Mr. Newbery's story books?"

"Yes. *Little Goody Two-Shoes* is my favorite."

"Is it nearby?"

"Yes, on the chest under my little sewing box."

The bed frame made a tiny creak as the ropes suspending the mattress relaxed when she got up to fetch it.

"Would you read me chapter four, please? It is very short."

"Very well." Clarity leaned forward into the candlelight to search for it.

Harriet whispered eagerly, "Page eighteen."

Clarity noted how this was likely significant but set it aside as she read very softly, "'Chapter four: How Little Margery Learned to Read, and by Degrees Taught Others.' Little Margery saw how good and wise Mr. Smith was, and concluded that this was owing to his great learning: Therefore she wanted of all Things to learn to read. For this Purpose she used to meet the little Boys and Girls as they came home from School—"

Harriet proved correct, the chapter was only three pages long, and two of those had woodcut illustrations covering half of them. Yet Harriet look so relaxed at the end that Clarity thought she had fallen asleep again, but when she stopped reading, Harriet opened her eyes and whispered, "May I tell you a secret?"

"Of course, my dear."

"I am like Margery. I, too, have a secret plan to learn to read." She motioned with a finger for Clarity to lean closer. "I must whisper it right in your ear."

Clarity found her smile growing as the confidence passed between them. "Of course I will help you learn, darling. Never fear, I will discuss it with your father, and we will see what we can work out. Can you sleep now?"

"Oh, yes."

Clarity knelt down to her level. "You are a very grown-up and thoughtful little girl." She did not add her amazement to hear Harriet talking like a miniature adult.

"Thank you for bringing me up. Good night."

Clarity was uncertain whether the child was capable in this frozen house of reaching out for affection, and so kissed her on the forehead. "Good night, my darling."

For just a second Harriet beamed, her first artless act of the night, and closed her eyes.

Clarity gathered her dress again and descended the stairs, to find the company disbanding in the hall. "Oh," she said to Dr. Dwight, "I fear I have missed out on more learned discourse."

"As when you were little? Ha! I suspect that you understood more of what passed around you than you let on."

She took his hand. "All children do, don't you think?"

"I know it may seem a bit early to break up our gathering, but many, other than yourself and mother, have come from distant points, and we must allow them to return home before the hour is too terribly late."

Clarity helped her mother arrange her cloak, after which Mrs. Marsh finally extended her hand to him. "Dr. Dwight, the evening has been as stimulating as it was entertaining. We are so delighted that you invited us." Freddy had brought the sleigh to the front door and Dwight helped her up into it.

Seeking out Clarity, Obookiah bowed. "To you me bid very good night, Mrs. Putnam."

Clarity recognized his restraint, and extended her hand in the modern way. "Good night, Mr. Obookiah. I have so enjoyed meeting you."

He took her hand, again surprised that she had offered it. "Thank you."

Discreetly she leaned forward. "And just between us, I rather like Miss Clear Day."

Obookiah smiled but knew better now than to laugh, bowed again, and backed away.

Mrs. Marsh had already snuggled beneath the blanket in her sleigh as Beecher accosted Clarity at the front door. "My dear Mrs. Putnam, may I offer you a small word of caution?"

Clarity was arranging the hood of her cloak over her hair. "Of course, Reverend."

"Henry Obookiah has made great strides toward civilization since coming to the Lord. But there are still many things he does not understand."

"Yes?"

"He is a young man, with a young man's desires, and should you become too friendly with him—" Beecher was clearly struggling. "If we can get him home, among his own people, perhaps he can marry, but no one has yet put it to him plainly that he shall never have a white woman. He does not understand the difference in color, in his yet degraded condition."

Clarity looked full into Beecher's eyes set in his face like melting wax. "You mean in his innocence?"

Beecher winced. "I mean, in his lack of sophistication. It would be easy for you, however unwittingly, to lead him into . . . impossible expectations."

She extended her hand. "I shall take heed. Mother is waiting, good night."

Freddy helped her into the carriage, and tucked a blanket around their legs and under their feet. "Daughter," said Mrs. Marsh suddenly, "this was a day that the Lord hath made, and I did not rejoice in it. We are bundled warmly and the night is beautiful. How would you feel about just taking a short ride?"

Clarity made a mighty attempt to hide the earthquake that rocked her, for she had never known her mother to do anything spontaneous. "I should like it," she said. "I should like to very much. Freddy, would you be willing?"

Meriden had the reins in hand. "That would be well. The horses have had no exercise today. Where shall we go?"

"Do you know," said Mrs. Marsh, "it has been many years since I have been out to our pond. With moonlight and the snow? I should like to see it. You know its location, I believe, Mr. Meriden?"

"Indeed I do," said Freddy. He flicked the pair lightly with the reins and turned up the North Road toward Goshen at an easy canter.

It was six miles to Goshen, but their pond tract lay not quite so far. Almost at once Clarity was lost in thought, which turned to the strange young man she had conversed with and perhaps befriended. She had not ever deeply considered the largeness of the world, that there were whole societies with ancient ways of living of which she had no understanding—a world of deep mystery. It seemed a great mistake to think of the English or the Americans as innately superior, the English with their imperial hauteur, the Americans with their clinging to slavery. Surely this darker sea of humanity extended across all races, each capable of unspeakable cruelty and depravity, yet surely susceptible to the elevation of kindness. Bliven had told her something of this when he returned from the Barbary Coast, told her of the customs of the Berbers— people in some ways still savages, yet people who prostrated themselves and prayed five times each day. She knew no one who prayed five times a day.

These Sandwich Islanders, Henry Obookiah's people, seemed to have never heard of the Lord God, yet they were a people to whom the original language of the Bible was closer to their native tongue than English was. Could it be that there was something in their innocence, also, that was closer to God? Could it be that there might be ways in which they were in fact closer to God than Beecher was, with all his chilly fussing and pettifogging?

"You are very pensive, my dear."

Clarity had not noticed that her mother had taken her hand for some minutes, and smiled quickly. "Yes, I suppose I am."

She imagined that the evening's events presented her with a new sewing box, tightly packed with topics to think on. She agreed to own it and to think on them, and so allowed herself for the moment to settle back and enjoy the moonlight and snow, and sleigh bells, and the rolling pale fields as they glided by.

A mile short of Goshen, Freddy turned the horses east down an unmarked lane, faint but perceptible under the snow. It soon began to follow a tumbling brook, into a patch of forest, where the water broadened into the pond, frozen blue-white, where Freddy reined in the horses in a clearing.

"Oh, yes, I remember," said Mrs. Marsh quietly. "Do you know, Daughter, this is where your father and I started our life together."

She did know very well, from many tellings. "I cannot imagine anything more romantic, Mama."

Mrs. Marsh removed a gloved hand from beneath their blanket and pointed. "I know the cornerstones of our little house must still be in those trees over there. Your father inherited this tract, and when he went into business he rode every day into Goshen and back again. His family were the founders of Litchfield, but he did not want to just follow along on what they had done, and he removed himself until he did well enough to move back on more independent terms."

"Yes. I imagine that is a reason why he overcame his objection to my desire to marry Bliven. He saw a little of himself in him."

"I did not know until many years later that he placed a mortgage on this property to buy his first stake in the trading company. I have so little head for gambling, I should have died from fear. He did not tell me until he safely held the deed again."

Conversation faded, and but for a snort from the horses, and the small distant tumble of water as the pond flowed out into the brook from beneath its frozen crust, the silence was utter. "I was not very brave, you see," Mrs. Marsh continued after a time. "I mean, who among us can know where life will take us? Look at that young man tonight, from the Sandwich Islands. From where he started, how could he have ever imagined being here now? Either God has a plan for us, or it is a fantasy. Yet look at his life, who could say it is not the product of design?"

"Yes," said Clarity. "Indeed." She had no idea that her mother was also thinking upon Obookiah.

"I have had a good life, Daughter."

"Mama! Please, do not sound so final. Let us hope you have many good years left with us."

Mrs. Marsh squeezed her hand, but delayed responding. "Yes. I have. I have had a good life. Yet, I should have been happier, had I not been afraid. Thank you for your trouble, Mr. Meridan, you may take us home now."

Back in town, Freddy saw Mrs. Marsh safe into her house, then turned south past their livery stable to Putnam Farm, where Clarity was out of the carriage before he could descend to help her. She reached up and pressed two silver dollars into his hand. "Thank you for your extra trouble."

"Oh, now, Mrs. Putnam, you needn't. I was happy to do it."

She curled his fingers around the coins. "I know I needn't, and I know you were. Ha! In my church we do not celebrate Christmas, but I am coming to think that this has become less a point of theology, and more an affectation to stick our noses in the air and show everyone how holy we are, and that cannot be a good thing. So let us think of this as a little acknowledgment of the season."

"Then I thank you kindly, ma'am, and I wish you a happy Christmas."

# 10

### New Year's Broadsides

On the weather deck of the *Java*, Bliven was taking in some fresh air, reflecting on it being almost the last day of 1812. The sea was nearly calm, with the swells low and easy, the wind light and northeasterly; it was coming on nine o'clock in the morning. The thin green line of the Brazilian jungle was visible to their northwest. They were before the wind under easy sail, in company with an American prize they had recently taken, whose crew was confined in the cable tier. Bliven had heard Kington say that they would put into São Salvador to unload their prisoners and register their prize before coming back out to resume hunting. The gun crews were occupied below in holystoning the deck, and rinsing it off with water pumped up by the elm trees. Sam would be on his hands and knees with them, physically able but no doubt in a barely contained disgust.

"Deck! Deck!" The shout came down from the masthead.

Kington himself was on deck to answer: "What do you see?"

"Sail, to the south, about six miles."

Kington and First Lieutenant Chads strode to the rail and raised their glasses. Without the advantage of height, all they could see was a speck of white on the horizon. "What do you think, m'lord?" asked Chads.

Kington calculated quickly. "The *Bonne Citoyenne* should still be in Salvador repairing from her grounding. I know of no other vessel traversing these waters. Make all sail to catch up with her."

Bliven observed the staysails being set and realized they must be giving chase. An hour went by before the call came down again. "Deck!"

"What do you see?"

"She has changed her course, now making southeast!"

"What can you make of her?"

"A large ship, sir! I would say a frigate!"

Bliven edged his way aft as he casually leaned against the rail, to better overhear the talk on the quarterdeck. After a quick look Kington tapped the end of his glass in his other hand. "Well, Mr. Chads, why do you think she would do that?"

"She has seen us and wishes to escape, sir?"

"No, Mr. Chads, she is luring us into international waters. If she is American, she will not want to engage us in the territorial waters of a neutral. I would wager anything that is what is transpiring. Signal the prize crew to take their ship into Salvador, and once she breaks off, set your stuns'ls and take up the chase."

"Very good, m'lord."

In another two hours, coming upon noon, it was clear that not only were they gaining on the ship rapidly, but that their chase had shortened sail to allow it, and again come to a port tack to take them farther from land.

Chads peered steadily at her through his glass. "It is a frigate, sir, and a frigate that heavy can only be an American. She is hoisting signals, but I don't recognize them."

Bliven's heart leapt. The *United States* and the *President* were with Rodgers in the North Atlantic. That left only one forty-four, the *Constitution* herself.

"Well, hoist our own signals and we'll see if she shows her colors."

"Very good, m'lord."

Bliven saw the flags flutter aloft, which he knew would be unintelligible to their quarry.

"Mr. Putnam," he heard Kington call out. "Come to the quarterdeck, if you please."

Bliven obeyed very willingly. "Captain—forgive me, I mean, my lord?"

Kington pointed with his glass at the vessel they were approaching. "You will have seen that we have taken up the chase of what we believe is one of your ships. Take a look through my glass, please, and tell me if you can identify her." He handed his scope to Bliven.

What he saw in the lighted circle of the glass elated him beyond description, but he did not answer for several seconds, enjoying studying her from stem to stern. She had shortened sail to allow the British to catch up, and she had cleared for action. He returned the scope. "Yes, sir, as I well know from her figurehead, it is the

*Constitution*, forty-four, last I knew under command of Captain Isaac Hull, a very formidable seaman."

Kington tried to smile, but it appeared more a leer. "Formidable seaman, is he?"

"Yes, sir. I had the good fortune to be aboard her when he eluded the entire Halifax squadron last autumn, and also when he defeated and sank the *Guerriere*, Captain Dacres." Surely, he thought, if he threw out enough bait, this preening peacock would fatally take it.

"Captain, she is unfurling colors, indeed she is American!"

Kington and Chads both studied through their glasses. Even without a telescope, Bliven could see the American flag trailing from the spanker boom, almost as large as the sail itself.

"Well," said Kington, "as much as I loathe to credit an American with gentlemanly behavior, he shortened sail to allow us to catch him, he steered into international waters to avoid violating a neutral, and he has shown us his colors with unmistakable theatre. He has sent us an engraved invitation to battle, and we are going to oblige him. Beat to quarters, Mr. Chads. Mr. Putnam, you will oblige me to confine yourself to the berth deck for the duration."

"As you wish, my lord. You are holding my crew in the cable tier. May I at least warn them to prepare themselves for a battle?"

Kington considered it, preferring to refuse. "Very well, but you may see them for a moment only. Do not tarry, do you hear?"

"Of course not, thank you."

Bliven descended to the cable tier on the orlop. "Boys," he said as they gathered, "we are shortly in for a fight. It is with the *Consti-*

*tution*, so this ship must lose. Do not worry, I will make sure you are not trapped down here."

He ascended by the forward ladder, and in walking aft paused by Sam's gun. "Mr. Bandy, how are you faring?" It seemed wise to maintain their charade.

"Well enough, Captain, I thank you, but for a sprain in my ankle."

"Oh? Let me see." He knelt and felt the ankle and a short ways higher, and flexed his foot. "Sam," he whispered, "it's the *Constitution*. We're about to take a hell of a beating. If we collide, I am going to jump for it. Are you with me?"

"Jump for it?" hissed Sam. "That is insane!"

"Are you with me?"

"Oh, hell, of course I am with you!"

"Do as they tell you. I think there is going to be such confusion we can run right out." Bliven stood up. "I will tell Dr. Kite about it," he said loudly. "He will have a look at it when he has an opportunity."

Bliven ascended back to the quarterdeck and approached Kington, who was surprised and not pleased. "What is it? I thought you went below."

"My lord, it occurs to me, it would be a great courtesy to relieve your American pressed men of the obligation to fire upon their own flag."

Kington's jaw went slack with surprise. "Are you mad? Of course not, that is out of the question. Now get below, sir!"

"My lord, the same kindness was extended by Captain Dacres of the *Guerriere* to his American captives."

"What! Yes, and look how that ended for him. Now get out of here!"

They were interrupted by the clapping boom of a shot from the *Constitution*, which a few seconds later they heard whiz through the rigging. Kington's attention deserted Bliven in an instant, and that look came over him, that mad, predatory, intensely alive look that he had seen before. Kington glanced aloft. With the wind from the northeast he could adjust several points to starboard without disturbing the canvas. "Mr. Chads, they are too far for the carronades, but they are in range of the eighteens. Come to starboard until your port guns bear. Fire a broadside and then return to this heading."

"Very good, m'lord."

Bliven heard the orders relayed and felt the ship enter a turn, then braced himself against the staccato broadside of the fourteen port eighteen-pounders. Kington studied their target through his glass and then exulted, "You've hit her! Good shooting!"

"Thank you, sir. May I recommend the identical maneuver, to port, sir?"

"You may indeed. Ready your starboard broadside and yaw to port. Ease off the yards if you need to."

The ship swung through ninety degrees before the starboard broadside boomed out. Bliven could imagine how Sam felt about having to fire on his own ship.

"You've hit her again, by God! Magnificent!" crowed Kington.

Two more shots from the *Constitution* sang through the rigging without effect. *Why doesn't she turn? Why doesn't she answer?* Bliven wondered with anguish, and then he remembered how Hull fought the *Guerriere*. He held his fire until he absolutely crushed her at a single stroke with overwhelming weight of point-blank twenty-four-pound broadside.

"We hold the weather gauge," said Kington with a note of triumph. "Close on her and we will rake her."

"Yes, m'lord. Yes, of course!"

*Java* was lighter and faster, but just as she overreached the *Constitution* and could turn across her bow and rake her, the American wore completely around to the west and prevented it. *Java* matched the turn, and still faster came again, this time on *Constitution*'s weather beam, threatening again to cross her path and rake her, but the American wore again and ran southeast.

"Bastard," shouted Kington, and again matched his turn, only this time, instead of coming upon his beam, he turned short and delivered a withering stern rake across the *Constitution*'s quarterdeck.

Less than a third of a mile now separated the two, and Kington could not judge the effect of this broadside immediately. Bliven was nauseated at the course of the battle, until he saw the *Constitution* emerge from behind the smoke, her main and fore courses suddenly dropped in a surge of speed, and deliver a thundering broadside, twenty-fours and carronades together. Bliven dove to the deck as the salvo carried away *Java*'s headsails, jibboom, and bowsprit together, and that and the sheer weight of iron crashing into her brought her to a dead stop.

And now the *Constitution* closed, firing at will, holing *Java*'s hull, carronades stripping her rigging, Marines in the fighting tops picking off crewmen. Kington himself went down with a musket ball in the shoulder but struggled to his feet, screaming, "Lay your helm aweather!" It was obvious to Chads that this would bring her before the wind, and with that the only chance to escape the slaughter by crashing into the *Constitution*'s stern.

There was a pause now in the firing as no one's guns would bear. It was slow, it was inexorable, that *Java*'s stem crunched into the *Constitution*'s taffrail, her forward speed arrested so suddenly that most of the men standing were thrown from their feet. *Poor Hull*, thought Bliven suddenly, *his cabin will be wrecked again*. The silence was brief, it was eerie, when the *Java* was rent by a mighty, popping crack as the foremast split, its height so great that its fighting top crowded with Marines seemed to plummet only slowly to the spar deck, through the grate to the gun deck, and through that hatch to the berth deck. The chorus of screams was audible all the way down until all lay in a heap of limbs and torsos, the whole pile seeming to struggle to move as the injured attempted to crawl from beneath the dead.

Bliven flew down the ladder to the berth deck and rushed into the debris before any could follow. "Lie still, you are hurt," he urged. "Help is coming. Be quiet, now, help is coming." None noticed him slip two loaded pistols into his coat pockets.

A gray-haired surgeon's mate appeared from the cockpit below, and Bliven helped him move one of the wounded to the ladder. "Wait, now," he exclaimed, "you're that Yankee Doodle. This is very kind of you, I'm sure."

"I would take this one next, he seems hurt the worst."

"Thank you, laddie," said the surgeon's mate. "You go on, now, we'll manage here."

In the confusion, no one took notice as Bliven emerged from

the waist ladder onto the gun deck. Sam saw him coming and was on his feet, ready. Bliven handed him a pistol. "Forward ladder, forward to the heads and try to get across!"

The one Marine still standing guard at the waist ladder saw them running forward in a crouch. "Halt!" he cried.

He was still leveling his musket when Bliven turned and fired his pistol, the ball striking him in the center of the chest and sprawling him backward. There was no opposition at the forward ladder, and they ran up into the confusion and wreckage of the spar deck. The *Constitution* loomed high before them, but just as they reached the stump of the bowsprit it wrenched slowly free.

Sam looked across and saw the American gunners holding the lanyards of their stern chasers and knew he had but a second to decide. He screamed, "Jump!" and the two sailed over just as the ripping discharges filled the space between the two ships.

Bliven was conscious even as he hit the water that he must not plunge too deep, and he began flailing his hands to surface from the instant he submerged. Back on the surface, water slung from his hair as he searched about. "Sam! Sam!"

He had been on his right and had struck the water first, and flatter. Bliven sucked in air to fill his lungs and dove, swimming in that direction, seeing nothing. He surfaced again. "Sam!" He heaved in several more breaths and dove again, deeper, just seeing Sam's white shirt and blond hair sinking ever so slowly. Against the sting of the salt in his eyes he seized hold of Sam's arm and pulled and kicked to the surface with all his strength.

Back in air he wheezed a loud breath, just took note of an ugly discolored wound on the side of Sam's forehead, and began pulling him toward the *Constitution*'s side. It was also apparent that after the ships separated, they had begun to twist back upon themselves, and high above them another full, deafening broadside poured into the stricken *Java*. More to the moment, he realized that the two giants were drifting closer to each other, and if they were caught between the *Java*'s hull and the *Constitution*'s flaring tumble home, they would be crushed like beetles.

"Help! Help up there! Help us!" He pulled Sam toward a line that trailed down the *Constitution*'s side and seized it. "Help us!"

He did not see who it was that threw a length of net over to him and, after he clung to it, walked him aft toward the boarding ladder.

Two stout sailors descended it and seized Sam's limp form under his arms, and with a grip so tight that they must leave bruises hefted him up to the spar deck. Bliven followed, shivering, quickly enough that when he gained the deck he saw Sam being carried at a run, disappearing down the waist ladder.

A sailor threw a heavy blanket over Bliven's shoulders. "Are you all right?"

Bliven scrubbed at his face and hair with the blanket. "Thank you, yes." He glanced about just long enough to get his bearings, and walked quickly to the quarterdeck.

There the officer in command was facing obliquely away from him, observing the receding stern windows of the *Java*—or what remained of them. He turned upon being hailed, and Bliven nearly fainted from shock. "Mr. Bainbridge!" he cried. Bainbridge, the reckless incompetent, as he remembered, who lost the *Philadelphia* at Tripoli.

"Mr. Putnam!" Bainbridge answered with equal surprise. "You it was we fished out?"

"Yes, sir."

"How came you—"

"I was in command of the *Tempest*, twenty, when the *Java* overhauled us and we had to engage. We were overwhelmed; I and the surviving crew were taken prisoner."

Bainbridge pursed his lips sourly. "Bad luck, then, you had no chance. And who was that with you?"

"Samuel Bandy, an American merchant captain pressed into service aboard the *Java*. He was formerly in our Navy; we served together in the Mediterranean."

"Yes, I remember the name. Are you all right?"

"Yes, sir, I thank you. Now, if you please, Captain, may I recommend that you direct your fire against *Java*'s mizzen? When we fought her I am sure we once struck her mizzen and damaged it, and since being taken prisoner I can tell you that it is not well spliced."

Bainbridge regarded his opponent across the short distance still separating them. *Java*'s courses had been reefed in the clearing for action, even as had his own. Her topsails were well holed from his raking fire and were leaking wind, so *Java*'s roundly filled spanker was the larger part of her propulsion. At this short distance they had every hope of bringing it down. "Mr. Chance!" roared Bainbridge. "Load your carronades with bar shot. Concentrate fire on her mizzen. Keep at it till you bring it down."

*Mr. Chance*, thought Bliven. *How wonderfully appropriate.*

A shouted affirmation came back. Powder monkeys had just

deposited charges of grape in the garlands beside the carronades, and now they were sent scurrying below to return with bar shot.

"Look there, Putnam"—Bainbridge pointed—"she's coming 'round for more, she's not done. That is most obliging."

Suddenly Bliven noticed something terribly amiss. "Captain, where is your wheel?"

"Shot away," answered Bainbridge. "Luckily, we were already where we wanted to be. I've got men below, wrestling the tiller."

In a rush, the enormity of this calamity seized him, and Bliven realized why Bainbridge had positioned the bosun where he had and was barking orders rapid-fire to brace up the port or starboard topsail yards to catch or spill the wind—he was guiding the ship in a way to make it easier on the men below who were working the tiller, steering the ship by the sheer power of their muscles. Bliven found his earlier critical opinion of Bainbridge diluted in his wash of admiration for such seamanship.

Suddenly from the gun deck beneath them, the *Constitution* rocked with a deep, roaring broadside from the twenty-fours. Almost simultaneously Bliven saw a brown wooden shower rise from the *Java*, splinters large and small, bits of hull and railing, before the scene was obscured by the pungent hanging pall of smoke that the wind began only slowly to clear.

From this white cloud came a singing spit; a small splinter of wood twirled up from the pine deck between them where a musket ball had bit into the wood. Involuntarily, Bliven jerked to the side, but Bainbridge stuck fast on his two feet. "Lieutenant of Marines!" Bainbridge's voice was loud but he was not shouting.

"Yes, sir!"

"It is bad enough that I stand here with a British ball in my ass, I do not propose to have my toes shot off as well. Direct your men in the tops to fire on their tops. Clear their sharpshooters out of there. They will have to take their shots through the tops'ls, but they must manage best they can."

"Yes, sir."

A sheet of flame erupted from the carronade farthest forward, followed instantly by a spray of railing, and a hole popped open in *Java*'s spanker but did not seem to catch the mizzenmast. *Constitution* was passing her only slowly, giving the guns time to sight individually on the target and each try their luck. In the course of the slow, rolling broadside, they shivered *Java*'s mizzen twice before a third hit caused it to split. The wind that filled the spanker caused the mizzen to lay over to starboard, creating confusion on the quarterdeck.

Bainbridge loped forward a few steps, one hand pressuring against his wounded hip, the other gesturing with his telescope. "Huzzah, boys! That's good shooting! Well done!"

He was answered by a cheer from the crews at the carronades.

"Bosun!" barked Bainbridge.

"Sir!"

"We are going to lay off for a while. She cannot go anywhere and cannot run up on us. She has cut up our rigging something fearful. Get to work on it, fast as you can. Ha! And look here, gentlemen." He pointed to their own mizzenmast, indicating a hole where an eighteen-pound ball had smashed clean through. "Look here. Hit it dead center but didn't bring it down. That is wondrous. Have the carpenter splint it; think of Dr. Cutbush working a broken leg."

"Right away, Captain."

As the *Constitution* sheared away, the *Java* ventured one more broadside with the half of her guns that remained in action but managed only to set their own fallen canvas afire. Dismasted and wallowing, it was apparent that she was going nowhere. Slowly the *Constitution* wore off and hove to, as the bosun, his mate, and four of the most able seamen fanned out, armed with marlinspikes and a deep knowledge of the lines and knots required. Others paid them lengths of new line from below as the damage was cut away. They began with the standing rigging, for if without their support the masts became overburdened, they could snap as surely as if they had been felled by shot; they moved on to the running rigging to regain controls of the sails, and slowly the whole vast web of rigging reappeared as though woven by a great invisible spider. Yet, it was the hole just breezed through the mizzen that became the talk of the weather deck as men wondered aloud if the ship was charmed with invulnerable masts as well as an impenetrable hull.

"Lieutenant Putnam." Bainbridge turned to speak to him, and Bliven saw a streak of red blood on the captain's upper trousers that had been hidden by his coat, and realized that Bainbridge had indeed been shot in the hip.

"Your pardon, sir, I am now master commandant."

"Oh? I was not aware. Well, good. We have things in hand here. Would you care to go below and see to your friend?"

"You are most considerate, sir, yes, I would." He had just started toward the after ladder when *Java*'s side erupted with an explosion, not a large one, which they concluded must have been a powder charge intended for a gun, touched off by the deck fire. Bliven clattered down the ladder, past the gun deck to the berth deck, and down again to the orlop, where he saw the cockpit brightly lit forward.

"Well, bless my soul!" Cutbush smiled, excited but quiet. "I saw Mr. Bandy and wondered if you could be far behind."

Cutbush snatched impatiently at Sam's too-tight trousers. "Get these off him," he said urgently to the surgeon's mates, even as he turned his own attention to opening a beat-up cabinet and extracting a small mahogany chest with brass fittings. He turned back around, hefting the mahogany box, to find the mates struggling to peel the trousers around Sam's ample butt. "No, no," he snapped, "you'll pull him in two! Cut them off! Mr. Putnam, I can use you. We must raise his feet and lower his head. Here, raise the plank where his feet are." Bliven did as he was bidden, as Cutbush wedged a small medicine box under it, leaving Sam's head about eight inches lower than his feet. "Now pull his shirt off over his head, quickly, and begin pressing on his back. We want to work his lungs."

Bliven peeled the tail of the soaked shirt upward over Sam's back and his sodden hair, stretching his arms out and pulling the sleeves until the shirt fell to the deck with a soggy splat. In the illumination of the battle lamps Bliven saw the still-livid red scars on Sam's white back and understood that he had been lashed with a cat, even as he realized that the wounds were likely old and since healed. Bliven pressed and released, slowly and forcefully, and pressed and released. "Like this? Correct me!" His fear for Sam's life was surfacing despite his knowing that there was a reason for Cutbush's determined calm.

Cutbush did not look up from what he was doing to ask, "How on earth did you come to be here?"

Bliven stared at him as he compressed Sam's back. "We swam!"

Cutbush erupted in laughter. "All the way from home?"

"No, sir, we were prisoners on the *Java*. We jumped overboard after the ships became entangled."

"Well, there is a story there, I expect. You must tell it to me when we have leisure."

With Sam's trousers cut away, one of the mates was scrubbing him vigorously with dry toweling as Cutbush removed a tightly woven tube from the mahogany case. At its terminus he rubbed a brownish sort of grease, nodding at the other mate. "Spread his cheeks."

The orderly did as he was bidden, and Cutbush flinched up and away for an instant. Captive sailors held as virtual galley slaves he knew could not be too particular in their hygiene. He inserted two inches of the tube before telling the mate to release his hips, whose own pressure would keep it in place. From the same mahogany case he removed a cork from a small ceramic jar and took out a large measure of tobacco. With no wasted motion he packed the tobacco into a tiny glass jar with a tube coming out its bottom, lit it with a brand that he had held over a lamp, and fitted it under a glass bell. With his surgeon's precision, Cutbush fitted the free end of the first tube from Sam's anus to the front exit of a small bellows and attached the second tube from the glass bottle now filling with smoke to a round fitting at the rear of the bellows.

"All right, now," he breathed. Slowly he spread the handles of the bellows apart, which sucked air through the burning tobacco even as a smoker would inhale. When the bellows would open no farther, Cutbush slowly began to close it; a valve shut the smoke from returning backward and forced it into Sam's backside. He repeated the procedure slowly and gently, reciting quietly,

> *Tobacco glyster, breathe and bleed,*
> *Keep warm and rub till you succeed.*
> *And spare no pains, for what you do*
> *May one day be repaid to you.*

"Do you see how this works?" he asked the first surgeon's mate. "Yes, sir."

"You keep doing it, very slowly, until the tobacco is burnt down." Then, to the other one, he ordered, "Bring me that bowl."

With practiced precision Cutbush extended Sam's right arm, opened a vein with a scalpel, and doggedly recited the poem again as Sam's blood dribbled into the bowl. When he had taken a pint he bound the wound tightly and gave the bowl to the second mate to remove.

Cutbush noted a thin stream of water and drool issue from Sam's mouth. "Good. Putnam, keep at it until I tell you to stop."

Two decks above them they heard the deep, rolling broadside of each twenty-four in turn, and realized that they must have come about and returned to the fight. It was followed by the increasing rattle of musketry from the fighting tops as the Marines began dueling with their English counterparts. Bliven hoped that, as in the Revolution, the New World marksmanship of lifelong hunters would carry the day.

Suddenly all the men on the orlop ducked and caught their breath as a tremendous crash broke above and beside them, not the reports even of the twenty-fours but something louder and closer, a deafening, whacking bang that shook the hull planks beyond the diagonal scantling and sent a cloud of dust filtering down from where the oak knees supported the pine of the berth deck.

"God Almighty!" spat Cutbush.

"We have taken a hit," hushed Bliven. "They are going for our waterline. I can't see." He took up one of the lanterns and gave it to the second surgeon's mate. "Hold this up there." He pointed to the join at the top of the knee, as close as he could judge to where the noise came from. Bliven peered as best he could into the flickering shadows. *Constitution*'s waterline was just about opposite them, but he could discern no leak, nor even a distension. "Amazing," he whispered. He saw that a surgeon's mate had taken over pressing Sam's back, and Bliven went forward two more steps and held the lantern up to the other side of the knee that had been hidden in shadow, but found it equally undamaged. "I can't believe it," he said back to Cutbush. "No breach at all, thank God."

Then all was drowned out by another rolling, roaring broadside from the carronades farther above them. Those echoes had almost died away when their eardrums were all but crushed by a louder rolling broadside from the twenty-fours immediately above. "God," said Bliven, "Bainbridge is really letting them have it."

With intense attention Cutbush held a small mirror before Sam's nose and mouth, heaving an immense sigh as a light fog spotted it. "He breathes," he said. "Oh, he breathes." From his professional bearing one would have thought that he had no emotional investment in whether Sam lived or died, but now he gave himself away. He smiled wanly and relaxed. "He breathes."

A midshipman walked quickly over and made his respects. "Commander Putnam?"

"Yes?"

"Captain Bainbridge's compliments, you are wanted on the quarterdeck."

"Very well"—he returned the salute—"I will be along immediately."

He ascended the after ladder so quickly that his eyes had not enough time to adjust to his return to daylight, and he squinted as he approached Bainbridge, even as hard by he saw the *Java*, standing off and smoldering, her mizzenmast fallen over the starboard railing, the spanker blanketing much of the quarterdeck. "Captain?" Bliven saluted.

"Commander, she is wounded but has not struck. My chase gunner is killed. Get forward and take over. Continue firing as you can bring the chasers to bear, until you are ordered to cease."

"Aye, sir!"

Bliven sprinted forward, from the quarterdeck to the bow chasers, almost the entire length of the ship, thinking as he ran that

Bainbridge had altered their configuration with two eighteens forward. He stopped and seized by the shoulders a boy whose hands were at that moment empty. "Bow chasers, eighteens, bring me powder and grape! Hurry!"

At the farthest point forward on the spar deck, past the smear of blood that showed where the previous officer's body had been dragged to the forward ladder, the two eighteens loomed over the gates that dropped down to the heads. He glanced down at the open toilet holes that lined either side of the bowsprit to make sure no one would be incinerated in the guns' muzzle blasts.

Out of the corner of his eye he observed the gun crews sponging the barrels, which they completed as the boy emerged up the forward ladder laden with a six-pound lead canister of powder and charge of grape. He was followed by a second boy similarly laden, and Bliven realized the boy had shown the initiative to snatch him in tow so that both guns could be loaded. As soon as the burdens were deposited in the garlands Bliven ordered, "Load!" and then aside said, "What is your name, son?"

"Ward, sir. Thomas Ward."

"Well done, Ward. Now get below and bring me another round, quick!" He sent him off with a push and a slap on the butt. "You, too!"

He turned to see the gun crews had quoined the guns up level, rammed home the lead cans of powder and the charges of grape, removed the quoins and had taken up the lanyards to run the guns out. "Wait! You have taken out the quoins. Put them back in!"

"Sir," protested the chief of the gun crew, "the barrel is elevated to cut up her sails and rigging."

Bliven was silent for a second, shocked at being disputed. "Don't argue with me, she has no sails left. Crow up the guns and place the quoins! Bring them level!"

"Yes, sir." The crew chief directed the operation but did not seem to have his heart in it.

Happy for the advantage of firing lanyards, Bliven took up the first one and began gauging the ships' respective rise and fall in the swell. On the *Java*'s quarterdeck he descried blue-coated officers gesturing the sailors, trying to organize some order from their chaos. They had extinguished the deck fires and cut some of the fallen canvas overboard. Bainbridge was wearing ship to starboard to bring the vessel back into the fight, and the range was still extreme for eighteens.

He knelt at the sights, waiting and calculating. Bliven heard Bainbridge roaring from the opposite length of the ship. "Putnam, why aren't you firing?"

Bliven raised his left hand behind him to indicate that he had heard while sighting steadily down the eighteen's barrel. He could not fire willy-nilly, he was dependent upon the swell. With his right hand holding the lanyard high, he had to wait for his own deck to level, at a time when *Java*'s stern rose on a crest. "This," he hissed to himself, "will mark paid to you—you—arrogant—British—"

After repairing her rigging and set to fighting sails, *Constitution*'s starboard turn brought her to a heading west-southwest toward the immobile *Java*'s port bow. On this heading shots from the bow chasers would pass down *Java*'s port quarter and miss her entirely. Bliven could not tell whether Bainbridge meant to pass down her port side and smother her with their own port broadside or turn across her bows and deliver an even more devastating bow rake from their starboard broadside.

Only when he heard Bainbridge shout, "Port your helm," and the order repeated down the after ladder to the tiller room was he certain that the sight from his bow chasers would sweep forward from *Java*'s stern to bow. As the sight crept from open sea horizon onto *Java*'s quarterdeck, he leapt to the side and yanked the lanyard. The eighteen-pounder erupted with a deafening roar and the tremendous kick of its six-foot recoil that would have crushed him had he stayed where he was. In a second he had vaulted over the housing that covered the bowsprit's insertion to its footing and fired the second chaser as well.

The wind blew the gun's smoke quickly off to larboard, allowing Bliven to witness three men in blue coats spin and fall as the charge of grape sprayed across Kington's quarterdeck. "Confusion to you, you bastards," he whispered.

*Constitution*'s port turn brought her starboard broadside close upon *Java*'s bow, and Bainbridge was seconds from ordering a horrific rake from carronades and twenty-fours alike. Suddenly a large white sheet unfurled from her bow toward the water, and in the moment that Bainbridge hesitated to deliver his *coup de grâce* a second white sheet was raised from a jury-rigged spar.

"Hold your fire!" roared Bainbridge. "Hold your fire!" The order was relayed below to the twenty-fours on the gun deck and the officers gathered on the quarterdeck, watching the activity on their wrecked enemy. The battle had lasted for just over two hours, from shortly before two in the afternoon, and it was now after four.

"Mr. Putnam, I need my lieutenants here, and you are senior anyway. Take a boat over and ascertain their intentions."

"Yes, sir. I'll want to take a Marine with me."

"Of course. Bosun, lower my gig. And Putnam?"

"Sir?"

"Put on a fresh shirt and coat, you are still wet. We are close enough the same size, get down to my cabin and supply yourself from my wardrobe."

The gig was bobbing gently at the foot of the ladder by the time he came back on deck, and it was a short pull over to the wrecked *Java*. He felt his hackles rise as they approached, for the water around her was tinged red, as though the floor of an abattoir had been washed down, and as they tied up he could see chunks of flesh and body parts slowly sinking. Entering her open waist, he was helped aboard by a non-com and escorted to the quarterdeck. The carnage was less than he witnessed on the *Guerriere*, but still enough to make him wish never to see such horrors again.

Lieutenant Chads was standing by her wheel, apparently waiting for him, and Bliven saluted as he approached. "Are you in command, Lieutenant?"

"Yes, sir. Captain Lord Kington has been wounded, we fear mortally, and has been taken below. You have won the day, sir, we are forced to strike our colors. My sword, sir."

Bliven reached out and took it. "Thank you. What are your casualties?"

"Twenty-two killed, wounded over a hundred, several more of whom are like to die."

"Do you know if you are sinking?"

"I do not believe so, but further inspection will ascertain the fact."

"Well," said Bliven, "if you please, take me down to see if your captain is able to confirm your surrender."

"Of course." Being but a light frigate, *Java*'s orlop was scarcely four and a half feet from deck underfoot to the deck overhead, dimly lit by battle lanterns—a suitable crypt for the life of a ship to extinguish itself in. Indeed, as he made their way forward to the cockpit Bliven was aware of all the smells of a dying vessel: rising bilge, the distinctly different odors of burning wood from burnt powder, all given a sickening reality by mixing with the odors of dying men—blood, vomit, uncontrolled bowels, the cries for aid and the groans of the wounded and dying heard above the deep creaking of the timbers twisting unnaturally at their joints as *Java* began to settle.

Bliven passed his own men, still waiting in the cable tier. "Boys, the fight is over, and we have won. You will be going home very soon, bear with us." Very briefly the cries and groans were drowned out by the lustiest of cheers.

He found Kington lying on the plank laid across two barrels, a white cloth with no cushion beneath him. Bliven had seen blasted and rent men before, but none so torn as this who still clung to life, and sentience.

"Dr. Kite," Bliven hailed him.

"Mr. Putnam! What? How did you—"

Bliven cut him short. "I am your prisoner no longer, I changed ships when we collided. I have returned to take your surrender.

"Captain," Bliven said, loudly enough and clearly enough that

Kington's eyes rolled and met his, and registered his recognition. "Captain, your first officer has surrendered your ship. It is apparent that you are in extremis. Will you confirm the surrender of your vessel before you leave this world?"

"Not to you!" It was shocking that a dying man could muster such ferocity, his eyes as hard as blue marbles, his teeth clenched against the bubbles of blood that foamed with each breath, his chest doggedly, forcibly expanding to suck in one more breath and one more breath before surrendering to the darkness. "Where is the surgeon?"

"I am here, m'lord."

At the surgeon's lightest touch to his bloody hand Kington seized it with the most clinging violence.

"I am here, m'lord."

"I desire the chaplain."

"He is killed, m'lord."

Kington was too far gone to register disappointment. "Hear me, then. I wish it to be known that I met my end in a manly way, and that my last thoughts were of my King, and the Navy."

"I will, m'lord."

"Captain." Bliven spoke up again and the hard blue eyes focused on him. "Have no fear, I shall also report your courage and fortitude to my superiors. All will know that you fought your ship bravely to the last."

Kington regarded Bliven's crisp new attire, the ruffled shirt brilliant white even in the dim lamplight, the deep blue coat and gold cordage. To the extent that his dying face could register emotion, it showed displeasure. Like lightning he seized the front of Bliven's shirt, pressing the back of his hand and arm across his stomach, leaving a crimson streak of his blood.

"To remember me by," he croaked. His tiny laugh became a cough, and then a strangle. It was shocking how fast his soul fled once he released it. His chest heaved, twice, and three times, before he entered a spastic shudder and then ceased all movement, his eyes open.

Bliven studied his face for several seconds. "Ill-gotten bastard to the end," he said, more in wonder than anything else that one man's soul could contain so much venom.

"Do not fret, young Yankee Doodle," said Kite. "His pain was exquisite enough to satisfy even you." He lifted up the sheet that covered him, to reveal his pasty torso pierced by three balls and also by two large splinters, one piercing his chest and one his belly, and then he reached down and closed the eyes. "He served policy. The policy may be right or wrong, but he did his duty."

Bliven's eyes did not leave the body. "No, he enjoyed it."

*Yankee Doodle,* thought Bliven in a flash. How much was revealed in those two words, that dated epithet: that the British had never accepted Yorktown and the Peace of Paris, that they still thought of America as theirs by right, to be retaken, and he knew that those American newspapers were correct when they printed that this war with England was, in truth, their second War for Independence.

The heat and pall of smoke pressed with greater urgency from the berth deck above. "Dr. Kite," said Bliven, "I need not tell you your ship is in danger. You must get your wounded and your people out of here. Once you are topside we will transfer you."

"Yes," he responded quickly. "Yes, thank you." His eyes darted about the dimness, searching out means to evacuate the men from the coming inferno. Many of his wounded were too broken up to be lifted by legs and armpits, and the first ones to be injured were still lying on the stretchers. "Boys!" Three of their powder monkeys had been slightly wounded, and once the battle ceased sought the refuge of the cockpit. "You, and you two, get to the sail room, bring back canvas. Cut it into pieces large enough to carry a man. Do you understand? Quickly, now!" They would not have far to go, for the sail room lay among the orlop deck's bow compartments.

As they clattered forward into the bow's curve, Bliven shot a look about, and up the after ladder, satisfying himself that the fire if it could not be arrested was in no imminent danger of reaching the magazine. He paused, listening for any gurgle of water swirling unseen below in the hold. If there were such a sound the powder should flood before it could blow up.

He started up the ladder but then hissed, "Damn!" He stopped and backed down the few steps he had climbed, and descended the dark hatch into the hold. He peered about and, seeing no lamps, returned to the orlop and seized hold of one. Back in the hold he descried the ribs of the ship, smaller and smaller in the forward perspective, and the glint of tons of sheet copper that now would not line the bottom of the seventy-four abuilding in India, but saw no movement. "Is there anyone down here?" he shouted. "Is there anyone down here? For your life, now, speak up!" All he heard was the slosh of water and, looking down, he saw the sheen of water between the ribs, seeming no more than unemptied bilge. If the hull was not tight it was nearly so, and she would float long enough to evacuate in an orderly way.

He raced back up the ladder, swung the heavy hatch shut, and secured it. "Have you enough men to carry your wounded?" he shouted to Kite.

"Yes, thank you, we will begin taking them on deck."

Bliven started to ascend toward the spar deck, but seeing the wardroom, stopped to entertain a wild thought. He ducked into the tiny stateroom he had lately occupied, and there his thought was rewarded. In a quick reach he scooped up his mahogany dressing box and secured it under his arm before continuing up.

———— // ————

Back on the *Constitution*'s quarterdeck, Bliven conveyed *Java*'s surrender, and the sword. "The captain is killed," he told Bainbridge. "The surgeon, Dr. Kite, will be ready to transfer the wounded shortly. The ship will not imminently sink, but she is wrecked and will burn to the waterline. We will have to take on her crew as prisoners."

Bainbridge made a sour face. "Are you certain?"

"Yes, sir, I am sure she is lost."

They both would have much preferred to keep the crew on their own ship and take her in as a prize, but even if she could be saved, they could not trust her to reach a harbor farther than Brazil. The Portuguese were neutral in this conflict, but neutral with a decided tilt toward the British. If they took her in to São Salvador or Recife there was no guarantee she would not be handed right back over to their enemy.

"Very well. Have the carpenter make a secure area around the cable tier. We will have to hold them in close confinement until we can get them ashore. And then have him make certain to bring her wheel over. We'll use that to get home."

"Captain, you will have to make it a large area. She is carrying passengers, a general bound for India and his staff, and supernumeraries, and the crew he took off my ship. We will have to take on about three hundred, I'm afraid."

"Oh, God damn! Why did she even chase us down when she had passengers?"

"Well, you know how some captains are about running to a fight. How is Mr. Bandy, do you know?"

"He is recovering. Give my instruction to the carpenter and you may see him. And Putnam."

"Sir?"

Bainbridge lowered his voice. "I cannot stand to see a fine ship burn in agony. When all the prisoners are aboard, blow her up."

Bliven saluted. "Very good, sir." He found the carpenter in the hold, hoisting a lantern to the curvature of the hull, frame by frame, confirming that their *Constitution*'s hull had taken this hellish pounding, and was undamaged. He acknowledged that he would prepare a space for prisoners about the cable tier, even as he looked toward a larger job when the *Java*'s wheel was bought over to replace their own that had been shot away, and would have to be engaged to the tiller.

In the cockpit, Bliven sat by Sam until, at length, his pale blue eyes opened languidly. Consciousness then returned in a rush, and without moving his head his eyes shot about the compartment.

"Sam, Sam, be still. You are all right. You were wounded, we have been taken aboard the *Constitution*; we are in the cockpit. Dr. Cutbush has been working on you."

Sam gained control of his breath as he slowly remembered— beating to quarters on the *Java*, chasing down the *Constitution* and seeing her gunports open, the awful silence before the eruption of broadsides. As he could not remember coming aboard this ship, he had to assume that someone had brought him. At length he sighed and said, "Oh, hell, Putnam, did you save my life again?"

Bliven pondered the question, and the advantage that it gave him, but quickly decided that such a double obligation would be more than Sam could live with. "No. No, quite the opposite. You saved my life. If you had not flown at me when you did and taken us overboard, we would have been staring face-on into a full salvo from the chasers. We would have been rent in pieces by splinters."

"Oh, good." He knit his brow. "My head hurts very badly."

"The *Constitution* fired just as we went over. One of the balls smashed into the *Java*'s railing, and a piece of it fetched you an almighty wallop on the head on your way down. You surely have a concussion, but Dr. Cutbush believes you will have no permanent injury."

"We won the battle, then?"

"Utterly."

"What of that Captain Lord Sir Almighty Majesty Turdbucket?"

Bliven looked down. "He is dead."

"Good, I hope it hurt. Bliv, I swear these British—" Sam sucked in his breath in something like a panic. "Oh, Jesus! Oh my God!" He grabbed at his stomach and twisted onto his side, revealing his naked butt as the sheet slid off, and before he considered whether

he could arrest it he ripped a flatulence both percussive and singing, one that extended its note as he pressed on his belly. Worst of
all, he looked behind him and saw a distinct pall of smoke. "What
in God's name? What in the—"

Bliven was helpless but to screech in laughter, even as he
squeezed Sam's hand. "Well, after Naples I never thought to see
Vesuvius again, but now I have!" He wanted to say more but could
not, for he could not breathe and just gave himself over to the
paralysis of hysterical mirth.

Like a shot, Cutbush was on them. "Hush now, quiet! Mr.
Bandy, you are awake. How are you feeling?"

"My head hurts like the devil."

"And will for some days. You took a nasty blow. I am going to
keep you very quiet until we are certain that you are not bleeding
beneath the skull."

"What . . . just happened?"

"Mr. Bandy, I had to administer a tobacco glyster. Tobacco is a
stimulant; forcing the smoke into your bowel is the fastest way to
jolt your system, speed things up, get your respiration going again.
Of course, what goes in must come out, hence the odor wafting
about just now of, em, a mixture of . . . stool and tobacco."

"Carolina's finest." Bliven was scarcely able to get the words
out. "On both counts! Haaa!"

Cutbush pulled Bliven to his feet. "That's enough now, get topside and make yourself useful. Mr. Bandy is out of danger." He
knew that was not true. If indeed he was bleeding in his brain
he could have a seizure and die at any second. In his medical case
he had a circular trepanning saw to make openings in a skull to

relieve pressure on the brain, but he had never used it and prayed he would never have to.

"Doctor, my own surgeon on the *Tempest*, his name is Gabriel and I believe you know him, he is among my crew held on the *Java*, I'll have him sent to you straightaway, I imagine you can use him."

"Indeed I can, indeed I can."

"Dr. Cutbush?"

He spun around. "What is this, a reunion? You look familiar. Do I know you?"

"Not for some years. Launcelot Kite, sir, surgeon of His Majesty's Ship *Java*, whom you have just destroyed. We met long ago, in Philadelphia, you had charge of the hospital there."

"Ah, yes." The light of recognition came over his face and he advanced with his hand outstretched. "I do remember. You were an estimable fellow, good student, quite the boulevardier, as I remember."

They shook hands. "Yes, I fear so. Try not to remember too much of me, then." They laughed. "My ship is wrecked but they say will not sink, and we are transferring our injured. It will be a great imposition, I fear, and you must let me tender my services to help you."

"Very kind," said Cutbush. "Very kind." He looked fitfully about. The cockpit below was full of their own casualties and he did not want to move them. "Use the forward ladder as you bring them aboard. I will appropriate some of the forward hammocks to enlarge the sick bay until we can get you ashore."

"Yes, that will be very well, thank you."

"At least I assume we will put you ashore. I'm not certain where we are. Perhaps Recife would be the closest port, I don't know. Mr. Putnam, we have killed and wounded of our own, and I desire Dr. Kite to stay here and assist me in treating them. If you have no other duties, would you supervise this transfer of their casualties? You will trust to handle them as gently as can be done."

"I'll just make certain the captain approves."

"Yes, of course," said Bainbridge when he was asked. "Go to it, take the longboats and the cutters, see if you can get them off by dark. If the ship will last, we can finish with the rest in the morning."

———— // ————

The task required until noon the next day, and when he was certain that the ship was entirely abandoned, Bliven set a fire in the orlop above the magazine, having first moved a few quarter-casks of powder proximate enough that her last moment could not be far distant.

When he returned, he found that Bainbridge had finally allowed himself to be treated, and lay bandaged in his cabin.

"Captain Bainbridge?" Bliven saluted.

"Come in, pull up a chair and sit by me."

"Captain, the *Java* is entirely abandoned, I set an explosive charge that the fire will reach before long. Your wound—do you need anything?"

Bainbridge looked surprised at such a solicitation. "Thank you, no, I shall just be sitting on pillows for a few days."

"Captain, they tell me that you held the deck all night, with a ball in your hip and a bolt in your thigh from when the wheel was shot away. You refused to be treated until all the dangerously wounded were seen to."

Bainbridge made no reply.

"That was gallant of you, sir, but I hope you will not make a habit of taking such risks with your life."

"Ha. I did not feel so dangerously wounded, and I knew it would have a good effect on the men. You see, Mr. Putnam, I am well aware of what people think of me. Hull was a popular captain, I am not. In fact, the crew nearly mutinied when I took command. I am thought an unlucky captain, you see, because I have lost two ships. Holding the deck will go a distance to remedy that, I think."

"Yes, I see." Bliven hesitated. "Then, may I ask you something?"

"What is it?"

"When I left the *Constitution* in Boston, after we put the *Guerriere*'s survivors ashore, Mr. Hull seemed very much in his element, almost a part of the ship. He was keen and anxious to put out again, at once. Was he taken ill, that he was relieved?"

Bainbridge took a long sip of sherry from a glass on the bedside table and raised up on an elbow. "Do you know, Commander, I am truly not a fool?" He raised his hands before Bliven could protest. "You have never spoken publicly against me, and I give you that credit, but I know well what you and Preble thought of me in the Mediterranean."

"On my honor, sir, I did not mean to imply—"

Bainbridge waved it off. "Never mind. After you were ordered to Charleston, Hull received a letter, containing the news of his brother's death. That brother left a widow and children, for whom Hull is now the only support. He knew that I was in command of the Navy Yard at Boston, which is proximate to his brother's family. As bitterly as it grieved him to do so, he himself made the request to change places with me."

Bliven nodded sadly. "What a heavy blow for him."

"I did not go angling to take his command."

"No, sir."

"But I would be telling a lie if I said I am sorry to have it."

"Captain, allow me to say that whatever my thoughts were in the past, when I came aboard yesterday, and saw you fighting this ship without even a wheel to steer her—my God, that was the finest piece of ship handling I have ever witnessed."

Bainbridge extended his hand. "Thank you, Commander. Will this put to rest any past between us?"

Bliven took his hand. "With all my heart, sir."

"A good night to you, then."

Bliven stood back and saluted. "Good night, sir."

———— // ————

The *Constitution* flew swiftly home, departing São Salvador on January 6, 1813, after landing her prisoners and resupplying, and tying up at the Long Wharf in Boston on February 27. The most difficult farewell for Bliven was from Cutbush, with whom he had renewed a fast friendship. "Are you staying with the ship, then?" he asked.

"Oh, yes," said Cutbush emphatically. "Having sailed in this majestic vessel again, I have come to regard her as almost indestructible, but the men are not. We owe them the best care that can be got, and for the time being, that would seem to be me."

"So say I," agreed Bliven, "and everyone I know."

"Ha! My thanks. And what about you? What is next for you?"

Bliven shrugged. "I confess, I have not an idea in the world. Probably nothing until there is an inquiry into how I lost the *Tempest*. If I am found at fault, I will be at the Navy's mercy."

"Ha! Well, rash action is a cashiering offense, cowardice is the capital offense. Whatever happens, at least we know you won't be shot. Ha!"

"Hm! No, at least I won't be shot."

Cutbush caught the note of sadness in Bliven's voice and responded to it. "May I tell you a great secret?"

"Of course."

"Say nothing to anyone or I will be ruined."

"You have my word."

Cutbush leaned forward. "My conclusion," he near-whispered, "after long observation and experience, is that the celebrated naval commanders—the ones for whom gold medals are struck and who are given triumphal parades—are either mad, or else go mad. My young friend, I would be very happy to learn one day that you never went mad."

Bliven smiled wryly at the deftness of his touch, to give advice without giving advice. It recalled to him Cutbush's fondness for Galen, and that ancient Roman's steadfast belief that madness could be defeated through conversation with wise elders. "After a time, who knows? Maybe they'll send me back out to the Atlantic if they can find me a ship, or I hear they are assembling a squadron on Lake Ontario, maybe they will send me there. Things are heating up in the Mediterranean again. Algiers is on their third little king since the war and he is not happy with how things were left. Or, there are still pirates in the Caribbean, albeit they are lying low now owing to the greater war. I may turn up anywhere, but I hope I do get some time at home first."

When they shook hands Cutbush took his tightly and laid his left hand over Bliven's. "Mr. Putnam, life is uncertain. We do not know whether we shall meet again in this life."

Bliven smiled. "You said that to me once before."

"So I did," Cutbush admitted. "It is how I say good-bye. I have found it always best to suspend friendships in a tidy fashion. You are still young, have you ever lost anyone close to you?"

Bliven shook his head. "Acquaintances killed in battle, but none of my immediate family, nor closest friends; my wife's father was the nearest."

"Well, I have, and when you do you will discover that once they are gone, gone, too, will be the opportunity to assure them that they meant something to you. I hope we do meet again, but if we do not I want to leave it with you how much I have enjoyed knowing you."

Bliven was taken aback by such openness, such frankness, indeed he thought he knew no other who was capable of it, but it warmed him and made him feel that he was in the presence of an extraordinary man. "Doctor," he said, "I have a suspicion that you have just told me something quite profound, and that it will bear pondering over in quiet moments. We New Englanders are reticent with our emotions; perhaps it is the cold climate we live in. But here in your quiet sick bay I will confess that I feel precisely the same about you. If we do not meet again, be assured I will never forget you." He smiled suddenly and broadly. "Nor the lemon in your tea, nor your fondness for ancient physicians. And besides"— he traced a line across his lower belly—"I will always have a certain scar, and a silver coin, to remember you by."

"Good-bye," Cutbush said and laughed heartily, and Bliven knew that was partly because he was amused and partly because that was the way people should part, in case it should be their last parting.

*Good-bye* echoed in his mind as he walked slowly back to the wardroom. Yes, there was an art to saying good-bye that he had never mastered, and now it had been taught him.

## ~ 11 ~

### *Home*

**B**ack in Boston the *Constitution* was besieged by crowds who came to admire her, and Bliven prowled the Navy Yard's receiving office for two days, after which the commandant conceded that he would have no orders until it was decided how to proceed over the loss of the *Tempest*. With permission for a leave safely folded in his pocket, he loaded his trunks and sea bag onto the stagecoach for Providence and thence along the familiar coastal post road.

Four other passengers affected not to be studying him, but Bliven often caught them in sidewise glances; evidently they were perplexed at his constant, faint, enigmatic smile. "No doubt," said one lady at last, "you are smiling because you are going home after a long absence."

He answered, "Indeed yes, ma'am." The truth was, however, that he was comparing the long, deep rolling of the ship at sea to this unpredictable lurching and jerking of their interminably slow coach and concluding that the former suited him better, or would, were he not homeward bound.

In New Haven he oversaw the driver in depositing his baggage at the station porch, and he entered to make the transfer.

"Why, it is Mr. Putnam!" Strait's voice cried from behind his ticket counter. He raised a gate and advanced, his hand extended. "It is so very fine to see you, Mr. Putnam. How are you?"

"I thank you, Mr. Strait, I am well. How are my parents, have you seen them?"

"Yes, often! They are very well indeed. I expect you know your father suffered a small apoplexy some months ago, but he is remarkably recovered. He often holds court in your tavern, registering his political opinions. He is becoming quite the sage." He laughed suddenly. "Or irritant, depending on your point of view!"

"Yes, he relishes both. And my wife?"

"Come, let me prepare your ticket. I see her less often, but she stays quite busy about the town. She helps your parents and her mother, and she has taken a most keen interest in church affairs. I deliver some parcel or other to her most every week. You are homeward bound, I gather?"

"Yes, just as fast as I can get there."

"May I say?" Strait was suddenly almost shy. "We understand from your family that you have been in the *Constitution*. We have all read of your victories. Most thrilling!"

*Yes,* Bliven thought, *apparently you have not read of my defeat, and the men I suffered to be killed.* "That is very kind of you, thank you."

"Here we are." Strait handed him a token and Bliven fished in his pocket and handed over three silver dollars. "We will be leaving in about an hour, do make yourself comfortable."

The late afternoon was dry but gray and cold, when the coach proceeded up the South Road into Litchfield. Gazing out the coach window, Bliven's eyes met his father's when he was yet fifty yards from stopping, giving him a full view of Benjamin getting to his feet. Both halting and with energy, pushing up from the bench with one arm while pulling himself up on a crutch with the other.

"Oh!" was all the older man could say as they drew near. "Oh!" Bliven wondered even as he embraced him how many more homecomings there could be. One would be a blessing, two a miracle.

"Father, why are you sitting out on such a dreary day? You will catch your death. Surely to be indoors by the fire would be more congenial."

"Well"—Benjamin drew back but held on to Bliven's forearms—"I have two reasons, to be truthful. The first is I knew, ask me not how but I knew, that one day very soon the coach would toss you off, so I sit out and watch the stage pass because I wanted to be the first to greet you. The second is"—he leaned forward intimately—"I sit out because the house is possessed."

"What?"

"Truly! There is an imp who wreaks about unrestrained. It is about so high"—he held a hand out, palm down, about three feet off the ground—"it noses into everything, and it is a font of riddles and unanswerable questions. Before the Throne, it was sent to torment me."

In a terror Bliven wondered if his father had suffered a third apoplexy that had damaged his mind, and the letter warning him of it had never reached him. "Father, what on earth are you—" Before he could finish, the front door flew upon. "Mother!"

She raced down the steps, cleaning her hands on her apron, although more from habit than need, for she had just washed. "My boy, my darling!" They hugged tight and kissed on both cheeks.

He held her back and regarded her. "Mother, you look wonderful."

She patted his shoulders. "Your homecoming is well timed, my son. We are having a fine fat goose for supper. Are you hungry?"

"Ravenous."

"Commander?" Bliven spun around at the address to see Mr. Strait levering one of his trunks off the edge of the coach. In his younger years Strait would have fetched it down and deposited it at the door himself, but now he felt well enough acquitted to merely hand it down, followed by his sea bag and the two further trunks.

Bliven took the sea bag and balanced it on his shoulder. "Thank you, Mr. Strait. When you get to the tavern please help yourself to a tankard of cider, with our compliments." He spun around awkwardly, for the sea bag was heavy. "The tavern is still ours, I trust?"

"Oh, my, yes," his father assured him. "Its commerce sustains us most admirably."

"Well, then, good day to you, Mr. Strait. Again, my thanks." They mounted the steps, leaving the trunks outside for the moment. "Is Mr. Peters still running it?"

"Indeed, he is. Mind, we did almost lose him, once. He got it in his mind to go study law from the celebrated Mr. Reeve."

"Great heavens! Tapping Reeve is still holding school?"

"He is."

"Lord, he must be older than granite by now."

The elder Putnam stopped short. "He may well be, but that is not a criticism that I would level at anyone anymore. But young Mr. Peters did not find old Mr. Reeve's law school to his liking. Many do not, you know, but have not the courage to walk away. He appeared most loath to return home and have his people think him a failure. I put it to him that he might wish to stay on a while longer as he considers his future. He has his board and lodging at the tavern, and he labors honestly, for the most part."

"For the most part?"

"Oh, I suspect he helps himself to an extra dollar here and there, but I do not complain for in fairness he works harder for what we pay him than may be entirely just."

The coach rumbled slowly on, and his mother held the door as he hefted the sea bag inside and set it down. "I am glad to hear it goes well, but if we have been taking advantage of him we must square our account. Where is Clarity? Is she about?"

"She is in your room," she said. "I expect she did not hear the coach."

Benjamin added with a note of caution, "Beware, she is with the imp."

He passed quickly through the keeping room, rapped three times, and opened the door. "I have heard that a sailor's wife lives here. Where is she?"

"Bliven!" she exclaimed, and flew out of her chair toward him. "Oh, my love!" They kissed tightly and he was stricken with his madness that he could ever leave such an embrace, the feel, the taste, the softness of lips, the scent of powder and perfume, his gratitude for her and for her need of him. "Safe home," she sighed, "safe home, oh, God be praised!" He thought again of those African lizards that change color, and thought he now understood how they could do it so quickly.

Bliven beheld the tiny form perched on a chair at the side of her writing desk, and realized that his father had not gone mad. "And who is this?" he asked.

Clarity held out her hand toward her. "Harriet, come here, darling, I would like for you to meet my husband, Mr. Putnam. Commander, may I present Miss Harriet Beecher?"

The child hopped off her chair and approached him, and he realized that, yes, there was no mistaking whose child this was. She bore the reverend's same downturning mouth and sliding eyes. She held out the sides of her skirt and dropped into a curtsey. "How do you do, Commander?" she said gravely. "I have heard so much about you."

Bliven would have been astonished at such correct behavior from a child of eight, let alone this small, and wondered what manner of changeling this was and whether his father might have been right. Still, he bowed gravely. "Mistress Beecher, the pleasure is mine." He held out his seaman's hand, and Harriet let her tiny hand disappear into it.

"Harriet," said Clarity, "would you like to go feed our chickens now?"

"Oh, yes," she said eagerly. "I would like to. But I know it is really because you wish to be alone with the commander."

Clarity scooted her gently toward the door. "Ask Mother Putnam to put some corn in your pail for you."

As she reached the door Harriet turned suddenly. "It was very nice to meet you, Commander Putnam."

"Mistress Beecher"—he bowed again—"may I look forward to our better acquaintance?"

"Oh, yes, but please, you may call me Harriet, for I am but four years old."

She disappeared and shut the door behind her, leaving him to ask, "Was that a human child?"

Clarity laughed softly as she nestled as deep in his arms as she could mold herself. "Yes, she is precocious. She is a delight to teach."

He noted the word *teach* and shelved it to investigate later. "Poor child," he said.

"What do you mean, 'Poor child'? She has the greatest abilities of any girl her age that was ever seen."

He shrugged lightly. "Is it not bad enough that Beecher's sons should grow up to look like him, but this poor little girl, too?"

Clarity stood back suddenly, her eyes boring into his. "Harriet does not know that she is not pretty." She studied him for a reaction. "And I will lay waste the man who tells her."

His broad smile reconciled her and she drew close again. "Allay your fears, my love. She shall never hear it from me. But do I gather she is something of an inconvenience to my father?"

She pulled back again. "Oh, he has started on 'the imp' again? Pooh! Don't you believe it. Wait a few seconds and you shall see." She led him within a few steps of their back window that looked out upon the hen yard, from where they could watch discreetly. Through the sheer curtains Harriet skipped into view, followed a moment later by Benjamin on his crutches, her pail of corn suspended from the fingers of one hand. The dozen chickens knew what their presence signified and came running on outstretched legs from all directions; Benjamin gave her the pail and she cast the corn about like a sower, her peals of laughter audible through the windowpanes.

Bliven and Clarity could not hear what they were saying, but it was apparent that they were avidly engaged. "Well, upon my word," breathed Bliven, "will you look at that?"

Clarity stood with her back to him, squeezing her hands on his arms as he wrapped them about her. "She has given him a new interest in life, you see? When nothing else could. He was declining, and that has been arrested."

"I am so happy to see it." With small steps and his arms still holding her he backed toward their bed; with one hand he braced two pillows against the headboard, lay down, and she cuddled against him. "But she is here for schooling? Surely Beecher can afford a governess to look after that growing tribe of his."

"Four older brothers," she allowed, "but they have little in common with her."

"Does she not have two older sisters as well?"

"Catharine and Mary," she refreshed his memory. "They must look after their mother. Mrs. Beecher is not well." She shrugged. "Mrs. Beecher is never well. And Harriet, with her nature, is under foot. They do not appreciate her prescience or her abilities. They put her aside and tell her to play, but to her learning is play."

"If Mrs. Beecher is unwell," he growled, "perhaps the reverend could give her a rest from popping out children like so many corn muffins."

"Well," she said with a sigh, "they are being fruitful and multiplying." Her eyes met his in a meaningful way.

"Oh, I see. Shall I understand, then, in looking after Harriet, you are practicing for our own children?"

She rested her head on his chest. "God may yet bless us."

He rolled her on her back and kissed her deeply. "And is it not written somewhere," he asked, "that God helps those who help themselves?"

He kissed her throat and could feel her breath turning shallow. "I am certain I have heard it," she said, "but I do not believe it is in the Holy Scriptures."

"An oversight, perhaps."

"Tonight, then, we must renew our efforts, dearest."

He looked longingly down the length of her form. "After dinner?"

"Ha! Yes, we must keep up your strength."

Shortly in the keeping room they sat down to clam chowder, and then roast goose, with rice and gravy, and sweet potatoes.

Clarity realized with a start the she had forgotten to inquire into what must be, to him, the most important subject. "What of your ship, dearest? Your *Tempest*, is she in Boston?"

Bliven's blood froze with the realization that they could not have heard, for news of the *Tempest* could only have reached home five days ago, with them. "No, my love, I came home on the *Constitution*."

As usual, it was his mother whose apprehensions rose first. "And what of your ship, my son, your command?"

It took him a moment to frame how to say it. "She was lost, Mother, off the coast of Brazil."

Dorothea went pale and set down her fork and knife. "What?"

"We were overhauled by a British frigate with twice our guns. We fought, but the *Tempest* was sunk. We were taken prisoner, and then several days later that ship was overtaken by the *Constitution* and sunk, so we were rescued."

She laid her hand on his. "Did you lose many men, my son?"

He glanced up and saw her studying deep into him. "Yes, Mother, I'm afraid we did."

"But *you* are all right?"

"Yes, I was not wounded." He felt as much as heard the sigh that Clarity heaved beside him.

"And how is this for Providence?" Bliven was determined to put the moment behind them. "Our friend Sam Bandy was also a prisoner on the English ship. He had been taken at sea and pressed into service, and was taken with me onto the *Constitution*. He is on his way home to South Carolina and his family, even now."

"I am so glad," said Clarity quietly. "I am glad that his wife will soon know the depth of relief that I am feeling, at this moment."

After a last course of syllabub, and the dishes being washed, Bliven's father rose on his sticks. "Well, my dears, the excitement of the day has drained me quite completely, and left me ready for bed. Will you come, Mrs.?"

"I will be along directly. I will just trim the goose for what we can use tomorrow."

The keeping room was soon left dark, with Bliven and Clarity alone in their chamber, grateful that his parents had retired early to their portion of the house, and aware that it was at least partly by design to give them privacy.

In a very few moments they were in bed, the moon visible through the window, and he began exploring her, as he always did, easily imagining it as their first time.

She luxuriated in his touch and then asked languidly, "Is it not true that Captain Cook was at sea for years at a time, yet he and his wife managed to have six children?"

"What?" He was amazed, withdrawing his hand from within her night dress and laying it flat on her belly. "How do you come to know of Captain Cook?"

"At church," she answered. "We have a convert from the Sandwich Islands, a native but highly educated. He told us of his homeland, which was discovered by Captain Cook, and that set me to reading about him." She moved his hand up to her breast. "And I am married to a naval officer, after all, so of course I want to learn more."

Bliven regarded her deeply. He wanted to nest her in his arms and talk with her endlessly, yet he also wanted to mate with her like an animal in a barnyard. He shook his head slowly, savoring the dilemma of having a woman whose conversation was as alluring as her body.

"Commander." Her voice brought him back into focus. "Forgive me, but oughtn't you to batten down the hatches?"

"How do you mean?" He had no idea.

"Perhaps you want to lock the door."

—⫻—

"Fire!" Bliven's own hoarse bellow awakened him with a start, sitting bolt upright in his bed, his chest heaving for breath.

"Dearest?" Clarity was sitting beside him, her hand on his bare shoulder, pale in the moonlight that streamed through the window.

He stared at her dumbly for a few seconds, coming back to the present. They had fallen asleep after their lovemaking, and he was conscious of nothing since. "Oh, I am sorry, my love. I woke you. I . . . I suppose I was dreaming."

"Are you all right? Look, you are soaked with sweat."

"Yes. Yes, it was nothing."

"It was hardly nothing. Do you remember it? Can you tell me about it?"

"No. I don't know." The moon had moved noticeably, but it was not yet late. Bliven swung his feet out of bed, crossed over to the porcelain basin and poured some water into it. He washed his face, then soaked a cloth and swabbed his neck, shoulders and chest as Clarity watched him intently.

He returned and kissed her lightly. "Go back to sleep, my love. I think I shall sleep better after a little walk, get some fresh air."

"Of course, dearest," she assented, but in a voice that she hoped would convey that her alarm was not allayed. "Wrap warmly."

He dressed, donning outermost a scarf and coat, and exited quietly, walking toward town until he reached the green. There was little frost, but what there was made the grass crunch underfoot, until he paused to decide which way he would go. A short distance on he regarded the house that unthinking he knew he wanted, two dark stern clapboard stories, and a room added to one side with a door and window, within which a light shone.

Bliven mounted the three steps and knocked, lightly, rather hoping it would not be heard and he could excuse himself from this errand. He had just backed away when the door creaked open. Lyman Beecher was still as fully clothed as he was during the day, except for the dressing slippers on his feet. "Commander Putnam!"

"You were on your way to bed. Please forgive me, I should not have disturbed you."

"Nonsense, I was having tea. You must join me." He reached out onto the stoop and took Bliven by the arm, tugging gently. "Come inside."

Bliven's eyes darted around the room, obviously Beecher's study and sanctum, with shelves crowded with books—books that ordinarily would have excited his curiosity, but of which he found himself vaguely afraid, for they must contain the raw materials for Beecher's forbidding sermons, his windows into heaven and hell. The chamber was connected to the darkened parlor beyond by a door that stood open.

Steam rose from a silver teapot that rested on a tray, in company with a tiny pitcher of cream and bowl of sugar. Beecher set a cup onto a saucer and poured. He stepped away and opened a cabinet, and extracted a blackish-green bottle, peculiar for its perfectly round globular bole beneath a long, slender neck that Bliven recognized instantly as rum from the West Indies. "A small fortification, perhaps?"

Bliven stared in astonishment. "Truly, sir, you are a man of God, yes."

Beecher's face wrinkled up into a smile and deep chuckle, the first relaxed moment in which Bliven had ever observed him. Beecher pulled the cork from the bottle and they heard its tiny gurgle through the long neck as the honey-colored rum spiked the tea. Beecher looked at him, suddenly serious. "I trust this confidence will be respected."

"No one will ever know, I give you my word. Oh, thank you." Bliven took the cup of tea and sampled it, and found the blend surprisingly compatible. After a few seconds' reflection it made sense, for many people put sugar in their tea, and rum was distilled from the molasses. The affinity was similar. "No fortification for you?"

"Not tonight. It is true that I am well known as a temperance man, and to be sure, drunkenness is a sin and the cause of numberless domestic agonies. Yet alcohol is a component in many of our medicines, and to you I will confide that sometimes, just a drop of rum in my tea helps me sleep, when I am troubled."

"There are nights when you are troubled?"

"Many."

Bliven felt his façade crumbling. "Then I should not add to it," he said quietly.

"My friend, did you come to me because I am your minister? If so I should be glad of it, for that is my job. Won't you tell me what is on your mind?"

If Bliven had spent long planning on such an interview as this he would have been prepared, but now he was simply caught up in it and found himself grateful that Beecher was practiced enough to have made him comfortable. "Have you ever been in battle?" he asked at last.

"Ah, for a man like me, trying to live a godly life and persuade others to it is battle, but of the sort you mean, no, I have not."

"Few have, hereabouts. The generation that fought the Revolution are passing away. Some have fought Indians, but that is about all." He knit his brow. "In our last battle, it was just before the new year, we were challenged and engaged by a British frigate. It was a fierce fight, I fired the last shot, I raked her quarterdeck with grape, killing the captain and others. Reverend, the battle was all but over. I did not have to take that shot. I fired it because my blood was up and I wanted to kill him. Understand me rightly, I *wanted* to kill him. I perhaps did not know it then, but I know it now."

Beecher nodded solemnly. "Let me ask you something very pointedly"—he set his tea down—"and answer me honestly."

"Very well."

"At the moment you fired that last shot, had she struck her colors?"

"She had not."

"At the moment you took that last shot, did you observe any activity about her deck that would lead you to believe she was imminently to strike her colors?"

"No, I did not."

"So she could have been standing off to make repairs and then resume the fight, is it not so?"

"Yes, that is true. We had done the same."

"Thus it is possible that your final shot, killing her captain and confusing her command, might have been what carried the day."

"Yes, I cannot deny it is possible." Bliven felt his emotions breaking like a dam, and he began weeping. "But that is not why—I did it. I did it—because I wanted to kill him. I wanted to kill him, and I did."

Beecher leaned close but did not touch him.

Bliven drained his cup; the tea would have scalded him, but the rum had cooled it. "You don't understand yet. When he sank my own ship a couple of weeks before, during the battle, I had a boy, Turner, a powder monkey, he was ten years old. He had just delivered a ball and charge to one of the guns. He stood up to go below for another. And then, there was a spray of blood, too fast to see how it happened, a ball took away his hips and bowels. His legs stood there, and his body above, but with open air between them—and then all fell into a pile." He sobbed. "But he was still as conscious as you or I sitting here, and he lay there, looking about, until he died."

"God in heaven," whispered Beecher.

"Do you know why he came into the Navy? His parents were dead. His relatives could not afford to keep him, he had already learned to lie and steal and do for himself. On my ship he came to look to me for—" He could not finish the sentence. "When that captain came to take our surrender—he did not send a lieutenant, he wanted the satisfaction himself—he saw what was left of Turner, and he told his Marines, 'Throw that overboard,' and they did, the pieces of him. Sir, he was a child, he had hopes, and things that amused him. Despite his bad start, he deserved some chance at life. 'Throw that overboard,' indeed! He walked around Turner's blood to take my sword, and I had to give it to him. My surviving crew and I were taken prisoners onto his ship.

"Later, when he fought the *Constitution*, the ships collided. My friend Sam and I managed to get aboard her. The officer in charge of the bow chasers was killed, and the captain ordered me to take over." He felt his calm returning to him. "And after the *Java* was reduced, I saw that captain on her quarterdeck. I fired that last spray of grape, because I wanted to kill him."

Beecher laid his hand on Bliven's knee. "My friend, you are too young a man, altogether, to be called upon to retain such terrible memories."

"When she struck her colors, I was sent over to take her surrender. I found the captain in the cockpit, laid on a plank; the surgeon was attending him although there was nothing to be done. He was appallingly cut up, and in agony, and I felt no pity." He hung his head. "None. No pity. What am I becoming?"

Beecher was silent for several moments, and Bliven knew that he was composing, arranging his thoughts oratorically, intending to persuade, as in one of his sermons. "Commander," he said at length, "some night, when you are cruising upon what you imagine might be the deepest part of the ocean, some night, at midnight under a new moon when there is no light, no light at all, walk over to the railing and look down into the water. Study it. Contemplate it. My young friend, there are corners of the human heart that are infinitely blacker than the deepest abyss. All men are vulnerable to it. You are prey to it. I am prey to it. The darkness wants us all."

"You?"

"I perhaps more than you, for I am held to a higher standard. Can you not see, placing ourselves in service to the higher Being is the only salva—"

"Why, good evening, Commander Putnam!"

Their dual gazes shot up to the door into the parlor as Harriet's barefoot, nightgowned little form emerged from the gloom.

"Harriet!" snapped Beecher. "Child, I swear if you ever actually stay in the bed once you are put there—"

"I am sorry, Father, I heard voices."

Bliven caught Beecher's arm. "No, please allow it." He stood to his feet and bowed. "Mistress Harriet, I am so sorry if we disturbed you."

"Not at all, I am delighted to see you." She curtsied. "I shan't keep you, I only wanted to wish you a good evening."

"You are most gracious. I hope we will meet again soon. Good night."

"Good night, Commander. Good night, Father."

"Good night, child."

Bliven and Beecher looked at each other, laughing softly at the innocent joy she took in playing at adult manners. "Children," Bliven sighed. "Children, to raise them, gently—are they not what gives us the hope to keep going?"

"Our savior said as much, suffer the children to come unto me, for of such are the Kingdom of Heaven." They were quiet for some moments. "Commander, until this night, I do not think I entirely approved of you."

Bliven took that in. "Nor I you, Reverend. Nor I you."

# ACKNOWLEDGMENTS

I was grief-stricken at the retirement of my editor at G. P. Putnam's Sons, Christine Pepe, who managed *The Shores of Tripoli* so well and got this project well under way. I am once again indebted to Putnam's president, Ivan Held, who placed this book, and me, in the care of Alexis Sattler, who has proved to be that wonderful combination of editorial eye and probity with a light touch. My thanks continue to my agent, Jim Hornfischer, who brought me this project that is turning out to be one that my whole career's training has pointed me toward. And thanks of course to my cadre of readers, who are the first to let me know if I left threads hanging out of the story: Craig Eiland, Greg Ciotti, Evan Yeakel.

# FURTHER READING ON THE WAR OF 1812

Dudley, Wade G. *Splintering the Wooden Wall: The British Blockade of the United States, 1812–1815.* Annapolis: Naval Institute Press, 2003. Tight, scholarly focus on the British blockade.

Dudley, William S., ed. *The Naval War of 1812: A Documentary History.* Washington, DC: Naval Historical Center, 1985. Well-annotated transcripts of hundreds of Navy documents; gives a reader a better perspective from the point of view of the participants.

Forester, C. S. *The Naval War of 1812.* London: Michael Joseph, 1957. A perspective from the British point of view, eminently readable, from the author of the Horatio Hornblower novels.

Hickey, Donald R. *The War of 1812: A Forgotten Conflict.* Urbana: University of Illinois Press, 1989. Scholarly interpretation with exhaustive documentation.

Jenkins, Mark Collins, and David A. Taylor. *The War of 1812 and the Rise of the U.S. Navy.* Washington, DC: National Geographic, 2012. Richly illustrated and deeply contexted, the best single-volume introduction to the conflict.

Long, David F. *Ready to Hazard: A Biography of Commodore William Bainbridge, 1774–1833*. Hanover, NH: University Press of New England, 1980.

Lossing, Benson J. *The Pictorial Field Book of the War of 1812* . . . New York: Harper & Brothers, 1869. A rare book but a treasure if one can find it; leaden, as was the style of the time, but exhaustive and documentary.

Maloney, Linda M. *The Captain from Connecticut: The Life and Naval Times of Isaac Hull*. Boston: Northeastern University Press, 1986.

Roosevelt, Theodore. *The Naval War of 1812* . . . Annapolis: Naval Institute Press, 1987, repr. Fast-paced and often argumentative, as TR himself often was, but written with great feeling and excitement.